THE SWICK AND THE DEAD

Loch Lonach
Book Two

DEDICATION

This work, the second in the series, is dedicated to the health care professionals and drug interdiction units on the front lines of the war against drugs. In this I include everyone who works to reduce the suffering caused by the use of illicit drugs of whatever form. God bless you all.

In addition, I wish to thank:
- The Firewheel Fictionistas Writers' Group for their invaluable support and assistance
- Members of the Scottish community here and across the world, my inspiration and foundation
- My content experts and beta readers, especially those who helped with the Spanish that appears in this volume
- My long-suffering editor and brainstorming partner, Mary Foster Hutchinson, without whom none of these books would have been possible

ACKNOWLEDGMENTS

The font used on the covers, in the titles, and for the chapter headings in this series is PR Uncial, created by Peter Rempel. It has been a continuing source of delight throughout this endeavor and I am happy to have this opportunity to tell him so. Vielen Dank!

The Mackenzie Dress Clan Tartan is listed as WR1981 on the Scottish Tartans World Register.

Davy Crockett's famous line is from his speech after losing his Tennessee seat in the U.S. Congress (11 August 1835), "Since you have chosen to elect a man with a timber toe to succeed me, you may all go to hell and I will go to Texas." As quoted in *David Crockett: The Man and the Legend* (1994) by James Atkins Shackford, Introduction, p. xi

"Hell hath no fury . . ." – William Congreve, *The Mourning Bride*, Act III, Scene VIII

"Revenge is a dish best served cold." – Meyer, N. (Director). (1982). *Star Trek II: the wrath of Khan* [Motion picture]. Australia: Paramount. Khan, citing a Klingon Proverb

"Loved not wisely . . ." – William Shakespeare, *Othello*, Act 5, Scene 2.

"The road to Hell . . ." – Proverb

DISCLAIMER:

Dear Readers:

This is a work of fiction. That means it is full of lies, half-truths, mistakes, and opinions. Any resemblance to any actual person, living or dead, is unintended and purely coincidental.

Similarly, the businesses, organizations, and political bodies are mere figments of the author's overactive imagination and are not in any way intended to represent any actual business, organization, facility, group, etc.

Dallas and Austin both exist, but the reader is warned that the author has re-shaped Heaven and Earth and all the mysteries of God to suit herself and begs the reader, for the sake of the story, to overlook any discrepancies in fact.

The Swick and the Dead

Loch Lonach Mysteries Book Two

by Maggie Foster

"Nowhere is wisdom more necessary than in the guidance of charitable impulses. Meaning well is only half our duty; Thinking right is the other, and equally important, half."
— Samuel Gridley Howe

"Most of the evil in this world is done by people with good intentions."
— T.S. Eliot

Cover design by M. Hollis Hutchinson

Foster, Maggie.
    The swick and the dead: Loch Lonach mysteries, book two /
    Maggie Foster

ISBN (pbk)
    ISBN-13: 978-0-9989858-1-7
    ISBN-10: 0-9989858-1-3

ISBN (epub)
    ISBN-13: 978-0-9989858-4-8

Fonts used by permission/license. For sources, please visit
MaggiesMysteries.com

Swick

From the Old Scottish swik, deceit (1420), swyk (1513), sweke (1514), to deceive, a deceiver.

CAST OF CHARACTERS

Ginny Forbes	An Intensive Care Unit (ICU) nurse at Hillcrest Regional Medical Center
Sinia Forbes	Ginny's mother
Jim Mackenzie	An Emergency Room (ER) physician at Hillcrest
Angus Mackenzie ("Himself")	The Laird of Lonach, Jim's grandfather
Tomas DeSoto	A Drug Enforcement Agency officer
Hue Tran	A Dallas Police Crimes Against Persons Unit Detective
Phyllis Kyle	The victim, an ICU nurse at Hillcrest
Marjorie Hawkins	ICU Head Nurse at Hillcrest
Lisa Braden	An ICU nurse at Hillcrest
Grace Edmunds	An ICU nurse at Hillcrest
Luis Perez	An abandoned five year old
Clara Carpenter	A Political Activist
Fergus Stewart	Second cousin to Ginny, a *gallóglaigh*

Loch Lonach is a Scottish community established before Texas became a Republic in the geographic region that would become Dallas. It has retained its culture and identity. Loch Lonach boasts its own schools, police force, churches, and other civic institutions. The head of the community is the Laird, currently Angus Mackenzie.

Thursday, Journal Entry

"Okay. I'm ready. If she'd been satisfied with merely blackmailing me, I could have overlooked it, but she's getting too close to the truth and that I cannot have. I've got people counting on me. I'm their contact to the money, to the good life, to not going to prison. They need me. The planning is complete. I have all my ducks in a row. With just a little bit of luck, by morning this particular problem will be behind me. So, off to work! Write at you later."

Chapter 1

Day 1 – Thursday night / Friday morning
Hillcrest Regional Medical Center

Death surrounded her. It hung in the very air she breathed. It slid across the tile floor and seeped around the corners, into and out of the rooms where the patients lay. It was there, always, waiting.

One a.m. in the Medical ICU at Hillcrest Regional meant the beginning-of-shift tasks were done and the patients settled for the night, as much as was possible. The ceiling lamps glowed at quarter-strength, casting muted shadows. Voices ebbed and flowed as the staff went about its business and the alarms, turned down as far as they would go, were swiftly silenced, to give the illusion of peace.

In some of the rooms frail humans fought for life, in others they slipped toward death. Ginny Forbes, RN, hovered outside her patient's door, grimly determined that he would live, at least until the dawn. After that—well, death isn't the worst thing that can happen to a man.

She frowned at the calculator, then ran the math again. In the glow from the monitors, her skin was the color of green tea. Her eyes, behind thick lashes and lowered brows, could barely be seen, pale and cold and hollow, to match her mood. Once she was sure she had the right dose, she put on the protective clothing mandated by hospital infection control policies and stepped to his side.

She was halfway through the carefully timed injection when she heard a sound just outside the door. Her head snapped up, but there was no one there. No one checking on her. She frowned. It was bad enough to be afraid of making a mistake. Even worse to be afraid of being caught.

Glancing down at the syringe, she found she had inadvertently pulled it out of the intravenous line port. She swore to herself, changed the contaminated access device for a clean one, and finished the injection. When it was done, she pulled off the gown and gloves, stepped out of the room, and accessed the computer link.

"I start classes in January. I've already explained to Ms. Hawkins and asked her to cut back my hours so I'll have time to study."

Ginny looked up to see two nurses emerging from the break room, coffee in hand.

"What are you going to focus on?"

"Patient safety, of course."

The first speaker was Phyllis Kyle, a velvet-covered

steamroller quietly saving the world. Her companion was Susan Reed, a level-headed collector of human foibles.

"Well, duh. What in particular?"

"My proposed dissertation topic is 'Best Practices for Spotting Nurse Imposters.' It's ridiculous that anyone can get away with pretending to be a nurse, but there's at least one in every *Bulletin*."

"What made you chose that topic?"

Phyllis shrugged. "Oh, you know. Someone said something last summer and it got me thinking."

"Did she give you any trouble, Hawkins, I mean?"

"She didn't look happy, but the big bosses want us to continue our educations, and they're paying for it, so she had to give in. She'll manage. She always does."

They passed out of earshot and Ginny went back to work, scowling at the computer displays. It was taking her twice as long as it should to complete her assigned tasks. Not that she could pack up and leave if she finished early. It didn't work that way. And it wasn't as if she didn't *want* to do her job. Usually she did. Usually, she was good at it.

She dragged her mind back to her task, wondering why she was having so much trouble concentrating. Knowing the answer. Trying to ignore it, to turn her back and move on.

"Hello."

Ginny started, twisting toward the voice. She found her heart pounding and her breath tight in her throat, but it was only Jim. He was wearing a lab coat over his scrubs, embroidered with *Dr. Mackenzie, Emergency*, proof that he was both legitimate and on duty.

"You scared me."

"So I see." He frowned slightly. "I was wondering if you could take a break."

Ginny shook her head. "Not at the moment. Maybe later."

He kept his voice down, in deference to the hushed hour. "Would you like me to get you something from the cafeteria?"

Ginny shook her head. "No, thank you. I'm not hungry." She smiled at him, trying to pretend she was all right.

He stepped closer and she could smell the faint scent of the emergency department on his clothes, a mixture of bandages and betadine and not-quite-fresh skin.

"You need to eat."

She nodded. "I know. I brought something."

"You also need to take a break."

"I will."

"When?"

"Another hour at least."

He didn't raise his voice, but she could hear the note of authority in it. "Find someone to relieve you."

"I'm fine, Jim. Stop worrying about me."

He reached out and brushed her cheek with his fingertip. "I can't help it," he said. "It's an occupational hazard."

She smiled in spite of herself. "Just let me catch up so I'll be ready for my admission."

He sighed and slipped a power bar into her hand. "Here. Better than nothing. I'll check on you later."

She watched him leave, her brow furrowed. She didn't want him hovering, didn't want him telling her what she should do, didn't want him reporting back to the Laird. And the only way she was going to get him to stop trying to help was to prove she didn't need it.

* * *

Nine hours later, Ginny sat with her head down on the conference room table. It was two hours past her bedtime and, in spite of the situation, she was having trouble keeping her eyes open. Somebody had to go last, she supposed, and she'd made the mistake of staying behind to help pick up the pieces. Stupid conscience.

She heard the door open behind her, then felt a hand on her shoulder.

"Ginny?"

She pried her eyes open and looked at Jim. His face was close and a bit distorted, seen sideways like this. He looked upset.

"I just heard what happened."

Ginny sat up, then rolled her head, trying to work the kinks out of her neck. She leaned back in the chair and swiveled around to face him.

"I left you a message."

"I got it. I've been catching up on some paperwork, waiting for you."

She sighed. "I have no idea how much longer they want to keep me. You'd better go home."

He shook his head. "Not without you."

"Okay, but you can't say you weren't warned." She put her head back down on the table and shut her eyes, but wasn't allowed to fall asleep. He put his hands on her shoulders and started rubbing and it felt really good, but that, too, was interrupted.

"Miss Forbes?"

She followed the police officer to the interview room and gave her statement, as well as she could through the haze of exhaustion, then, finally released, she let Jim lend a strong arm, steer her to his car, and drive her home.

"I'll see you this evening."

"I'll be there."

She closed the door to her bedroom, pulled the shades on the windows, and turned out the light, plunging the room into darkness. By touch she undressed and slid between the covers. She curled up on her side, willing her muscles to relax, to let her sleep. It wasn't until she was almost there, eyes closed, just on the point of dropping off, that the full horror of the situation broke through her defenses.

It was just chance that Ginny had been the one to find the body. It could have been anyone, but it had been her. And, once seen, there was no unseeing it. Phyllis was dead, murdered, and she, Ginny, was one of the suspects. The tears slid out from under closed eyelids and rolled down her cheeks. She let them go.

* * *

CHAPTER 2

Day 1 – Friday afternoon
Forbes residence

With a huge gasp, Ginny came awake, sitting bolt upright in bed, staring into the darkened room. She was sweating and shaking, struggling to breathe and despising herself for it. She wasn't the target this time. What did she have to be afraid of?

She pushed her hair back from her face, then relaxed onto the pillows, trying to talk herself down. Phyllis. It was Phyllis who was dead, strangled, in the ladies' room at the hospital. Not just any ladies' room either, the one *inside* her Intensive Care Unit. Ginny swallowed, allowing herself to remember what she'd seen.

Cyanosis—the bluish tinge that meant no oxygen was getting to the victim's brain. Swelling—as the blood fought to overcome the stricture around her neck it had spread to the surrounding tissues. Filmed eyes—like cataracts, except for the broken blood vessels. Protruding tongue—a gargoyle on the roof of a medieval cathedral. Blood—on her hands and neck where she had torn her own flesh as she fought for life. A wire—like some grotesque parody of a twist tie, clamped in place and impossible for her to remove, not alone. She had died alone. Unless her killer had stayed to watch her die.

Did murderers really return to the scene of the crime? Or insert themselves into the investigation? Had the murderer stood and watched as they tried to resuscitate Phyllis?

The faces surrounding the scene had been stiff with horror and grief and fatigue. A few were openly curious. Most were silent.

Ginny shivered. Who could have done such a thing? She closed her eyes, but could not dismiss the image of that death.

* * *

Friday evening
Cooperative Hall

The next item on the ceilidh program was *Waverley* and the assembled clan evidently approved the choice. As soon as announced, the dancers raced across the floor, grabbed their partners, and skidded gleefully into position in the set. Those not dancing tapped their toes on the wooden floor or clapped their hands in time to the music. The fiddler added a jigging movement to his bowing and smiled and smiled and smiled.

Ginny smiled, too. Her eyes followed the dancers as they chased each other across the set (kilts and tartan sashes flying), weaving in and out of the line of standing dancers (an illegal move, but who was there to stop them?), then dashed back to place, arriving just in time to burst into laughter as the dancer at the bottom of the set inevitably got left behind at the start of the new rotation. Scottish Country Dancing had the power to make the heart sing, most of the time.

They were only halfway through the evening, but Ginny had opted to sit out the rest of the dances in favor of talking over the murder. Her best friend, Caroline, was across the table from her, Jim was on Caroline's right, the Laird of Lonach sat beside Ginny. They all looked worried.

"They cannot be serious!" Caroline shoved her blonde curls back from her face and nailed them in place with a headband. Ginny had seen that gesture before. Whenever she was agitated, Caroline took it out on her hair.

"The Medical Examiner puts the time of death between three and five a.m. Phyllis hadn't done any of the four o'clock vital signs, so she was probably already dead by then. Everyone who was in the unit during that timeframe is a suspect."

Jim had already heard the story, extracted from Ginny on the way home. It was Caroline asking the questions.

"How did you find her?"

"When she didn't show up for shift change, we starting hunting. The break room was an obvious place to look."

"I thought she was in the ladies' room?" Jim asked.

Ginny nodded. "Both of the restrooms are accessed through the break room. I did the ladies' while Peter checked the men's. The handicap stall was locked. I peeked underneath and saw her slumped in the corner. I had to wriggle under the door to get to her and the police are mad at me for messing up their crime scene, but I thought she was just taken ill or something."

"Understandable." Caroline nodded. "The bathroom is inside the breakroom, which is inside the ICU, right?"

Ginny nodded.

Caroline raised one eyebrow. "I expect the police think that narrows the field very nicely."

"If they do, they're wrong. Normally the ICU is badge-only, but they had the doors propped open last night because of the heavy traffic." She looked across at Caroline and raised both eyebrows. "Don't let anyone tell you a full moon doesn't make a difference. It does!"

Jim nodded. "Someone could have gotten in and out again without being noticed."

"Bonnie Prince Charlie could have shown up in full Highland dress, with a piper, and we wouldn't have noticed. We were too busy."

"Ye had four admissions, I think ye said." Himself had turned his chair so he could face the group, his feet solidly on the floor, his walking stick planted between his knees, brushing the hem of his kilt. His hands, one on top of the other, lay on the knob of his cane.

Ginny nodded. "Two of which were mine, and two Code Blues. On top of that, we had the photographer from Human Resources. He told us he was assigned to get pictures of the night crews with the Christmas decorations and was going from unit to unit collecting images to use in marketing and advertising. The Night Supervisor introduced him and stayed long enough to make sure she was in some of the photographs, then disappeared. We had to order him out of the way at least twice. He wanted action shots. I don't know when he gave up and left."

"Ye knew th' dead lass, I think?"

"We were friends in school." Ginny's face clouded. "Two boys at home, ages three and five. Whoever did this should be strung up!"

They all nodded agreement.

"What happens next?" Jim asked.

"We wait for the police to finish processing the body and the scene. They closed the Unit, moved all the patients, and sent us home with instructions not to leave town."

"But surely you have an alibi! All those witnesses!"

Ginny gave Caroline a pitying smile. "Without turning around, can you tell me who is dancing at the moment?"

"Well, no, of course not."

"You know the dancers. You see them every week. Did you notice if anyone was missing tonight?"

Caroline shook her head.

"It wouldn't take more than fifteen minutes to kill Phyllis and hide the body. Whoever did it probably can produce witnesses who would swear she—or he—was right there, in plain sight the whole time."

"What about the cameras and that photographer fellow?"

"The police are looking at the images. Let's hope they find something. In the meantime, all we can do is wait." She looked across the table at Jim. "At least you're off the hook."

"Why is he off the hook?" Caroline asked.

"Because he wasn't on the Code team last night."

Jim nodded. "I had my hands full, though. We had the usual drug overdoses and schizophrenics and someone who wanted to save our souls, plus four car wrecks, a venomous snake bite, two anaphylaxis, one corneal abrasion, two heart attacks, and at least a dozen viral illnesses with no primary care provider. No gunshot wounds and no sexual assault last night, which is a surprise, but we did have one person who 'accidentally' sat on a foreign object."

Ginny snickered. She was fully aware of what oddities could come through the doors of a big city Emergency Room, especially at night, on a full moon.

Caroline turned to Jim. "Did you have to go up to the ICU and pronounce death?"

He shook his head. "Day shift got that honor. I was in the back, catching up on charting."

"Well," Caroline continued, "the obvious thing to do is catch the killer as soon as possible, so you can all go back to normal." She looked significantly at Ginny.

"Who? Me?" Ginny shook her head. "No, thank you."

"You solved the last murder that happened at Hillcrest."

Ginny shifted in her seat. "Not exactly."

"You and Jim."

Ginny exchanged glances with Jim. It was true. Between the two of them, they had caught a murderer, but it had come at a price.

"I think we should give the police a chance to do their job," Jim said. "If they need our help, we can step in later." He came around to Ginny's side of the table. "Come on. I'll take you home."

Her mother let them in. Ginny said goodnight to both, climbed the stairs, and slipped into her bedroom. She dropped her purse on the chest of drawers and sat down on the end of her bed. *There ought to be a law*, she thought to herself. *Unless you choose to be a policeman, one murder per lifetime, no more.* She could hear Jim and her mother murmuring, discussing her, no doubt, then Jim's footsteps on the stair. He tapped on her door.

"May I come in?" He stuck his head around the edge of the door and she nodded.

"I have a favor to ask," he said.

"What is it?"

"I want to spend the night in your guest room."

"There's no need."

He took a step toward her. "You know your mother talks to Himself?"

She nodded. The Laird had been acting *in loco parentis* to her and her brother ever since their father had been killed.

"She told him you were having nightmares."

It was inevitable that the Laird's acknowledged heir, Jim, would be included in the confidence.

"It occurred to me that discovering a murdered woman in the bathroom might trigger one."

Ginny rose and stepped toward him. He opened his arms to her, enfolding her in a warm hug.

"I'll be all right," she said.

He kissed the top of her head. "I know you will. I just want to be close tonight."

She sighed, then broke out of his arms, and pushed him toward the door.

"Go home, Jim."

"I can't help if you won't let me."

"We'll talk tomorrow." They had a date to meet for lunch.

He turned at the head of the stairs, slipping a finger under her chin and lifting it until she could not avoid looking into his eyes.

"Call me, if you wake in the night."

She nodded, then watched him descend the stairs and be let out by her mother. He cared and he wanted to help, but it was time he stopped treating her like an invalid.

The sight of her friend, dead, could easily have triggered a breakdown, but it hadn't. The professional in her had surfaced, calmly in control after months of being gone. She had turned a corner at last and all it had taken to do it was another murder.

* * *

Cħapter 3

Ginny stirred her coffee slowly, counter-clockwise, watching the cream make swirls of pale light that faded into the darkness. Good coffee was as soothing as it was stimulating: a chemical enigma. She inhaled the fragrance and let it seep into her soul.

"Another slice of ham?"

Ginny raised her eyes from her cup. Her mother was adding ham and eggs to her own plate, not looking at Ginny, her face serene. It was a gift, that face, the ability to look serene no matter what the trouble.

Ginny nodded, accepting a small slice of ham and a spoonful of eggs, then helping herself to cantaloupe, as a counterpoint to the protein. She picked up her fork and took a bite of the eggs, taking her time, concentrating on the taste and aroma and texture.

Eating had become a challenge and she'd been shying away from admitting it, but it had to be faced. The pain she felt was psychosomatic, a construct of the emotional pain. Good food was a pleasure, she told herself. Worth the trouble and necessary for health. She nibbled on the cantaloupe.

"How are you holding up, darling?"

Ginny gave her mother half a smile. "Phyllis is dead and I'm suspected of murdering her. What do you think?"

"I think you're handling it splendidly."

Ginny frowned. "Jim doesn't. He thinks I'm a mess."

"Is that why he wanted to spend the night?"

"He figures if he can catch me in a meltdown, he'll know better how to manage my condition."

"Sounds like a physician. Why did you send him home?"

Ginny's brow wrinkled. "Are you familiar with the term, *enabling*?"

"Yes."

"Well, that's what he's been doing. Every time I face an issue, or an obstacle, or a challenge, he's there, trying to smooth the way." She scowled. "All he sees is an emotional cripple."

Her eyes dropped to the kitchen table, her mind returning to the scene that had taken place here, right here. The one that made her stomach ache. She picked up her spoon and poked at the coffee cup, reluctant to admit her worst fear.

Her mother waited patiently, and after a moment, Ginny took a deep breath and asked the question that was haunting her. "What if I can't do it? What if I can't bounce back?" She looked up. "Jim's not imagining it. I *am* an emotional cripple. I can't trust myself at work. I can't force myself to face the ice. I can't let Jim touch me without fighting down panic."

Mrs. Forbes nodded. "First, I have full confidence in you and so does Himself. We both think this is temporary. Second, you have the blood of heroes flowing through your veins. That hasn't changed. You're just a wiser version of the person you were."

Ginny studied her mother's face. The Scottish blood to which she referred included some of the boldest of the

Highland clans. Men—and women—who had fought on both sides of the Atlantic and, if the stories were to be believed, never once considered giving in to anyone. Some days it was a lot to live up to.

Her mother continued. "You're not going to be happy until you take back what Hal took from you and none of us can do that for you. But you don't have to do it alone. You have me and Himself and Caroline. And you have Jim."

Ginny squirmed. "I wish he'd lighten up. He's so serious."

"I think he feels responsible."

"He thinks he can fix everything."

Her mother's mouth twitched. "He's too intelligent and too well trained to believe that." She smiled. "But I think you're right that he wants to." She put down her coffee and crossed her arms on the table, looking directly at Ginny. "It hurts him, to see you in pain."

Ginny scowled. "I don't like it either."

"It would be a kindness, to him, if you'd let him feel useful."

Ginny's frown deepened. Her role as dutiful daughter and licensed nurse and one of the Lonach community meant she had an obligation to the Laird's grandson. The question was, did it take precedence over her obligation to herself? She fought down an urge to whine. She was too old for that. Besides, it had never worked with her mother anyway.

She nodded, then rose, and cleared away the dirty dishes. "I'm going over to Phyllis' house for a condolence call, then out to the Homestead, then lunch with Jim."

"All right." Mrs. Forbes rose and held out her arms.

Ginny let herself be hugged and kissed, then said goodbye and headed for the garage. She and her mother had a good relationship, with mutual respect on both sides, but Ginny didn't tell her mother everything. There was another reason Ginny didn't want Jim controlling her life. She'd made a promise to herself—to dig out of this blue funk, regain her self-esteem, and prove to the world she was a survivor. On her own. By herself. Whatever the cost.

She sighed heavily. What it would probably cost was her pride and that was the only thing that had kept her going since October, her stubborn, mulish, arrogant, Scottish pride. If that went, what was she going to use for courage?

* * *

Saturday midmorning
Kyle residence

The woman who opened the door to Ginny looked enough like Phyllis to confirm the family relationship: ash blond hair, hazel eyes, lean and lanky build. Ginny shifted the bags of groceries to one hand and held out the other. "I'm Ginny Forbes. We spoke on the phone."

"Rachel Amante, Phyllis' sister." She gave Ginny a wan smile. "This is so kind of you! Please come in."

Ginny headed for the kitchen. "I've brought casseroles and frozen dinners and stuff for the kids." She set her packages down on the counter and faced the other woman. "I'm so sorry for your loss, and my own. Phyllis and I were in school together. I'm really going to miss her."

"Who's there?" The voice was almost as ugly as the expression on the man suddenly appearing in the kitchen doorway.

Ginny looked at the newcomer. He must have been six feet tall and, under better circumstances, a good match for Phyllis. At present, he was unshaven, dressed in rumpled jeans and tee shirt, his spiky blond hair in disarray, his eyes wild. Even from here, Ginny could smell alcohol on his breath.

THE SWICK AND THE DEAD

"Is she from the hospital? Tell her to get out!"

"John, please! She brought food."

"We don't need her food!" He stepped toward her and Ginny took a step back. She would gladly have complied with his demand, but he was blocking the exit.

"I'm very sorry to intrude on your grief, Mr. Kyle. I'll go."

"Damn right, you will! Coming here again."

Ginny hadn't been over before, so she was a bit confused by the accusation.

"It wasn't her, John. It was the other one."

John blinked, then swallowed, then seemed to deflate. "Sorry." He straightened up again immediately and stuck his finger out, pointing it at Ginny. "But you tell that woman not to show her face around here again."

Ginny nodded. "I'll do that." She slipped sideways toward the door and Rachel took the hint, stepping between her and the bereaved man, to let her out.

"Forgive him. He's very upset."

Ginny nodded. "Please let me know if I can do anything to help. You have my number." She took her leave and headed for her car, wondering what had caused the outburst and whether the other person from Hillcrest was someone she knew and whether she had any obligation to do anything about the situation.

* * *

Saturday late morning
Loch Lonach Homestead

The grass was dappled with moving shadows cast by the live oaks that edged the Homestead exercise ground. The earth on which she sat was dry and the insects had retreated. With the sun out, white clouds adrift in a sapphire sky, and the air sweet on her face, it was easy to imagine it was a spring day, rather than deep winter in Texas.

"Ginny?"

She looked up as Caroline approached, in period costume and obviously working. It was equally obvious that Ginny, clad in sweats, was not.

"What are you doing here?"

Ginny motioned toward the field. "Watching the lesson."

Caroline dropped to the earth, put her hand to her eyes and focused on the closest pair of combatants.

"Oh! That's Jim, isn't it?"

Ginny nodded.

Caroline grinned. "Well I can understand why you might want to watch *that*."

Both men were wearing white tee shirts, kilts, and body armor in the form of thick padding. They edged warily past one another, then moved in suddenly, the sound of metal on metal punctuating the moment of impact.

Caroline cocked her head to one side. "Are they regimental?"

Ginny grinned. "No, they're both wearing briefs—black—as per regulations."

Caroline's brow furrowed. "Is it my imagination or has he been working out? His muscles look bigger."

Ginny nodded. "He has figured out he must look the part as well as be able to wield both musket and sword, for which he needs muscles."

Caroline nodded, watching the blades flash in the sunlight. "Not bad. Who's he fighting?"

Ginny looked over at her friend and smiled. "Don't you recognize him?"

Caroline squinted, studying the other man. "Tall, lean,

strawberry blonde. He looks familiar."

"He should. That's Alan."

Caroline started. "Alan? My Alan? Well, not mine, but Alan Christie?"

"Yes, dear."

Caroline's eyebrows rose. "I don't think I ever saw him on the field, just indoors. He looks older. What's Jim teaching him?"

"It's the other way round. Alan is teaching Jim."

Again Caroline looked startled. "Really?"

"Alan is our best swordsman. He's also a gifted instructor." Ginny watched Caroline's face undergo a series of adjustments. As recently as last October Caroline had been hiding from Alan, thinking him unsuitable as a companion, even for dinner. She had done some growing up since then and appeared to be doing some more right now.

"Hmmm." She withdrew her gaze from the field and focused on Ginny. "Speaking of edged weapons, what about you? Are you back on the ice, yet?"

Ginny reached up unconsciously and brushed a wisp of hair away from her left ear, her fingers tracing the scar that had formed as a result of her fall.

"No."

"Why not?"

"Because Jim was talking helmets and I refuse to wear one."

"You can understand his position."

"I can, but it's not going to happen."

She'd had a good excuse—two of them—for delaying her return to the ice. Her cracked ribs had needed time to heal, and she'd had to order new skates, since the crime lab had cut her old ones to pieces.

Actually, she *had* been out to the rink, to be fitted for the new boots then have the new blades positioned. Steve had let her watch and shown her there was no chance they would move. If she fell again, it wouldn't be the skate's fault.

"Do you want me to go with you?"

Ginny smiled at her friend. "No, but thanks for the offer." She needed to go alone, so no one would see how badly she sweated at the prospect.

Caroline's eyes drifted back to the field. "You haven't told me yet why you're here. Is it a secret?"

"Himself asked me to evaluate Jim's progress."

Caroline frowned. "That strikes me as awfully cold-blooded, considering."

Ginny shrugged. "It was never a sure thing."

"Jim doesn't know, does he?"

"No, and don't you tell him."

"I won't." Caroline looked around. "You know what everyone's going to think, don't you?"

"That we're an item."

"Are you?" Caroline's voice was carefully neutral.

"I'm off men at present."

Caroline nodded. "I can understand that. Does Jim?"

Ginny shifted uncomfortably. "We haven't really talked about it."

Caroline lifted an eyebrow. "Everyone assumes you and he will end up together."

Ginny gave a non-committal shrug. "There are a lot of eligible women in town. He doesn't have to settle for me."

Caroline turned to face her. "Oh, I think we all know what *he* wants. The question is what do *you* want?"

Their conversation was interrupted by the approach of the two combatants. Ginny reached into her bag, pulled out water bottles, and handed them over as Jim and Alan dropped onto the grass. She turned to Alan, who was eyeing Caroline with a tentative smile on his face. "Caroline, I think you and Alan already know one another."

Caroline nodded and Ginny was amused to see the beginnings of a blush.

"Hello," Alan said.

"Hello."

Ginny turned back to Jim, leaving Caroline to fend for herself.

"How did you do out there?"

"He did just fine," Alan answered her. "Especially since he's years behind the curve."

Ginny smiled at the look of annoyance on Jim's face. He had yet to learn that good-natured teasing was part of the package.

"Well, it isn't my fault. You have no idea how odd it feels to aim for someone's liver with the idea of cutting it out of his body without anesthesia."

Everyone laughed, but it was true that the physicians among them had trouble with the idea of deliberately inflicting mayhem on an enemy, even a hypothetical one.

Jim lowered the water bottle and caught her eye. "Maybe you should learn how to handle a sword," he teased. "That way you could skewer me if you wanted to."

"Auch, she knows how," Alan volunteered. "She just knows she couldn't beat either one of us with cold steel and has sense enough to use her pistol instead."

This was true. Ginny was a dead shot with her nine millimeter semi-automatic. So, for that matter, was Caroline.

"Are either of you gentlemen hungry?" Ginny asked.

"I am," Alan said.

"Me, too."

"Then may I suggest the four of us go get something to eat?"

"Oh! I can't!" Caroline said. "I have to be back on duty in ten minutes."

Alan smiled at her. "I tell you what. Let's go pick up something from the kitchen and show the tourists how to eat with our fingers." He rose gracefully and held out a hand to Caroline. She let him pull her to her feet, then waved to Ginny.

"We'll finish our conversation later."

Ginny watched the two of them move off in the direction of the compound, chatting easily, and thought how much more mature Alan seemed. She crossed her fingers for her friend.

"What were you talking about?" Jim asked.

Ginny turned her head and looked at him. "You, of course."

He sighed heavily. "I'm getting tired of being the subject of everyone's curiosity."

"I'm afraid you're stuck with it." Ginny dimpled suddenly. "She wanted to know if you and Alan were properly dressed under your kilts."

Jim choked on his water.

"And I was able to assure her I had seen enough to put her fears to rest."

He was laughing and coughing at the same time.

Ginny watched him long enough to make sure he was in no danger, then got up and held out her hand.

"Come on. It's lunchtime and you need a shower."

He rose and stood looking down at her, still laughing. "I knew I had a lot to learn about this place. I just didn't have any idea what that included."

"It's a good thing you're a fast learner."

"I have a good teacher."

"Alan? Yes. He's as good as they get."

He stepped toward her. "I wasn't talking about Alan."

She raised an eyebrow. "Before you come any closer, you should know there are three people over there watching us."

"Oh." He sighed. "It will have to wait, then." He picked up his jacket, then took her arm and led her off in the direction of the parking lot. When they were out of earshot, he said, "When are you going to let me kiss you, Ginny?"

She felt her throat tighten, but tried to keep her voice light. "You've kissed me."

"As I would a sister, yes. When are you going to let me *really* kiss you?"

She closed her eyes and tried not to panic. Caroline was right, she needed to decide what she wanted. It wasn't fair to string Jim along if she had no intention of letting him get close.

"You mean like Hal used to?" Maybe she should let him. It might help her make up her mind.

"If by that you mean as a pale candle is like a roaring fire, then yes."

She looked up, surprised to find a poet's soul in this physician's body. "Are you such a good kisser, then?"

He smiled. "My skill has been admired. Envied, even." He slid his arm around her waist and pulled her close, leaning down to whisper in her ear. "And I guarantee, my bonnie lass, once *I* have kissed you, you'll never think of that man again."

She couldn't help laughing. "Promise?"

"I promise."

His lips brushed her ear as he straightened up and Ginny found her mouth dry and her heart racing. She recognized the physiologic response to a perceived threat. Fear, then. Remembered fear or fear of the unknown. Or perhaps it was something else. Whatever it was, it was distracting. She concentrated on not tripping over her own feet.

* * *

CHAPTER 4

Day 2 – Saturday noon
Restaurant

Jim sat across the table from Ginny and watched her eat. He'd finished his meal and was sipping coffee, his mind on the murder. He hadn't seen the body, hadn't been invited to, but he'd seen cases of strangulation and had a pretty good idea what the victim must have looked like. He ached at the thought that she'd had to face that by herself.

"Nice day."

Ginny looked up and smiled at him. "Very."

She had declined the services of the grief counselor at work. Jim wasn't surprised. The Scots took care of their own and the suggestion had come from one of the outsiders.

"Would you like to go for a drive this afternoon?"

"Can't. I have to be at the police station at two."

"What do they want?"

Ginny poked at her salad. "Statements, signatures, DNA samples."

Not for the first time he wished they were at a point in their relationship where he could insist he go along.

"How about tomorrow, after church? I want to look at sailboats and I'd like your help."

She looked up in surprise. "Mine? What can I do?"

"If I'm going to teach you how to sail, I need to make sure you can reach everything."

Their eyes met and Jim got the impression she was wondering if it was safe to go out in a small boat with him.

She nodded slowly. "Okay. Sounds like fun."

Jim refilled her coffee cup. "Did you get any sleep last night?"

She shrugged, her eyes back on her meal.

"Ginny?"

She looked up, then back down at her plate, then set her fork down and pushed the plate away.

Jim frowned. "Aren't you going to finish that?"

"I've had enough."

His frown deepened. She had started October in robust health, her curves firm and round, her cheeks rosy, her eyes sparkling. Since then, she'd been steadily losing weight. He made a mental note to keep difficult conversations away from mealtimes. "Well, if you're not going to eat, let's talk."

She crossed her arms on the table and leaned on them. "All right, Jim. Talk."

He reached over and put a hand on her arm. "I'm so sorry this happened. The last thing you need is another murder. If I had known, I would have come up with a medical excuse and sent you home. That way you would have been out of the worst of it."

Ginny shook her head. "We were already short-staffed. I couldn't leave."

"Or brought you down to the ER and put you to work there."

"Same comment."

"Or stayed in the Unit and tried to prevent the murder."

He saw the corner of her mouth twitch.

"My hero."

He glowered. "Whoever did this had better hope we don't meet in a dark alley. I might give him a taste of his own medicine."

"That would *not* be a good idea. Leave it to the police."

He leaned toward her. "It was a cowardly thing to do, kill a woman then leave the body for someone else to find. He doesn't deserve police protection."

"Maybe not, but that's the price we pay for civilization."

Jim tried to keep his voice steady. "It might have been you."

Ginny pulled her arm away, shaking her head. "No. The one thing we know for sure is that the murderer meant to kill Phyllis. The room was well lit. He couldn't have mistaken her for someone else."

"It might have been a random choice."

Ginny's brow furrowed. "Much as I hate to admit it, the list of suspects precludes a random attack. It was one of us, Jim. That implies a motive."

"It wasn't *you*."

He saw her quick smile. "Are you sure? You weren't there."

"Ginny, my love, your face gives you away. If you were guilty, you'd be confessing by now."

"Well, as a matter of fact, I didn't do it." Her smile faded. "I had no reason to. I liked Phyllis."

Jim shook his head. "That's not a barrier to murder. Maybe you were jealous of her. Or she was getting on your last nerve. Or she rebuffed your amorous advances."

Ginny looked startled. "Where did you get *that* one? Too much time on the Internet?"

Jim laughed. "Romance novels. People bring books into the exam rooms to read while they're waiting and leave them behind. We have a collection and sometimes, when there's a lull in the action, I'll pick one up and look through it."

She raised a sardonic eyebrow. "I'll stick to mysteries, thank you."

He smiled. "They seem to stick to you, too."

"Very funny." She made a face.

Jim felt his heart lift at her tone. "Okay. Levity aside, what are we going to do about this?"

"You—nothing. And I will do as little as I can get away with."

"I want to help."

"I know."

"Did you sleep last night, Ginny?"

"You already asked me that."

"You didn't answer." Jim waited, watching a variety of expressions cross her face as she considered what to tell him.

She shrugged. "I had a nightmare, but it didn't last long. It was just unpleasant."

He lowered his voice. "Tell me about it."

"No."

He dropped the pitch again, using a technique he'd learned in school. He had a warm, rich baritone that he could use to good effect when interviewing nervous patients. "Please?"

She studied him for a moment, her brow furrowed, then shook her head. "I'm sorry, but I have to go or I'll be late for my appointment. Take me home, please."

Jim checked the time. She wasn't wrong. Even if he could have persuaded her to tell him what was in the nightmare, he didn't have enough time to follow through on it. He would have to try again later.

* * *

Saturday afternoon
Dallas Police Substation

Ginny presented herself at the police station at two p.m., as instructed. She allowed the technician to collect her DNA and fingerprints, looked over her statement, corrected one or two minor details, signed it and turned it in, then found herself face to face with the investigating officer.

"Detective Tran! Did you draw the short straw on this one?"

Tran Thi Hue—trim, petite, and just shy of forty—shook her head. Her straight black hair, cut to frame her face, swung gently, then settled back into place; very neat, very professional. She had been the officer assigned to investigate the trouble last October and had proved a subtle and tenacious sleuth.

"I requested the assignment."

Ginny smiled. "I'm happy to hear that." She took the seat indicated. "So what's next? Waterboarding? Bamboo under the nails?"

Detective Tran gave her a dry look. "No need. I already know you did not do it."

Ginny grinned. "Because I'm such a bad liar!"

"Correct."

"In that case, why did you want to meet with me?"

The older woman leaned forward. "I would like your help in this investigation."

Ginny raised her eyebrows. "What could I possibly do to help you?"

"I would like to have someone on the inside. Someone who knows how an Intensive Care Unit works. You could spot discrepancies I would likely miss."

"Are you looking for something in particular?"

"A way to narrow the suspect pool, if that is possible."

Suspects.

Ginny had heard of the walls closing in but had never experienced it for herself. She did so now. They weren't very nice walls, either. Painted a dull, industrial green, cracked and peeling, with white scratch marks at chair level, the room contracted around her, pressing on her, making it hard to breathe.

She sat very still. Amateurs were always a nuisance in a police investigation. They tipped off the wicked and messed up the evidence and accused the innocent, to the consternation of all. In literature and movies they were a laughingstock, many of them caricatures, so they wouldn't be mistaken for genuine detectives.

She had played that role last October and it had almost gotten Jim killed.

But there were times when an expert assisted with an investigation. There was precedent. She drew in breath and the walls retreated.

She rubbed damp palms down her thighs. She could run. She might even be able to hide, but she couldn't escape. Her cooperation was being requested by the one person with the greatest right to do so, one to whom she owed thanks and a civic duty. Ready or not, she was back in the investigation business.

Ginny forced her smile into place and nodded. "Where would you like to start?"

"Tell me about the victim."

Ginny spent the next ten minutes describing Phyllis: her work ethic, her personality, her home life.

"Were you friends?"

"School chums. Sometimes we ended up taking a break at the same time and would fall into conversation. Nothing outside of work."

"Why is that?"

Ginny shrugged. "I'm Homestead. She wasn't."

Tran nodded. "Can you think of anything she might have said or done that could make an enemy of someone at the hospital?"

"You think it was one of us."

"We are not ruling out any possibility, but we are considering the most likely first." She studied Ginny's face, her eyes narrowing. "Do you know something?"

Ginny nodded slowly. "I think I might." She explained about her reception at the Kyle household.

"He mistook you for another woman?"

"A woman from Hillcrest, apparently."

"Did he mention a theft?"

Ginny blinked. "No. Just that she wasn't welcome. Why do you ask?"

"Because we have not yet found Mrs. Kyle's purse."

"Did you look in her locker?"

Detective Tran flipped through the file on her desk. "The officers on the scene reported they had asked for and received her personal belongings. It does not specify whether that included the contents of a locker. I will follow up on that. See? I knew you would be useful."

Ginny nodded. "What else can I do for you?"

Detective Tran set the notebook down and fixed Ginny with a steady gaze. "If you can do so discreetly, see if anyone at the hospital knows anything that might have made Mrs. Kyle a target."

Ginny swallowed. "Wouldn't it be better to let the police do that? I wouldn't know the right questions to ask."

Detective Tran gave her a shrewd look. "I have seen the way your mind works. You will do very well."

Ginny felt she could have done without the compliment.

She had one more card up her sleeve. She played it now. "For me to be of any real use to you, I will need access to the evidence."

Detective Tran nodded. "So you can look for incongruencies."

"Yes."

She smiled, then rose and gestured for Ginny to follow her. "Come with me."

Two hours later Ginny headed for her car, thinking hard. The crime lab was still processing the scene, still tracking down persons who could assist them in their investigation. What's more, it seemed doubtful that the biological exemplars they were collecting would help. In a place as public as a bathroom in a hospital, there were thousands of stray bits of DNA.

Ginny's eyes narrowed. If *she* were planning to murder someone in a hospital bathroom, she'd wear Personal Protective Equipment—the gowns, masks, and gloves that were everywhere. No one would think twice about someone in scrubs grabbing a set and hurrying off to take care of an unspecified patient. The PPE would both disguise the wearer and prevent the transfer of DNA.

Ginny pulled out of the parking lot and headed for Loch Lonach, still thinking.

Scrubs. No help there, since all the staff had to buy their own uniforms. If you weren't picky, you could buy new scrubs at the grocery store and used ones in second-hand clothing outlets. But even if the murderer had gone to the trouble of buying the professional grade, color matched versions Ginny and the rest of the Hillcrest staff wore, so what? Unless a set of scrubs could be found on a particular person, covered in the victim's DNA, it wasn't even circumstantial evidence. What she needed was a motive. Something that made it necessary for Phyllis to die.

She glanced at the lake as she drove by. The sailboats were out. They ran before the brisk Texas wind; full canvas deployed, bows cleaving the green water, heeled over to catch the sky. Jim's motive for wanting to buy a sailboat was easy to understand. Ginny could almost taste the adrenaline. Too bad she didn't feel the same way about tracking down Phyllis' killer. She would do her best, but she wasn't going to enjoy it.

Organizing what she already knew could be done in private. Asking questions could not. And they weren't going to be innocuous questions, either. What did you have for dinner last night? Where are you going on your vacation? Did you happen to kill Phyllis?

Nor was there any reason to expect her coworkers to cooperate. It wasn't as if she had any genuine authority. She was probably going to be told to go to Hell. She pulled the car into her garage, closed the door, and went inside.

Her head was already hurting, the tension starting at the base of her skull, then spreading down her spine and across her shoulders. Was there any way she could fulfill her promise to Detective Tran without actually poking any hornet's nests? Because she'd learned that lesson the hard way and didn't want to do it again. Let someone else get stung this time.

Even as the phrase formed in her mind, Ginny knew she couldn't turn the responsibility over to anyone else. If she ever wanted to be able to look herself in the mirror again, she would have to do it herself. She felt her stomach churn and wondered if she was up to it.

* * *

Saturday afternoon
Forbes residence

Ginny dropped into a kitchen chair, crossed her arms on the table, and put her forehead down on them. "Why is everyone pushing me so hard?" She heard her mother sit down across the table from her.

"Is that a real question?"

Ginny looked up. "Yes. I don't understand why everyone won't just leave me alone."

"Because we care about you."

"Detective Tran doesn't. All she cares about is solving this murder."

"You do her a disservice. I was very impressed with her last October."

"October! October! Why won't anyone let me forget about last October?!"

"Because you haven't gotten over it, yet."

Ginny sat up, throwing her hand out in exasperation. "Do you know what Caroline did? She suggested I solve their crime for them. Like I was some sort of miracle worker. Wait until she hears that Tran has pressed me into service. She'll be on my back until everyone is either dead or in jail."

Ginny put both hands down flat on the table. "I am NOT an investigator!"

Her mother cocked her head to one side. "No?"

"NO! I'm not a private eye, or a police officer, or an assistant district attorney. I'm a nurse."

Her mother got up, poured a cup of coffee and set it down in front of Ginny, then resumed her seat. "You're also a genealogist."

Ginny reached for the sugar and cream. "Yes."

"And you spend a fair amount of your time at the hospital

figuring out what's going on with your patients, many of whom cannot tell you what they need."

Ginny wrinkled her nose. "True."

"In both of those settings you investigate."

"All right. I'll give you that, but this—*this* is not my job."

"You're angry."

"Yes! It's NOT fair! Isn't it bad enough that Phyllis has been murdered and all of us are suspects? Why is it *my* responsibility to find out who did it?"

Mrs. Forbes caught Ginny's eye and held it. "What are you afraid of, Ginny?"

"Nothing!" Ginny set her cup down and rubbed her forehead. "Everything!"

"Tell me."

Ginny swallowed, then tried to explain. "Can you imagine how hard it will be to work with these people if they think I'm spying on them? Most of them—maybe all of them—are innocent."

Mrs. Forbes nodded. "I see your point. Is what you can do for Detective Tran valuable enough to outweigh the disapproval?"

Ginny sucked in a breath. "I don't know. Why did she have to single me out?"

"That's easy. Because you showed her what you can do."

"You mean that spreadsheet?"

"I mean you showed her you can think, even under pressure."

"Most ICU nurses can do that."

Her mother smiled. "You sank your teeth into the puzzle and didn't let go."

Ginny made a face. It was true.

"You've been doing that since you were a little girl. Stubborn. Determined. I used to have to pry you away from whatever it was you were doing to get you to eat."

Ginny felt her mouth twitch. That, also, was true.

"I think, if you asked them, everyone on that suspect list—except the guilty party—will be happy to have this resolved as quickly as possible."

Ginny sighed. "That doesn't mean they won't resent my prying into their private lives."

Her mother lifted her coffee cup to her lips. "In my experience, if you ask people for their help, they're happy to cooperate. It's when someone tries to trick them that they get angry. It seems counter-intuitive when you're looking for a killer, but what's needed is transparency."

Ginny snorted. "That ought to be my middle name. I can't hide a thing from anyone."

"Just be yourself."

Ginny nodded slowly. "So, full steam ahead and hope that whoever killed Phyllis doesn't do the same to me."

"I'm betting you'll get there first."

Ginny lifted a sardonic eyebrow. "Let's hope you're right." She finished her coffee, then rose from the table. "I think I'll get started on my notes for Detective Tran." She paused in the doorway, then turned back. "How did you get to be so wise?"

Her mother smiled, a bit crookedly. "I'm afraid it comes with experience."

Ginny nodded, then sighed. "I seem to be getting quite a lot of experience in murder. Let's hope I can put it to good use."

* * *

CHAPTER 5

Day 3 – Sunday morning
Auld Kirk

Sunday morning dawned flawless, the sky brilliant with winter sun and the weatherman predicting a ten percent chance of snow in time for Christmas Day. It added a cheerful note to the holiday preparations.

Ginny and her mother were sharing a hymnal, singing, in parts, the carols that accompanied the Advent season. Because of her work schedule, Ginny was not free to participate in divine service every week, but she was a trained chorister and never missed an opportunity to sing along, especially the descants. Most she knew by heart, so it was no surprise to find her eyes straying from the page to the front of the sanctuary.

Among the duties of the Laird of Lonach was the responsibility for reading the Sunday Lessons. As a result, his place was in the front pew on the right hand side of the church. As his heir, Jim's place was beside him.

Ginny studied the pair. They were of a similar height, with the same broad shoulders, though Jim's filled his suit jacket more completely than did the older man's. Both stood ramrod straight, the white head on one side, the dark blonde on the other, bending to the page, then looking up at the ceremonies going on behind the altar.

The hymn ended, the Laird took his place at the lectern, and the congregation settled down to listen. The subject was courage.

Ginny bit her lip. She was not feeling brave. She should be back to normal by now, but she wasn't, and it scared her. She dropped her eyes to the prayer book, scowling at it, and tried to concentrate on the lesson. Trying to focus, praying for help, and guidance, and courage, and finding only silence.

* * *

Sunday late morning
Streets of Dallas and environs

Jim pulled out of the parking lot at his apartment, half his mind on the hazards of driving in a city the size of Dallas, the other half on Ginny. The physical wounds had healed, but the psychological wounds remained. Hers showed. Did his? He frowned at the thought.

He'd been focusing outward. It was easier that way. Much easier to concentrate on work and Ginny and the learning curve at the Homestead than to face mortality. Who wants to admit he will die someday, could die at any moment?

If he was honest with himself, part of his frustration with Ginny was having to wait for her. He wanted to wed her and bed her and get children on her *now*, rather than later, to make sure he got the chance. Because he might die without warning. Almost had.

Jim swallowed hard and glanced at the speedometer, then eased his foot back. People died on the Dallas roadways every day, but he'd rather not be one of them.

He pulled up in front of Ginny's house, seeing the door open and Ginny emerge. She was wearing brown slacks, ankle boots, and a pumpkin-colored sweater with a subtle texture that caught the December light and made it look soft, even from a distance. He wanted to touch it, touch her. He got out, came around the car and opened the door for her.

"Are you ready?"

She nodded, her eyes on his face. "What is it, Jim?"

He slid a hand across her back, caressing the cashmere. "I'll tell you after we're rolling."

Jim had identified several sailboat retailers in the DFW area. The most likely were on the highway between Dallas and Denton. That gave them a good thirty minutes of driving time in which to talk. She waited to open the conversation until they headed north.

"So, what is it that put that grim look in your eye?"

"I hate feeling like a failure."

He heard the surprise in her voice. "You? The miracle worker who managed to defeat certain death?"

"Me. The man who can't cure cancer or prevent closed head injuries or persuade you to confide in him."

"Oh."

Jim had been thinking about what he was going to say. "I had hoped taking some of the load off your shoulders would help you heal. Grandfather tells me that was a mistake."

She shook her head. "Not at first. You handling the medical decisions—that helped."

He reached over and took her hand. "Thank you for that."

"But," she said, "it's time I went back to taking care of myself."

Jim waited long enough to be sure his voice didn't betray him. "Does that mean cutting me out of your life?"

"Is that what you're afraid of?"

"I'm not afraid—" Jim stopped himself. "Can we find some

middle ground?"

She pulled her hand back. "Can you stop treating me like a half-wit child?"

Jim frowned. "When I see something that can be corrected, I feel obliged to mention it."

"Mentioning is not what you've been doing."

"I made a promise I would take care of you."

She sighed. "Jim, you're not at fault in this. It's just time I took back the reins."

Jim was trying not to think about all the times he'd had to let a patient leave without treatment, knowing she would never return. "You want to make the decisions."

"About myself, yes."

He nodded, more to himself than to her. Whether he liked it or not, informed consent was a tenet of best practice in healthcare.

She continued. "I want you to feel free to make suggestions, but not expect that I will do whatever you say."

"Even if I'm right and you're wrong?"

"How are we going to know who's right if we don't try both ways?"

Jim bit off the retort that rose to his lips. This was no ignorant patient off the street. This was a trained ICU nurse. "Okay. I make suggestions, we talk about it, you decide. Will that do?"

"It's a start."

Jim felt a stab of annoyance. "What else do you want?" The question sounded peevish, a small child whining, and Jim kicked himself when she didn't answer. "I'm sorry, Ginny. I didn't mean that the way it sounded. Talk to me. Please."

He heard her take a deep breath. "Does that work both ways? Are *you* willing to talk to *me*?"

Jim glanced at her, the corners of his mouth turning down.

"I'm not the one having nightmares."

"That's what I thought."

"What?" he demanded.

"You're too proud to admit you're human."

Jim squirmed. "I cried."

"Did you?" She sounded interested.

He nodded. "That's why I had all those tissues in my pocket."

"And why you were gone so long."

"Yes."

There was a pause. "You've never talked about it. Not to me."

"You had enough going on."

She turned toward him. "You cut me off, Jim. Every time I tried to ask, you changed the subject. So I stopped trying."

Jim admitted to himself that he hadn't wanted to face his feelings, hadn't felt he needed to. He glanced at her then put his eyes back on the road and eased off on the accelerator, again. The highway was typical of Texas, permanently under construction, and filled with the unrelenting Dallas traffic, sprinkled with suicidal drivers. He took a careful breath.

"All right. Having established that I don't have the slightest idea what I'm doing, can you tell me what you need, to help you move forward?"

She was silent for a moment, then answered him. "I need to feel competent again, to be able to rely on my own judgment. I need to face my fears and overcome them. And I need—somehow—to find a way to trust you."

Jim felt his heart leap in his breast. "You can trust me, Ginny. Absolutely." It was hard to be convincing without being able to make eye contact, but he hoped his tone of voice conveyed the depth of his feelings.

"You're not the problem. I am."

"But I can help. How to build trust is one of the things we studied in medical school. It starts with listening."

She sighed. "Men, even doctors, don't want to listen to a woman complain. They want to fix the problem and move on."

"Is that what you need? Someone to listen to you? Because I can do that."

"You have better things to do with your time."

He took a breath. "We've known each other for—what? Two months? Two and a half?"

"About that."

"Yet I feel as if I've always known you, as if we were friends before we met. I care about you. I want to do whatever it takes to help you get well. If you need to talk, then we'll talk. Or, you talk and I'll listen."

He waited through the long silence that followed. Eventually, he heard her stir.

"Trust requires being vulnerable," she said, "on both sides. It's sort of like emotional blackmail. I let my hair down and expect you to reciprocate. Men hate that."

Jim frowned. "You're right. Men hate emotional blackmail, but *people* need to be able to unload on one another, to be honest with someone they trust. It's the nature of the beast. Even men need that so, unless you fight dirty, I don't see a problem with being vulnerable. I'm just not very good at it."

"Okay," she said. "Assuming you mean that—"

"I do."

"—I'll go first." She took a breath. "I know I need to put this behind me, but every time I try to act normal, especially at work, I find myself making stupid mistakes."

"And catching them."

She nodded. "Yes, thank Heaven, but it scares me."

He nodded. "You need to rebuild your trust in yourself."

She threw her hand out. "How am I supposed to do that? I

missed all the warning signs. Worse, actually. I ignored them. I deluded myself, lied to myself. How am I *ever* supposed to trust my own judgment again?"

Jim took a minute before answering. "Trial and error. You try, you fail, you learn. You try again." He looked over at her. "You have to believe you're going to be all right."

"Eventually, yes, but I need time and everyone's pushing me: you, Tran, Mother."

Jim blinked. "Detective Tran? What does *she* want?"

"She wants me to spy on my coworkers. To root out their dirty little secrets and report back to her."

Jim frowned. "And you don't want to."

"No, but I can't get out of it."

"Why not? She can't force you to help." He heard her sigh.

"Because I owe her for what she did for me, for us. If she hadn't been willing to listen to you, there's no telling who else might have died."

"I see your point." The problem with Ginny, Jim thought, was that she could think straight. It was hard to argue with her conclusions.

"Okay, my turn." Jim took a breath. "You're right. I'm afraid of losing you." He glanced over, finding her eyes on him, then put his back on the road. "I'm afraid the minute you don't need me anymore you'll leave and never come back. Because of what he did." He took a breath.

"I understand you're not ready to trust a man and I'm willing to wait, but in the meantime, I'm going to do everything in my power to prove you *can* trust me." He reached over and slid his hand over hers, entwining their fingers.

"I want you to feel safe with me, Ginny. Safe enough to be yourself. Believe me. I will never hurt you."

"Not on purpose."

"Not ever. I want you to feel free to ask me for help, or a

hug, or to scream at me in frustration. Whatever you need to get you back to where you were before."

She sighed. "I'm not the same person I was."

"No. Neither am I." He looked over at her. "Better, I hope. Give me the chance to prove it."

"I'm afraid you won't like the new me."

The corner of his mouth twitched. "Is the new you a serial killer?"

"No!"

"A slattern?"

"No."

"A self-righteous know-it-all?"

"A frightened, humbled used-to-know-it-all."

He looked at her in sympathy. "I know the feeling." He pulled the car into the parking lot of the sailboat shop, turned off the ignition, then faced her.

"I have one more thing I want to say. Ginny Forbes, you and I can't go back to the way we were before and I wouldn't want to. I'm glad we were thrown together, and I want that to continue. I know I have a lot to learn, but I also have things I can offer, if you'll let me."

She nodded. "I want this to work, too. I just don't want you to think you have to fix me. That's *my* job."

Jim nodded. "Promise you'll come to me if you need anything."

She looked at him then nodded. "On one condition—that you do the same."

"Agreed. Now, let's go see if we can find a toy boat to put in my stocking."

* * *

Sunday afternoon
Sail Shop

They spent the next two hours looking at sailboats and Jim saw several that might do, but he didn't fall in love with any of them. He decided to wait until summer, when the selection would be better. Also, he was having trouble concentrating.

He'd never had a companion on his boat before. It had always been just him and the vessel and the elements. It gave him an odd feeling to see Ginny walking around the display models, absorbed in the search. She seemed to be enjoying herself, peering into the interiors, asking questions, trying out the deck chairs. If he got his way, she would become a part of every aspect of his life. He would have to learn to share his toys and, as an only child, he'd had little chance to learn how.

She was testing him, too, descending the ladders too quickly. When he realized what she was up to, he turned the tables on her, blocking her exit, forcing her to jump and trust him to catch her. When he had her in his arms, he found her trembling. She buried her face in his shirt and he held her, stroking her hair until she stopped shaking.

"I'm sorry," she mumbled. "I want to trust you. I *do*."

"I know. Just give it time."

On the drive back, they talked about the boats, Jim explaining the types of sail craft and the ways they could be used. He let his passion show and glanced over to find her smiling at him. "Am I boring you?"

"Not at all."

"It gets under your skin."

"My skin is not made for spending much time on the water. I burn if you look at me sideways."

"That's what you get for being a redhead. Sunscreen is available, as are sleeves. Do you get motion sick?"

"No, though I've heard anyone can get seasick under the right conditions."

"Even that can be handled. How about some dinner?"

It was emblematic of their medical training that neither Jim nor Ginny had any trouble going from vomit to veal without missing a beat.

"Will you buy me a steak with garlic bread and iced tea and a nice salad?"

He smiled over at her. "Whatever you want."

She met his eye. "Let's start with dinner."

Jim was just opening his mouth to reply when his phone went off. He pulled it out, glanced at the number, then handed it to Ginny.

"Put it on speaker."

"Hello?"

Himself's voice answered. "Auch, Ginny, is it you, lass?"

"Yes. Jim's driving, but we've got you on speakerphone."

"Aye, well lad, listen then. There's a bit o' a situation at th' Hillcrest ER and I've a mind ye should go find out what they're talkin' aboot. Something tae do wi' a bairn. Can ye go?"

Jim glanced over at Ginny and sighed. Dinner would have to wait. "Yes," he replied. "We can be there in fifteen minutes."

"Let me know what ye find."

"Yes, Grandfather."

He watched Ginny end the call. "Guess I'll have to owe you that steak."

She smiled at him. "That's all right. I'll be just as happy with drive-through chicken."

* * *

ChApTER 6

They pulled into one of the parking spaces reserved for ER physicians.

"This way." Jim led her through the ambulance bay and into the back of the Emergency Department.

"Jim! I thought you were off tonight." Richard Lyons handed the x-ray he was holding to one of the nurses and turned toward them.

"I am. My grandfather said you had an issue with a child. Have you met Ginny Forbes?"

"I've seen your name on the schedule, but I don't think we've been formally introduced."

Ginny shook the offered hand. "I work nights."

"Ah, that explains it." He smiled, then turned back to Jim. "We've put him in a treatment room, to give him some privacy." He led the way. "And I had Bryan look him over. He seems healthy." They stopped outside Room Six.

Jim nodded. "So what's the problem?"

Dr. Lyons' brow creased. "According to the boy, his mother brought him here, sent him inside to wait for her, then never appeared. A nurse noticed him in the waiting room. She asked

him where his mother was, after which she got one of the
security guards to do a grounds search. No sign of trouble.

"The security footage shows the boy getting out of a white
sedan, but no shot of the license. There's no answer at the
phone number he gave us. And no one has seen a woman
answering her description." He reached over and opened the
door.

Ginny looked past the men to see a small boy sitting on the
exam table with his knees drawn up and his head down on
them. The sitter rose when she saw them, then gathered up
her purse.

"I'm sorry. I have to go."

Dr. Lyons thanked her, then turned his back on the boy,
lowering his voice. "Since then all he's done is cry. Not that I
blame him."

Ginny put a hand on Jim's arm. "I've got an idea." She
hurried out to the car, grabbed the take-out, and hurried back.
It was no longer piping hot, but that was probably a good thing.
She gestured toward the boy with her head. "Let me try."

She shut the door on the two men, closing herself in with
the child, then put the food down on the countertop and
pulled the lid off. The aroma filled the room. She helped herself
to a drumstick, and began to nibble.

She had positioned herself so she could see the child
without actually facing him. She worked on her drumstick for a
moment, then fished out another and held it out in the
direction of the exam table. "Are you hungry?"

When the child didn't respond, she set the second
drumstick down on a napkin and put it where he could reach it,
then picked up her own, making lip-smacking noises.
"Ummmm!"

She caught the gleam of a small eye peeking at her over the
edge of his sleeve. "Go ahead. Help yourself." She went back to

eating, licking her fingers as well as her lips.

He reached down to pick up the drumstick, then bit into it, abandoning caution in the natural response of a small child to fried chicken. Ginny smiled and fished out another piece, placing it where the first had been.

"My name's Ginny. What's yours?"

He hesitated, his eyes on her, then went back to chewing.

Ginny moved the bucket over to the exam table so he could reach, wiped her fingers on a napkin, and settled down in a chair, leaning back, her fingers laced and resting on her belly.

"What we need now is pecan pie." She cocked her head at the child. "Too bad we don't have any."

He was working his way through a third drumstick, using both hands and all ten fingers.

"Ice cream would be good, too."

He looked up at that.

"Maybe we can get some later." She watched him wipe his hands on his shirt, noticing it had started the day a good deal cleaner than it was now. "Did you go to the park today?"

He shook his head. "Sunday school."

"Me, too." She lifted her nose and took a sniff. "Are you sure you didn't go to the park? I think I smell some sort of animal in this room."

He shook his head vigorously, his eyes on hers.

She touched her nose. "You see this nose? This nose knows!"

He smiled at that. "The zoo."

"Aha! I knew it! You rode a zebra."

He shook his head.

"A lion."

"A goat," he volunteered.

Ginny let her eyes grow big. "You rode a goat?"

He shook his head. "I petted a goat and fed him some milk."

"In a bottle?"

"Uh huh, and then we saw some penguins and a tiger and a bear."

Ginny smiled. "Sounds like fun. What was your favorite animal?"

"The helefant."

"The elephant? Did you feed him, too?"

The child shook his head. "He was big and he made a noise."

Ginny nodded. "I've heard that noise. It's loud and if you're not careful he'll try to push you around with his trunk."

"He tried, but he couldn't reach me!" The boy smiled triumphantly.

"Good job! What's your name?"

"Luis."

"Good job, Luis! That's a nice name. What's your last name, Luis?"

"Perez."

"Are you thirsty, Luis?"

He nodded and accepted the bottle of water Ginny offered.

"Where's your momma, Luis?"

"Don't know." His face clouded.

"Maybe we can go find her."

He shook his head, then burst into tears.

Ginny got up from her chair, leaned against the side of the exam table, and carefully gathered the child into her arms.

"Mama said to wait for her here."

"Are you sick, Luis?"

He shook his head.

"Or hurt?"

Again, he shook his head, rubbing his damp nose on his sleeve.

"Well, she must have had a good reason. Can we call her and find out?"

"Tried." He started crying again. "I want to go home."

"That sounds like a really good idea. Let's see if we can figure out how to get you home." She went over to her purse, pulled out her phone, and dialed Jim.

"How's it going in there?" he asked.

"Luis has had dinner, and would like to go home, and I was wondering if that's a possibility."

"We haven't figured out what to do with him."

"Can we continue this discussion at my house? I think he'd be more comfortable there."

"Hang on."

Ginny could hear Jim's voice in the background, then returning to the phone.

"I'm coming in."

She heard the call end, then the door started to open, slowly, so as not to startle the boy. Jim stepped in. She went back to stand beside Luis.

"Hello, Luis," Jim said. He sniffed the air. "This room sure smells good!"

The boy looked warily at Jim, then turned his face into Ginny's shoulder.

Jim walked over and looked down into the bucket of chicken. "Ummmm! Fried chicken! I can hardly wait, but I want to eat mine in comfort." He smiled at Luis. "Let's go find a nice, warm kitchen."

Ginny took a hasty swipe at Luis' hands and face, then she and Jim got him into his coat. Ginny held out her hand and Luis put his in hers, then moved in close, leaning against her.

They didn't have a child seat in Jim's car, so they were forced to put Luis in the back with the belt fastened as snuggly as Ginny could get it to go. Jim set the childproof locks, then waited while Ginny got in, closed the door, and put on her seatbelt.

She looked at their passenger. "Ready?"

The child nodded.

"Okay. Let's go."

* * *

Sunday evening
Forbes residence

"Mother?" Ginny called. "We have a guest."

Mrs. Forbes met them in the kitchen.

"This is Luis. He's had some chicken. Do we have any milk we can offer him?"

"Of course." Mrs. Forbes smiled at the boy. "Come sit over here."

The child was reluctant to be touched by another stranger, but they managed to get him seated at the kitchen table with milk and cookies while Ginny slipped into the other room to try to locate his mother.

She dialed the number Luis had given her. No answer. She left a message explaining who she was and how she and Luis met and asking Mrs. Perez to call as soon as possible.

Back in the kitchen she found Luis finishing the last of the cookies, her mother tossing a salad, and Jim polishing off the chicken. She put her hand on the boy's head and ran her fingers through his dark curls. No obvious neglect. No sign of abuse, mental or physical. He was appropriately wary of strangers and started asking about going home the minute she appeared.

Ginny explained she had left a message for his mother.

"And I've called Himself. He's on his way over," Jim said.

Ginny sat down where Luis could see her. "Did your momma tell you when she'd be back to pick you up?"

He shook his head.

"Tomorrow?"

Another shake.

"What about school?" All the area schools were preparing for the Christmas break, but it hadn't started yet.

He shrugged.

"Does your momma take you or do you go on a bus?"

"She takes me."

"What time?" Ginny was thinking she might catch someone who knew something if she could figure out where the boy was supposed to be the next morning.

He shrugged again, the details of carpooling of no concern to him.

Jim was making himself useful, dishing vanilla ice cream into four bowls. He handed them around. "What school do you go to, Luis?" he asked.

"Our Lady."

Ginny glanced at her mother. "Kindergarten?"

Luis nodded.

"Where is the school located?"

Luis shrugged.

Ginny rose and made her way upstairs to her computer. She did a quick search of the kindergartens with any variant of the name "Our Lady" and compiled a list. No sense trying to call tonight. They would all be closed.

When she got back to the kitchen, her mother had disappeared, Jim was washing up, and Luis was emptying his pockets onto the (now vacant) cookie plate. She took a chair next to him and watched. It was an eclectic assortment of the things one might find in a small boy's pocket: a toy car, two nickels and four pennies, a red crayon, a plastic card, a folded piece of lined paper, dirt, and a turtle.

"What is this?" she asked.

"My stuff."

"Okay. Why are you putting them on the cookie plate?"

"Seymour's hungry."

Ginny watched as Luis tried to coax the turtle out of his shell with cookie crumbs. "Why did you name him Seymour?"

"'Cause if he sticks his neck out he can see more."

"Ah." She rose, pulled a lettuce leaf out of the salad bowl and gave it to Luis. "Try this," she said, then picked up the plastic card. It was a pre-paid phone card upon which someone had written Luis' address and telephone number.

He was having some luck with the lettuce, she could see the tip of a tiny snout peeking out from the turtle's shell. She unfolded the piece of paper and read the note.

God forgive me for doing this, but I am desperate. If they find me, they will kill me, like they killed Phyllis. She is dead because of me, because of what I told her. She said there was a Safe Haven law that allowed her hospital to take in children whose mothers cannot care for them. Take Luis, please, and keep him safe until I can come for him. Please, please do not call the police. They will use him to get to me. Tell him I love him. Tell him—God willing—I will come for him. ¡Dios te bendiga! ¡Santa María, madre de Dios, ten piedad de mí! En nosotros dos. Maria Perez.

Ginny handed the note to Jim, who read it, his eyebrows rising. He looked up and caught her eye. "This woman knew Phyllis Kyle?"

"It certainly looks like it."

"Joey."

Ginny looked at Luis. "What?"

"Joey Kyle and Pe'er."

"Do you know Joey Kyle?"

Luis nodded. "He's in my class at school."

A shadow had appeared in the kitchen doorway and Ginny

watched as Jim handed the note to the Laird, who looked at it, then crooked his finger at Ginny. She followed him into the living room and sat down facing him.

"Poor wee lad. What's his mither gotten herself into, I wonder?"

"The question is, what do we need to do about it?"

"A bed fer th' nicht first, I think." Himself pulled out his phone and set to work.

Ginny took the opportunity to peek into the kitchen. She found Luis on Jim's lap. The child was getting tired and, as a result, fractious.

"I want to go home!"

"As soon as possible. I promise."

Jim was talking to Luis, looking relaxed and natural, as if small boys were a routine part of his life. Ginny hadn't seen him at work in the ER, but she'd heard he was good with children. She smiled to herself then rejoined her mother and the Laird.

"Ginny, lass. The shelter can tak' him, but not 'til th' morrow. Sinia tells me ye can put him in Sandy's room."

Ginny nodded. Her brother was grown and married and living in Atlanta so his room served for guests. "What about the police? She said not to call them."

"If th' woman has vanished, they'll ha'e tae be told sae they can search fer her. I'll tak' care o' that."

Ginny nodded, then went to tell Jim and Luis about the arrangements. She found them building a terrarium.

Jim looked at her, smiling. "It's just a temporary shelter for Seymour, but he'll be a lot more comfortable than he was in Luis' pocket." When they were done, Jim carried the boy upstairs and showed him the bed and bathroom and tucked him in. Ginny made sure Seymour's new home was stable and visible. She had no illusions about how important that tiny lifeline was going to be over the next few days.

She saw Jim and his grandfather out, then went back to Luis' room. She had left the light on and could see him, curled up on his side, his eyes squeezed shut. Ginny went over and sat on the edge of the bed.

"Do you want me to stay with you?"

He peeked at her, then nodded.

"Okay." She settled down in the chair, thinking hard.

Maria Perez knew Phyllis Kyle. Knew her well enough to entrust her child to strangers on Phyllis' word alone. Maria believed her only chance of saving her child was to dump him and run. If what Maria believed was true, then Phyllis' murder took on a whole new dimension. Murdered, because of what Maria had told her and Maria running for her life. What could she know that would be that dangerous?

Luis spent the next hour sneaking peeks at Ginny to make sure she was still there, then finally drifted off to sleep. Around two a.m. he awoke, crying. She wrapped her arms around him and held on, rocking him until he was quiet, then crawled in beside him, acutely aware of how rapidly a world could dissolve around a child's ears. She understood. It had happened to her. She pulled him close and kissed his curls as he slept.

* * *

CHAPTER 7

Day 4 – Monday morning
Forbes residence

By Monday morning a dismal, gray front had moved in, blanketing the entire north Texas area with patchy fog and a shivering damp. Her mother had to work, so Ginny took charge of Luis, making sure he was clean, warmly dressed, and fed.

Sinia Forbes taught history for the Lonach Independent School District on Monday, Wednesday, and Friday mornings, then for the Dallas County Regional College District on Tuesday and Thursday afternoons. Ginny worked three twelve-hour nights per week and every other weekend at the hospital. Between the two schedules, there were days they didn't see one another.

At nine a.m. Ginny opened the front door to a trio of authority figures. Himself introduced the strangers.

"Mrs. MacGregor runs th' Lonach Children's Emergency Shelter. She'll see Luis gets everything he needs." The Child Protective Services representative was nearer fifty than forty, short, plump, cheerful, and smelled of fresh bread, with a hint of cinnamon.

"This is Officer Ventura. He would like tae tak' yer statement." Ginny nodded to the policeman. He was in his early thirties, dark complexioned, with a tight, earnest expression that made his smile seem forced.

"Please come in."

She took them into the kitchen, then left Himself and Mrs. MacGregor with Luis while she spoke with the policeman. The officer listened carefully, consulted his notebook, then stowed his recording device. Ginny hesitated. "May I ask if anyone has looked for Mrs. Perez, yet?"

The police officer looked Ginny over, then appeared to make up his mind. "We checked out the apartment last night. There's no evidence of a disturbance. No reason to think she isn't just away for the weekend. Except for the boy, of course." He touched his cap, then strode off down the sidewalk.

Ginny watched him get in the patrol car and drive away, realizing she had no idea how many missing persons there were in the DFW area. The population was too fluid and too likely to be flying under the radar. It was at least possible Mrs. Perez was already dead, which would be a really dirty trick to pull on Luis, especially at Christmas.

Ginny poked her nose into the kitchen to find the Laird and Rose MacGregor talking to Luis. He had apparently taken to Mrs. MacGregor as he was sitting in her lap, showing her the turtle and explaining that it liked to eat lettuce.

"How old are you, Luis?" she asked. "Five?"

"Five-and-a-half!" He emphasized the difference.

"Of course. Any brothers and sisters?"

He shook his head.

"Where's your father?"

"Mexico."

Ginny left them to it and went upstairs. She stripped the bed in Alex's room, then turned, her arms full of linens to find Himself watching her.

"A verry engaging child," he said.

"Yes." She dumped the linens in the basket.

"I ken tha' look. Ye'd like tae find the bairn's mither fer him."

Ginny's eyebrows rose. "What can I possibly do that the police can't do better?"

"Talk tae him, fer one. Between you an' Rose MacGregor, ye might find oot something worth knowin'. Ha'e a wee keek aroond, fer anither. Ye've an eye fer detail, as I ha'e reason tae know." He lifted an eyebrow at her. "'Tis a verry useful talent, that one."

Before Ginny could answer, the doorbell rang again. This time it was Jim, bearing gifts in the form of clothes and toys suitable for a five-and-a-half-year-old boy. Luis accepted the gifts cautiously and Ginny got the impression some adult had tried to buy him off in the past. He looked up at her. "I want my bear."

"You have a Teddy Bear?"

Luis nodded. "He sleeps with me."

"Where is he?"

"At home."

"Do you have a key to your apartment, Luis?"

He nodded, reached into his backpack, and produced a perfectly normal looking door key.

"May I borrow it, please?"

"Mama told me to keep it safe."

Ginny nodded solemnly. "I'll make sure you get it back, but I need it to go get your Teddy Bear. Is he on your bed?"

Luis nodded. "I want to go with you. I want to go home."

Ginny held out her arms and Luis came to her. She gave him a big hug and a kiss. "I know, sweetheart," she said, "but it will be faster if I go get him for you. Trust me."

* * *

By ten a.m. Luis had been packed off to Mrs. MacGregor's, Angus had excused himself, saying he had business to attend to, and Ginny was left to deal with the Teddy Bear—and Jim.

He planted his feet on the kitchen floor and crossed his arms on his chest, his eyes steadily on hers. "This is a bad idea."

Ginny blinked, suddenly aware of how tall he was, and how strong his biceps looked. If he chose to use those muscles against her, there would be nothing she could do to stop him. She swallowed. "The child needs his bear."

Jim frowned. "Whatever trouble that woman has gotten herself into is likely to be dangerous. She's scared. You should be, too."

"We have no idea what her problem is," Ginny pointed out. "If we go look, maybe we can find a clue."

Jim uncrossed his arms and came over to stand looking down at her. "The police have already searched the apartment. If there was something there, they would have found it." He lifted a hand and reached for her cheek.

Ginny took a step back. His gesture had raised a ghost in her mind and her skin crawled. She fought back the fear, reminding herself that this was not the same man, but she couldn't hide the dilated pupils or the racing pulse that meant her instinct was urging her to run.

She dropped her eyes to the floor, telling herself he wouldn't hurt her, no matter how sorely tried.

"I'm sorry, Jim. I didn't mean to do that."

"I know."

She heard the subtle change in his voice—the frustration, carefully controlled. The man had an amazing amount of self-control, but it was a bitter pill to swallow to know she had forced him to use it.

"The reason Detective Tran asked me to help," she said,

"was because the police might overlook a detail that would mean something to an insider."

His words, when he spoke, were measured and reasonable, even though, technically, he was arguing with her.

"Detective Tran specified the ICU."

Ginny could feel her heart beating against her ribs, but she stood her ground. She lifted her eyes to his. "Yes, she did and this may be a wild goose chase, but Maria thinks Phyllis was murdered *because of her*. I'd like to know why she said that."

"Even if it puts you in danger?"

Ginny sucked in a breath. "You're the one who said the only way I was going to get my confidence back was by taking chances. Trial and error. Well, I'm trying."

She watched Jim's brow furrow, his eyes on her. It was more than a minute before he spoke and when he did, it was with a note of misgiving. "Okay, but you're not going alone."

"I hadn't planned to," she said. "Come on."

* * *

Monday midmorning
Streets of Dallas / Perez apartment

Jim pulled the car onto the freeway and headed for one of the less affluent parts of town. He took a deep breath and held it to the count of ten, then let it slowly out, feeling his heart rate settle back to normal. Letting Ginny take risks was a necessary part of her healing, but he wasn't happy about it.

The circumstances of the missing woman's departure suggested an imminent threat, and a deadly one. Ginny poking her nose into the other woman's affairs could attract some very unpleasant attention. Maybe he should have put his foot down, forbidden her to go. He felt an almost irresistible urge to protect her, from herself, if necessary. He glanced over to find her eyes down on a scratchpad, pen in hand.

"What's that?"

"I'm making notes for my report to Detective Tran."

Jim took another breath, making sure his voice was steady. He had not missed how pale her cheeks were. There was nothing wrong with her understanding. "Are you nervous?"

She let the notepad sink into her lap, looking out at the passing scenery, then at him. "Yes."

He reached over and took her hand. Even with the heat on, her flesh felt cold. "You don't have to get out of the car. I can go get the bear."

When she spoke, her voice was low and tightly controlled. "You're wrong, Jim. I have to face this. All of it. I'm sick of feeling helpless and stupid and afraid."

He gave her a quick smile. "Okay. We'll go together."

They turned into the parking lot of the apartment complex and located the correct building. Concrete blocks and metal railings had replaced the single-family homes that had stood here for the better part of the last century. The few remaining trees looked barren, and the earth as if it hadn't brought forth anything live since the walls went up. Empty playground equipment stood in the muddy yard, fringed by abandoned toys. Jim could hear adult voices echoing in the concrete corridors, sounding as flat and gray as the surroundings.

"This way." He led Ginny toward an exterior staircase.

The Perez family lived on the second floor. Jim counted off the numbers, then slid the key into the lock.

"María, ¿eres tú?"

A woman stuck her head out of the doorway of the next apartment, looked them over, then disappeared.

"Think she's calling the super?" Ginny asked.

"Or the police." Jim opened the door and let them in.

The place wasn't immaculate. A five-year-old lived here, after all, but it wasn't trashed, either. Ginny headed for the back of the apartment, returning in a moment with the stuffed bear.

Jim stood in the middle of the main room and looked around. The central heat was still on, but the burners on the stove had been turned off and there were no dirty dishes in the sink.

Ginny set the bear down on the table next to the door and crooked a finger at Jim. "Come see what I found."

He followed her into the sleeping areas; two bedrooms, one bath. The larger was clearly Maria's. Ginny walked over to the bookcase, pulled out a massive tome, and held it up for Jim's inspection. His eyebrows rose.

"Nursing textbooks?"

"In English and Spanish, and there's more." She pointed to a certificate on the wall. "I have one just like that at home."

Jim looked at it more closely. "It's a certificate from the State of Texas."

"From the State Board of Nursing, to be exact. She's a Registered Nurse."

There was a knock on the door.

Jim gestured for Ginny to lead the way, flipping the lights off as they went. The door was already swinging open to reveal the neighbor who had spoken to them standing behind a man with a bunch of keys on a ring. The man blinked in surprise.

"Who are you?"

Jim held out his hand, introducing himself and Ginny, and explaining their errand.

"His bear? Oh, of course."

The woman pushed forward. "Is he all right?"

Ginny nodded. "Yes. Can you tell us where his mother is?"

The woman and man exchanged glances, then the woman

shook her head. "No. She just left."

The man straightened his back and gestured toward the door. "You go, too."

Jim looked at him for a moment, then dug a business card out of his wallet. "If you see Maria, will you give this to her? Luis is safe. She can find him by calling me."

"Sí, if we see her. You go now."

Jim took Ginny's hand and moved in the direction of the door. She grabbed the bear and followed. The man stepped aside to let them by.

Once out in the corridor, Jim pulled Ginny in front of him, herding her down the stairs and into the car. He could feel the eyes of the other two on their backs and was not surprised to see faces peering at them from behind curtains that were hastily replaced when he looked in their direction. He put the car in gear and headed home.

"Whew! That was interesting."

Ginny nodded. "Do you think they know where she is?"

"I couldn't tell. Maybe. At least we gave her a way to contact us, if she wants to."

"And we found something." Ginny slipped her notepad out of her pocket and turned it so Jim could see. "I wrote down her license number. Maybe the Board of Nursing can help."

* * *

CHAPTER 8

Day 4 – Monday noon
Forbes residence

Ginny asked Jim to drop her off at home. There were a number
of things she wanted to do, among them, think.

She put on a load of laundry and tackled the kitchen,
cleaning away the morning's debris, then chopping vegetables
and sorting them into plastic containers. That done, she began
to rearrange the refrigerator, pantry, and spice shelf.

When Mrs. Forbes returned, she settled down at the
kitchen table and watched for a few minutes. "You look like a
long-tailed cat in a room full of rocking chairs."

Ginny sighed, put the spices back in the rack, then sat down
across from her. "I feel like one."

"What is it, darling?"

Ginny took a deep breath. "How could anyone do that?
Dump her son and drive away?"

"She said she was desperate, and I believe her."

"*You* couldn't do that, not to Alex, or me, could you?"

"If I had to, yes, I could." Mrs. Forbes took a sip of her tea.
"Have you decided how you're going to handle Jim?"

Ginny shook her head. "He agreed the only way for me to
regain my confidence is to take risks, but he still wants to

decide which and when. He's behaving as if we're married."

Mrs. Forbes set her cup down, eyeing Ginny. "Do you want to be married, Ginny?"

She thought about it for a minute. "Yes."

"Do you want children?"

"Yes."

"Do you want Jim?"

Ginny considered the question, probing deep, trying to come up with an honest answer. "He has many fine qualities."

Her mother smiled. "Yes, he does, and he will be Laird."

Ginny squirmed. "That's not the problem."

"Then what is?"

It took Ginny a minute to find the right words. "I can't know if he's really who and what he seems to be."

Her mother sighed. "We can't know that about anyone, except in retrospect, but he's Angus' grandson. That should count for something."

"He's a stranger. Angus hasn't seen him since he was a child. He was raised outside Lonach, outside any Homestead. There's no telling what he may believe or be willing to do. Do we know what drove his father off?"

Sinia Forbes shook her head. "I don't. Does Jim?"

"I don't know. I haven't asked him."

Her mother sighed, then smiled. "Well, there's one thing I *am* sure of. That man loves you and wants to marry you."

Ginny sighed. "That's what I thought last time."

* * *

Monday early afternoon
Hillcrest Regional Medical Center

Jim had a meeting. It was inconvenient to be pulled in on his afternoon off, but he didn't have to report again for another twenty-four hours, so it could have been worse. The subject of the meeting was fentanyl.

"Where's this stuff coming from?" The speaker was another ER physician. Jim had met him (and most of the rest of the medical staff) when he hired on, but hadn't seen him since. His name was Devlin Jones, known as 'DJ.' He was a large, ruddy, aging patrician, a fixture in the community. Not Homestead, but born and bred in Dallas. He owned the remnants of a local ranch, now within the boundaries of one of the suburbs, though it had been open land when he'd been born. He had a genuine Texas drawl, and a habit of 'talkin' country' that sounded odd to Jim's Virginia-trained ears.

"That's what we want to find out." The DEA agent was dressed in a suit and tie and was perched on the end of the conference room table, one leg dangling. Jim couldn't tell if this was habitual or an affectation, adopted for the benefit of the locals he now faced.

He had Washington written all over him. Around the same age as Jim, Agent DeSoto had the slick, no-nonsense haircut and physique that said he could run and was packing heat. He also had no concept of the traditional deference paid to elder statesmen in Texas.

"We already know about the synthetic fentanyl coming in from China," one of the white heads at the table noted. "Why focus on us?"

"What we're seeing in Dallas is not coming from China. The chemical signature is wrong. We're seeing high-quality narcotics clearly manufactured in the U.S. and they're not being combined with anything. That's suspicious. As you know, most dealers want to stretch their profits so they mix whatever they get with something else."

Everyone around the table nodded. They were familiar with the problems caused by this practice. One of the more common involved mixing crack cocaine with baking soda, powdered sugar, or powdered milk. These substances didn't always dissolve completely and, when injected, could form a solid mass that acted like a clot, cutting off the blood supply when the foreign material reached a tight spot in the circulatory system.

DeSoto continued. "If they're putting pure product on the streets, there has to be a reason, and it's only happening here. We want to find out why."

A middle-aged Indian woman leaned forward. Jim had worked with her twice and been impressed. She was intelligent, knowledgeable, and calm in a crisis. "The problem," she said, "is that the patients are not able to speak to us. So far, they've all been dead on arrival."

Agent DeSoto nodded. "From massive overdose."

Jim caught a movement out of the corner of his eye and turned to look at his boss. Even in scrubs, Dr. Lyons' military background showed. He pushed off the wall, drew his five foot ten into a precise vertical line, planted his feet shoulder width apart, crossed his arms on his chest, and addressed the agent.

"Let me see if I got this straight. You're telling us that Dallas has a drug problem no one else has."

"Right."

"And it's because the dealers are supplying pure, U.S. produced drug to the users."

"Right again."

"And the users don't expect that much active ingredient, which leads to accidental overdoses."

"Yes."

The medical director looked around the table, then back at the DEA agent. "I don't see how we can help you. If they're dead, they're dead."

The agent slid off the table and faced Dr. Lyons. "We want to put agents in all the Emergency Rooms in Dallas to interview the families and friends. We're hoping to get a lead on what's happening and why and who's responsible. We need your cooperation to help the agents fit in."

Several of the physicians exchanged glances. Agent DeSoto seemed to read their minds.

"We have a task force put together and everyone on it has basic medical training. We want to disguise them as techs and we expect them to do what they're told, to maintain their cover, for as long as needed."

Dr. Lyons looked around at his crew. "Any discussion?"

Jim watched as the gathering of physicians considered all the things that could go wrong with a plan like this. Eventually the Indian woman, Dr. Varma, spoke. "If there's even a hint this is a trap, they will eliminate anyone with knowledge of what's going on. That means us."

Agent DeSoto nodded. "We hope to have a swift resolution to this problem, but it's true it carries some risk."

Dr. Lyons raised a sardonic eyebrow. "Being an ER physician carries risks. We all know that. We just don't want to put targets on our backs."

Dr. Jones looked over at Agent DeSoto. "Would putting more security on help or hurt?"

"Could go either way. We don't want to alert anybody, but we could have extra help in-house and ready to respond if needed."

Jim leaned back in his chair and crossed his arms on his chest. Dr. Lyons looked at him.

"You have something you want to add, Dr. Mackenzie?"

Jim turned to face him. "The D.C. area has a lot of crime." Lyons nodded. He was aware of Jim's history. "Three years ago, some of the facilities decided to add bulletproof vests under the scrub tops." Jim took a breath, remembering a particularly hairy night that had seen one death and a number of injuries among the Emergency Room staff. "They work and we were able to work in them." He met the medical director's eyes. "But they aren't cheap."

All eyes were on the medical director now. He scanned the room. "Is that what it would take?"

There were nods from almost everyone around the table.

"I think we'd all feel better if we knew we weren't gonna die the first time someone came in guns a-blazing," Jones said. "It would give us time to duck."

Lyons nodded, then looked at Agent DeSoto. "I'll take it to the Hillcrest hospital board. You'll have your answer tomorrow, one way or another."

* * *

Monday midafternoon
Forbes residence

Later that same afternoon, Ginny sat in front of her computer, her fingers poised to write down whatever she came up with. She had dutifully called Detective Tran and relayed the question about Maria Perez's nursing license, and been told it would be added to the list.

"Anything that might have made Mrs. Kyle a target," Tran had said. If Maria was right, and Phyllis was killed *because of her*, then there was clearly a motive, but without Maria to tell them what it was, Ginny could only guess.

She frowned to herself. If Detective Tran was right, it was one of them. Someone she worked with. Someone who could brutally and cold-bloodedly kill another human being, then walk away and blend in with the crowd. A very small crowd.

Miserable as that thought was, it gave her a starting point. One of the people who'd been present last Friday morning had a connection to both Maria and Phyllis. Maybe not directly, but—if Maria was right—it was there.

* * *

CHAPTER 9

Day 4 – Monday midafternoon
Jim's apartment

Jim had gone home and was now sitting, staring at the wall, thinking of Ginny. He'd promised he wouldn't order her around, and he meant to do less of it, but she'd announced today that she needed to face her fears and this was one both of them had been avoiding. She needed to get back on the ice.

She was physically healthy, and he knew she'd had her skates replaced. The last time he'd brought it up, she'd stormed off, but then, the last time, he'd been insisting she wear a helmet.

He could still see her as she'd looked, lying in the hospital bed, unconscious, then concussed, then merely hurting. He didn't want to risk that, any more than she did, but it was absolutely necessary she face that fear. She wouldn't be able to face herself until she did.

He took a deep breath. It was like surgery; pain for a while, then healing, then strength. She would understand that. There was no sense in putting it off any longer. He pulled his phone out and got to work.

* * *

Monday late afternoon
Dallas Ice Arena

Ginny sat in the passenger seat of Jim's car. "Where are we going?"

"You'll see."

He'd announced he was taking her to dinner, but nothing else. Her curiosity had gone into overdrive, but she recognized an immovable object when she saw one.

Ginny studied his face. He sat with his lips pressed firmly together as if he didn't trust himself to speak, but she didn't catch on until twenty minutes later when he pulled up in front of a building she knew all too well.

"We're here." He pulled into a parking space, got out, walked around behind the car, and reached into the trunk. Ginny felt her throat tighten as she recognized her skate bag.

He opened her door and held out his hand.

"What are you doing with my skates?" She heard the sharp edge to the question, but was too busy trying not to panic to do anything about it.

"I had your mother get them out of your car for me."

Ginny was having trouble breathing. "I'm not going in there."

He set the bag down on the pavement, slipped an arm around her waist, and pulled her out of the car. "We need to get past this."

"Not now. Not like this."

He put his hands on her shoulders and turned her to face him. "You shook me today, Ginny. You reminded me that I can't do this for you, much as I want to."

"Jim, *please*."

He pulled her into his arms. "I can't imagine how frightening this must be for you, but I know you can do it. Your mother says you love to skate and you've missed it."

Ginny could feel her heart racing, her eyes suspiciously damp. "You promised you wouldn't tell me what to do anymore."

"I'm not going to let you ignore this, any more than I would let you ignore a hot appendix. This needs to be faced."

Ginny was shivering, in spite of her warm winter coat. He was right. She needed to skate, to prove to herself she could.

"I don't want you to see me like this."

"I promised I would do whatever you needed, to help you heal. Lean on me, Ginny. Let me help you."

Lean on him! He had no idea what he was suggesting. She should give him his wish. That would teach him. She pulled back and looked up into his face.

"On one condition."

"What is it?"

"You skate, too."

"I don't know how."

"It doesn't matter. You said you'd help. I need you out on the ice, with me."

She saw the corner of his mouth curve up.

"All right. If that's what you need, that's what we'll do." He picked up the bag and turned her toward the entrance.

Ginny found her head pounding and her conscience in crisis. Why had she insisted on his coming out on the ice with her? What did she hope to get from it? He couldn't help her. All he could do was find out how hard it was to skate. Why did she want him to know that? Because she was so frightened? Was this revenge?

He paid their admissions and his skate rental fee, then found a seat in the bleachers while Ginny slipped into the ladies' room. She kept an extra pair of hose in the bag. She put them on, then pulled her slacks over them, and added a headband to keep her hair out of her eyes. She looked at herself in the mirror, seeing a skater. She looked the part. It remained to be seen if she could act the part as well.

When she got back to the bleachers, she checked his skates, to make sure they were laced up and tied properly, then put on her own. She had to concentrate to keep her hands from trembling.

It was the first time she'd had the new skates on. New skates had to be broken in. She wouldn't have tried anything fancy under any circumstances. So, just the basics. Just get out there and stroke.

She moved to the boards and did a few stretches, then turned and faced the ice. God! Was she really going to do this?

"Ready?" Jim put his arm around her waist.

She stood at the gate wanting to run, knowing she couldn't, not with him there. She swallowed then stepped over the barrier and onto the frozen surface.

I can do this, she said to herself. *I can do this*. She held onto the boards and watched as Jim followed and suddenly knew why she had insisted on his being there. She needed to teach him. Having to focus on him would help her control her fear.

She spent the next ten minutes showing him the way the figure skates worked and explaining how to control the physics. "Did you go skating as a child?"

"Yes, but all I had was hockey skates. This is different."

"You're right. It is."

She pushed off, her eyes on him, and demonstrated a simple stroke. She went back to collect him, coaxing him away from the wall.

"Put your hands on mine and look at me. Don't look down."

She skated backwards, swiveling, both feet on the ice, holding him on line and making sure he didn't get too far off balance. A treacherous little voice in her head taunted her. *This isn't skating. You'll never skate again. Not the way you used to.* She shoved the thought aside.

"You're doing fine. Turn your foot to the side and push gently. Bend your knees. Look at me, not at your feet."

They made one complete circuit of the ice in this manner. When they got back to where they had started, she let Jim grab the boards and hang on for a bit.

"I had no idea! It looks so easy on TV."

Ginny laughed shortly. "Those effortless movements you see are the result of raw talent, excellent coaching, and a lifetime of practice."

"Go skate for me," he said, nodding at the ice surface. "Show me what you can do."

She shook her head. "Not today." She explained about the new skates.

"All right. I won't expect triple axles, but I need a moment. Once around the park, then come get me."

Ginny took a deep breath, then nodded.

She was tight, very, very tight, and that was very, very dangerous. She needed to loosen up. She started around the rink. It had been two months. Two months and a twisted ankle. Two months and a twisted ankle and a cracked skull. She blinked hard, trying to clear the memory out of her mind. She pushed carefully, first with one foot, then the other.

The new boots were stiff. If she wasn't careful, they would raise blisters. She bent her knees and pushed again. Nice blades. They bit the ice and pulled her around the curves effortlessly. Very nice. She took a deep breath and looked at the other skaters.

It was a public session and there were too many people on the ice. No chance she could get away with anything, even if she'd been willing to try.

She glided toward the boards. The edges were really sweet.

She curved back, being careful to stay out of everyone's way. Gentle swing rolls, into the center and back out. Nothing dangerous. No speed, no sudden changes of direction. She completed the circuit and went back to Jim, who was gripping the barrier as if his life depended on it. He put an arm around her waist, pulling her to him, giving her a hug.

"You look good."

"Your turn."

"Mine? I can't even stand up."

"It's much harder to balance standing still than it is moving. Come on. Basic stroking." She pulled him away from the side and took him around again, coaching him on posture, foot position, and how to use his muscles. He was being a very good sport, trying to follow her lead and smiling at her between bouts of panic. She let him retire to the boards and stroked back out onto the ice. She was breathing easier now.

God, it felt good! She found herself settling into old habits, found herself picking up speed, found herself stretching and lifting and shifting her weight. It was all coming back. She turned on the ice without conscious thought, then dropped into a lunge, then headed for the boards and did some kicks.

She pulled her leg up and moved it into spiral position, then brought it around on the edge-change-edge. It was too crowded for that move, and she was too out of shape to be sure she wouldn't fall, so she contented herself with one smallish spiral of the straight line variety, but in good position, then into the center and turns again, slowly, but correctly. Then, without thinking, she was into the backwards crossovers, picking up speed and stepping into a spin, then curving into a pivot to finish with a full stop in the center of the ice, just as she used to do.

She looked up, hunting for Jim. He'd gotten off the ice and was standing in the doorway, his eyes on her, a huge smile on his face.

Ginny felt a rush of warmth in his direction. She hadn't done *anything*, but she felt as if she'd summited Mount Everest. And she'd been able to do it because of him. Because he believed in her. She raced over, jumped off the ice, and threw herself into his arms, knocking both of them to the mats.

"Oh, Jim! Thank you!"

"You're welcome!" He was laughing, his arms around her as she covered him with kisses, on his neck, his cheeks, his lips. Then, suddenly, he was kissing her, seriously, passionately, the two of them locked in an embrace, unaware of the sight they made for the other skaters until someone reached down and offered Ginny a hand to help her to her feet.

She stood, quivering with the emotions coursing through her, and watched as Jim rose, thanked their helpers, and assured them that neither he nor she was injured.

He turned to face her and Ginny saw a warmth in his eyes that certainly had not been there earlier. He held out a hand and she let him pull her to him, settling into his arms, her head on his shoulder.

"You did it," he whispered in her ear. "I knew you could."

Ginny closed her eyes, letting the joy wash over her. She was back on the ice and he had kissed her and for the first time since October it seemed just barely possible that everything was going to be all right after all.

* * *

Monday late afternoon
Perez apartment

She stood in the apartment and looked around.

"The police came?"

"Sunday night."

"Did they speak with anyone?"

"Sí, Señora Jefa. But no one knew anything. Then a man and a woman came. This morning."

"What did they want?"

"El oso del niño."

She considered this for a moment. "The child is how old?"

"Cinco, Señora Jefa."

Too young to be on his own. Whoever had the boy probably knew his mother and where to find her. "What did this man and woman look like?"

The manager raised his arm. "Tall. So. And pálido. The woman, she had long red hair, in a braid. I sent them away."

"What else can you tell me?"

"The man, he left this." The manager fished a business card out of his pocket and held it out to her.

She looked at it, her eyebrows rising. James Mackenzie, MD, Hillcrest Regional. She slipped it in her pocket, then faced the manager. "Wait for me outside."

He bobbed his head and left, closing the door behind him.

She searched the apartment, but there were no drugs and no clues as to where the missing woman might have gone. She was pretty sure she knew what had happened, but she needed to get all her ducks in a row before she reported in. They would have to respond, of course. And quickly.

* * *

CHAPTER 10

Day 4 – Monday / Tuesday night shift
Hillcrest Regional Medical ICU

When Ginny reported to the hospital on Monday evening, she
was still thrumming from the afternoon's adventure, by which
she meant the kiss. She hadn't even thought about it at the
time. It had seemed so right, so natural to kiss him, to show
him how happy she was. And he had responded in kind, then
with more enthusiasm, and she had found her eyes closed and
her head spinning. She caught her breath at the memory.

Jim (God bless the man—and she meant that) had been
patient. She'd been his patient, of course, during the months of
healing and only a monster would move in on a woman unable
to defend herself. But he'd been more. He had let her curl up in
his arms and ache with the devastation; had refrained from
making light of the situation, recognizing the depth of the
betrayal; had let her pull away when he touched a nerve,
without abandoning her.

She sighed to herself. After the euphoria died down, she'd
remembered his promise not to make decisions for her. He'd
broken it, but he'd been right, so maybe she was wrong, at
least about this one thing. She was inclined to be lenient, as
long as he didn't do it again. He'd lavished compliments upon

her, and apologized, and she hadn't seen him that happy in months. She smiled to herself and turned her attention to her job.

It was her first shift back at work after Phyllis' death and among the things she'd found in her e-mail box was a note from Detective Tran, giving contact information to use if the police station number was busy. Network security had automatically sent a copy to the ICU Head Nurse, Ginny's boss, and to Human Resources. Ginny made a note of the alternate number, then moved on. Her concentration was broken by a muted squeal of feminine delight.

"Oh! They're so cute!"

Someone had brought in a box of puppies.

"Look at them! Aren't they adorable?" Four nurses surrounded the box, each cuddling a puppy. Ginny's mouth twitched at the sight.

Grace called to her. "Come on, Ginny. Don't you want to hold one?"

Ginny found she did. She rose, walked over, and looked down at the remaining three pups. Grace rescued pit bulls and these were typical of the breed, modified by an unspecified male parent. "How did you come to have puppies?"

"The usual way. The last bitch I adopted turned out to be pregnant. Come on. Hold one and tell me you don't want to take it home." Grace scooped up a puppy and handed it to Ginny, who tucked it up against her cheek. It squirmed in her hands, turning to lick her ear.

She played with the pup for a few minutes, then put it back in the box. "Sorry. Can't take on an animal at the moment. And you'd better get them out of here before you get caught."

Grace nodded. "They're going to the shelter tomorrow, but I was hoping to find homes for some of them before that."

"Have you been down to the ER?"

"That's my next stop." Three of the other nurses put the puppies back in the box, but the fourth followed Grace to the elevator, making arrangements for transfer of ownership of the chosen animal. Ginny washed her hands of the dog hair and the incident, reflecting that Grace had a habit of thinking rules were made to be bent—in a worthy cause, of course.

The first few hours of the shift were easy. There was so much to do she didn't have time to think about the murder, but as the clock moved toward midnight and the night settled in, Ginny found herself looking at the other staff, rather than the patients.

Peter was new. African-American with a buzz cut, Marine tattoos, and one diamond stud in his left earlobe. He'd been employed at Hillcrest for four months and was one of the Respiratory Therapists acquired when the latest hurricane had driven refugees from their homes on the coast to the north Texas prairie. She didn't know him at all.

Dee, also African-American and also a Respiratory Therapist, had been here longer than Ginny. She didn't look old enough to have three grandchildren, but she'd started young so maybe that explained it. Solid, reliable, an open book. She would talk to anyone about anything, if they would only stand still long enough.

Both of them had been busy with the Code Blues. There was no chance either of them could have slipped away while those were going on. Ginny corrected herself. It was *possible*, of course, just not likely.

Ginny felt her skin crawl. She turned her eyes back to her work, trying to shake the memory of how many times she'd been told to butt out last time.

But this time is different, the little voice in her head argued. *Detective Tran has asked for your help. You have a duty to try. And—let's be honest here—you are the nosiest person I know, never satisfied until you find out what's behind everything.*

Ginny squirmed, admitting the truth of that accusation, then sighed. She could put together a time line. They'd gotten slammed just before two a.m. and the fun didn't ease off until close to six. Ginny didn't know which Respiratory Therapist had been assigned to which Code, but it would be in the logs.

She rose and checked on her patients, making sure they were safe and comfortable, which kept her busy until one-thirty, at which point she found herself with twenty free minutes. She let her mind drift back to the night of the murder.

They'd started the Thursday night/Friday morning shift with four of the twelve beds empty. Ginny'd had a patient in resolving Diabetic Ketoacidosis, and the first admission.

Phyllis had had two relatively stable patients; one renal failure on continuous dialysis, the other a multiple trauma, four days out, on a vent, with TPN and wound care with Contact precautions. Ginny glanced around the Unit, as if expecting to see the dead woman emerge from one of the patient rooms.

It had been hard not to hate Phyllis in nursing school. She learned easily and was the sort of leggy blonde who looked good in everything, which meant she could have her pick of male companions. But her laid-back Texas upbringing defused any real animosity. She and Ginny had been in the same study group and both had benefitted from the partnership. After graduation, they both applied to Hillcrest and both ended up in the Medical ICU. Ginny had been glad of that, too. Phyllis was calm and competent and night shifts were always quieter when she was on duty.

Ginny looked up as Alice flew by on her way to the med room. Alice was the opposite of Phyllis, a bombastic brunette with a penchant for noise. She had one of those laughs that could be heard over the alarms and an aggressive style of interaction that included the newly-minted wedding band set with diamonds that she flashed like a red flag at a bull.

On Thursday night Alice had drawn what turned out to be an expanding subarachnoid hematoma, who Coded, then had to be shipped off to surgery and transferred to the Neuro ICU. Ginny had stepped in to cover her respiratory failure patient until the first admission arrived. At which point Susan had taken over Alice's second patient, and lent a hand to help Ginny get her myocardial infarction settled in.

Susan was a plump fawn of a person, doe-eyed and mousey brown. She and Ginny had gone through orientation together, sharing lunches and tidbits of personal information. She saw everything, understood everyone, and had a wicked sense of humor she shared with very few.

Susan's admission that night, a motor vehicle collision from the ER with orders to prep for orthopedic surgery, but not until he cleared the cocaine from his system, turned out to be uncooperative, so she'd had to stay with him and was no longer available to help Alice, which meant the charge nurse had to take over.

The charge nurse was usually one of the night people, but Margot had called in with some sort of family emergency. So the Head Nurse, Marjorie Hawkins, had been forced to come in on her day off and fill in.

Physically, Ms. Hawkins was unremarkable. You could look right at her and not be able to describe her the minute you looked away. Medium height, medium build, medium age, medium brown hair and eyes. But she was good at her job, with a flair for the bureaucratic tasks required of a department head.

She'd been holed up in the office doing paperwork for the first part of the shift, but had to come out and play when her own admission arrived, also from the ER and also a motor vehicle collision, this one also an asthmatic. That put extra strain on the Respiratory Therapy department as they kept having to do breathing treatments, as well as cover the ventilators and assist with the Codes.

Ginny looked up as Margot approached.

"Have you seen Grace? She's MIA."

Ginny shook her head. Best not to mention the puppies. "She's here, though. I saw her earlier."

"Well, she'd better show up soon. I've got other work to do." She stalked off.

An alarm called Ginny to one of her patient's side. She dealt with the issue, collected the two a.m. data, administered the scheduled medications, charted, and ended up an hour later back at her table, watching the monitors, thinking about last Friday.

Grace had the last two patients that night, a vented lung cancer with metastasis awaiting a bed on hospice, and a patient with pneumocystis (immunocompromised and in Protective Isolation).

Grace lived up to her name. She was tall and willowy, with almond-shaped eyes and satin skin. She had been a model and had been married, but both of those endeavors had ended badly. She usually displayed a sang-froid that allowed stressors to roll right off her back, but Ginny had seen a darker side on the one occasion when Grace had completely lost her cool.

The fourth admission was the second MI and should have gone to the nurse with only one patient, Ms. Hawkins, but she was busy with charge nurse tasks and helping Alice and Susan. So the fourth admission (and a third patient) fell to Ginny, which put her over the top and racing to finish all her work on schedule. By which time it was four-thirty a.m. and *that* was when the cocaine abuser decided to rip out all his lines, trash his room, and die on them.

And—at some point during that chaotic night—Phyllis had

been murdered.

Murdered! Ginny rose and went about her tasks with the word floating in the air just out of sight. Someone had followed Phyllis into the restroom, wrapped a wire around her neck, and clamped it in place.

The police were leaning toward premeditation, the wire and clamp brought to work with murder in mind. But Ginny couldn't help thinking that, if you wanted to kill someone in an ICU, all you had to do was look around. There were lethal weapons in every direction.

"Did you hear the news?"

Ginny turned to find Lisa leaning over the back of the monitor desk, speaking to June.

"What news?"

"The police came Saturday afternoon and broke into Phyllis' locker and you'll never guess what they found!"

"Tampons?" June had a dry sense of humor that was lost on Lisa, but made Ginny's mouth twitch.

"No! Well, yes. They found her purse, but they also found drugs."

"Drugs? What kind of drugs?"

"Cocaine!"

June frowned. "Why would she have cocaine in her locker?"

"Well, isn't it obvious? She was using on the job! If she wasn't dead already, they would have to fire her."

June raised a skeptical eyebrow. "You really think Phyllis was snorting cocaine on the job and not one of us noticed?"

"Well, all right. Maybe she was just stashing it here until she could take it home."

"Where would she get cocaine? From our stock?"

"No. These were street drugs."

"How do you know?"

"Had to be. We don't stock cocaine in our medication

dispenser. That's a surgical, or maybe an ER drug, not ICU."

June nodded. "But it still doesn't make sense. If she wasn't stealing it from here and stashing it until the end of shift, why would it be in her locker? If she bought it on the street, she should either have taken it home or left it in her car."

"It was in her purse. Maybe she forgot to take it out."

June seemed unconvinced. "How did you find out about all this?"

Lisa pulled back, then lifted her chin. "I have my sources."

"Really?" June's voice was even drier than usual.

"Yes, really. What's more, someone called in an anonymous tip last Thursday. The Director of Nurses was already investigating."

"And your point is?"

"Well, maybe that's what got her killed. Something to do with the drugs. It's a good thing she's gone. If the media found out, Hillcrest would be in big trouble. Maybe someone wanted to hush up the investigation."

"By killing her? That's not going to stop an investigation. Besides, the autopsy will tell us whether or not she had drugs in her system."

"Well, all I've got to say is, if one of us had to be killed, it's a good thing it was someone who needed killing." And with that remark, Lisa stalked off in the direction of her assigned rooms.

Ginny smiled when June rolled her eyes toward the ceiling. Lisa could be a lot to deal with. Still, it was a disturbing thought. Who among them had decided Phyllis needing killing? Because someone certainly had. Ginny looked around.

It wasn't the same ICU crew tonight; Margot was back and Susan was off. Some the patients (and their families) had gone and new ones taken their place. The Code Team members, the physicians, and the night supervisor all rotated duty. It could have been any one of them and it would take some doing to eliminate them from the investigation. As of this moment, the only person she *knew* was innocent was herself.

Ginny pulled her phone out of her pocket and scrolled to the audio recording software. What she had in mind was a memorial collection, the kind where everyone contributed a memory of the dearly departed. If she could pull it off, it might even be a nice gesture, something to give John Kyle. But what she hoped to do was find someone who might say something in an unguarded moment. A clue that could be handed over to Detective Tran.

She made sure her patients were stable, then made the rounds of the nurses on duty. With each one, she explained the memorial idea, recorded the responses (or accepted a promise of an e-mail when the interviewee had more leisure), then asked if he or she had heard about the cocaine.

Ginny was no psychiatrist, but not one of them (other than Lisa, of course) seemed to be hiding anything. They were all interested and willing to help. She was kept busy the rest of the night recording tidbits those on duty the night of the murder had forgotten to tell the police, and rumors those who had not been there had come across since.

Several had heard about the drug seizure, but none had been in the Unit at the time. Ginny would have to ask the day shift about that.

They had questions for her, too. Did the police have a favorite suspect? Was there any forensic evidence? A man or a woman, for instance? No? Not even that? So it could be anyone. There were a number of worried expressions.

Ginny documented carefully, making notes of her own thoughts alongside the accounts. It was just as interesting to hear what the others were asking her as their answers to what she was asking them.

Her mother had been right. The innocent among them

wanted this mystery solved, and quickly. They didn't like the idea that there was a murderer among them. No one said it, but everyone seemed to be wondering if the murderer would strike again and—if so—who would be next?

* * *

CHAPTER 11

Jim's apartment

Jim had his feet up on the bed, pen in hand, writing his latest medical journal article. He was the sort who could concentrate, ignoring distractions, but even he had limits.

He swore mildly, finished his sentence, then rose to investigate the incessant knocking that was interrupting his work. He found the Laird on his doorstep. He stepped back, opening the door to a swirl of heavy wool and cold air.

"Are ye deaf, lad? I've been knockin' fer fifteen minutes."

"The doorbell works."

The Laird snorted. "It dinna th' time afore."

Jim smothered a smile. "I've had it fixed and you could have called."

"'Tis better ye see this fer yerself." The Laird flipped his cloak off and sat down on the edge of the couch.

Jim sat down facing him. "All right. What do you have to show me?"

He watched as his grandfather pulled a small plastic bag out of his sporran and extended it toward him. "This."

Jim peered at the contents of the bag, frowning. "Where did you get these?"

"Rose found them stuck on Luis this mornin', when she stripped him tae gi'e him a bath."

Jim looked up in alarm. "Is he dead?"

"Nae, th' wee nyaff's unharmed."

Jim pulled on a pair of disposable gloves, then opened the bag and drew out one of the wafers, inspecting it closely. It appeared to be a transdermal patch containing a potent narcotic painkiller, the kind used with terminally ill cancer patients. "He was wearing these?" Jim counted the patches, estimating the delivery dose.

"Aye. He told Rose he found the stickers and was playin' wi' them, but he's no sure how they got on tae his skin." Himself lifted an eyebrow. "I've a notion the lad kens a bit more than that, but he's no sayin'."

"Give me a minute." Jim moved to his computer and pulled up a reference site used to help identify medications. "Well, it certainly *looks* like fentanyl." He swung around in his chair. "Was he sick? Any symptoms?"

"Nary a one. Perfectly normal wean, and I'll eat my hat if he dinnae ken he shouldna hae been playin' wi' them."

"You spoke to him?"

"Aye. Rose found them, and recognized them. Her mither, I think, uses something like. She tells me it gave her quite a turn, but the bairn was fine so she called me instead o' takin' him tae th' emergency room."

Jim frowned. "If these are used, then the amount of narcotic in them might be significantly diminished, but he could still have absorbed some of the drug. Where did he get them?"

"Ah, weel, that he hasna said."

Jim picked up the patch again and examined it closely. "There's an expiration date, but no lot number. We might be able to trace the manufacturer, but we'd need the box it came from, or someone with more experience than I have."

"Wha' aboot th' pharmacy at th' hospital?"

Jim nodded. "We can try." He set the patch down and looked at his grandfather. "He wouldn't talk to you? Or Rose?"

The Laird shook his head.

"Then he won't talk to me, either. What we need is Ginny."

"Aye, but she's asleep."

Jim nodded. "With your permission, I'll take these in with me when I go to work tonight and see what I can find out." His brow furrowed. "It's interesting that it's fentanyl."

"Why is that, lad?"

Jim looked up and met his grandfather's eyes. "Because it's fentanyl that brought the DEA to Dallas."

His grandfather nodded. "And on th' same subject, th' board approved yer request fer protective vests. I'm told th' DEA is deliverin' them this afternoon."

"That was fast!"

"Ye'll want tae make sure ye get one that fits."

Jim nodded. He remembered the routine.

His grandfather rose, pulling his Inverness cape over his shoulders. "Jim—" The Laird caught Jim's eye and held it. "Dinna tak' chances, lad. No wi' this."

Jim let his grandfather out, then went back to his writing, thinking about Agent DeSoto's plan. He didn't mind running a few work-related risks: germs, punctures, even an irate patient once in a while. He *did* mind having to worry about drug runners. He hadn't told Ginny, or his grandfather, but he'd been shot in the chest that night in D.C. If he hadn't been wearing his vest, he wouldn't have lived through the experience, and, even with the vest, it hadn't been any fun.

* * *

Tuesday afternoon
Hillcrest Regional Medical Center

Agent DeSoto had them cornered in the largest of the Hillcrest conference rooms. On this December afternoon, the DEA agent stood with his back to the sylvan views of north Dallas, his expression grave.

"It's imperative that none of you talk about this operation. Not even to each other. Lives hang in the balance, yours, perhaps. My agents, certainly."

The room was lined with agents. Jim let his eye roam over them. They looked ordinary enough, the sort of faces you'd see at the park or a football game.

Jim frowned to himself. What was missing was the enthusiasm he usually saw in young people assigned to the Emergency Room. Most loved it. There was a romance to it, especially at night. The patients would come out of the darkness, in fear and pain. Sometimes they were in crisis and the team had to move fast. Sometimes the trouble wasn't immediately apparent and you ended up with a surprise, and then you had to move very fast indeed. It got the adrenaline pumping and made you feel alive.

"The agents will help you select a vest. You're to wear them while you're on duty, every minute."

Someone stuck a hand in the air. "What if we get hot?"

"If you take it off, you take a chance on getting killed."

"Are you going to teach us what to do if someone pulls out a gun?"

"It's the same drill you've already practiced. Active shooter—run, hide, fight."

Jim's mouth tightened. He hoped it wouldn't come to that.

"You all know where the safe zones are."

There were nods all over the room. The Saturday Night

Knife and Gun Club was a well-known phenomenon in any big city Emergency Department. The gangs would exchange fire, then bring their injured to the hospital, and continue the battle in the ER waiting room. As a result, modern ER doors were fitted with metal detectors and equipped with armed guards, windows facing the waiting areas were bullet-proof, and most of the walls were concrete.

"Okay. These vests are all new, no embedded bullets, so you can move through the metal detectors without setting off the alarms. Wear an undershirt to minimize contact with the fabric and make sure your scrub tops are loose enough to cover your torso when bending and reaching."

Over the course of the next hour Jim and the other ER staff members were fitted for vests and instructed in how to adjust them for maximum effectiveness. They were also told exactly what the vests could and could not do.

The design would not protect them from bullets to the head, arms, legs, hip, and groin. One lucky shot to the femoral artery would result in a sudden reduction in the Hillcrest medical work force. The synthetic fiber used to produce the lightweight body armor would not stop a determined assault with a knife, though it would take real power to stick a blade through the heavy twill fabric covering the armor. Nor would the vests offer protection from blunt force trauma to the chest, which could send the wearer into a lethal dysrhythmia, no penetration required.

Jim tried not to think about it. The vests would do what they were designed to do, protect the major organs in the torso from penetrating injuries. The system wasn't perfect, but it was a whole lot better than nothing.

* * *

Tuesday Evening
HQ of the North TX Distribution and Support Region

The night felt empty. No moon hung overhead and no stars, not even a wisp of gossamer cloud to show where the earth ended and the sky began.

She stood, as was required in his presence, and waited. Nonsense, of course. Very out dated. She stood, but she refused to drop her eyes to the carpet, insisting on meeting his gaze, especially now.

"You are sure?"

"I'm sure the woman is missing, along with one set of the counterfeit fentanyl patches. I've been told the man who came out to the apartment knows where the boy is. I could question him, but it might draw attention to the situation."

"I agree. Besides, I have another way to discover the boy."

"What about the woman?"

"What of her?"

"I think she could be a problem. I could take care of that."

The man behind the desk studied her face. "You would need my help."

She crossed her arms on her chest. "I thought you wanted us to do our own dirty work."

He nodded. "So I do, but not if it brings the police down around our ears." His eyes narrowed. "No. I will decide when and what to do about her."

"As you wish." She handed over the business card.

"You may go." He made a dismissive gesture with his hand, his eyes on the card.

She nodded, then let herself out of the room. Once she was in the parking lot, she drew a deep breath. Considering the potential consequences, that hadn't gone so badly.

The key was the boy. Once in their custody, he could be

used to draw his mother out. But sooner would be better than later. Perhaps, if she found the boy first—

She drove home planning how to control the gossip that was undoubtedly running through the organization like wildfire. Most would know not to listen, but there were always a few too stupid to understand what was good for them. Well, she would put a stop to that and without danger of police interference. Then she would see what she could come up with to settle the other woman, quietly. Because he was right. Too much police interest was not good for business.

* * *

Tuesday night
Hillcrest Regional Medical Center

Jim caught up with Ginny just before midnight. He'd left one of the fentanyl patches with the night shift pharmacist, and another with the lab, extracting a promise that it would be tested for chemical content before dawn. A third was destined for DeSoto and the DEA labs. The remaining three were in the plastic bag he showed to Ginny.

"Could he have gotten them out of a trash can?" he asked.

Ginny shook her head. "I don't think so."

"Why not?"

"These haven't been used." She pointed to the non-sticky surfaces. "The rule is that the person who administers the medication—and that includes family members—puts his or her initials, the date, and the time on the patch, to prevent overdoses. These are unmarked."

"Could the marks have been rubbed off?"

Ginny tipped the patches back and forth in the light. "No dents and no trace of residual ink." She handed them back.

"My best guess is, no, these are not discards."

"Which means he got hold of fresh patches." Jim gave Ginny a sober look. "I know he's only five, but that child needs to understand this is not a game. His mother is missing and those patches may be the only clue we have to finding her. You're the only person he'll talk to. Get him to tell you where the patches came from."

Ginny sighed. "I'll do my best."

The night was fading into dawn when Jim made his way back to the ICU. He set the baggie with the remaining three fentanyl patches down on the desk in front of her. "Luis is safe. There's no active chemical in any of them."

Ginny's brow furrowed. "Why would anyone want fake fentanyl patches?"

"Good question. Let's hope we find a good answer."

* * *

CHAPTER 12

Day 6 – Wednesday morning
Hillcrest Hospital

Where another might have pictures of family, Marjorie Hawkins had portraits of herself, in SCUBA gear, holding up rare, exotic seashells.

"Is this new?" Ginny asked, admiring a delicate specimen, brilliant in pinks and golds.

Her boss nodded, smiling. "It's a Calico Scallop. I picked it up just off Bunkum Bay."

"Monserrat?"

She nodded. "On the Caribbean side."

Ginny sighed, wishing she had the resources to go sailing in the Caribbean. Someday, maybe.

Ms. Hawkins motioned to a chair, then settled down behind her desk and faced Ginny. "I'm sending you to Austin."

Ginny nodded. The two of them had been talking about the need for more preceptors and how it would be cost-effective to have someone in-house to train them. Ginny was the obvious choice. She'd been helping new nurses (those just out of school) and new recruits (experienced nurses just hired on) to get up to speed in the Medical ICU for two years.

"It will mean a rotating schedule for you, so you can work

with nurses on both shifts, and more money, of course."

"I don't mind rotating, as long as I get Friday evenings off."

Ms. Hawkins smiled ruefully. "Not this week, I'm afraid. The conference starts on Friday morning and runs through Sunday noon."

Ginny wrinkled her nose. It was not possible to drive from Austin to Dallas during rush hour on a Friday. The traffic would make the entire I-35 corridor a parking lot.

"Okay, maybe not *this* Friday."

"Here's the conference schedule." The Head Nurse handed over a sheaf of papers with yellow highlighting on the pages. "Network where you can and make nice."

Ginny nodded. She understood how the industry worked.

"Thank you for staying late to talk with me. I appreciate your flexibility."

"I'm happy to help in any way I can."

"I know it." She paused, eyeing Ginny. "You and Phyllis were friends, weren't you?"

"In school, and we got along well here. I feel really bad for her family." Ginny sighed. "It's a good thing she had a sister in town. Her husband isn't coping well."

"You've seen him?"

Ginny nodded, explaining about the condolence call. "And I have no idea who it was that upset him so much."

The other woman sighed. "I'm afraid I did that."

"You?" Ginny's eyebrows rose.

"I went over on Friday to see if I could pick up some files Phyllis had taken home with her. I wanted to make sure there were no HIPAA violations."

Ginny nodded. Those could be expensive.

"But he wouldn't let me look." Ms. Hawkins' eyes narrowed. "I wonder if you could pick them up for me."

Ginny blinked. "I suppose so, if I knew what to ask for."

The Head Nurse leaned forward. "Anything that has a Hillcrest identifier on it, paper and electronic versions. And anything that looks like it might be a legal issue. It would be a kindness to take them off that poor man's shoulders."

Ginny nodded. "I can try. How soon do you need them?"

"Today would be best. Just put them all in a box and bring them to me. I'll sort through them here."

"I'll see what I can do."

The Head Nurse rose and Ginny recognized her cue, happy to be dismissed promptly. Rose MacGregor was expecting her and she wanted to make a quick stop before going over to the shelter.

* * *

Wednesday morning
Loch Lonach Children's Shelter

Ginny sat beside Luis at the kitchen table and watched him eat cereal. Seymour rested on a rock in his terrarium, apparently enjoying the spectacle.

"Do you know why I'm here, Luis?" she asked.

He shook his head and kept on eating.

"Those stickers Mrs. McGregor found on you, they didn't belong to you, did they?"

He looked at her sidelong, then shook his head, then went back to his cereal.

"You're not in trouble, but I would like to know where you got them. Will you tell me?"

Mrs. McGregor had searched Luis' belongings and found nothing.

Luis reached for his milk, finishing it with a minimum of fuss. Ginny was glad to see he had a good appetite. She reached into her bag and pulled out the gift she'd brought. She showed the sticker book to Luis and saw his eyes light up.

"I like stickers," Ginny said, then started to flip through the book. "They're shiny and have bright colors and clever pictures." She showed him the page she was looking at, full of dinosaurs.

"Roaaar!" She lunged toward the child and he responded by giggling.

Ginny went back to flipping through the pages. "Here are some about Santa Claus. It looks like someone went up to the North Pole and took pictures of his elves. That's probably because Christmas is coming." She saw Luis' eyes focus on the page and held it out so he could see.

"Here's Santa's sleigh. See the reindeer? They have names." Luis looked at her.

She pointed to each animal as she ticked them off the list. "Dasher and Dancer and Prancer and Vixen and Comet and—"

"Cupid and Donner and Blitzen!" Luis finished triumphantly.

"That's right!" Ginny smiled at him. "Would you like to have this book of stickers?"

He nodded, but made no move to take it from her.

"I brought it for you, because of the other stickers, because we had to take those stickers away, and I wanted you to have some stickers you can keep."

"For me?"

"Yes." Ginny set the book down and pushed it toward him. Luis reached over and picked it up.

"Will you sit in my lap, Luis?" Ginny asked.

He nodded, his eyes on the book. Ginny slid her arm around his waist and pulled him over, wrapping her arms around him.

They spent the next ten minutes turning pages and exclaiming over the pictures. As Luis relaxed, he became more vocal, pointing out items of particular interest.

"Do you want to wear a sticker?" Ginny asked.

The boy nodded.

"Okay. Which one do you want to start with?"

He flipped through several pages then pointed. "This one!"

Ginny carefully peeled off the T-Rex and applied it to his arm. "There!"

He grinned up at her. "Roooaarrr!"

Ginny laughed and gave him a quick hug. By the time they had been all the way through the collection, Luis was wearing stickers on both arms, both knees, his cheek, and he had put one on Ginny's forehead. "There!" he said, smiling up at her.

"So where did those other stickers come from?"

"Envelope."

"From the mail?"

He nodded. "A blue one."

"Do you still have the envelope?"

"It was Mama's."

"It was something she sent to other people?"

He shook his head. "They were for her. I wasn't supposed to touch them." He had his eyes back on the sticker book now.

"Someone sent her the blue envelopes?"

He nodded.

"How did you get one of the blue envelopes?"

He gave her a sly look. "Took it."

"Why did you do that?"

"It was for her, for Christmas."

"You wanted to give her a present?"

He nodded.

"So you took one of the blue envelopes because they were special, just for her."

He nodded again. "A special Christmas present."

"When did you take the blue envelope?"

He shrugged.

"Where did you put it?"

"In my jacket."

"Okay, then what happened?"

His face clouded. "Mama went away." He dropped the book and turned in her arms. "Mama went away and left me."

Ginny wrapped her arms around the stricken child and hugged him, murmuring that it was going to be all right, his mother would come home to him. She hoped it was true.

When he settled down, she stroked his hair. "Did you look inside the blue envelope, Luis?"

He shook his head.

"Then how did you find the stickers?"

"They fell out."

"Why did they fall out?"

"It tore. I didn't mean to. I wanted to show her the present so she'd come home." He was crying again. "I didn't mean to tear it."

Ginny rocked him back and forth, soothing him. "So when you saw they were stickers, you decided to put them on you, to see if they would bring her home." Ginny understood magical thinking.

He nodded, wiping his nose on her shoulder. He pulled back and looked up into her face, his eyes still brimming. "I'm sorry." The tears spilled over. "I won't do it again!"

She pulled him to her, her heart aching. "Oh, Luis! This isn't your fault."

"I wanna go home. I want my Mama!"

There was no way Ginny could tell this child her worst fears. "It's going to be all right, Luis. We'll find her and bring her home."

"Promise?"

"I promise." Ginny looked up in time to see Rose MacGregor cross her fingers, but she couldn't tell whether it was to invoke good luck or invalidate a promise they might not be able to keep.

* * *

Wednesday morning
Kyle residence

John Kyle looked better than he had when she'd last seen him, but the grief was evident in every line.

Ginny leaned toward him. "You asked me to make sure that woman from Hillcrest didn't come back. I can do that."

He looked at her, his eyes empty of tears. "I'd appreciate it."

"She wanted to pick up some materials Phyllis brought home. If you'll trust me with them, I can take them back to the hospital and you won't have to think about it."

He nodded. "Work stuff."

"Yes."

"She was always doing something. Never knew her to be still, not for a moment." He swallowed. "She was working on something to do with getting enough nurses to fill in here in Texas. Something political." His eyes filled with tears. "Could that be why she was—"

Ginny reached over and laid a hand on his arm. "The police are looking for a reason. If there's anything you think they should know, tell us."

John Kyle wiped his face with his hand, then dug around in his pocket, looking for a tissue. Ginny pulled a box over and handed it to him.

He blew his nose, then continued. "She said there was a vote coming up in the legislature. That it was going to be unpopular." He controlled himself with an effort. "I didn't care.

I didn't even listen. I should have been more supportive."

It was a story Ginny had heard many times before. Too many people took the good things in their lives for granted, until it was too late. "Do you think I could look at those files?"

He nodded. "Take them. Take them all." He rose and led her into a room set up as a home office. He moved swiftly, making a pile on the desk. Ginny let him work, knowing it was helping, even if only a little.

In the end, she needed a box to hold all of them. He carried them out to her car and put them on the back seat. Ginny turned to face him. "Thank you."

"You find him, whoever did this. You find him."

Ginny nodded soundlessly. That was two promises she'd made today she saw no way of keeping.

When she got home, Ginny collapsed into bed, promising herself she would look at both problems when she woke up. As she relaxed into her pillow, she found herself grieving for all of them. Poor little Luis and his friend, Joey, and Joey's father.

The odds were seriously against her, but Ginny knew, whatever happened from here on out, there was no way her conscience would let her walk away. It wasn't just her own self-respect anymore. She had given her word. She would have to keep it, or live with the guilt for the rest of her life.

* * *

Chapter 13

Day 6 – Wednesday evening
Forbes residence

Ginny slept until dinnertime. Like most night workers, she bulldozed through her assigned shifts, then collapsed, hoping to recover in time for the next round. It usually worked, but she was already beginning to wonder if she shouldn't be looking for a less grueling schedule.

After dinner, Ginny settled down at her desk and opened her computer. She made a précis of what John Kyle had told her about Phyllis' interest in politics, set up a timeline and a list of possible sources of information, and filled in some of the blanks on her means/motive/opportunity spreadsheet. She was soon staring at several pages of notes.

She added a few comments, then set the murder aside and turned her attention to Luis.

On the assumption that the disappearance of Maria Perez was somehow connected to Phyllis' murder, Ginny started a mind map.

Mind maps do not follow linear formats. Instead, they allow the user to link one idea back to another (or many others) as the ideas occur to them. Ginny mapped *location* (both Luis and Phyllis had a connection to Hillcrest), *Maria* (Luis' mom and

Phyllis' friend), *occupation* (both Maria and Phyllis were nurses), *timing* (Maria went missing after Phyllis' death and referred to that death as if it had some importance to her), *unknown enemy(ies)* (Maria fled someone and appeared to think Phyllis was killed by the same or similar someone), and *illicit drugs* (Luis found wearing fake fentanyl patches and Phyllis' purse found with cocaine in it).

Ginny took a moment to examine her work. Not a bad start but there were some dead ends. Why were Luis' patches fake? What spooked Maria Perez? Was Phyllis connected, somehow, or was her death unrelated and Maria mistaken on that point? What did Phyllis have to do with the nursing shortage?

Ginny leaned back in her chair, her brow furrowing. She didn't pay much attention to what happened in state politics. In some ways, the less she knew, the happier she was. But when it was something to do with the Board of Nursing, she had to pay attention.

Four times a year the Board published a bulletin with updates on laws affecting nurses in the State of Texas; announcements about programs, projects, and workshops; information about nursing education; articles of interest to nurses; and notices of disciplinary actions. It was always entertaining to see who had gotten into what kind of trouble.

Ginny opened a browser and pulled up the most recent issue, finding no one she knew on the 'naughty' list and a very dry description of some upcoming legislation having to do with expediting applications for nursing licenses for foreign nurses. She printed the article off for further study and set it aside.

There was one more thing she absolutely *must* do before she went back to bed and that was go through the pile of material John Kyle had given her, so she could hand the Hillcrest stuff over to Ms. Hawkins tomorrow before leaving for Austin. She sat down on the carpet, with the box beside her, and started to sort.

The files with a Hillcrest identifier were an eclectic lot. Among them were the human resources department policies on new hires, including proposed revisions to licensure verification processes (some of them fifteen years out of date), nursing department lists of continuing education dates and deadlines, and contact information directories for Hillcrest staff covering the last ten years. Interesting, but nothing that looked like a HIPAA violation. All of these went into pile number one.

The second pile was made up of things having to do with nursing reform and other political issues. Ginny went through this with attention, but found nothing more recent than last year and nothing that sounded as if it had anything to do with the nurse shortage.

The third pile addressed Phyllis' graduate school plans. Among other things, Ginny found a stack of articles on imposters in healthcare, including a collection of Board of Nursing *Bulletins*, all open to the imposter alert page, and a calendar marking the class schedule with handwritten notes about which shifts Phyllis wanted to work in January.

Ginny paused, then dug out the January schedule for the Medical ICU. Phyllis was not on it, which was odd because it had been posted before Phyllis died. An oversight, perhaps?

The last pile was stuff unrelated to the hospital or nursing. Mr. Kyle had included mailings, advertisements, and some private letters in his haste. The letters would need to be returned. Ginny sorted through the junk, decided it was safe to discard most of it, put the Hillcrest files into the box and stood up, stretching.

Because of being sent out of town, she would be on day shift until the middle of next week. The sooner she got to sleep, the easier it would be to stay awake on the road tomorrow. Hillcrest first, then Tran, then drive to Austin. Then

Friday, Saturday, and Sunday morning conference, then drive home in time to attend the Christmas party at the Jumping J ranch. Then two days off to make up for having to work through the weekend.

Not much time left for investigating. She hoped Detective Tran wouldn't need her for a day or two.

* * *

Wednesday late evening
Hillcrest ER

"Got one!"

Jim followed the DEA agent down the corridor and into the exam room. It was a teenaged girl, just barely arousable, clearly under the influence. The nurse handed Jim the triage paperwork.

"What did she take?" The DEA agent asked.

"This." She tossed him a baggie with a dusting of white powder inside. "The friend who brought her in said she'd injected it. She thinks it was fentanyl."

The agent took the bag, then retired to a back room to do a field drug test on the material. He was back in five minutes.

"Positive."

"Okay. Add fentanyl to the drug screen." They had already medicated the patient with a second dose of naloxone.

So sophisticated had opioid drug abusers become that they carried their own supply of antidote with them when they went to shoot up. The young woman accompanying this patient had produced an auto-injector she had used to keep her friend alive while waiting for the ambulance. Jim and the DEA agent took her into a private room to talk while they waited for the patient to wake up enough to speak for herself.

"I'm Dr. Mackenzie," Jim said. "What's your name?"

"Keesha."

"That was quick-thinking on your part, Keesha. You probably saved Jasmine's life."

"Well, like, you know, you hear things." The young woman shrugged, her eyes darting from Jim to the agent, then back again.

"What sort of things?" Jim asked.

"You, know. Things. So we, like, got the drug."

"You mean the naloxone?"

"Yeah."

"Do you know where she got the fentanyl?"

"No." Keesha's eyes were no longer on Jim, focusing instead on her shoes.

Jim leaned forward, resting his forearms on his thighs and clasping his hands loosely between his knees. He was deliberately trying to look harmless.

"It would help us to know where to look for her dealer. Do you both buy from the same person?"

Keesha was twitching now, squirming in her seat. "I don' give up my sources. Y'all knows that."

Jim nodded. "Normally we wouldn't even ask, but there's a problem."

She swiveled a white eye in his direction.

"There's someone targeting drug users, killing them, deliberately." He watched Keesha's eyes grow wider. "Whoever it is needs to be stopped."

"I can't tell y'all. I wouldn't make it home tonight."

"No one will know it was you." Jim waited, watching the young woman squirm. "If you can help us find him—or her—you can save more lives, just like you did for Jasmine tonight."

Keesha jumped to her feet and started pacing. "It's not like I knows," she said. "But I hear'd something, on the street."

"What did you hear?"

"There's, like, a war on. New guy says the old guy wants us dead and it ain't safe to buy from him no more. Says his stuff is better. Safer."

"Is it true?"

Keesha's eyes grew wider and her cheeks taut. "Yeah. It's true. They's droppin' like flies out there. It ain't safe." She went back to pacing, her hands moving spastically along her arms, then down the sides of her legs.

"Keesha."

She turned abruptly to face him. "What?"

"Have you taken something tonight?"

She wrapped her arms around herself. "No. Hain't I done told you it ain't safe?"

"When was your last dose and what did you take?" It was clear she was in the first stages of withdrawal from something.

She stared at him, her mouth falling open.

"Let us help you." Jim rose and stepped toward her. She backed up against the wall and stood staring at him, then, very slowly, nodded.

"I don't feel so good."

"We'll take care of that." Jim very gently took her arm and steered her out of the consultation room and into the system. When he had her settled and had checked on Jasmine, he located the DEA agent.

"Do you need me for anything else?"

"Nope. Thanks Doc. That was a real nice job in there. Maybe enough to persuade one of them to give up the dealer."

"Let's hope so," Jim replied. "You heard the lady. They're dropping like flies out there."

* * *

CHAPTER 14

Day 7 – Thursday early morning
Hillcrest Cafeteria

"Mind if I join you?"

Jim looked up from his tray to see one of the nurses from the ER smiling at him. He gestured at the three empty seats on the other side of the table. "Help yourself." He went back to his meal, thinking he had a number of charts left unfinished and, if he wasn't careful, he would have to stay late to complete them.

"You're new, I think."

Jim looked up again, realizing that the blonde was trying to engage him in conversation. He nodded. "Sort of. I started last summer."

"Lisa Braden." She stuck out her hand and he shook it. "ICU, mainly, but I float to the ER. I've seen you there."

She was not his type. Too brassy and too aggressive, but he was aware that, in any job, making enemies could be a bad idea. He smiled. "And we're very grateful."

This much was true. The dynamics of an acute care facility like Hillcrest required that nurses be able to work in more than one area. The critical care areas routinely covered for one another, but ER nurses notoriously hated both floating to ICU and taking care of ICU patients who landed in the ER. They liked the "treat 'em and street 'em" variety.

The blonde seemed to have forgotten to get herself something to eat. She was toying with a soda, her arms crossed on the table, her just-barely-covered breasts resting on her arms.

"You're really good," she said. "I've been around a lot of ER docs and you're the best I've seen." She smiled at him.

Jim smiled back. "Thank you." It had been a while since he'd had anyone throw themselves at him and he was finding it amusing.

"We heard what happened, about the virus. I'm glad you're all right."

Jim sighed inwardly and changed the subject. "I haven't had much chance to get to know Dallas. What is there to do around here?"

"Oh! Well, there's Billy Bob's, of course, and the stockyards, and Southfork, and the State Fair, and gobs of nightclubs and good places to eat. What do you like to do?"

"Billy Bob's, is that where they have the mechanical bull?"

She grinned. "Yeah, and Country and Western dancing. Can you Two-Step?"

Jim shook his head. "No, sorry."

"Other kinds of dancing, maybe?" She looked at him coyly.

Jim studied her face for a moment. He did not want to encourage this woman. "Scottish Country Dancing," he said. That should put her off.

Lisa blinked. "Scottish what?"

"Do you know Ginny Forbes?"

Lisa nodded.

"Has she ever mentioned what she does on Friday nights?"

Lisa's brow furrowed. "I don't think so."

"Well, she and a hundred other Scots get together every

Friday night. The dances are made up of intricate patterns that require the cooperation of everyone in the set and the footwork has its roots in French ballet. It's quite a sight."

Lisa looked dubious. "You do that, too?"

"I try."

Jim saw a vertical line appear between Lisa's eyebrows.

"Is it hard?"

Jim nodded. "Very."

"Hmmm. Could I come watch?"

"Sure. It's open to the public."

She nodded, then changed the subject, holding out her hands for his inspection. "Which do you like better, the right or the left?"

Jim glanced at her nails, then looked closer, then averted his eyes, reminding himself he was a grown man and a physician.

"Sorry." He gathered up his tray and stood up. "Got to go back to work. Nice to meet you, miss."

"Lisa. See you later." She was smiling at him, pleased with his reaction to the images painted in miniature on her blood red nails.

Jim hurried off, making a mental note to report her nails as a health hazard. They had certainly interfered with his appetite.

* * *

Thursday morning
Police substation

Ginny was sitting in Detective Tran's office, copies of her notes in front of her, fidgeting. She'd been thinking about transparency and how to use it to catch a killer.

"Here are the bios—all I could remember about each of the

people who were in the Unit that night. Here's the summary of the shift and the timeline. And this is my Means / Motive / Opportunity spreadsheet, which you've seen before and which is essentially empty because I can't think of a single reason why anyone who works at Hillcrest should want Phyllis dead."

Detective Tran nodded, looking over the work. "These are very clear. Thank you."

Ginny then handed over the second set of notes, explaining about Luis. "He says the patches were intended for his mother, but I don't know how reliable his testimony is. Dr. Mackenzie is following up with the DEA agent. Here," she set down the third group, "is what I've been able to get from John Kyle, plus my mind map. And I'm working on a way to gather more personal information about Phyllis' relationships with her coworkers, but that's going to take some time."

"Uncovering the truth usually does." Detective Tran looked up from the mind map, then set it aside and leaned back in her chair, her eyes on Ginny. "You have something else to say?"

Ginny nodded, then took a breath. "Since everyone at the hospital already knows I'm working with the police, I was wondering if you could use me to pass along selected bits of information—or misinformation. Baiting the hook, as it were, to see if we could draw someone out."

Detective Tran studied her for a moment, her eyes narrowing. "You would be willing to let us use you in this way?"

Ginny nodded.

"Have you spoken with anyone about this idea?"

"No."

Detective Tran thought for a moment longer, then shuffled through her folder and pulled out a file, handing it to Ginny. "This is the forensic science report from the crime scene. It reveals nothing of use and, if the killer learns that, he may let down his guard."

Ginny nodded and rose from her chair. "I'll get started on this right away."

"Miss Forbes."

"Yes?"

"Discretion is called for. We want to lull our quarry into a false sense of security, not frighten him into precipitate action."

Ginny nodded. "I understand." She did, too. Cornered prey tended to attack.

* * *

Thursday morning
Forbes residence

"I'll get it." Ginny made her way to the front of the house and opened the door to Jim. "What are you doing here? Shouldn't you be asleep?"

"I heard a rumor you were being sent to Austin. May I come in?"

"Of course." She showed him into the living room and watched him sink onto the sofa. The morning sun pricked out the shadows under his eyes. "Hard night?"

He started to laugh. "You wouldn't believe what happened. One of your colleagues has decided she likes me." He described the scene in the cafeteria.

Ginny started laughing. "Her fingernails?"

"Yes. I'm going to have to keep an eye on her!"

"Should I be worried?"

"No," he said, still grinning. "Anyway, that's not why I came. Grandfather called me and said you'd be missing the ceilidh this week."

"Where *does* he get his information?" Ginny shook her

head.

"In this case, from me." Her mother appeared in the door. "I told him about you being sent to Austin for the conference. Morning, Jim." She set a tray down on the table in front of them. "I thought you might like some coffee." She smiled, then retired, leaving them alone.

"I want to go with you."

"Why?"

He frowned. "I'm not sure. I just have a bad feeling about this."

Ginny shook her head at him. "I'll be in the conference the entire time."

"We could eat together."

"Not breakfast and not lunch and not some of the dinners. It's all included in the package."

He sighed, then leaned toward her. "The truth is I don't like the thought of you going off on your own while this business about Luis and the drugs is unresolved."

"The timing is a little awkward, I agree, but I turned everything over to Detective Tran this morning. Call her if anything comes up."

He reached out and took her hands in his. "Will you call me?"

Ginny felt a twinge of annoyance. "Jim, this is work. Just like a regular shift. I don't call you to check in during those."

He looked at her seriously. "I just want to hear your voice. To reassure me you're all right."

"I won't have time to get into trouble. I drive down, check in, report for classes all day on Friday and Saturday and half of Sunday, then I drive home. If it will make you feel better, I'll touch base with you once a day. I'll be doing the same with Mother, so you can check in with her if we miss one another."

He nodded. "I can live with that. But—" He pulled her out of her chair and onto his lap, then wrapped both arms around her. "Before you go, I want to remind you what you're leaving behind." He bent to kiss her.

Ginny felt her eyes close and her blood pressure rise, and lost track of time for a moment, but they were in her living room, with her mother in the kitchen. When she came up for air, she broke out of his embrace and pulled him to his feet.

"Get some sleep. I'll call you tonight." She pushed him toward the door.

"All right. I'll go, but I hold you to your promise." He turned on the threshold, kissed her again, then strode down the sidewalk, got in his car, and drove off.

Ginny closed the door, turning to find her mother smiling at her.

"Tuna for lunch all right with you?"

"Yes, please." Ginny could feel the heat rise in her cheeks, but her mother was already headed for the kitchen and didn't see. She put the subject of Jim's intentions aside and concentrated on her trip. There were still some things she needed to do. She hurried upstairs to finish packing.

* * *

CHAPTER 15

Day 7 – Thursday evening
Host Hotel, Austin

The host hotel in Austin was crawling with attendees. Ginny checked into her room, then made her way down to the banquet hall.

She approached the white skirted registration tables and found the section of the alphabet under which Forbes would be filed. She signed the sheet, told the attendant her name, and was handed a badge and a bag full of materials.

"Breakfast starts at seven-thirty and the first lecture at eight. You'll find banquet and two lunch tickets, one for each day, a voucher for one dinner in the hotel, and the break-out session room assignments behind your badge. Don't lose it."

"I won't," Ginny promised.

"No special dress code, but there will be photographers throughout the weekend. The Board wants this one documented. You have been warned!"

Ginny grinned. "Thanks."

"The bar is that direction and the pool is heated, if you remembered to bring your suit." The attendant ran a finger across the page, made a tick mark next to Ginny's name, then frowned slightly. She looked up from her paperwork, the expression on her face changing abruptly. "Wait!" Her eyes narrowed, then widened. "You're Ginny Forbes!"

"Yes. Is there a problem?"

"No! Gosh, no! It's just we've all heard what happened in Dallas and you were there."

Ginny felt her throat tighten. "Heard what?"

"About the murder, of course. You were right there. On the scene. You can tell us about it."

Ginny picked up her registration materials, forced a smile, then shook her head. "There's nothing I can tell you that wasn't already in the news."

"But—" The official looked at the woman waiting in line behind Ginny, then took a breath, smiled, and said, "I hope you enjoy the conference."

Ginny found an empty table, dropped her papers, then made her way to the bar. Ghouls! Was everyone going to take that attitude? Was she some kind of weird celebrity? The answer, as it turned out, was, yes.

"Excuse me, but I couldn't help noticing. May I join you?"

Ginny looked up at the woman who stood smiling down at her. It was impossible to tell from her clothes, makeup, or jewelry, exactly what level of administration she belonged to, but there was a definite corporate air about her, with an underlying hint of something else.

Ginny motioned to the seat across from her.

"I'm Becky Peel, the Hospitality Chair. I hope your room is comfortable?" The hand she extended had a tattoo on the forearm, just above the wrist and Ginny recognized the symbol as that of the Navy Nurse Corps. A veteran, then.

Ginny made polite noises, wondering what was behind her new friend's enthusiasm for the company of a stranger. The woman came right to the point.

"I expect you're going to find a lot of people looking forward to meeting you."

"Why is that?"

"Because most of us have seen dead bodies, but very few have found a corpse in a bathroom. There's bound to be some professional curiosity. So tell me. What was it like?"

Ginny felt her jaw tighten. She really didn't want to talk about it, but she'd been instructed to make nice, so she obliged with a description of what they had found when they got the handicap stall door open and could see Phyllis' body.

Becky continued to ask technical questions about the subsequent police investigation, how they had handled the patient work load, who had been called in, and so forth. Ginny found an audience collecting around them as she answered these and other questions.

The inquisition lasted for the better part of an hour with two free drinks appearing at Ginny's elbow as gestures of appreciation. When she had exhausted the Q&A, the group fell into discussion about the incident, allowing Ginny to listen for a while.

They made some good points.

What they were concerned about, of course, was that it had happened to one of them, a nurse, while on duty, and in a restricted access area. If a murderer could get to Phyllis, he could get to anyone.

"Who did it? Do the police have any leads?"

Ginny shook her head. "There's no useable forensic evidence. Every one of us has been in that bathroom a hundred times."

"But it must have been cleaned at some point. Wouldn't they be able to narrow the field by seeing who was in there since the last time housekeeping came in?"

"We'd like to think that, but, no. They don't wipe down every surface every time. There were dozens of finger and handprints on the doors and walls. The floor had hair left over from people who haven't worked there in a year. The ceiling fixtures had DNA from the maintenance crew and there were unidentified specimens that probably belonged to visitors. They took swabs from all of us, for comparison, but there was no way to rule anyone out."

A youngish woman with coal black hair wrinkled her nose. "Geez! Remind me to be more careful next time I use the restroom at work!" There was scattered laughter.

"What about the cameras? Every unit has cameras these days."

Ginny nodded. "The police pulled all the video, but I don't know if it showed anything. No one has been arrested."

"And the body? Anything left on it?"

"Nothing, other than the wire. They think the killer was wearing Personal Protective Equipment, including shoe covers. They looked for footprints on the tile, to see if they could narrow it down to a man or a woman by shoe size or footwear tread, but there was nothing."

"A man? I thought it was the ladies' room?"

"It was, but with PPE on, everyone looks alike and the break room is used by both men and women. No help there. It could have been a tall woman, a short man, or a trained monkey."

The young woman with the black hair suddenly sat up straight in her chair. "They could use the inside of the discarded PPE! That would tell them who to look for."

Ginny smiled at her. "If we had it, yes. Housekeeping emptied the receptacles just before the end of shift. The bundles were collected and incinerated before we knew she was missing."

"Hrmph. Good luck for the murderer."

"Good timing, perhaps. He or she may have known about that routine."

They all nodded.

"No skin cells under her nails, I gather. And no hair caught in the ligature."

Ginny shook her head. "Not the murderer's anyway." There had been traces of nitrile, undoubtedly off the gloves the murderer had used, but the skin under Phyllis' nails had been her own. She had tried to claw the thing off before she died.

"What I want to know," Becky said, "is how the murderer, whoever he was, had the balls to kill someone in a hospital ICU, right under the noses of that many medical professionals. Suppose someone had heard or seen something? It was a very risky thing to do."

The conversation flowed on in this vein through dinner and dessert. The party broke up early, though, with murmurs of alarm clocks and early classes.

"I'll see you tomorrow." Becky nodded goodnight.

Ginny gathered up her possessions and went to her room. Once she was settled, she picked up her phone and called her mother, reporting a safe arrival, the room number, and the weather in the area. After that was done, she dialed Jim.

"I've been waiting for your call."

"Well, there's nothing to report."

"Really?" He sounded skeptical.

"What?"

"I knew I could tell you were lying if I was looking at you, but I've just realized I can tell from your tone of voice as well."

Ginny squirmed, unable to think of anything to say.

"Ginny?"

"Yes, all right. There was something."

"Tell me."

She recounted the cross-examination and her discomfort at

discussing Phyllis in that manner. "I guess I'm over-reacting."

"No, you're not. I can forgive the clinical interest, but someone should have realized how rude they were being."

"They're worried. They all seem to think it could have been one of them."

"Well, they're not wrong. I've been worried about letting you go back to work."

"Jim—" She started to remind him it was not his call, but he interrupted.

"Someone my size wouldn't need a wire, just his hands."

The thought made Ginny uncomfortable and she tried to turn the conversation. "Jim—"

"All you'd have to do is let the wrong person know you were on to them and—"

Ginny snapped. "JIM! That's enough!"

He burst out laughing. "That's more like it!"

His tone was warm with affection and Ginny found herself smiling in spite of the irritation she felt. "Remind me to punish you when I get home."

There was another rush of laughter. "That sounds interesting. What did you have in mind?"

"I'll think of something."

"I can hardly wait."

"Goodnight, Jim!" She hung up on his reply, but, on the whole, was satisfied with the exchange. If he felt comfortable enough with the subject to tease her, he must not be too worried and of the two, she'd rather he was teasing than hovering.

Having kept her promises to her mother and Jim, Ginny now turned to her obligation to Detective Tran. She pulled out her phone, plugged in the earphones, and set about transcribing the recordings, moving steadily through two night's worth of reflections about Phyllis, being careful not to alter the language and taking note of pauses or other breaks in the flow. Most was innocuous, some sentimental, but one comment caught her attention.

Grace had said she and Phyllis had not seen eye to eye on political issues. She could not approve of Phyllis' attitudes, and it was a shame she couldn't be talked out of them. Ginny had asked for clarification and Grace had shrugged. "I just meant she believed in what she was doing."

Ginny closed the files, put the project away, and settled down with her bedtime book, but her mind kept wandering. What kind of political activity had Phyllis been up to? Had it gotten her killed? And why had the murderer chosen the ICU restroom? Surely there were safer places to ambush an enemy? At the mall, or the lake, or the hospital parking lot. Any of those would have been safer. Why had the murderer felt compelled to attack Phyllis in a place and at a time where the suspect pool would be limited to a couple dozen people? As Becky had pointed out, it was a very gutsy move. Either that, or very stupid.

* * *

CHAPTER 16

Day 8 – Friday lunchtime
Conference Hotel, Austin

The speaker had a political agenda. Most people in Austin did. It was the state capital and chock full of people with causes, in this case, Mexicans.

Texas was full of Mexicans, some here legally, others illegally, all with their own agendas. The speaker waxed poetic on how responsive Texas health care had been to the plight of non-English speakers in need of medical attention. The number of Spanish-speaking nurses was climbing, but was still far too low. So they (whoever 'they' were) had facilitated the recruitment of Spanish-speaking nurses from Mexico. She had statistics. Lots of them. And an enthusiasm the organizers apparently shared, though not all of the audience seemed to agree.

Ginny looked around the room. There were eight nurses at each of the round tables, arranged in no particular pattern. Not all of the faces looked happy.

When the morning session was over and the lunch buffet laid out, Ginny returned to her seat to find at least one dissenting opinion. She listened as a pair of nurses talked quietly about problems they were having in Houston in the long-term care facilities. Ginny made eye contact with them and was tacitly invited to join the conversation.

"The number of errors is way up. They may speak Spanish, but not enough of them can function in English."

"Where are they coming from?"

The older nurse shrugged. "Hard to tell. The organization that vetted them has a strong lobby in the state legislature and is insisting on confidentiality."

Ginny was puzzled, and said so. "Doesn't the Board of Nursing need to know what school they graduated from?"

The younger nurse nodded. "They provide all the necessary information for credentialing and are required to pass the licensure exam in order to practice in Texas, but there are far too many gaps in their education. It's as if they crammed for the NCLEX, got the license, then forgot even the most basic material."

"That doesn't sound safe."

"It's not, but we're not allowed to criticize. The people behind it are convinced that any nurse, especially one who can speak Spanish, will do, and it's politically incorrect to disagree. But there've been enough incidents that the Board is starting to collect data. It will be interesting to see how many of the deaths correlate directly to this particular stream of foreign nurses."

Their discussion lasted for the remainder of the lunch break. Ginny listened, but with her attention split between it and the other people at her table. The topic, though serious, was only marginally relevant to the reason she was here. She would not be training new nurses to work in long-term care. She filed the comments away and concentrated on networking.

* * *

Friday noon
Hillcrest Regional Medical Center Cafeteria

Marge Hawkins collected her lunch tray and sat down at the table in the corner of the Hillcrest cafeteria, as she always did. She had a professional journal with her, open to an article on the mounting problem of fentanyl abuse in urban areas.

"Interesting reading."

She looked up to find one of the hospital pharmacists sitting at the next table, his eyes on the journal.

"Yes." She went back to her reading.

"I understand that most of it comes from Asia."

"So it says."

"Funny thing. With all that cheap poison available, it seems odd that someone is making fakes."

Marge raised her eyes to the pharmacist, her brow wrinkling. "Fakes?"

He nodded. "We had something that looked like fentanyl patches come through here two days ago, but they were fakes. No active drug at all." He had turned toward her, relaxed, comfortable.

"I expect you'll find they were from the School of Nursing supply."

He shook his head. "Nope. Thought of that. Those are all labeled as bogus. This looked like the real thing."

"What would be the point of counterfeit fentanyl patches?"

The pharmacist shrugged. "Can't imagine. You?"

She shook her head. "If not for training, I have no idea."

"May I join you?"

"If you don't mind my continuing to eat while you talk. I have to get back for a meeting." It was her standard excuse.

"We've met, but I doubt you remember me." He held out his hand. "Jonathan Simpson."

"Marge Hawkins." She closed the journal and set it down on the table. "Where did the patches come from? Were you able to tell?"

"Nope. One of the ER docs brought them in. Wanted them tested. But we couldn't identify a source."

"An ER doc? Where did he—or she—get them?"

"He, and he didn't say."

"Which one was it, do you know?"

"No. Sorry. One of the night shift crew. Why do you care?"

"I was just wondering if they might have been used for a prank, you know, a gag of some sort."

"Hallowe'en. It's a thought. I'll suggest we widen the search to include costume shops."

"Theater, too. Some of the movie props are very realistic."

"So they are." He smiled at her. "You're a sharp cookie."

"Thank you. Do you still have them?"

"No. At least, I don't think so. You might ask the Medical Director what happened to them." He leaned toward her across the table. "I've seen you around. Nice gams."

She blinked. "Surely that term is out of date?"

He grinned. "I like old movies. How about you?"

They chatted film noir while she finished her meal, his suggestions becoming less and less veiled as the encounter progressed. Marge kept her cool. It was one of the things she was good at. When she finished, she picked up her tray and her magazine, and took her leave.

"So when can I see you again?" Simpson asked.

She gave him a bland smile. "The minute 'gams' comes back into common use, I'll give you a call."

* * *

Friday evening
Austin

As soon as they were dismissed, Ginny headed for the parking garage. If she wanted to visit the State Cemetery while she could still see the graves, she would have to hustle.

She drove out into the street, meaning to cross under the highway on Eleventh, but found she had come out on the wrong side of the hotel, on Tenth Street, which was one-way and headed in the wrong direction. She proceeded to the next intersection, intending to turn right on Red River and right again on Eleventh, but found *that* route blocked by police barricades.

She was mildly annoyed, but it was Austin and rush hour and she was near the State Capital, so police barricades seemed only to be expected. She followed the officer's directions.

She could have turned right on Trinity Street, which was one-way the correct direction, but didn't see the sign in time to get into the right lane and the next, San Jacinto Blvd., was one-way the *wrong* direction. After that, she moved over to make sure she was in the appropriate lane and carefully turned right at the next intersection, on Brazos Street, which took her straight to the State Capital—where there was a demonstration in progress.

She only had one block to go, then one more right turn to get onto Eleventh Street, so she gritted her teeth and stuck it out, creeping along at ten miles per hour. This gave her plenty of time to read the pickets.

There were, apparently, two opposing camps. One was clearly in favor of House Bill 1712, which appeared to be calling for stricter control on the use of foreign nurses. The other was obviously opposed to the Bill, with slogans such as, "Equal

Rights for Illegals" and "We Need More Nurses."

The demonstration explained the lecture they'd gotten earlier about the use of Mexican nurses in Texas. Clearly, it was a hot topic. So hot, in fact, that Ginny found protesters pounding on her windows, shouting at her to side with them and vote for/against the Bill. She watched as two of them got into a fist fight right in front of her car, then, joined by supporters from both sides, as the fight became a brawl.

The police moved in swiftly with tear gas and rubber bullets, one of them gesturing to her to get out of the way. Ginny tried to obey, having to brake repeatedly to avoid hitting the protesters. It was with relief that she managed to get clear of the disturbance and head at last for the cemetery.

She was shaken. Not actually frightened, but not happy about some of the expressions she'd seen pressed up against her windows. It was not her problem at the moment, but how long would it be before her ICU was full of foreign nurses who couldn't speak English? Dallas was not immune to the problems caused by Texas sharing a border with Mexico. She shrugged the images out of her mind as she pulled into the parking lot at the State Cemetery.

Genealogy was one of Ginny's hobbies, visiting cemeteries—a form of recreation. She headed off across the grounds, searching for the ancestor she knew was buried there. The stone was in good condition and the site well cared for, so she took a picture, then spent some time wandering, reading the markers, and soaking in the sounds of the coming night.

The gloaming in a cemetery always had a special feeling of timelessness, heightened by the presence of those for whom time no longer held any meaning. She found her nerves settling down and her thoughts returning to the problem of the foreign nurses.

Texas had always been a place for emigrants to go when

things got tough. Davy Crockett's famous line, "You may all go to hell and I will go to Texas," was plastered everywhere. Three-quarters of her own ancestors had arrived in the area before it became a Republic and the last quarter not long after, all seeking a chance for a better life.

The Texas of that time, however, was not a place that welcomed newcomers. The government was (to put it politely) constantly in flux. The neighbors were hostile, and the land was wild and dangerous. It had taken a special breed to settle here and build the nation that was to become a legend.

Times had changed, of course. In the Texas of today, over a hundred years' worth of laws were in place to safeguard both natives and newcomers. To judge by what she had just seen, however, the pressure of change still had the power to stir emotions.

Ginny found it interesting that many of the same complaints she had heard today mirrored the complaints found in the records of those early years. She stood for a moment on the edge of the rise and looked across the cemetery to the city beyond. The place had history. Especially here. In this quiet corner devoted to the honored dead, the echoes of war could be heard. Texas had seen a lot in the way of conflict, and had forgotten none of it.

The rosy tints of evening had gone and the last pale blues were fading from the sky as Ginny turned and made her way down Heroes' Hill toward the gates and the parking lot. She was startled (and almost twisted her ankle in consequence) by the sound of an explosion. Several, in fact, in rapid succession. She looked around, but at first could see nothing. Then a column of smoke caught her eye, followed by tongues of flame which seemed to be growing, reaching into the darkening sky.

In the gloom, it took her a minute to figure out which direction she was facing. Once she had identified I-35, however, she knew what she was seeing. The Texas State Capital complex was on fire.

* * *

CHApCER 17

Day 8 – Friday evening
Ceilidh, Cooperative Hall, Loch Lonach

Caroline nudged Jim's arm and pointed across the room with her chin. "Get a load of that."

Jim turned to see what she was pointing at and raised an eyebrow. He hadn't given Lisa an address or directions to the Cooperative Hall, but there she stood, just inside the door, looking around.

Jim turned his back on her and faced Caroline. "Maybe we should rethink the open-door policy."

"She's headed this direction. Oh, wait, Jean has intercepted her." Jean Pollack was the Matron for the Loch Lonach Homestead and had, among her other responsibilities, the duty to greet outsiders.

"She's pointing at you, Jim. Do you know her?"

Jim sighed. "I'm afraid so." He put a noncommittal smile on his face and turned to greet the visitor, looking her over as she crossed the floor. She was wearing an aggressively cowgirl outfit complete with denim skirt, suede cowboy boots, and leather fringe, and she was not alone. She was accompanied by a younger woman, dressed in jeans, tee shirt, and sneakers, carrying a camera.

"Jim!" Lisa called and flashed him a dazzling smile. She strode across the room, oblivious to the dance patterns and was almost run down by a chase currently going on in the sets. She stepped aside, startled, then fixed her eyes on her quarry and plowed ahead.

"Jim!" She tried to hug him, but he managed to stick his hand out to forestall her. She took it and pressed it to her chest, obliging him to use a bit of force to retrieve it. "Well, you see I'm here."

"I see that."

Lisa turned and indicated her companion. "This is my sister, Mary Jo." The younger woman smiled shyly up at Jim.

Lisa flashed him another dazzling smile, showing off excessively white teeth straight enough for a toothpaste commercial. "I hope you don't mind. She's majoring in photography at school and they've got an assignment coming up. I suggested this—" Lisa gestured at the room "—might make a good subject."

Jim turned to Mary Jo and gave her a genuine smile, holding out his hand. "I agree, though, if you want to catch the flavor of the dances, I hope you brought a really fast camera."

She blushed, then nodded.

"Caroline is an expert and I'm sure, if you asked her nicely, she would be glad to answer questions for you."

"Of course. What would you like to know?" Caroline put an arm around Mary Jo and steered her toward the top of the room, leaving Jim to deal with Lisa.

"The website said the dancing started at seven." Lisa looked around. "Is it always this crowded, and this noisy?"

Jim nodded. The band was playing a reel, using bodhran and pipes for emphasis, and the effect was rousing.

Lisa watched until the end of the dance, then turned back to Jim. "Do all the men wear skirts?"

"Kilts are normal clothes for the Scots. You'll see them at the parties, at the Games, and on any formal occasion."

She reached out and started to stroke the fur on the sporran Jim was wearing. "And what's this?"

Jim caught her hand and put it back at her side. "It's a form of pocket."

Lisa stepped closer, looking up at him from under unnaturally thick lashes. "And is it true—?" She was interrupted by the approach of three woman, all running toward Jim, laughing and calling to him.

"Jim, Jim! My turn. You promised!"

Jim smiled at the approaching harem. "Ladies, this is Lisa. She's new. Can you find her a partner?"

One of them smiled at Lisa and took her hand. "Sure! Come on. I'll give you a crash course in what you need to know to dance with us." She hauled Lisa onto the floor and could be seen showing her hand and foot positions.

Jim smiled at the remaining two women, allowing himself to be pulled onto the floor by one and promising the next dance to the other. For the next half hour he was caught up in his own lessons. He was behind the curve here as well as on the battlefield, but was rapidly catching up and was never without a willing teacher.

He was deep in the intricacies of strathspey footwork when he became aware of a mild exodus from the floor. There seemed to be something going on in the media room. Those who had been to see hurried back into the great hall to report. Jim looked up to see his grandfather beckoning to him. He excused himself from the dance and obeyed the summons.

"What's up?"

"Come." His grandfather led him into the media room and pointed to the big screen TV. Jim fell in at the back of the crowd, listening to the announcer.

"The bombs went off in the midst of a riot," the man was saying. "We're being told this demonstration has been in the works for months, with nurses coming in from all over the state. Both supporters and opponents of HB 1712 were throwing punches and the police were trying to break up the fight." The image behind the reporter showed a domed building and the ribbon across the bottom identified it as the State Capital in Austin, Texas.

"As a result, it's unclear whether either side was the target, or whether this was a repeat of the ambush on police we saw in Dallas a few years back, or whether it's an act of terrorism. Over a hundred people have been dispatched to area hospitals with burns and shrapnel injuries. There are twenty confirmed dead, but that figure is likely to rise. We won't show you, but the street is filled with body parts, so it's not possible to get an accurate count at present."

The image pulled back to show a darkened Austin street lurid with flames. There were several buildings on fire, emergency crews trying to put them out, police trying to clear the area, EMS trying to treat survivors. The voiceover continued.

"All area hospitals have activated mass casualty plans and crews are being flown in from San Antonio, Houston, and Dallas to help. Locals are asked to stay away. A hotline has been set up for families who may be trying to reach protest participants."

Jim was no longer listening. He grabbed his phone out of his sporran and dialed Ginny's number, telling himself there was no reason to think she was involved, other than she was a nurse and in Austin. That and the prickling sensation on the back of his neck.

When he got no answer, he took a breath, then tried again, leaving a message for her to call as soon as she could, then turned to his grandfather. "I have to call the hospital."

"Aye, lad. Go."

Jim grabbed his coat and headed for home, trying Ginny again as he went. He called Hillcrest and was able to get past the switchboard by using the number for Richard Lyons, who was coordinating the relief effort.

"I want to go," Jim told him.

"You're scheduled to work this weekend."

"I'm on the Disaster Response Team and I want to go to Austin. Find someone to cover for me."

"Okay. Get over here. The chopper leaves in forty minutes."

Jim hung up the phone, pulled into a parking space at his apartment, and jumped out, calling his grandfather as he mounted the stairs, to let him know what was happening.

"I don't know when I'll be back."

"It's all right, lad. We'll hold down the fort."

Jim changed clothes, threw an overnight bag together, then hurried to the hospital. He made it with ten minutes to spare.

"Glad to have you aboard, doc." The co-pilot helped him get strapped in, then settled into his own seat.

Jim had been in a medical evacuation helicopter before. He put the ear protectors on and made sure his harness was tight, then looked at the other team members, nodding a greeting to the physician, a burn specialist he knew slightly. The nurse also turned out to be from the burn unit.

Jim took a deep breath and tried not to think about what they would find when they got to Austin. He watched the night stream by the windows of the helicopter, the lights of Dallas fading, to be replaced by the lights of Waco, then Austin.

Hundreds, thousands, maybe, of nurses hurt. And her hotel was near the capital. And she wasn't answering her phone.

He fought down panic. While he was waiting to hear from her, he would do what he was trained to do. At least he'd be on the scene. It would be easier to get word, to search for her, to deal with whatever he might find. But until the crisis was over, he could do nothing, except pray that none of the body parts mentioned on the news turned out to be Ginny's.

* * *

Friday evening
Austin

Ginny hurried down to the car. Ten minutes had her in the hotel parking garage and another ten in the lobby, looking at the puzzled expressions on the faces of the people gathered there. The sirens had started. She could hear the wail as emergency vehicles began to arrive.

She went up to her room and threw her purse and coat down, then went back to the lobby. The video screens over the bar and in the lounge areas were all tuned to the news and reporters were trying to describe what they were seeing. Ginny joined the small knot of people in front of one of them and listened in.

"—at present. The fire department is attempting to bring in trucks, but the number of bodies in the street is making it hard to get close enough." The curvaceous blonde in the trendy winter coat looked pale, but that might just have been the effect of the bright lights on her face. "I'm going to go see if I can find out what happened." She turned in her high heels and tripped over something. When she looked down, the camera followed, showing a woman's arm, still holding hands with a man, well, half a man, both body parts lying in a growing pool of blood. The reporter stumbled, then fell, then retched. The picture cut away to the studio.

Ginny heard a noise and turned around to see the doors of

THE SWICK AND THE DEAD

the hotel open and a woman stagger in. She was covered in blood, holding her arm, and looked to be in shock. As Ginny watched, another arrived, then another, then two coming in through the garage doors, then movement from the hotel staff, coming out from behind the counters, shouting orders, guiding the victims to chairs or sofas or window ledges.

Ginny moved toward the victim closest to her, taking in the injuries, assessing the likely complications, calling for towels and water and EMS. She was not alone. The nurses staying in the hotel were being told, notified by friends or asked by the management to help out. Housekeeping appeared with gloves for everyone. Becky Peel appeared from the dining room and got on her phone. In twenty minutes she had turned the lobby into a full-scale triage area.

The fourth victim Ginny saw turned out to be someone she knew.

"Grace?" Ginny sat down beside her coworker and tried to make contact. "Grace, are you hurt?"

The other woman turned slowly to look at Ginny, her eyes glazed, then slowly focusing.

"Are you hurt?"

It turned out the answer was, yes, but not seriously. Grace had numerous cuts, some of which would require stitching, but no evidence of major hemorrhage or internal bleeding. No chest pain, no collapsed lung, no head injury.

"Were you protesting?"

Grace nodded.

"Did you see anything?"

"Just the flash of light, then blood." Her eyes grew wide. "So much blood!" She was rubbing her hands together, trying to get the blood off.

Ginny laid her gloved hands on Grace's bloody ones, stilling the motion. "We're going to take care of you," she said. She attached the triage tag, finished the paperwork that would accompany Grace to the hospital, then handed her off to the EMS crew.

Ginny dealt with the walking wounded until past midnight. When the last of the victims had been sent to the hospital, she and the other nurses collapsed onto the sofas. The barman brought over a tray of ice water. Snacks followed. There was very little conversation.

The management went from group to group. "If you will leave your clothes for the staff to collect tomorrow, the hotel will be pleased to clean them and return them to you. No charge."

Ginny nodded her thanks, then climbed to her feet. She wanted a bath and a stiff drink, and her bed. She went back to her room and got cleaned up, then reached for her phone. She had missed five calls from Jim and one from her mother. She called her mother first.

"I'm fine. We had casualties in the lobby and I was helping out. I'm sorry I couldn't call sooner. No. I have no idea what happened. I'll let you know when I do. I love you, too."

Jim wasn't answering his phone, but she was pretty sure she knew what he wanted. She tapped out a text message indicating she was fine and would try to reach him in the morning, then turned down the volume on the phone, shut off the light, and closed her eyes.

She was practically catatonic with fatigue. The only problem was, with her eyes closed, she couldn't help seeing the image of that reporter, and the body parts, and the injured she'd cared for that evening.

Someone had overreacted. Surely no one in Texas would kill so many and so indiscriminately over a disputed bill in the state legislature. There had to be more to it than that.

She moved restlessly in the bed, trying to find a comfortable spot. Anyone was capable of violence, of course, even nurses, but if this was a nurse, he or she was deranged. The people who went into nursing did so because they wanted to help, not hurt. Nurses didn't send shrapnel into crowds of unprotected protesters.

Besides, what nurse would set up shrapnel bombs knowing they would take out voters who were on their side? Kill the enemy, maybe, but not friends.

Ginny's eyes drifted open. Grace had said she and Phyllis were political enemies. Grace. Calm, cool, elegant. Except once. On that occasion she had managed to break an IV pole and that took some doing. They were made of steel and bolted together, intended for heavy use and heavy loads.

Ginny sat up and rubbed her face with both hands. It wasn't Grace. Violent she could be, true, but that outburst had been sudden and the result of severe stress and over as suddenly as it had started. A strangling required stealth. Like a bomb. Stealth and patience and the ability to hide in plain sight.

Ginny fell back into the pillows. It was a good thing she wasn't really a detective. She was starting to see murderers everywhere she looked. She closed her eyes and tried to count sheep. She had gotten to sixteen before she realized the sheep were all wearing scrubs. At twenty they also had stethoscopes around their necks. Red ones. At twenty-five, the stethoscopes had become red wires, dripping blood. She was sure that meant something. Something important. She should write it down, before it got away.

She rolled over and saw no more sheep that night.

* * *

Friday evening
Austin

It took Jim just over an hour of flying time in the helicopter to go from Dallas to Austin. With the take-off and landing, that put them on the roof of the big county hospital in Austin around nine-thirty. He was swept into the ER, his bag stashed in a locker, and an isolation gown thrown over his scrubs in fifteen minutes flat. The nurse assigned to help him also got him into shoe covers and a face shield before he could ask. He saw why as soon as he walked into the first patient room.

It was midnight before Jim could get away to take a bathroom break and grab a cup of coffee. There didn't seem to be any end to the patients still lining up to be seen. He tried Ginny again, still without success. He tossed back the coffee and went back to work.

By four a.m. the flood of patients had dwindled to a trickle and Jim was released to one of the call rooms to get some sleep. He checked his phone again and this time found Ginny's text message. He breathed a heavy sigh of relief, set the phone down on the table, and closed his eyes. The next thing he knew, he was being shaken awake.

"Dr. Mackenzie, there's a call for you."

Jim climbed groggily back to consciousness, reaching for his phone.

"Not that one. It's the house phone." The nurse picked up the receiver on the hospital line and handed it to him.

Jim rubbed a hand over his face. "Lo?"

"Jim, it's Richard Lyons. Sorry to wake you, but I need an update."

Jim glanced at his watch. Seven-thirty. Three hours of sleep. Just like residency.

He took a breath, then gave his boss a run down on what

they'd found; the types of injuries, casualty numbers (last he'd heard), and projected timeline.

"Sounds like you've got that under control."

"As far as the emergency care is concerned, yes."

"Good. Here's why I'm calling. DeSoto found out you were in Austin and asked me to ask you to do something for him."

Jim groaned under his breath. All he wanted to do at the moment was go back to sleep. "What does he need?"

"He wants you to talk to one of the docs at County. Here's his name and contact information."

Jim wrote it down on his hand. "What about?"

"Fake fentanyl patches."

* * *

Chapter 18

Day 9 – Saturday morning
Host hotel, Austin

The alarm went off too early for Ginny. If it hadn't been for the bombing, she would have been tempted to cut the conference and go back to sleep. Instead, she pulled herself awake and turned on the TV, hunting for news.

Most of it she already knew. They had found pieces of several bombs, each hidden in an abandoned bicycle. The explosive had been packed into the hollow tube of the frame and any empty space filled with nails, bits of broken glass, cut up aluminum cans, and other sharp objects, then the bikes had been chained to stands, lamp posts, and fences. They had been triggered remotely, which meant wirelessly, and they had been synchronized. The delay in the explosions she heard was caused by the size of the charges and the composition of the bicycles, but all had gone off, with lethal results.

Ginny was just finishing her braid, twisting the rubber band around the bottom when an image appeared on the screen that froze her where she stood.

"In a related story, the lead lobbyist for HB 1712 is unavailable for comment. Supporters are claiming foul play in the sudden disappearance of their spokeswoman, Clara

Carpenter. She was last seen one week ago. The police have no leads and there is speculation that her disappearance may be connected to last night's bombing."

Phyllis!

Ginny was unaware she was staring at the TV, her mouth hanging open. She shook her head. She must have been mistaken. It couldn't have been Phyllis. It was someone who looked sort of like Phyllis.

But, the other woman had disappeared one week ago. Phyllis had been murdered one week ago.

Ginny shook her head again, harder. It wasn't possible. Phyllis had a husband and two children, each with carpools and playdates, and laundry and cooking and all the other demands of married life. In Dallas. And she had a job, full time nights in the Hillcrest Medical ICU. In Dallas.

Ginny turned off the TV, glanced at the clock, and headed downstairs, thoughts tumbling through her mind. What had John said? That Phyllis was mixed up in something political. That he hadn't paid enough attention.

But surely he would have noticed if she'd been gone often enough and long enough to be running a political campaign of this magnitude.

But—Phyllis was dead. Murdered. And there had to be a reason.

Ginny turned left out of the elevator, located her assigned conference room, and found a seat. They had replaced the round tables with long rectangles, swathed in white linen and edged with ruffles in deep blue.

She put her materials down, then got in line for the breakfast buffet. She smiled vaguely at the other nurses, her attention still on the news cast.

Okay. Suppose, for a moment, it was true. Suppose Phyllis was mixed up in this House Bill whatever thing. Did it make sense to kill her?

Ginny could imagine a shadowy opposition gathered around a basement table planning to remove the political head of the movement. Extreme, but possible. If—somehow—Phyllis was the head of that movement, then a nice, quiet throttling, in a city far away from the media scrutiny surrounding the bill, might suit her enemies very well.

What's more, it explained why the murderer chose the ICU ladies' room. A hired killer would benefit from the change of venue, and a suspect pool, none of whom was guilty, but all of whom would come under suspicion. The real killer would be overlooked in the investigation of the innocent. The police would focus on the people who had access.

So, from that point of view, it fit. It was looking more and more likely that Phyllis' killer was an outsider, someone who had managed to get past the security, do the deed, then slip away without detection.

Ginny helped herself to breakfast with these thoughts churning in her brain and a niggling sensation of having missed something. It was the sort of feeling she got when she'd forgotten to do something, or write something down, or tell someone something. She knew the feeling well. She also knew she would have to wait for whatever it was to make its way into her conscious mind before she would know what it was. She settled down at her table, took a deep breath, then deliberately turned her attention to breakfast and the day's lesson, releasing her subconscious mind to work on the puzzle.

* * *

Saturday morning
Travis County Hospital, Austin

At nine a.m. on the morning after the bombing, Jim sat across the desk from a thin, pale man who seemed on the point of a nervous breakdown. His white hair looked as if he'd managed to pull several clumps of it out by the roots and there was an artery pulsing in his temple that bulged with each heartbeat. The nameplate on the desk identified him as Dr. Wingate, Medical Director for Travis County Emergency Responses.

"I'm getting too old for this," he said. He pushed a gallon-sized baggie toward Jim, who lifted it, seeing, among other things, the same fentanyl patches he'd seen in Dallas. "They're all fakes," Dr. Wingate said. "Good ones."

"Do we know who's making them?"

"Yes and no." The Director leaned back in his chair. "Border patrol intercepted a shipment coming up from Mexico last month. They took pictures of the cargo, but the courier somehow died—in custody—before he could talk. The truck went up in flames in the impound yard, and the seized samples in a warehouse fire."

"So where did these come from?" Jim asked.

"A woman. A nurse." Dr. Wingate leaned forward. "This has to stay confidential."

Jim nodded.

"Three days ago, we got a patient in the ER. Vehicle versus lamp post. She was still seizing when they brought her in. She's on life support, but there's no brain activity. When we went looking for next of kin, we found *that* in her purse." He tapped the baggie. "At first, we thought they were real and maybe had caused the seizures, but analysis showed no active ingredient in any of them."

"What made you suspicious?" Jim was thinking of Luis.

"The house supervisor took the bag to the pharmacy and asked them to try to identify the drugs. The pharmacist opened the bag and pulled out one of the cocaine vials, only to find it was leaking. He managed to spill some of it on his wrist."

"Careless."

"Yes, but not lethal, and there were a lot of broken vials in the bag. Anyway, he expected the skin to go numb. You know."

Jim nodded. In health care settings, cocaine was used as an anesthetic.

"Well, it didn't happen. That made him suspicious, so he tested the liquid, then the others. They're chemically inactive, every last one of them."

Dr. Wingate was rocking in his chair, the squeak making Jim nervous. "That's when I called the DEA. We arranged a handoff. He didn't want to come here, something about making targets of the hospital staff. I was supposed to meet him and hand over the fake drugs."

The Medical Director rubbed both hands on his pant legs. "It was his idea to meet during the demonstration, to blend in with the crowd." Dr. Wingate swallowed and Jim suddenly thought he knew where this was going.

"I was late. I was in my car and got stopped by the police barricades. I had to find a place to park and get out and walk.

"The DEA agent had chosen the Heroes of the Alamo monument because we could step inside and not be seen. I was just entering the Great Walk when all hell broke loose."

He swallowed. "You wouldn't believe the carnage. I've seen a lot in this profession, but nothing like that. Maybe in a war. I missed out on military service. Anyway, as soon as I could pick myself up off the ground, I ran."

He clasped his hands on his desk and fixed his eyes on them. "I called my contact at the DEA and told him what had happened. He said one of the bombs leveled the memorial.

Apparently, someone knew we were supposed to be there."

Dr. Wingate lifted his eyes and looked at Jim. "They want you to take this stuff back to Dallas with you, but I won't blame you if you refuse."

Jim pressed his lips together, eyeing the baggie, then looked up at Dr. Wingate. "Does the DEA think the bombers know who *you* are, or just the agent you were supposed to meet?"

"They had agents watching, taking pictures. The man I was to meet was seen talking to an older man in scrubs and a jacket just before the bomb went off. It's possible the bombers think I'm dead and the evidence was destroyed in the fires."

"Or they know who you are and that we've had this little chat."

Dr. Wingate nodded. "That's about the size of it." He took a deep breath. "We can disguise this meeting as a thank you to the Dallas volunteers or a promise to share what we learn from the post-mortem. Something like that."

Jim nodded. "The latter, I think, and I have a suggestion."

"What is it?"

"You give me half the contents of that baggie. Then you take the rest and leave town. You can mail them to the Dallas DEA office. That way we double our chances of getting the evidence into the right hands."

The older man licked his lips, then nodded. He pulled a manila envelope out of his drawer and reached for the baggie.

"Wait," Jim pulled a pair of nonsterile gloves out of his pocket. He slipped them on, then went through the contents of the baggie, picking them over and choosing ones he thought might have DNA or fingerprint evidence on them. Dr. Wingate held the manila envelope open while Jim filled it, then he sealed it and handed it to Jim, who took it and slid it inside his pants, under his scrubs.

"Okay. If they're watching, they know we've been talking,

but it doesn't have to be about fake drugs." Jim rose and walked toward the door, rumpling his hair. "Don't forget to smile at me."

Dr. Wingate pulled himself together and opened the door to his office. "We're so grateful for your help. I'll be sure to send you the data we collect on the disaster response and I'll look forward to hearing your suggestions."

"I don't know if they'll be of any use. You've done a great job with this emergency, but I'll be happy to look over the data and see if I have anything to offer."

"Safe trip home!"

"Thanks." The two men shook hands then Jim went back to the ER locker room, slid the envelope into an interior pocket in his overnight bag, put on his coat, and headed for the lobby.

He called Mrs. Forbes and got the name of Ginny's hotel, then gave it to the taxi driver. He was allowed to check in and order an early lunch from room service then hit the showers. He'd brought slacks and a turtleneck in addition to the scrubs, so he had something decent to put on later.

For the moment though, food and sleep took priority. He ate, drank two bottles of water, pulled the blackout curtains, and fell into bed, deliberately not thinking about the envelope concealed in his bag. Hopefully no one in Austin would realize he had the fake drugs in his possession. He also hoped they wouldn't be in his possession for long. He didn't want to end up like Dr. Wingate.

* * *

Saturday morning
Host hotel, Austin

Ginny was paying attention, but not hanging on every word.
The material being presented wasn't new and the handouts
covered all but a few points. She had her laptop open, muted,
and was using it to do a bit of investigation on the subject of
the two Phyllises.

She plugged HB 1712 into a search box and scanned the
results. There were a lot. By the next break she had assembled
a short portfolio on the missing woman. Her name was Clara
Carpenter. She was a nurse. She was active in many nursing
organizations and had made headlines when she took on the
foreign nurse problem.

For many years, Texas, along with the rest of the country,
had been importing nurses trained in other lands. Some
worked out, some didn't. Ginny already knew there had been
backlash when whole flocks of nurses from the same country
came in, were hired by one facility, and took over everything.
Clique didn't even begin to cover the change in culture in those
locations.

Nor did they assimilate. They brought prejudices and
practices with them which did not meet standard of care and,
sometimes, did not comply with local and federal laws. The
fresh-off-the-boat recruits had to be watched like hawks, to
make sure no patient suffered, and that defeated the purpose,
since they were usually hired by places that already didn't have
enough qualified nurses.

Ginny pulled up a picture of Clara Carpenter and slipped it
into the image search engine. Lots of hits. She looked carefully
at each one, trying to find some familiar face, or place, or
situation in the background. Nothing popped out at her. She
went back to the search engine and tried again, without the

name, hoping for a picture of Phyllis—and got two. The first was the one posted on the Hillcrest website as part of the staff directory. The second was Phyllis at her graduation from nursing school, tagged by someone and posted to social media.

With the images of Clara and Phyllis side by side, Ginny was even more impressed by the resemblance. They weren't twins, of course. They had different birthdates and hometowns and parents and schooling and addresses. One was married, with children, the other unmarried. One was famous, the other unknown. There was an odd similarity, though. Both had spent time in adult ICU nursing. They had that in common.

"But what does it all mean?"

"It means it's time for lunch."

Ginny hadn't realized she'd spoken out loud. She looked up to find Becky Peel at her elbow.

"Put that away and come rest your brain."

Ginny did exactly that, settling down to a better-than-average chicken salad and a lively anything-but-nursing conversation. She listened while she ate, then asked if any of the others could tell her about the demonstration she'd encountered the day before. They could.

"Nut cases."

"No, they're not! They believe in their cause."

"Like I said, nut cases."

Ginny listened to the exchanges and noted that Becky said scarcely a word. Well, she was acting as hostess, so she could hardly take sides, but it was interesting.

"Do you have plans for this evening?" Becky asked.

"Nothing special."

"Paul, my husband, is looking after the kids. What do you say we go sample some of the nightlife in Austin?"

"Sounds good." Ginny went back to the lecture, and her investigation, with her nose twitching. Becky Peel knew

something about those images—it had showed in her face—
and the invitation suggested she had something she wanted to
say to Ginny, privately. Good manners demanded that Ginny
listen.

* * *

CHAPTER 19

Day 9 – Saturday afternoon
Host hotel, Austin

Jim walked along the corridor reading the meeting room labels. He found Ginny in the third room he tried, her computer out, her nose down to the screen.

"May I help you?"

The woman who addressed him was clearly an official. She gestured for the two of them to step into the hall so they could talk. Jim explained he was hoping to catch Ginny to take her out to dinner and that his presence in Austin was unscheduled.

"They'll be through in ten minutes. Would you like to wait or shall I give her a message?"

"Wait, please."

She nodded, gesturing at a bench across the hall. He spent the time thinking through what he'd learned about the counterfeit drugs. A large shipment seized coming up from Mexico implied they were either being made there or imported through there. The destruction of the evidence and the person who could have told about it implied the stakes were very high, which implied a large-scale operation, and *that* implied cartel involvement.

The cartels were capable of anything, up to and including

the bombing at the capital, though how they had managed to get the rendezvous information was still a disturbing mystery. And where did the brain-dead nurse fit in?

Jim was still musing when the doors opened and the conference-goers poured out into the hallway. Jim set his thoughts aside and stood up, catching a number of eyes as he did so. When Ginny appeared, he stepped forward, into her path. Her eyes fell on him, registering shock, then delight.

"Jim!" She was burdened down with her study materials making it impossible to do more than give her a peck on the cheek, which he did, then took her backpack and shouldered it.

"What are you doing here?" she asked.

"I came down to give them a hand with the bombing victims and I was hoping you'd give me a ride back to Dallas."

"Of course! I need to drop my stuff in my room then we can talk. Come on."

They rode up in the elevator and Jim followed her into her room. Once inside he set the backpack down on the bed, then captured her, wrapped his arms around her and kissed her, thoroughly, feeling relief wash through him like a drug.

She tipped her head back and looked up at him. "What's wrong, Jim?"

"I was afraid you'd been caught in that explosion."

Her eyes narrowed. "Why?"

"Because it was Austin and nurses and you weren't answering your phone."

"I'm sorry. I had it off for the conference, then in my room while we dealt with the walking wounded. I texted you as soon as I could."

"I know and I appreciate that."

He saw her brow wrinkle. "You could have called the front desk and had me paged. Why did you hop a plane first and ask questions afterwards?"

"Helicopter," he corrected. "I had this picture of you in my head, surrounded by angry people."

As soon as the words were out of his mouth, he regretted it. He hadn't meant to tell her that. On the news they'd shown footage of the rioting, the faces hostile, followed by images of the terror caused by the bombing. But that one image, the one he hadn't actually seen, had overridden the others.

He saw her blink, saw her eyes narrow, saw her frown.

She pushed herself out of his arms. "Has this happened before?"

"Maybe." He was hedging. It had probably been nothing more than his imagination working overtime, because he was worried in general, and about her safety in particular. *That* had happened before.

She crossed her arms on her chest. "I wonder," she said.

There was a speculative look in her eye that made him uncomfortable. "Wonder what?"

"Do you know what the Sight is, Jim?"

He stood very still for a moment. The Second Sight. His mother had had it, and her mother and he had never considered for a single moment that a man might inherit that particular gift. He'd always dismissed it as an old wives' tale, but he knew what it was.

He looked at Ginny, aware there must be something behind her question. Normal people wouldn't leap to obscure Scottish folk lore to explain his wanting to come to Austin. His brows drew together. "Why do you ask?"

"Because I was there."

"*What?*"

"I got caught in the traffic around the Capital. I had to drive through the demonstration."

"You were there. You were in danger!" Jim felt as if he'd just been punched in the solar plexus.

"I left as soon as the riot started." She pulled a wooden pendant from inside her collar and showed it to him. "Do you know what this is?"

Jim touched the carved image of a tree suspended from a thin gold chain. "I've seen this before."

She nodded. "This talisman has been in my family for generations. The rowan is a portal tree. It guards thresholds and travelers. If you go back far enough, you will also see it credited with healing powers. I wear it at work, when I am ill, and when I am traveling." She caught his eye. "You can laugh at me, if you want to, but the Scots are a superstitious lot for a reason and *you've* just demonstrated one of them."

"Me?"

She nodded. "You felt the threat and acted on it. Without evidence, without confirmation. You, a scientist and a physician." She was smiling at him. "If I hadn't already known you were a Highlander, I'd know it now."

Much as Jim valued his Highland heritage, he felt that a gift like that, being able to tell when Ginny was in danger, might be enough to unhinge a man.

"Is there a way to get rid of it, the Sight?"

She laughed. "No. Sorry."

He ran his hand through his hair. "I feel as if I've stepped off a curb and misjudged the distance."

She tucked her talisman away. "You'll get used to it. Now, if you will excuse me, I'm going to change clothes. I have a dinner engagement."

Jim nodded, still overwhelmed at the thought that his mother's legacy might be genuine. He wondered whether *she'd* been able to tell when *he* was in danger.

He dropped into the desk chair to wait for Ginny to reappear. A dinner engagement. He frowned. He didn't want to share her with anyone this evening.

"Is it a private dinner or may I come?"

She had changed into slacks and sweater and was busy pulling on short boots. "I had planned to dig some information out of one of the locals. She might not want to talk in front of you."

"I would very much like to hear what your contact has to say. Can we tell her I'm safe to know?"

Ginny dimpled. "Are you?"

Jim remembered the fake drugs stashed in his room and felt his chest tighten. He certainly hoped so. "Yes. I'll even buy."

"Well, in *that* case. Come on! We're going to meet for drinks first."

* * *

Saturday evening
Sixth Street, Austin

Sixth Street was still the place to go in Austin. Ginny pushed open the door on a dimly lit gem of the dark wood and solid chairs variety. The piano player was sketching an arpeggio for a laughing female patron. In another moment she had begun to sing to him, in a rich contralto that matched the setting to perfection.

Ginny introduced Jim to Becky, followed her to a table, and came straight to the point. "You know something about that House Bill. I could see it on your face today."

Becky picked up her drink and took a sip, then set it down. "Nothing that can be proved. At least, not yet."

"Go on." Ginny leaned closer.

"Someone approached the Board. You know I work for the Board of Nursing, right? Well, she came in with a story of an underground railroad for, shall we say, marginally qualified nurses trained in Mexico. The suggestion was made that someone here in the U.S. was funding a project to identify young women willing to settle here in exchange for help getting a license." Becky looked up. "She brought a spreadsheet with statistics showing the number of injuries and deaths correlated to the dates of hire for the suspect nurses."

Ginny's eyebrows rose. If true, that would be a major scandal and probably actionable. "Wow."

Becky nodded, her eyes back on her drink. "That was three years ago. It's taken them this long to get a bill before the House and, as you can see, it's a hotly contested idea. On one side we have the people who are pushing for diversity and inclusion. On the other, the group lobbying for patient safety."

"What did the Board do?"

"The investigation is still ongoing."

"So, no police involvement."

"Not yet and there won't be unless some of the legislators get involved. Apparently, there's big money behind the project."

"How do you know all this?"

Becky looked up. "You've heard of Clara Carpenter."

Ginny nodded. "There was a news clip this morning. Someone thinks she's the victim of foul play because she was supporting the bill."

"Oh, she was more than supporting it. She helped draft it. She's the one who went to the Board."

"Do you know this woman?"

"I do. She's my sister."

* * *

CHAPTER 20

Day 9 – Saturday late evening
Sixth Street, Austin

Jim was keeping his mouth shut and the drinks coming. Becky Peel leaned toward them across the table, her eyes on Ginny. "You saw the news this morning?"

Ginny nodded. "I saw the picture."

"And I saw you researching my sister today when you were supposed to be paying attention in class."

"I can multi-task."

Becky smiled at her. "Okay. Why is he here?" She glanced over at Jim.

Ginny smiled. "This is my partner in crime. We're working with the police to solve Phyllis' murder."

Jim smiled at Becky, trying to look useful. He watched her take another swallow of her drink, studying them.

"Can he keep his mouth shut? Can both of you? I don't want Clara to end up like Phyllis."

Jim felt his pulse quicken. "*I* can." He cocked his head toward Ginny. "She's a chatterbox."

Ginny turned and punched him in the shoulder. "I am not!"

Becky laughed. "All right, you two. Knock it off." They set the discussion aside as their dinners arrived. When they were finished, Becky looked at the two of them. "How about dessert at my house?"

"That sounds lovely," Ginny said.

They got directions from their hostess, then worked their way south, down the interstate, over the river, and into a residential neighborhood lined with mature trees.

Becky closed the door behind them, then called to her sister. "Clara, I have someone I want you to meet."

She emerged from a back room, her long, rangy legs accentuating her lanky form and blonde hair. She held out a hand to Ginny, then to him.

"Hi! I'm Clara Carpenter."

Jim nearly dropped his teeth. If she hadn't been so warm, he would have sworn he was shaking hands with a corpse. Ginny seemed to have known, but he hadn't. Clara Carpenter was a dead ringer for Phyllis Kyle.

* * *

Saturday late evening
Peel residence, Austin

Ginny could sympathize with the shock she saw on Jim's face. She, too, found the resemblance unnerving and she'd been prepared for it.

"Please, sit down." Becky steered Jim over to the sofa, then sat down beside him. "Now you see why we're concerned about this murder in Dallas."

Clara nodded. "When I saw the announcement on the TV, I went into hiding. My first thought was that she was killed by mistake and the murderer was after me."

Ginny leaned forward. "Why? Phyllis was killed in the Hillcrest ICU, on a night shift. Why would you think the killer would mistake someone in that position for you?"

Clara and Becky exchanged glances. Clara answered.

"Phyllis has been standing in for me, pretending to be me. We're afraid someone followed her home."

Ginny knew she was staring, but she couldn't help it. "Phyllis was impersonating you?"

"Yes. So I could meet with some of the decision-makers without having to deal with protesters. I offered to pay her for it, but she refused. She said she was glad she could do something more useful than waving a placard at a TV camera."

"How many times?" Jim asked.

"Eight, total."

"How did you two meet?"

"At an ICU conference two years ago. We hit it off immediately and pretended to be twins. When this issue came up, she called me and asked if she could help."

Ginny frowned. "Do you honestly believe you have enemies willing to murder you?"

Clara nodded. "There's a great deal of money involved in this Mexican Nurse Pipeline. If it gets shut down, someone is going to be hurt, financially, I mean." Clara frowned. "What I don't understand is why they chose to kill her at work, rather than in some quiet alleyway. There are places in Texas lonely enough that she might never have been found."

Ginny nodded, then explained her theory about the hired assassin choosing the Hillcrest ICU as a way to cover his tracks.

Jim nodded slowly. "Well, that part of it makes sense, but how did he plan to get in? The ICU is usually locked."

Ginny shrugged. "Visitors come and go and I'm not sure anyone counts noses. Or maybe he planned to dress up as maintenance." She turned back to Clara. "It's been driving me crazy that I couldn't find a motive for anyone who had access to Phyllis to want to kill her, but if it was a mistake—" She shrugged. "And that still doesn't explain why they concluded you and she were the same person. Especially if you were seen together at an ICU conference."

Becky nodded. "After we thought about it, we decided they didn't. We think the murderer knew it was Phyllis, not Clara. We think she was the target."

Ginny felt her skin crawl. "Why?"

Clara reached over and picked up a small booklet, handing it to Ginny. "Because of this."

Ginny looked down to find the Texas Board of Nursing quarterly *Bulletin* in her hand. She glanced at the date, seeing that it was not the most recent issue. This was the one before, issued six months ago. She looked over at Clara. "What am I looking for?"

Clara opened the *Bulletin* to the featured article. "Here."

Ginny read the headline, then the author's name. Her eyebrows shot up. "Phyllis wrote this?"

Clara nodded. "I helped with some of the legal angles."

Ginny read through the two-page article, her heart sinking. It was an argument against using vulnerable Mexican nationals in the illegal and deadly drug trafficking going on between Mexico and Texas. She looked at Clara. "Did she tell you how she got this information?"

"She said she had a friend among the pipeline nurses. Someone who wanted out." Clara nodded at the *Bulletin*. "Those insider details, she didn't get those from me."

Ginny sucked in a deep breath. "I think I know who she got them from." She turned to Becky. "If I give you an RN license number, can you see if it belongs to one of the pipeline nurses?"

Becky nodded. "I can probably find out, but not until Monday. Get me the number and a way to get back to you."

"I can give you her name, too."

"Even better."

Clara leaned forward, her eyes troubled. "I absolutely hate the thought that Phyllis died because of me."

"Even if this is what got her killed, it's not your fault. Besides, it's just a theory and there are others." Ginny took a deep breath. "What happens now?"

Clara shrugged. "The vote is next week and, if that demonstration is any indication, it's going to be ugly."

Ginny hesitated. "Please don't think I'm giving you orders, but I'm going to suggest you stay in hiding until this is over. If the opposition thinks you're dead, they won't come after you."

Both Clara and Becky nodded.

"Okay. Now, I want to hear every single detail. From the beginning."

It took an hour for Clara to describe the entire history of the problem, during which Becky fed them chocolate cake and ice cream.

"So, House Bill 1712 is proposing stricter controls on the use of foreign nurses in Texas."

"Right."

"And there are some powerful people in Austin (who prefer to remain anonymous) who have set up a way for Mexican nurses to come to Texas to work."

Clara nodded. "All expenses paid. They agree to come in exchange for help with the NCLEX and the philanthropists behind the idea arrange all the necessary papers. Once the nurses get here, they're supplied with housing and jobs."

"And you know this how?"

Becky lifted an eyebrow. "There's a woman at the Board who's been bragging about it: how noble they are and how admirable it is to rescue these women and fill the need here at the same time."

"I heard there've been some problems in Houston."

"Yes. Some of these foreign nurses have made enough mistakes to attract official attention."

"How do you know *those* nurses, the ones making mistakes, are part of this pipeline?"

"Timing, mostly. We tracked the official documents—immigration, licensure dates, and so forth—on the problem nurses and found they had all come over the border and been placed in long-term care facilities in batches."

Becky interjected at this point. "When the Board started investigating, we found those particular long-term care facilities were all owned by either the same umbrella corporation or a sister version of it, all of the assets in holding companies. That caused some concern and we tried to dig deeper, but got stonewalled. Whoever is behind this has friends in high places."

Clara resumed her tale. "So we decided to tighten up on the credentialing, which the Board has the power to do without the cooperation of the employers. But it meant obtaining a resolution from the legislature so we could reach the necessary records. This protest is just one of the ways they've tried to stop us. I've heard rumors of threats to legislators' families, bribes to turn a blind eye, and suggestions that opponents will find their careers over."

She sighed. "Don't get me wrong. There are a lot of people in this town who do an awful lot of good in the world, but I can't help thinking that someone is using the do-gooders in Texas to do something that is not very good for the people of Texas."

* * *

CHAPTER 21

Day 9 – Saturday night
Host hotel

They took their leave of the sisters and drove back to the hotel. Jim followed Ginny into her room, closed the door behind him, then leaned against it, his eyes on her.

"Thank you."

She hung up her coat then turned and smiled at him. "You're welcome. What for?"

"For letting me come with you tonight. I would have been worried sick not knowing where you were or what you were doing or when you'd be back."

She laughed. "You sound like an old woman. Speaking of which—" She pulled her phone out and dialed home.

"Mom? Yes, sorry it's late. We were out having dinner. Jim and I. Yes, he came down to help with the emergency. I'll bring him home with me tomorrow." She looked at him. "Mother says hello." She turned back to the device. "Yes. All right. Yes. I love you, too. Goodnight."

She slipped the phone back into her purse. "There, that's done. Now where were we?"

"You had just called me an old woman." He dropped gloomily into the desk chair. "The truth is, I feel like one. This whole thing has gotten so much bigger than I anticipated."

She nodded. "Not just a simple little murder. Now it's a case of state law versus restraint of international trade."

He caught her eye. "I hope Clara's wrong. I hope—and this sounds awful, but I'm going to say it anyway—I hope Phyllis' murder turns out to be personal. I don't like playing spy."

Ginny looked up. "Who said anything about spying?"

Jim caught his breath and back-peddled hastily. "No one. It just has the flavor of a spy novel to me." He jumped to his feet, crossed to where she stood, and scooped her up in his arms.

"Jim!" she squeaked. "What do you think you're doing?"

He dropped her on the side of the bed farthest from the door, then settled down beside her. "Manning the gates. You sleep. I'll keep guard."

She curved toward him, her eyes on his face, a small frown forming. "You look tired. Did you get any sleep last night?"

"Three hours in the call room at the hospital and four here."

"Well, you look as if you could use more. Go back to your room. I'll see you in the morning."

He reached over and stroked her cheek with a fingertip. "Didn't I just tell you I wasn't going to leave you alone?"

She nodded. "I heard you, but I assumed you were exaggerating. You cannot spend the night in my room."

"Just for tonight. I promise I won't misbehave."

She shook her head. "Not gonna happen." She sat up and looked at him, frowning. "What's bothering you, Jim?"

"Nothing. I just want to be with you."

She rolled off the bed, came around, and tugged on his arm. "Up. Out. I need my sleep. I've got another half day of conference tomorrow."

Jim sat up, then swung his legs over the side of the bed and sat watching her as she tried in vain to pull him to his feet. Talk about not gonna happen. He could force the issue, but he had to admit that he really was tired and she was probably as safe here as anywhere in the city. He stood up.

"You'll lock the door."

"Of course," she said. "Come on."

"All right." It would be easier to think in the morning. "But come tuck me in."

"Jim!"

He had hold of her hands now, pulling her toward the hallway. "Come on. Tuck me in and kiss me goodnight."

"Jim! Someone might see!"

"We will walk decorously side by side in the public spaces. Come."

They made their way up to his room, two floors above. Jim fished out his room key, opened the door and started to enter, then froze. Someone had been in the room.

To help him sleep, Jim had covered the power button on the television with one of the ubiquitous hotel advertisements. When he opened the door, the bright red light caught his eye. He glanced down at the doorknob, seeing his *Do Not Disturb* sign still in place. Considering his late arrival and the fact that he'd slept in this room most of the day, it was unlikely that the intruder was the maid.

He pushed Ginny behind him and flipped on the light. The room was empty, but his make-shift LED cover was now lying on the floor. He went straight to his overnight bag, pulled the zippers open and looked inside.

The envelope was gone.

He grabbed his belongings, stuffed them into the bag, then grabbed Ginny's hand and pulled her into the hallway. "Come on."

"Jim, what's wrong?"

"We're leaving."

"Now?"

"Right now."

He took her back to her room and helped her pack, his mind racing. Someone had followed him here. Someone who knew what he was carrying. Someone willing to break into his hotel room to retrieve the evidence.

They checked out, rode up the parking garage elevator, and stepped out into the concrete structure. Ginny was leading the way, but glancing back over her shoulder, her face full of unspoken questions. It wasn't until Jim's eye fell on the car that he stopped. Retrieve the evidence, eliminate the witness.

"Ginny, wait."

She turned to look at him, her hand halfway to the trunk latch.

"Ginny, sweetheart, please, back away."

She stood without moving for a moment, her eyes locked on his, then did as asked. Jim sighed his thanks to whatever deity might be listening.

He motioned for her to come to him. When she did, he slid an arm around her waist and steered her back inside. It took him twenty minutes to locate Agent DeSoto. It took the Austin bomb squad only ten minutes to respond.

Jim was sitting in the hotel lobby with his arms around Ginny, fending off her questions, when the police officer approached.

"There was something there, all right, but it isn't a bomb. It's a tracking device." He held it out to show them. "Can't have been there very long either. The case is pretty clean." He slid a gloved fingernail along the edge of the plastic case, then opened it to show them the electronic device nestled inside. "Attached by a magnet. GPS locator. Available off the Internet. What do you want us to do with it? I mean, if it's evidence, we'll need to bag it."

Jim looked up from the device in the officer's hand. "Can

you give me a minute? I want to hand that question off to someone else."

Jim called DeSoto again and explained what they'd found. "The question is, do we give it to the police here or bring it to you, or what?"

"Let me think a minute."

Jim waited through the silence on the other end of the line.

"Dr. Mackenzie? Can you put the officer on the phone?"

"Sure." Jim rose and handed over the phone, explaining DeSoto's role. He watched as the police sergeant walked out of earshot, waited while the two officers of the law came to a decision, then took the phone back when it was handed to him.

"Here's what we'd like to do. The device is evidence and we want to preserve that for use in court so we have to maintain the chain of custody, but we don't want to alert the bad guys."

Jim listened as DeSoto outlined the procedure for bagging and tagging the device, then signing it over to him, to be held until he could turn it over to DeSoto or someone designated by him to receive it.

"Can you do that? It means leaving the evidence bag, tracker inside, in the car, so that whoever put it there won't notice."

Jim nodded into the phone. "We can slip it into the door pocket so it will stay put until needed. Can we figure out who put it on her car?"

"Possibly. Officer Weems is going to photograph the device and send me a copy of the image. With the serial number, we may be able to track the purchase. Get back to Dallas," DeSoto instructed. "I'll catch up with you tomorrow."

Jim hung up the phone, then accepted the evidence bag from the police officer, signing where indicated.

"Since this is going to be out of police custody, we would like to emphasize that whether or not this perpetrator is caught and whether or not he goes to jail, might hinge on your diligence. Please check on the bag regularly, in a private place like a closed garage, to make sure it's still safe. We would hate to let a criminal slip through our fingers because of a procedural glitch."

"I understand."

The officer nodded. "Have a safe trip."

"Thanks."

Jim held the door while Ginny got in on the passenger side of the car, then settled down to drive back to Dallas. They were an hour out before she spoke.

"Are you ready to tell me what's going on?"

He took a deep breath, then explained about the ambush at the state capital and his role as courier and how the disappearance of the fake drugs implied he was being followed.

She was silent for a long time after he finished. "You think they're planning to kill you?"

Jim shook his head. "No, at least, not yet. If they had wanted to, they could have gunned me down at any time. Or planted a bomb instead of a tracking device. Whoever this is, they wanted to know where to find us."

"Us?"

He reached over and took her hand. "It was your car. You and I were out on the town in that car until late, which means they knew which car to bug, and were ready to move in swiftly once we got back to the hotel. That requires resources and organization. We have to assume that, if they've decided I'm a threat, the same is probably true of you."

* * *

CHAPTER 22

Day 10 – Sunday two a.m.
Loch Lonach Homestead

They drove straight back to Dallas. With twenty minutes left in the drive, Jim pulled out his phone and called his grandfather.

"Homestead grounds. I'll meet ye at th' gates."

Jim looked over at Ginny. "What does he mean, 'Homestead grounds'?"

"The living history site is secure. The gates are locked and there are guards."

Jim steered toward the Loch Lonach Homestead, and pulled up at the gate, unsurprised to find Himself already there, fully dressed in kilt and Inverness cape even at this hour.

They followed his taillights through the historic village, then pulled into a small parking lot facing a one-story modern building. The Laird opened the door with a badge and thumbprint.

"Bring yer bags. Ye can stay here th' nicht. I'll bring ye groceries in the morn. Turn off th' phones 'til we can talk. 'Tis a safe zone, but cell lines are no secure."

Both Jim and Ginny nodded.

"Th' guards ken yer here and will no bother ye. I'll be back fer breakfast. Sleep."

Jim followed the Laird to the front door and got instructions for locking themselves in, watched the car out of sight, then turned off the lights. He found Ginny in one of the bedroom suites pulling the shades down on an unlit view of the back wall. She turned to look at him, and he saw her shiver.

"Are you cold?"

"No. Scared."

The suite was laid out in an "L" shape, with a sitting room on one leg and the sleeping area on the other. Jim guided Ginny over to the sofa, pulled off her coat and shoes, wrapped her in blankets from the bed, then settled down and pulled her into his arms. He held her, murmuring to her, telling her she was safe, until he felt her stop shaking.

"Sleep, Ginny. We're going to be busy tomorrow."

This time she didn't protest, just shifted against him, snuggling closer, and closed her eyes. She was warm enough for both of them and Jim relaxed into the cushions. He put his head down and studied the patterns of shadow and light that appeared on the ceiling.

Luis was the key. If his mother was involved with the fake drugs, there was a very good chance she was involved with the people responsible for the bombing.

Phyllis had described—in writing—a system that exploited and abused Mexican nurses, probably quoting Maria. If Phyllis had been killed for publishing cartel secrets, then anyone working on the case might be in danger. Alternatively, the killer might feel safe, having pulled off the perfect murder, leaving no forensic evidence, no witnesses, and a satisfyingly large number of innocent suspects.

Jim let his eyes wander, trying to think through the implications, but his brain just wasn't cooperating. Maybe DeSoto knew how the Mexican nurses and the Mexican drug cartel fit together. Jim's tired brain amended that thought. The question wasn't whether DeSoto knew or not, but what he planned to do about it. Presumably, they would find out tomorrow.

* * *

Sunday midmorning
Loch Lonach Homestead

At ten a.m. the next morning, Jim, Ginny, Angus, and Tomas DeSoto were gathered around the table in the safe house on the Homestead grounds, eating Sunday brunch. True to his word, Himself had brought groceries, then stayed to cook. Jim was pleasantly surprised at how good the food tasted.

"So," he said, wiping his mouth, "that's everything." He picked up his coffee and turned to face DeSoto. "Your turn."

DeSoto nodded. "What do you want to know?"

"I assume using me as a courier was your idea."

DeSoto nodded. "When I saw the explosions on the news, I called my Austin contact. He told me about the evidence drop and that it looked as if they either had a traitor on the inside of the Austin office or their intranet had been hacked. As a result, they had evidence they didn't want to hand to anyone in their organization."

Jim nodded.

"I called your boss, to see if he knew Dr. Wingate, because of the ER connection. He mentioned you'd flown to Austin to help out and would be in the same hospital. That's when I got the idea to use you as a courier. Whose idea was it to split the drugs?"

"Mine. I picked out the examples I thought we might be able to trace and suggested to Wingate that he mail the remainder to the Dallas DEA office, then disappear. Did he?"

"I don't know about the mailing. He's disappeared, all right. No one knows where to find him, but his car's gone and so is a big chunk of his ready cash."

Jim hoped very sincerely Dr. Wingate had managed to get out of harm's way. Which brought him to the real question. He licked his lips, his mouth suddenly dry in spite of the coffee.

"Am I in danger? Is Ginny?"

DeSoto shook his head. "I don't think so. The organization—and they are very organized—has its evidence back."

"Part of it."

"Yes, part of it, and they might want to ask you where the rest is. But, unless I misread the situation, this has been going on for some time. They'll be willing to take some risks, like disguising a hit on a DEA agent as part of a violent demonstration, but they're not going to attack you unless they have to."

"How did they know I had the drugs?"

"Ah! Now, *that* I can answer. Dr. Wingate's office was bugged. We found a listening device stuck to the back of his filing cabinet."

Jim felt his stomach clench. Someone had been listening in on that conversation. "Wait a minute. If someone was eavesdropping on us, they already know I don't have the rest of the drugs."

"Correct, but they may think you know where Wingate is."

"Oh."

"It narrows the field for us, though. We'll probably be able to trace that bug."

"And the hotel?"

"We think someone followed your taxi from the hospital. They'd have no trouble finding a maid willing to pick up a little extra money by letting someone into your room."

"What about the tracking device under my car?" Ginny

asked.

"We'd like to leave it where it is." DeSoto frowned. "Frankly, it has us puzzled. Once they knew about Dr. Mackenzie, it would be easy enough to follow him and see what car he was using, but we can't figure out what they thought they could learn by tracking you."

"Where to find Clara Carpenter?" Ginny suggested.

DeSoto nodded. "It's possible, but—according to my sources—she's not associated with fake drugs, just clamping down on incompetent nurses. The only thing she and the drugs have in common is Mexico and we're not even sure about that. I don't see a connection."

He sighed. "We searched the house of the woman in the wreck, the one who was carrying the fake drugs, but found nothing. Someone got there ahead of us. Those fentanyl patches you found on the boy are the only solid evidence we have at this point."

Jim looked over at Ginny, then back at DeSoto. "So what do you recommend we do?"

"Act normal. Go to work. Go Christmas shopping. Do whatever you would usually do."

"And wait for something to happen." Jim found his throat tight.

DeSoto nodded. He tapped the table with his fingertip. "We'll be watching, though. You shouldn't see any of our agents, but they'll be there. This is the best lead we've got and we won't let it—or you—slip through our fingers."

* * *

CHAPTER 23

Day 10 – Sunday afternoon
Jumpin' J Ranch

The Hillcrest Regional Medical Center ER/ICU Christmas party was usually held on the grounds of the *Jumping J* ranch, east of Dallas. It was the family home of Devlin Jones and still boasted enough acreage for horseback riding, skeet shooting, a bonfire, outdoor barbeque, indoor buffet, two-story tall Christmas tree, and a build-your-own bar. The doors opened at noon and closed only when there were no more guests on the grounds.

Jim wandered through the main part of the ranch house, nodding to some, speaking to others, thinking his colleagues ran to type. There was far too much booze in the blood flowing through the physicians' veins.

They had all learned to drink in medical school. It was a prerequisite for surviving some of the shifts they'd had to put in, some of the horrors they'd had to face. The nursing schools had added the seamier element to those parties, a handful of the attendees earning the reputation (perpetuated by the Hallowe'en costume industry) that all nurses were loose women. Jim hadn't met anyone he'd want to take home to his parents at any of those parties.

He turned a corner and spotted Lisa. She was marginally

clothed in what appeared to be a Christmas elf costume, with few details left to the imagination. He turned back, but it was too late. She'd seen him.

"Jim!" She hurried across the room, went up on tip toe, and tried to kiss him. Jim put his hands on her arms and pushed her away.

"I haven't had a chance to thank you for Friday night." She had raised her voice, a smirk on her lips.

"I'm glad you enjoyed the ceilidh." He also raised his voice, to make sure anyone who heard her also heard him.

She tipped her head sideways and wiggled her shoulders. "They seem very nice, your people."

He looked down at her, making eye contact and not smiling. "They *are* nice."

She pouted, her lips plump and stained with both lipstick and Bloody Mary mix. Her tongue came out and licked the drink off, slowly, keeping her eyes on his.

"You looked very handsome in your kilt." She tipped her chin up. "I love a man in a kilt."

Jim tried hard not to frown. He crossed his arms on his chest and took a half step back. She followed, reaching out and laying the hand that wasn't holding her drink on his bicep.

"It made you look, oh, more virile, somehow." She simpered.

Jim pressed his lips together, but he couldn't think of a crushing response to that because he agreed with her, as did the entire female population of the Homestead.

Lisa batted her eyelashes at him. "So does your vest."

He froze, then dropped his voice. "What vest?"

"The bulletproof vest, of course. There's something so macho about wearing one, about being willing to go into danger like that."

He grabbed her arm, not gently, and dragged her away from

the crowd, hissing at her. "Shut up!"

She looked startled. "Why?"

He was close enough to smell the alcohol on her breath and see the flush caused by inebriation. He put his mouth next to her ear and whispered. "Because people may die if someone finds out about that. You don't want to kill anyone, do you?"

He watched the color drain from her cheeks and almost felt sorry for her.

She shook her head.

"Then be a good little girl and go home. Sleep it off and don't mention those vests to anyone ever again."

She nodded, meekly, he thought, then tipped up her glass, finishing it in one gulp and gaining courage from it.

"I'll go when I like." She looked around the room. "I'm bored anyway." She looked back at Jim, defiance in her eyes, and raised her voice again. "See you later, darling."

Jim watched her cross the room, pick up her purse and head for the front door, downing another drink on the way.

"Dr. Mackenzie?"

Jim turned to find the woman he knew as Ginny's boss addressing him.

"Is there a problem?"

The ICU Head Nurse had not been included in the group of people who had a need to know about the sting operation. ICU nurses floated to the ER when there was a hole in the schedule and that had explained Lisa's presence three shifts in a row last week, but none of the ICU people had been included in the briefing sessions so none had been warned about the secrecy.

It was an oversight. DeSoto should have seen that coming. Hell, Jim should have. He was the one with experience.

"No."

Ms. Hawkins looked at the closed door, then back at Jim.

"I'm responsible for my nurses."

Jim sucked in a breath, then looked the Head Nurse directly in the eyes. "Lisa is an excellent nurse. I have no fault to find with her work."

The Head Nurse's eyes narrowed slightly, then she smiled and nodded. "You'll let me know if that changes."

"I will."

She turned and walked back into the crowd.

Jim hadn't seen any of the DEA agents at the party, which didn't mean they weren't there, of course. But it meant he would have to catch up with DeSoto at the hospital and explain Lisa's indiscretion. Hopefully they could contain the damage.

Jim's eye swept the side rooms as he turned back toward the party, and found Ginny standing in one of the doorways, her eyes on him. He swallowed hard, then walked over and stood looking down at her.

She raised her eyebrows, one dimple showing. "Have you been having fun with Lisa?"

Jim's eyes narrowed. "How much of that did you see?"

"Most of it, I should think."

"It's not what it looks like. That woman has been making a nuisance of herself ever since you left. She even came to the ceilidh on Friday night."

"I know."

Jim looked at her sharply. "How do you know?"

"Because Lisa sent me pictures of the two of you dancing together, drinking together, smiling at one another."

Jim's eyes widened in dismay. "I wasn't! I didn't!"

"They were waiting in my e-mail box when I got home."

Jim could feel his temper rising. "Show me."

Ginny pulled out her phone and accessed the e-mail account. She handed it over, the slight smile still in place, her eyes quizzical.

Jim studied the images, then handed the phone back.

"These are faked." He pointed at one where he and Lisa were cheek to cheek. "That never happened, and I have witnesses to prove it. *And*, she brought her own photographer." He explained about Mary Jo.

Ginny started laughing. "Poor baby! You *have* had a hard week! Don't worry. I'll deal with Lisa." She took his arm and steered him back into the party. "Come on. They're starting the Secret Santa, and I don't want to miss it. You never know what you might find under the tree."

* * *

Sunday afternoon
Jumpin' J Ranch

The party-goers were gathered around the Christmas tree, drinks in hand, watching the Secret Santa packages being opened and laughing with the recipients. A tin bugle went to someone known for blowing his own horn, a book on handwriting analysis to a nurse who frequently complained about the quality of hand-written chart entries.

Ginny was given a junior detective set, complete with fingerprint powder. Jim received a set of maps of the Dallas/Ft. Worth area, none of them accurate and all of them illustrated with suggestive caricatures of physicians enjoying themselves.

One of the men received software for his phone, which he instantly installed and demonstrated. Ginny watched in delight as he changed his voice to cartoon characters, then mechanical life forms, then a sultry female. A sudden movement caught her eye and she glanced up in time to see her boss watching the demonstration with a shocked intensity it didn't seem to deserve.

When the Secret Santa was over, Ginny went in search of

the powder room, which turned out to be located in the west wing of the ranch house. She lingered in the pink and white retreat, freshening her makeup, remembering.

She'd been disoriented, then comforted when she woke that morning in Jim's arms. He was still asleep and she lay there, careful not to move, breathing in his scent, feeling the rhythm of his chest as it rose and fell, examining the red-gold fuzz around his mouth. It was no surprise women like Lisa found him attractive. He *was* attractive. She took a last look in the mirror, thinking she looked less so, having suffered from not enough sleep for too many days. She gathered up her purse and opened the door.

"There you are! Come on!" Jim gestured for her to follow him down the corridor and out onto the porch.

"What's going on?" she asked.

"Didn't you hear it?"

"Hear what?"

"A gunshot."

She looked around. There was a small open fire in a stone pit, with abandoned drinks along the edge and evidence of marshmallow toasting, but the S'mores had been eaten and the revelers had moved on.

The BBQ grill was manned by a cook in a Christmas apron, his eyes on his work, his ears covered by red and green fuzzy muffs with battery-operated lights that twinkled. There was a wire stretching from his left ear to the pocket on that side and his movements suggested he had the sound turned up.

The sun hovered just above the horizon, throwing long shadows across the fields. Ginny spotted a cow chewing its cud.

As they got closer to the fence line, she lifted her nose and breathed in the evening. The sky was dotted with pink clouds and there was just a hint of rain in the air. Also, the smell of burning wood from the open fire (oak), and the smoke from the BBQ (mesquite), and hay, and dried leaves, and something else she had no trouble identifying, gunpowder.

She could hear something, too. Cursing and pleas for help, coming from the area beyond the yard.

"Who's that?"

"I don't know. I heard the shot and turned to follow the sound and found you in my path so I decided to take you with me."

"You're such a fun date!"

Ginny could see him now, a young man on the ground, rocking back and forth, holding his left knee in both hands.

Jim dropped to the grass and examined the knee while Ginny tried to see if there were other injuries. The young man grabbed Jim's arm.

"He shot me! He shot my knee!"

Jim looked up. "Call 9-1-1, and let DJ know where we are, and I could use a first aid kit."

"Right." Ginny pulled her phone out as she turned, explained to the 9-1-1 dispatcher, then hurriedly located their host.

"What? What's that?" Dr. Jones almost knocked her over in his haste.

"A young man. Says he was shot. Near the fence."

Ginny followed their host out the back door.

"Dad! He shot me!"

"Corey! Goddammit, Corey! What did I tell you—" He broke off. "How bad is it?" he asked Jim.

"Bad enough." Jim had pulled his shirt off and was using it to slow the bleeding.

Dr. Jones turned to Ginny. "Get hold of Harold. Tell him there's a trauma kit in the master bath, second cabinet, top shelf."

Ginny nodded and fled. Harold turned out to be in the kitchen, able to drop everything, and willing to help. They were both in the backyard again within five minutes. The ambulance took longer.

By then they had attracted a crowd of onlookers. Most had sense enough to stay out of the way. Ginny did what she could to help, listening to the young man trying to tell his father what had happened and being shushed repeatedly. When the ambulance arrived and she and Jim were allowed to move back, she caught his arm and pulled him into the house, then into the bathroom to wash.

"Where are you on your vaccines?" she demanded.

"All up to date." He was smiling down at her as she scrubbed his hands and arms with soap.

"Does any of this hurt?" She was hunting for breaks in his skin.

He let her dry him off, then examined his skin himself. "No obvious wounds, but I think it would be advisable to go get some gamma globulin. Want to come?"

"Yes."

She followed him to the coat room, then the parking area, then to Hillcrest. It was tedious waiting for him to get checked in as a regular patient, fill out the forms, and be seen by the ER doc on duty, but he took it with good grace and got what he— and she—wanted, a dose of medicine to help fight off any viruses that might have been lurking in Dr. Jones' son's blood.

He lifted an eyebrow at her. "So, Dr. Jones has a son who's an IV drug abuser."

"You saw the tracks."

"I did."

Ginny sighed. "Well, it's not the first time that's happened."

"No, and it's none of our business."

"Except for one thing," Ginny said. "Something he said while you were working on him. I don't know if you heard him. His father may have. He kept telling him to be quiet."

"What did he say?"

"He looked up at me and said, 'I should have listened to Phyllis.'"

* * *

Chapter 24

Ginny rolled out of bed on Monday morning and stumbled toward the bathroom. She ate breakfast, then headed for the Homestead Children's Shelter. Over coffee she explained her errand to Rose MacGregor.

"I need to find that blue envelope, the one Luis said he got the drugs out of. Have you seen *anything* that fits that description?"

"No, but I've nae searched all o' the lad's things."

"Is it all right with you if I look?"

"Of course. I'll help ye."

The dormitory was set up as small suites, with four rooms sharing a central bathroom. Luis' room was a cheerful mix of blues and greens, with pastel whales and fish along the borders and at child's eye-level. There was no closet. All the children used toy chests and alcoves for their possessions. It took Ginny and Rose fifteen minutes to assure themselves there was no blue envelope in Luis' room.

"Could he have stashed it in someone else's room?" Ginny asked.

Rose shrugged. "'Tis possible, but the ither children would

hae thrown it away, I think."

"So it's hidden somewhere. Let's check the bathroom."

"Ye do that and I'll check the ither three rooms."

The bathroom had cabinets and shelves and cubbyholes for shampoo and soap. Each child had a drawstring bag made of net, hung from hooks, again at child's eye-level. They were color-coded to match the towels.

Ginny went through the cabinets first. Nothing at ground level seemed to offer a place to hide an envelope so she worked her way up. The cabinets along the ceiling had padlocks and required keys to open them. Ginny went to find Rose.

"Naething in the ither three rooms. What o' th' bathroom?"

"I'd like to look in the locked cabinets."

"Surely the bairn could nae get into those?"

"No, but he might have stuffed something through the gap."

Rose obliged with the key and a step stool and watched as Ginny opened each cabinet in turn, making sure to lock them tightly behind her.

"What's this?" Ginny peered into the darkness of the fourth cabinet, the one that a five-year-old could presumably have reached if he was standing on the counter. "I need a flashlight, a pair of tweezers, and a clean manila envelope, please."

It took Ginny several tries, but eventually she was able to grasp a torn and badly wrinkled blue envelope and slide it out from between the frame and the side wall of the cabinet. She held it up for Rose to see.

"Looks tae be a blue envelope."

"And you're a witness to where it was found." Ginny held it by the corner, using the tweezers. She turned it this way and that, trying to see if it had a return address on it anywhere.

"This hasn't been through the mail."

"Is it the right one, then?"

"It's addressed to Mrs. Perez."

"Well, all right, then. Ane blue envelope found."

Ginny dropped it into the manila envelope, then locked up and handed the keys back. "Thank you for your help. I'll make sure the authorities get this." She climbed down, then turned to face Rose MacGregor. "I see no reason to tell Luis about this, do you?"

"Nane at all. He thinks his secret is safe. Let him go on believing so."

* * *

Monday morning
Brochaber

Ginny had gone straight from the Shelter to the Laird. She now sat in his kitchen with Luis' blue envelope in its manila prison between them. She had come here as a matter of course, because this was where one came, when one was in trouble.

"Send him away! He'll listen to you. Send him somewhere safe until this is over."

The Laird shook his head. "I canna do tha', lass."

"You heard what DeSoto said. The DEA is hoping the cartel will attack one or both of us, so they can catch them in the act. He's your heir. We can't afford to lose him."

Again the Laird shook his head. "Do ye think Jim would feel he was a true man if I sent him awa' and left ye tae face th' cartel alone?"

Ginny tried to imagine Jim's face. "No."

The Laird sighed, his eyes on her. "Yer faither died and there was naught tae be done, tae undo it. How did ye cope?"

Ginny wrapped her arms around herself and held on. "I closed my mind and tried not to see the body on the ground or the tree falling or his ruined face."

"And in th' days since?"

She thought for a long moment, then answered. "I look in the mirror and tell myself that being dead is easy. The dead aren't in pain. They're not frightened any more. They don't have the weight of the world on their shoulders." She sucked in a breath. "Being dead isn't something to fear. Being left behind is."

The Laird sighed, his expression softening. "Tis part o' life, tae be left behind when the generation ahead of ye moves on."

"I know, but Jim's my generation. He's not supposed to die yet."

The Laird smiled and nodded. "I tak' yer point, but I still canna send him awa'. Sae let's examine th' problem. What are ye afraid o', Ginny?"

She stood up abruptly and walked over to the sink, then turned back, leaning against it, facing him.

"Other than being murdered? Getting Jim—or someone else—killed because of what I did, or couldn't do, and having to live with that on my conscience."

"Because o' what happened wi' young Williams."

She nodded. "I'm afraid of making a mistake and that makes me afraid to make a decision. I never used to doubt myself like this, but I've proved how stupid I can be, and I'm terrified of doing it again."

"Ye trusted a man wha proved untrustworthy. Tha' can happen tae anyone. Ye must forgive yerself fer being human and go on."

Ginny screwed up her face. "If it were just me, it wouldn't be so bad, but it's not, it's everyone around me."

"Aye, I ken. Ye've a conscience tha' works o'ertime. 'Tis what makes ye wha ye are. But ye mustn't let it cripple ye, lass. Dinna let what that man did rob ye o' yer proper place in life."

Ginny knew her proper place—back in the trenches, saving

lives at work; ferreting out details for the police; accepting that people die, and living takes guts, and nothing comes with a guarantee.

"Sae what does yer conscience tell ye tae do?"

She sucked in a deep breath. "Stiffen my spine and face the danger."

The Laird nodded.

"But," Ginny continued, "there's a problem. Jim doesn't want me to."

"He seemed happy enough tae face the risks yesterday."

"For himself, yes, but he wants to protect me. As long as he's focused on that, he can't focus on his own safety. If you won't send *him* away, send me."

The Laird shook his head. "He needs tae face his ain fear and tha' includes losing you. Forbye, young folk need tae work oot how they're tae be wi' one anither and I'll no interfere wi' that."

She met the Laird's eye. "So, how do I get past this?"

He leaned back in his chair and looked at her. "What are th' possible outcomes?"

Ginny shrugged. "I live, I die."

"If yer deid, th' mess ye leave behind is someone else's problem, aye?"

The corner of Ginny's mouth twitched. "True."

"Sae 'tis only a problem if ye live. If ye live, what are th' possible outcomes?"

Ginny's brow furrowed. "It all comes out right in the end, or it all goes to hell in a handbag."

"If't all comes out richt, ye've nothing tae fear. Sae we only ha'e tae worry aboot it all going tae hell."

"Okay."

"What are th' odds?"

"Of it all going to hell? I have no idea."

"Who are ye fightin'?"

"The drug cartel."

"Who are ye fightin' with, yer allies?"

Ginny blinked. "The police, the DEA."

"And Jim and th' Hillcrest staff and the Homestead, all o' which ha'e yer back."

Ginny nodded slowly. She had the entire federal law enforcement system on her side, as well as the local authorities, and the massed strength of the clan.

"If ye mak' a mistake, if ye fall, ane o' them will tak' o'er fer ye. Ye dinna ha'e tae do it alone and ye dinna ha'e tae be perfect. Being Scots means being willin' tae try, even though ye may fail. And bein' prepared cuts th' chance o' that." He caught her eye and held it. "I've an assignment fer ye, lass. Go inta my office and fetch a pad and a pen."

Ginny did as told.

"Sit, lass, yer goin' tae write."

An hour later Ginny looked down at the action plan they had created and felt that she might, just might, be able to pull this off. The ideas they had come up with were specific, realistic steps toward an as-yet-unreachable (but a whole lot closer) goal. She rose and let Himself escort her to his door.

"I'll expect ye tae report back tae me on yer progress."

"Aye, Mackenzie." Ginny turned to face him, curtsied, then, throwing protocol to the wind, reached up and kissed him on the cheek. "Thank you."

He wrapped his arms around her and gave her a hug. "Yer welcome, lass."

* * *

CHAPTER 25

Day 11 – Monday midmorning
Hillcrest Medical Center

Ginny pulled into the hospital parking lot and headed for the elevators. She went first to the office of the ICU Head Nurse, Ms. Hawkins, explaining that she'd been interrupted during the last day of the conference, but that the organizer, Becky Peel, had made arrangements for her to watch a recording of the last session and get her certificate, and that she was sure she had learned a lot and could use the knowledge to help train new preceptors and she was very grateful for the opportunity, etc., etc., etc.

Marge Hawkins seemed preoccupied and a bit short-tempered, so Ginny beat a hasty retreat and headed for her next stop. She was standing at the elevator when the doors opened and Lisa got out. They both started.

Ginny hesitated for a moment, then smiled at her co-worker. "What are you doing here in the middle of the day?"

"What's it to you?"

Ginny raised an eyebrow. "If you're headed for Marjorie Hawkins' office, I suggest you be careful. She's not in a good mood."

Lisa mumbled something unintelligible, pushed past Ginny,

and took off down the hall.

Ginny shrugged, rode the elevator down to the Emergency Department, let herself in using her ID badge, and made her way to the nurses' desk. Item one on her action plan.

"I'm looking for Agent DeSoto."

"Room Three."

Ginny stopped in front of Exam Room Three. The door was cracked and she could see movement, but there were rules in hospitals about poking your nose in where you had no business. She was saved from having to make a decision by the door opening and DeSoto emerging, in the company of one of the ER techs. He looked at her, then turned to the tech.

"I'll catch up with you." He smiled at Ginny. "How may I help you this morning?"

"I have an early Christmas present for you."

He gestured for her to enter. "Step into my office."

Once they were inside, he closed the door. "I've appropriated this room so I'll have a safe place to talk. The cameras are disconnected, it's been swept for bugs, and it has a signal scrambler in place."

"Sounds cozy." Ginny handed over the manila envelope with Luis' envelope inside. DeSoto opened it, his eyebrows rising.

"Where did you find this and have you touched it?"

"Only with tweezers and shoved into the back of a supply cabinet at the Homestead Children's Shelter."

DeSoto nodded, his eyes on the contents of the manila envelope. "Good job!" He set the envelope down and eyed Ginny. "How are you holding up?"

"Well—" She hesitated. "Should I assume my phone calls are being intercepted?"

He shook his head. "I don't think they realize you're involved. You haven't worked the ER since the sting operation began and you didn't have any contact with Dr. Wingate in Austin." He crossed his arms on his chest. "However, you are linked to Jim Mackenzie."

"And Luis and his missing mother, who was receiving fake fentanyl patches from someone."

He nodded. "Was there something you wanted to tell me over the phone?"

"Something came up at the office Christmas party." Number two on her action plan.

"Go on."

"Devlin Jones has a son, Corey, who uses drugs and who knew Phyllis. He was shot in the knee yesterday by his pusher and is currently a patient here at Hillcrest. I'm on my way to talk to him now."

DeSoto considered this for a moment. "Maybe I should come with you. Do you know him? Will he talk more freely if you're alone?"

Ginny shook her head. "I don't think so."

DeSoto crossed the room, opened one of the drawers, pulled a tiny audio recorder out, turned it on, then spoke into the microphone, stating his name, location, and the date and time. He looked at Ginny. "This is legal if one half of the conversation knows it's happening. Do you consent to being recorded?"

Ginny nodded.

"Out loud, please."

"I consent to this interview between Ginny Forbes and Corey Jones being recorded by DEA Agent DeSoto."

He grinned at her, tucking the device into her pocket and arranging the microphone among the folds of her shirt. "Thank you. Let's go."

* * *

MAGGIE FOSTER

Monday midmorning
Hillcrest Medical Center

The young man in the bed looked uncomfortable and Ginny had seen enough pain to recognize the twin effects of a gunshot wound to a joint and the controlled withdrawal from a narcotic.

"Corey? We met yesterday, at the party. Do you remember?"

"Yeah, I do. Who's the dude?"

"Agent DeSoto and I are looking into the death of Phyllis Kyle."

"What about it?"

"You said something yesterday that made me think you might know her. Do you?"

"Yeah. She's my cousin."

"First cousin?"

"Yeah. My aunt was her mother."

Ginny nodded. "First, please let me say how sorry I am for your loss."

He shrugged.

"Phyllis and I were in nursing school together, and I worked with her. I'm an ICU nurse here at Hillcrest."

That got his attention. "Oh, yeah? Were you—uh—"

"I found her body."

His eyes widened. "Oh."

Ginny watched his brow wrinkle as he shifted restlessly on the bed. "She was okay." He looked up and met Ginny's eyes. "Just a nuisance, you know. Always trying to fix things."

"What kind of things?"

"Me, for one."

"You mean about the drugs?"

"Yeah."

Ginny waited, but he didn't elaborate. "What did you mean yesterday?"

"What?"

"You said you should have listened to Phyllis. What did you mean by that?"

Corey looked from her to DeSoto, then back. "She told me he was bad news."

Again, Ginny waited, watching Corey squirm.

"She told me I couldn't trust him." He threw out his arm. "It was only one hit, man. He could have waited."

"For his money?"

"Yeah. I was good for it. Well, Dad was."

"Your father's been paying for your drugs?" Ginny tried not to sound disapproving.

Corey nodded. "He's been trying to get me back into rehab, but he hasn't found a place, yet."

"If he does, will you go?"

Corey met her eyes, but said nothing.

"Is that what Phyllis wanted?"

He nodded, chewing on his lip. "Yeah. She always wanted the best for me. She liked me." He looked away. "Can't think why."

Ginny smiled at him. "I think I know why."

He looked at her, doubt showing on his face. "Yeah?"

"I think she saw what I see."

"What's that?"

"Someone who got in over his head and wants out."

He looked down, shrugging his shoulder at her.

"We can help you, Corey."

"Oh, yeah? How?"

"We can take the threat off the street, if you'll tell us who it is."

Corey started twitching in earnest at that one. "Christ, no, man! They'd shoot me in the head if they found out."

"What if we could get you into treatment somewhere they couldn't find you?" Ginny looked over at DeSoto. He nodded.

"We can do that," he said.

Corey looked at DeSoto, then at Ginny. "What'd I have to do?"

DeSoto answered. "After you're safe, we'd want you to tell us who your contacts are, so we can arrest them."

Corey looked at him, his eyes practically bugging out of his head. "You and what army?"

"I have resources I can call on. Starting now. We can put a man in the room with you, to guard you."

"He'd have to be SWAT, man."

DeSoto nodded. "Do we have a deal?"

"I gotta think about it."

DeSoto shrugged. "The cartel already knows you're here. What's to stop them from coming in and finishing the job as soon as we leave?"

"Shit. They don't want to off the paying customers." His expression changed. "'Cept that's what's happening. It's how I got in trouble."

Ginny exchanged glances with DeSoto. "Tell us."

Corey lifted a hand and rubbed the back of his head, his color fading. "Clark died. Some bad shit." He put both hands behind his head and held on. "Word on the street is there's one of the dealers pushing death, you know?"

Ginny nodded.

"And he was my regular. So, when I heard that, I disappeared. But he found me. Said I owed him for the last batch, but I didn't use it so I didn't owe him, right?"

"You didn't pay him."

"No. Didn't think he'd find me, did I?" Corey's eyes were darting from side-to-side, his upper lip moist with sweat.

"You went to your father?"

"No. To Phyllis."

"Why Phyllis?"

"'Cause she told me to."

"She told you she'd help if you were in trouble."

He nodded. "We arranged to meet. Not at her house. A place we knew about. But he found me. I lit out of there and hid. Called Dad. He was furious." Corey rubbed his hands up and down the back of his head. "He said—" He fell silent.

"What did he say?"

But Corey seemed to have hit a wall. His arms came down, crossed on his chest, his eyes on Ginny, his mouth closed.

"What did your father say, Corey?"

"You promised me a guard."

Ginny glanced over at DeSoto, who nodded, then rose and stepped out of the room.

"Okay, he's gone to arrange the guard. What did your father say, Corey?"

"He said Phyllis must have let the cat out of the bag." Corey licked his lips. "Said he was going to have a talk with her, about keeping her mouth shut. Said he was going to make sure she didn't do anything that stupid again."

* * *

Ginny stared at Corey. "Did I understand you correctly? Your father told you he was going to shut Phyllis up?"

Corey looked at her, then away, his eyes sliding toward the floor. "He didn't mean it. He was livid. White-headed boy and all that."

Ginny sucked in a deep breath, reminding herself that this was all hearsay and a drug addict was not considered a completely reliable witness. "All right. Listen, Corey. We're going to take care of you and, in exchange, you're going to rehab and you're going to make Phyllis proud. Got that?"

He nodded.

The door opened and DeSoto re-entered, an armed police officer in tow.

"This gentleman is going to stay with you while I make our arrangements," he told Corey. "It would be safer—for you—if you told me the name of the man who shot you, so we can pick him up now, rather than later."

Corey looked from Ginny to the police officer to DeSoto, then nodded. "Dr. C.—cause of the crack. C for crack."

"Where can I find him?"

"Under 66, top of Lake Ray Hubbard."

"Any particular time?"

"Every night, round one a.m."

Ginny rose, then leaned over and patted Corey's arm. "Thank you. We'll take it from here. You stay tough."

He reached over and grabbed her arm, his reflexes lightning fast. "They're gonna kill me soon as you leave."

Ginny shook her head. "No. They're not. We're going to take that threat off the streets and put him behind bars, and no one is going to know how we found him. Trust me on this one."

He studied her face, then nodded, then released her arm.

"If I don't check back with you," she said, "it's because Agent DeSoto has managed to hide you from me as well as everyone else, but I'll still be working for you, behind the scenes. Do you believe me?"

He nodded slowly. "Okay."

On impulse, Ginny bent down and kissed him on the cheek. "That's from Phyllis, with love." He blushed, but nodded.

"Okay. Bye."

Ginny took her dismissal and left, Agent DeSoto in her wake. She peeled off the recording device and handed it to him.

"Thanks for your help," he said. "I'll get right on this." He took off in the direction of the elevator.

Ginny turned more slowly and made her way back to the parking garage. She had a lot of thinking to do. Dr. Jones had been in the Medical ICU at the time Phyllis was killed. He'd been leading one of the Code teams. She'd seen him, and his name would undoubtedly be on the records.

But, was it even possible? Could a man sworn to *do no harm* have throttled his own niece, no matter how mad he was at her? Ginny certainly didn't want to think so.

She drove home, went upstairs, pulled out her investigation spreadsheet, and got to work. In the course of a weekend, she'd gone from no motive to at least two. How many more would she find, if she kept digging?

* * *

CHAPTER 26

Day 11 – Monday afternoon
Hillcrest Medical Center

Marjorie Hawkins glanced at her watch, then back at the door to ER Exam Room Three. She'd been told she could find Agent DeSoto inside. She pressed her lips together. She had every right to be here, a mandate, really, since it involved one of her nurses. She waited until the hallway was clear, then knocked on the door.

"Come in."

She let herself in, and eyed the man who stood before her. She had seen him in conversation with Dr. Lyons at lunch last week. She stepped forward.

"Agent DeSoto? I'm Marjorie Hawkins. I'm the Head Nurse over the Hillcrest ICUs."

He extended his hand. "Ms. Hawkins. I'm happy to meet you at last. I've heard a lot about you." He gestured to a chair. "Please."

She sat down, then leaned back and crossed her legs. She had good legs and was wearing a wool skirt that draped nicely over her knees and thighs, displaying the shapely calves and slim ankles she had inherited from her grandmother. She worked hard to maintain a softly professional appearance, aware that she had little else to offer in the way of physical charms.

"How may I help you?"

"It's about one of my nurses, Lisa Braden. On Sunday, at the Christmas party, she was overheard mentioning something about bulletproof vests. I met with her today and she told me all of the ER staff have been wearing them."

"That is correct."

"May I ask why?"

"For their protection."

She narrowed her eyes. "My nurses have never needed that sort of protection before."

He spread his hands. "I owe you an apology, Ms. Hawkins. When this problem first came to our attention, we thought it would be confined to the Emergency Room. I should have realized the ICU staff might float down here, and included you in the planning. I hope you will forgive the oversight." He smiled at her, a charming smile, and she almost smiled back.

"I don't like the thought of my staff in danger. We need them too much, and they are hard to replace. Perhaps," she said, "if you could tell me what's going on, we can come up with a plan."

He studied her face for a long moment, then nodded. "We're interviewing drug users that come to the ER, trying to identify the source of the drugs. The nurses are caring for the patients and not directly involved in the interviews, but they may be in the room when one of the patients says something. We're asking everyone to use discretion."

Marge nodded. "Shall I speak with my nurses?"

"I think not. We can talk to them on an 'as needed' basis, but I thank you for the offer."

"If, as you say, there is limited danger to the nurses, then why the vests?"

He shrugged. "An excess of caution. Hillcrest has a good security force and—so far—we've had no trouble. Was there anything else?"

"Yes. I don't normally get a copy of the staff schedules for the ER, but, under the circumstances, I would like as much advance warning as possible. If we can control the number of nurses who float, we can contain the gossip. Can you get me a copy of this month's schedule?"

"Let me ask." He was gone five minutes, returning with a folded sheet of paper. He handed it to her. "Please let me know if you have any other concerns."

She rose, shook his hand, and let herself out.

When she was back in her office, she took a look at the staffing schedule, then pulled up the Hillcrest directory. She sent copies of two of the photos to her personal e-mail account, then closed the program and tucked the schedule into her purse. She would scan that and add it to the file this evening.

She pulled out the cell phone dedicated to her second job and selected a number. "I have the information you asked for. I'll send it this evening." She disconnected and put the device away. She would include a brief summary of what Lisa Braden and Agent DeSoto had told her as well.

There was no way she could manipulate the schedule to ensure Ginny Forbes would float to the ER this week. There were no openings, and she could not force the issue. On the other hand, James Mackenzie would be on duty both of the next two nights. From six p.m. to seven a.m. anyone who might want to find him would know where to look. After that, it was out of her hands.

* * *

Monday afternoon
Forbes residence

When Ginny sat down at her computer on Monday afternoon to research Lisa Braden, she had no thoughts beyond trying to find a polite way to warn her off of Jim. Not because Jim was her, Ginny's, property, but because he was being distracted. Himself had added this item to Ginny's action plan toward the end of the hour, as a result of a comment Ginny had made about the scene at the Christmas party. The Laird had frowned, then thought for a moment, then suggested Lisa was a problem Jim didn't need right now.

Ginny had a number of tools loaded on her primary computer that let her search more thoroughly than a simple search engine could manage. She started with the images.

Lisa had sent pictures of Jim and herself cozying up to one another at the ceilidh. Ginny pulled them out of her e-mail box and dropped them, one-by-one into the image search utility. Not surprisingly, Lisa had posted them on social media websites, with comments about how *nice* Jim had been to her, and his smile seemed to support her claim. If Ginny hadn't known better, she would have believed the evidence of her own eyes.

She added "Christmas" and "Xmas" and "party" to the search parameters and was not surprised to see the elf costume again. Ginny pulled each image into her photo manipulation software and examined it for discrepancies in the background and alignment. These did not appear to have been tampered with, but Jim didn't appear in any of them. A wide variety of other men did.

One search led to another. There were *lots* of pictures of Lisa enjoying herself in public. Ginny waded through an hour's worth of Lisa in almost a hundred images, all just this side of indecent, then stopped collecting them. She had established a pattern going back several years and didn't think she needed more. She was about to shut the search down when a familiar face caught her eye—John Kyle, cheek to cheek with Lisa.

Ginny enlarged that image and took a good look at it. Lisa's image manipulation skills must have improved over the years. This one, stamped as Christmas six years ago, was rougher, with discrepancies in the resolution and background, as well as an image fragment she seemed to have been unable to erase completely, a woman's hand, wearing a ring Ginny recognized as Phyllis' engagement ring.

Ginny sat back and thought for a moment. Lisa was a man trap, but not a very good one. On one level, it was a sad tale of loneliness and desperation. On another, it was disturbing. If Lisa knew she was making up these relationships, then she was merely pathetic. But if she had crossed the line into delusional thinking, then she was dangerous. Dangerous enough to—?

Ginny caught her breath. No. This was a functioning ICU nurse. If she was mentally deranged, someone would have spotted something. But jealousy *was* a motive for murder. Had been since the dawn of time, and John Kyle had married Phyllis, not Lisa.

Ginny's mind was suddenly filled with famous quotes. "Heaven has no rage like love to hatred turned, nor hell a fury like a woman scorned." "Speak of one that loved not wisely but too well." "Revenge is a dish best served cold."

But—and this was a big but—did Lisa have the wherewithal to wrap a ligature around Phyllis' neck and pull it tight? Phyllis was six inches taller than Lisa and in good physical condition, whereas Lisa had been heard to brag she had never crossed the threshold of any gym of any sort. Even using leverage, would Lisa have had the strength needed? That sounded like a question for the forensics specialists.

Lisa had been in the ICU that night. Ginny'd seen her, so the next step was to find out if Lisa had been in the ICU *at the time of the murder.* She also wanted to explore a bit of anecdotal evidence on the subject of jealousy.

Ginny frowned at her computer. All she'd meant to do was let Lisa know her attentions to Jim were unwanted and she might find the consequences of pursuing him uncomfortable. Now Ginny had to do a lot more research before she could sit down with Lisa and have that heart-to-heart chat.

She glanced at the clock. Would it do any good to go talk to John Kyle? What could he tell her that might either rule Lisa in or out? It would probably upset him, and Ginny didn't want to do that. Tran first, she decided. If Lisa wasn't on the suspects list, then she didn't have to go farther.

DeSoto hadn't seemed concerned about Ginny's phone being hacked, but she was taking no chances. She picked up her purse, told her mother where she would be, got into her car, and drove to the hospital.

There were small conference rooms on each floor, equipped with hard-wired telephone lines. She settled down in one and reached for the phone. Detective Tran answered almost immediately.

"Miss Forbes. I did not recognize this number."

"I'm avoiding using my home or cell numbers."

"A good thought. What can I do for you?"

Ginny explained her question about Lisa.

"One moment." Ginny heard the sound of a drawer, then Detective Tran's voice.

"Yes. She was on Code Team One that night and in the Medical ICU at the time of the death."

Ginny swallowed. "Thank you."

"Miss Forbes, I have been in contact with Agent DeSoto. He

told me about your adventures in Austin. I would like to remind you that you are not required to put yourself in danger for this investigation. It might be prudent to withdraw."

Ginny took a long breath. "Detective Tran," she said, "I have no intention of risking my life, but I would rather not withdraw until *after* I've talked to Lisa about leaving Jim alone."

Ginny could hear the smile on the other end of the line. "I will be interested to hear how that goes. Please let me know if you find out anything relevant to the death of Mrs. Kyle."

"I will."

Ginny hung up and headed back to her car. Lisa had been there, in the Unit at the time of the murder. Which meant Ginny needed to go have a wee chat with John Kyle after all.

* * *

CHAPTER 27

Day 11 – Monday afternoon
Kyle residence

On arrival, Ginny found John Kyle at home, Phyllis' sister, Rachel, visiting her brother-in-law, and both of Phyllis' sons playing in the backyard.

"I'm so sorry to trouble you again, but a question has come up. It's about a woman. Do you know Lisa Braden?"

John made a face. "I do. We were dating when I met Phyllis. She did not want to go quietly."

"Did she make threats toward you or Phyllis?"

"Not threats, really. Just said some childish things like, 'you'll be sorry,' that sort of stuff."

"There was no restraining order or anything like that?"

John snorted. "No need. Phyllis was really good at being nice to people. Eventually Lisa got tired of getting no reaction from her—or me—and stopped showing up."

"You knew she worked with Phyllis, right?"

He nodded. "But Phyllis never said anything to give me any concern." He frowned. "Was she hiding something from me?"

"I don't think so. I worked with both of them and never saw a thing."

Rachel's face had changed as John spoke. Ginny asked John

a few more questions, but he didn't seem to have anything to add to the investigation. She took her leave.

Rachel volunteered to see her to her car. When they were out of ear shot, Ginny turned to face the other woman. "What is it you didn't want to say in front of John?"

"He doesn't know, but Lisa made threats, in writing, some of them very specific. Phyllis showed me the letters, but made me promise not to tell. She didn't want to upset him. She also didn't report them to the police, or even to Hillcrest. I told her she should, that a woman who could suggest such things didn't need to be taking care of patients, but she said I was overreacting."

"How long ago was this?"

"Six years ago, when they got engaged, then for a while after the wedding, then nothing until last year."

"What happened last year?"

Rachel's brow furrowed. "I don't know." She turned to face Ginny. "Phyllis came to me last summer, asking if I'd take the boys for a while so she could spend some time with John. They were gone for ten days."

"Why did that worry you?"

"Because Phyllis wouldn't give me a reason for it. I tried pumping John, but he didn't seem to have any idea what was behind it. He was just thrilled they got a vacation, just the two of them."

"Had they been having difficulties in the marriage?"

Rachel shook her head. "Not unless you consider having two small boys a difficulty."

"Phyllis loved those boys. She talked about them at work. Doted on them."

Rachel smiled briefly. "Yes, well, I took them places—the park, the zoo, you know."

Ginny nodded.

"And Lisa was there, watching us. Stalking, actually. It gave me the creeps. I took pictures of her, and reported her to the cops, and she disappeared. I asked Phyllis about it when she got back. She laughed it off, but she looked worried all the same. I think Lisa was threatening her, threatening her family."

"Did she tell John?"

Rachel lifted an eyebrow. "I think she mentioned it, but you know what she was like. She could pull the fangs on a rattlesnake and make the serpent like it." Rachel blinked suddenly. "John was a happy man; happy in his marriage, happy in his wife, happy in his sons." She looked at Ginny. "Can you help us?"

"I don't know, but I'm going to try." The two women exchanged hugs, then Ginny got in her car and headed back to Loch Lonach, trying to make sense of what she'd heard.

What did Lisa hope to gain by threatening Phyllis' boys? A mother would do almost anything to protect her children, but that wouldn't include divorcing a perfectly good husband. If Lisa's goal was to get John Kyle, she wasn't thinking clearly. Because killing Phyllis didn't mean John Kyle would marry Lisa. At least, no sane person would believe that.

Ginny swallowed hard, realizing she no longer wanted to confront Lisa. Instead, she was beginning to be afraid of her.

* * *

Monday afternoon
Forbes residence

Ginny put the drink down next to Jim's elbow, then pulled up a chair. He was seated at her computer, looking over the images of Lisa.

"She was threatening Phyllis?"

Ginny nodded. "Sounds like it."

Jim zoomed in on the image Lisa had posted of him smiling at her. "I can see where she cropped this one." He pointed at the change in pixel density. "But I have to admit, she's good. If she goes to prison, maybe she can start a business from inside."

"Bite your tongue! Can you imagine the publicity?"

His smile faded. "You're right. It wouldn't do the hospital any good."

"Is it possible? Could she have murdered Phyllis?"

Jim shrugged. "Anything is possible." He turned to face her. "What about Devlin Jones? Do you really think he could have strangled Phyllis?"

"According to Corey, he was spitting mad."

Jim's face reflected his doubt. "He's an ER physician. He knows about drug users and he'd understand if Phyllis was trying to help."

Ginny met Jim's eye. "Do you know the man, personally?"

Jim frowned. "No, I'm just pointing out he had other things he could try before resorting to murder."

"It's his only son at stake, and he's been hiding him, protecting him, paying for his drug habit. He wouldn't be happy if Phyllis made that job harder."

Jim nodded, looking unconvinced. "It's also possible someone from the drug community wanted Phyllis dead so she couldn't rat them out."

Ginny frowned. "I refuse to believe Phyllis was running with a bad crowd, but I *can* see her telling the authorities what she knew. Maybe Detective Tran can find out if Phyllis was talking to the local drug squad."

Jim nodded. "Good idea. So, that's how many possible murderers?" He picked up a yellow pad and started a list.

Ginny held up a finger. "One, Phyllis killed by person or

persons unknown because she was mistaken for Clara Carpenter. Clara doesn't want it to be that, and I don't blame her. Two, Phyllis killed by jealous ex-lover of her husband. Except Lisa waited six years to take her revenge. Not exactly a crime of passion."

"She may not have been mentally unstable until now."

"Scary, but true. Three, Phyllis killed by her uncle for exposing his darling son to both the authorities and the drug dealers."

Jim's brow furrowed. "If this was fury, why not just shoot her on the ranch and bury her in the woods?"

"That would make more sense, wouldn't it?" Ginny added a finger. "Four, Phyllis executed by drug dealer (or agent of same), to keep her from telling the authorities whatever it was she knew about the local drug scene or—possibly—as a lesson to other illicit drug buyers not to stiff the dealer. Five, Phyllis killed by hired hit man because she was speaking out against the Mexican Nurse Pipeline."

Jim looked up. "If that's what happened, we're going to have trouble proving it." He added another number. "Six, John Kyle, for reasons as yet unknown."

Ginny protested. "He's not on the list!"

"The police always suspect the spouse. It's required."

She shook her head. "He has an alibi. The older boy, Joey, woke in the night and decided to call his grandmother and ask her to bring him a truck for Christmas. The grandmother spoke to the boy, then asked him to put John on the phone. There's a record of the call and the testimony of the grandmother."

Jim leaned back in his chair. "If I were writing this story, I'd have some nefarious way to wake that child and the grandmother, then slip out, do the murder and go back to bed with no one the wiser, but at the moment I can't see any way to work it."

Ginny sighed. "Well, all we can do is hand our suspicions to Detective Tran and let her sort out the evidence. You're staying for dinner, of course."

"Of course, but then I have to go home, to bed." He grinned at her. "Alone this time."

"Hush! If someone overheard you, they might get the wrong idea."

"I never laid a hand on you."

Her brows rose archly. "No?"

"You know what I mean."

"I do."

He caught her hand, pulling her into his arms. "Say that again!"

"Say what?"

"I do."

"Not today." She broke out of his embrace and headed for the kitchen. "Dinner in ten minutes."

* * *

Monday evening
Loch Lonach Gun Range

It was nine p.m. and the winter night shrouded the concrete tunnel in shadows that flickered with the wind. The smell of gunpowder lingered in the air, visible as wisps of smoke and bits of paper drifting to earth. Ginny leveled her weapon and squeezed off two more shots, this time placing them in the forehead of the paper target. She and Caroline were running neck and neck on points, but Ginny's were the better groupings: neat, precise, well controlled. She moved the target farther away and finished the box of ammo, then cleared her weapon, brought her target in, packed her equipment, tidied up the bay, and made her way to the common room, Caroline only a few minutes behind her.

When they were both seated at the tables, weapons disassembled and cleaning in progress, Caroline looked up and caught her eye. "You seemed pretty intense this evening. Something on your mind?"

Ginny inspected the patch she was using on the barrel of her gun, then went back to scrubbing. "What would you say if I told you there was a woman moving in on Jim?"

Caroline started laughing. "I'd say she has no chance, unless you have definitely decided against him, and you haven't. Anyone I know?"

"Um hmmm. The cowgirl who came to the ceilidh last Friday night."

"That one! Well, I can't say I actually know her, but I did get an eyeful. What does Jim have to say about it?"

"That he's innocent, of course."

"If he needs a character witness, I'm willing to tell you what I saw."

Ginny looked up. "Which was?"

"Can you spell 'squeamish'?"

It was Ginny's turn to laugh. "Actually, it's not Jim's behavior I'm concerned with. It's hers."

"She got hauled out onto the dance floor by Jane, who pretty much kept her occupied and—as I recall—Jim left early and alone."

Ginny nodded. "So he told me, though not in those words." She finished her task, reassembled her weapon, checked it carefully, then put it away. After which she leaned back in her chair and fixed her eyes on Caroline. "May I ask you something completely inappropriate?"

"Sure."

They had been friends since elementary school. There was

very little either did not know about the other.

"Have you ever been tempted to kill another woman for stealing your man?"

Caroline finished what she was doing before replying. "You're assuming I've been in that positon."

"I know you have."

"Are you, perhaps, referring to my first summer away from home?"

Ginny nodded. No one had pressed charges, but Caroline had come home early, with cuts and bruises she had never bothered to explain.

Caroline draped one arm over the back of her chair and crossed her legs. "I left her alive."

Ginny grinned. "I know that. I also know you put her in the hospital."

Caroline lifted an eyebrow. "She did the same to me, but it was mostly accident. That Colorado slope we were having our discussion on turned out to have some very sharp stones at the bottom of it."

"Why did it come to blows?"

"Shoves. Because she was lying."

"So you hit her."

"Heaven forefend! I asked her to refrain from spreading false tales and explained carefully that to continue was not in her best interest."

Ginny's brow furrowed. "What did she hope to gain by lying?"

"The contested male. It worked, too. He wouldn't have dumped me if he hadn't believed her."

"She stole your property by bearing false witness."

Caroline wrinkled her nose. "Well, he wasn't my *property*, but I had kind of hoped he might be."

"How long did it last?"

"What? The relationship?"

"Your fury."

Caroline shrugged, a small smile playing at the corner of her mouth. "If you mean, how long before I got over him, about two months. If you mean, have I forgiven her, not yet."

Ginny's eyebrows rose. "But that was years ago!"

Caroline shrugged again. "It's the principle of the thing. Dirty, underhanded tactics and the triumph of evil. I never get used to that." She studied Ginny in silence for a moment. "Why are you asking? I mean, why now?"

Ginny met her eye, then told her the whole of her suspicions about Lisa Braden, by the end of which Caroline was frowning.

"Mentally ill, really?"

"Do I know? Jim says if she was really off her rocker someone would have noticed."

"I don't suppose you can get her a referral to a psychiatrist."

"Not unless she snaps in public. What I wanted to know from *you* was how long a woman can hold a grudge."

Caroline brushed that aside with her hand. "Forever, but hiding it can become a strain."

"She'd be living a lie."

"Yes."

Ginny's brow furrowed. "And if the lie was challenged, it would increase the stress."

"*When*, not *if*. Things like that have a way of getting out."

Ginny pulled her mind back from Lisa and focused on Caroline. "Speaking of which, have you told Alan, yet?"

"Told him what?"

"That you've decided he's not that bad?"

Caroline arched an eyebrow. "We're working in that direction."

"You'll let me know if I can help?" Ginny smiled sweetly.

"I'll let you know you can keep your nose out of my business!" Caroline's brow descended. "Going back to Lisa. If I were you, I'd go talk to that sister."

Ginny considered this. "You think she knows something?"

"Maybe. Sometimes sisters do and sometimes they don't."

"What makes you think she'd tell me anything?"

"I spent an hour with her last Friday, and I came away with a good impression. She's someone I'd like to know better."

"I see." This was no small praise from Caroline. "Okay, I'll take it under advisement."

Caroline rose. "Come on, let's go get a burger. Killing people always makes me hungry, even paper ones. Can't think why."

"It's because we've been taught to eat what we kill and paper tastes terrible."

"You may be on to something there. Unless it's dipped in chocolate, of course."

"Of course." The two girls gathered up their possessions and headed out.

* * *

CHAPTER 28

Day 12 – Tuesday morning
Coffee shop

"Thank you for agreeing to meet with me," Ginny said. "I'm afraid I need your help. It's about your sister, Lisa."

Mary Jo Braden nodded, the look on her face suggesting this was not the first time she'd heard something of the sort.

Ginny took a breath and plunged in. "Lisa is under suspicion of murdering someone at work, and I'd like—very much—to be able to change that."

"I know. She told me."

"The police have been going over all the available evidence. So far, they can't eliminate her."

Mary Jo's face settled into a grave concern. "Does what I say to you count as evidence?"

"It might. Do you know something that can help us?"

Mary Jo's face clouded. "Maybe. You may have noticed, Lisa spends a lot of time on how she looks."

Ginny nodded.

"That includes her nails and she's always pretty vocal when she breaks one. They cost a lot at the salon where she goes." Mary Jo was frowning heavily. "She broke one that night, at work."

Ginny took a careful breath. "Are you sure it was that shift?"

Mary Jo nodded. "She came home Friday morning, after the police let her go, swearing at the nail, saying she'd caught it on something during the Code. She said she had to go have it replaced, and it was going to cost her a fortune, and she was really mad. She wouldn't have said that if she was guilty, would she? She'd hide it from me, if she tore it while—you know. Right?"

Ginny nodded. "I would think so, yes." She was thinking it wasn't proof, but any murderer with half a brain would be worried about leaving evidence at the scene. If Lisa had broken a nail during the struggle with Phyllis, she might have picked it up and put it in her pocket, and, if she was worried Mary Jo might notice, she might have made up a story to cover the missing nail. So *not* finding the broken nail wouldn't tell them a thing. It would only be useful if the police *had* found it.

"Okay. I'll pass that on. Now can you tell me whether Lisa was mad at anyone in particular?"

"I don't think so. She doesn't confide in me. Not much anyway. And she wouldn't tell me if she'd killed someone. Would she?" Mary Jo's face paled as she said it, but she didn't amend her comment.

Ginny shook her head. "I wouldn't think so, but we've heard a rumor Lisa was jealous of the dead woman. Can you shed any light on that?"

Mary Jo's eyebrows rose. "Why would she be jealous?"

"Because the man she wanted chose the dead woman instead of her."

"Oh! You mean John Kyle."

Ginny nodded.

"She was furious about that, for about six months, then she moved on."

"One of the witnesses reports Lisa made threats."

"What kind of threats?"

Ginny was deliberately vague. "Ways to get John back."

Mary Jo shook her head. "She didn't need to do that. She has someone else."

"A steady?"

"Yeah. Two years now."

Ginny blinked. "Do you know who it is?"

"Of course. Isaac Zimmerman."

"The guy from Human Resources?"

Mary Jo nodded. "I introduced them. He and I met at a photography class. He's very good, sells his work to the news media. Lisa picked me up one night from school and he was there." She screwed up her face. "I got the idea it was serious. He's been taking her places, nice places. She usually comes in smiling, when she comes in at all."

"You two share a house?"

"An apartment, yeah."

"Mary Jo, will you do something for me? Keep your eyes and ears open. I want something that will definitively prove Lisa isn't our killer."

Mary Jo nodded. "I want that, too. If I find out anything, I'll let you know."

* * *

Tuesday midmorning
Hillcrest Regional Human Resources Department

Ginny knocked on the open door and was invited in. "Mr. Zimmerman?" He rose to greet her.

"That's me. How can I make your day better?" He gestured toward the guest chair, then sank into his own, leaning on his desk, smiling at her.

Tall, dark, and handsome. The curly black hair gleamed, almost aggressively healthy. The light blue eyes were set an attractive distance from the straight nose and balanced above a wide, generous mouth. He was clean-shaven and neatly dressed and Ginny could see the appeal. She smiled back.

"I'm hoping you can help me clear up a few things. I'm Ginny Forbes." She saw his eyes kindle in recognition, but he did not interrupt. "I know you've been taking publicity photographs for the hospital, and I'm told you're really good."

His smile grew wider. "Thank you to whoever that was."

"Mary Jo Braden."

Both his eyes and his smile softened. "She's a nice kid."

"Yes, she is. She said you're dating her sister, Lisa."

He nodded, his smile suddenly wary.

"Lisa is under suspicion in the death of Phyllis Kyle."

He nodded again, this time with nothing but alert interest in his face.

"I'm trying to prove Lisa could not have done it, and I was wondering if you had any photographs that could help me."

He shook his head. "I turned over all my images from that night to the police. If they haven't found anything, it's probably not there."

Ginny nodded. "But you might see something they missed. You have the eye."

His lips twitched at the compliment. "I looked at them carefully, for the same reason, but didn't spot anything. Sorry."

Ginny's brow furrowed. "Is there anything you can give me, anything at all that would clear her name?"

He studied her for a long moment, as if trying to decide whether to trust her, then spoke. "There is a very good reason why she could not have committed that murder."

Ginny's eyes narrowed as she studied him. "But you can't

tell me what it is."

"No, it would be a breach of confidence." He gestured around his office. "My position prohibits it."

"I see." Ginny rose and held out her hand. "Thank you for your time. If you find you can get past that barrier, whatever it is, and exonerate Lisa, please call me or Detective Tran. We would be very happy to be able to take her off the list."

"I'll do what I can."

She took her leave and made her way to the parking garage. He knew something. Too bad she couldn't pry it out of him, but there was someone else who probably knew what it was. Lisa. If she could be persuaded to tell.

* * *

Tuesday noon
Braden residence

Isaac Zimmerman crossed the atrium, rode the elevator up to the third floor, strode down the hall, and rapped on her door. He had called ahead, to make sure she was home and receiving visitors, then stopped for Asian takeout on the way over. Lisa opened the door to let him in.

"Hi, lover! Come for a little midday snuggle?"

He set the food down, took her in his arms and gave her a kiss. "That's what I've come to talk about."

"I was teasing."

"I know."

He helped her set the table, then watched as she tucked away a healthy portion of the noodles and chicken. Her appetite was still good. That was something. She added a bottle of wine to the meal.

"Are you sure you should drink that?"

She shrugged. "If it kills me, at least I had a good last meal."

"Lisa, it's time to tell."

She shook her head. "I don't want anyone to know."

"I understand, but you have to. They need to know why you couldn't have killed Phyllis Kyle."

Lisa frowned. "I wish I had."

"You don't mean that."

She met his eye, then sighed. "No, I don't." She poured herself another glass of wine then settled down on the sofa. He dropped down beside her, throwing his arm around her shoulders.

"It's weird," she said. "Sometimes I want to rip someone's throat out with my bare hands. Like when I was watching her kids at the zoo. I wanted to be her so badly it hurt, actually hurt. Other times, it's like nothing matters."

He pulled her into his arms. "We're going to get through this."

She closed her eyes, letting him set the glass down on the table. "The odds are against us."

"If we ignore it, you'll die."

"We all die, and this way would be quick."

He gave her a hug. "Call me selfish, but I want more time with you."

She looked up at him. "You mean that?"

"I do."

Her brow furrowed. "The surgery may kill me."

"I'm betting it won't."

"It could leave me with brain damage."

"We've got the best neurosurgeon in the country right here in Dallas. Let's call him and set this up."

She shook her head. "Not until after Christmas. The literature says to wait until everyone is over the holidays before scheduling anything important."

"If you have another attack, we'll have to do the surgery on an emergency basis."

"I know, but I'm willing to take the chance. It's just a little while longer."

He gave her a hug. "Then at least take care of yourself. No more emotional upsets."

She sighed deeply. "You know I can't control that, right?"

"Yes, but the doctor said if you stayed quiet and kept your blood pressure down, there might not be any more episodes. I can get him to prescribe Valium, if you need it."

"I'll think about it."

"You should also think about taking some time off from work."

"I'm going to have to do that after the surgery. Let me have a few more days of pretending to be normal."

"I've been thinking about the future," he said. "I'd like to go away, start fresh somewhere else."

She looked at him. "Leave your hobby behind?"

"Not the photography."

"That wasn't what I meant."

He took a deep breath. "Yes. I think it's time to give that up. I've got a nice little nest egg and, if I can get a new job in a system where no one knows me, I think I can settle down to a normal life and still make ends meet."

"Kids and a mortgage and medical bills."

"Don't you worry your pretty little head about any of it. We'll be fine. Your job is to get through this surgery and the rehab, so you can take care of our children."

She smiled. "That sounds nice."

He kissed her head. "Let's tell the police the truth, so they can cross you off their suspect list and stop asking awkward questions."

"I don't want—"

"Just the police. No one else, and they don't need to share that information."

She was silent for a long time. "You're afraid they'll find out, aren't you?"

He nodded. "The deeper they dig on you, the more likely they are to stumble over me. If we're open with them about you, they'll be satisfied."

She looked at him. "You were there that night, too."

He nodded. "But I was thrown out before she went missing, so I'm not a suspect. You are, and we need to change that."

"Who told you I was a suspect?"

He hesitated for a moment. "Ginny Forbes came to the office today, asking questions."

"That interfering bitch!" Lisa sat up, her eyes furious. "She should keep her nose out of other people's business or she may find herself getting hurt—again!"

"Lisa, sweetheart, calm down. Please? Here, relax and let me hold you." He pulled her back into his embrace. "Ignore her. Don't let her upset you."

"She pisses me off. She's such a goody-two-shoes. Thinks she's better than everyone else."

"She's not worth having a stoke over. Ginny Forbes will get what she deserves. Never doubt it."

He held her gently until she relaxed. It was the aneurysm talking, the blood leaking into the space around the amygdala. (He had learned that word from the doctor, then spent a week looking it up.) Keep her calm, he had said. Keep her blood pressure down. And no sex.

Isaac lifted her hair and brought it to his lips. When they made love again, he promised himself, it would be without fear, and with the rabbi's blessing, and for the purpose of having children. God allowed for redemption in his chosen people. If he turned over a new leaf and sinned no more, that would be enough.

He would start looking for a new home today, a new place to start a new life. One without temptation, perhaps. Yes, that might be a good thing, finding a job that didn't have the kind of temptation he'd fallen victim to. Because he was a victim. God couldn't really expect human beings to be that strong. After all, original sin was His idea. What he needed was to move quietly away from this city—and this police investigation—and try again somewhere else.

* * *

CHAPTER 29

Day 12 – Tuesday noon
Forbes residence

"Is there any way we can eliminate some of these people so I won't feel so useless?"

At the end of her last conversation with Detective Tran, Ginny had asked for and received (via courier) several packets of information, with a reminder that she was not to share them with anyone other than Jim without express permission. The first was a list of the people considered to be present, and therefore suspects, on the night Phyllis was killed.

"You can cross your own name off the list," Jim said.

"Really? Are you sure?" Her tone dripped sarcasm.

"Hey!" He reached over and took her hand, tugging on it until she looked at him. "I'm sure."

Ginny nodded. "All right, but it doesn't help much. How are we supposed to narrow this down?"

"We need more clues."

"You mean like a string of bodies, each bloodier than the last, as the serial killer comes unglued?"

Jim shook his head. "No more bodies, please. Other kinds of clues. What else did Tran give you?"

Ginny handed over a six-page report. "Here are the crime

scene forensics. Most of them, anyway. In addition to a sea of DNA, none of which can be identified, they say Phyllis had no drugs in her system when she died. Not even an aspirin. So she wasn't using and there goes that theory. Also, she wasn't working undercover for the drug squad. I asked."

The next stack contained twelve pages. "These are the notes on the video and still images. They're supposed to identify every person who appears in any image collected that night." The third sheaf was only ten pages long. "This is similar, except the data was pulled from the ID badge locators."

Jim made a face. "Did Detective Tran give you any idea what she wants us to do with these?"

"She said she wouldn't know a clue if it bit her on the nose. She wants us to figure out who was where they shouldn't have been. Or vice versa. And that's not all."

Ginny hefted the remaining stack of files, deciding it must weigh nearly a pound. "These are the witness statements. The only bright spot is that she provided the entire collection in digital form as well, the better to search it with, my dear."

"Wow."

"And they say policemen don't earn their money." She set the papers down and leaned back in her chair. "What we need is a plan. How are we going to untie this Gordian knot?"

"Cut it."

"Ha, ha."

"I'm serious," Jim said. "Cut to the chase. Means, motive, opportunity."

"We've been over all that."

"So we do it again."

She sighed. "Okay. The means was strangulation. What does that tell us?"

"That she was killed by someone strong enough to twist that wire around her neck, and cold blooded enough to leave her dead body in the corner of a hospital bathroom." Jim frowned heavily. "That still upsets me more than I care to admit. She was so close to help, and none of us knew."

Ginny nodded. "Tran says the lab is still examining that wire for clues, but so far they haven't found anything useful."

"Okay. Motive."

"To stop her from talking? White hot rage? Jealousy?" Ginny shook her head. "I don't find any of them very convincing, and there's no smoking gun."

"Which leaves opportunity." Jim's brow furrowed. "It's almost a closed room puzzle, though the list of suspects is larger than in the mystery books."

"And the door was propped open."

Jim picked up the list of suspects and a pencil. "All right. Tell me who these people are."

"Four of them are ICU nurses who were working that night: Alice, Susan, Grace, and Ms. Hawkins. I am omitting myself—and Phyllis, of course."

Jim checked off the names as he came to them. "Okay. Who else?"

"Dr. Jones and Dr. Candajar, both of whom were running Codes. The two Respiratory Therapists, Peter and Dee. The Human Resources guy, Isaac Zimmerman. The House Supervisor, both Code teams, and a lab tech who acted as runner."

"You're forgetting the patients."

"None of our patients were off camera for a moment, not even the guy on cocaine. That rules them out. Ditto the families, who were all pushed out to the waiting room when the first Code started and weren't let back in until day shift got there."

"Where are the cameras located?"

"There's one in the hall facing the Medical ICU entrance.

Then one at each end of the Unit. And one in each patient room, trained on the bed. But none of them is a continuous video recording. They all take an image every few seconds and the ones in the hallways pan back and forth."

Jim nodded, studying the printout. "All four of the ICU nurses show up coming and going about their lawful business."

"Yes, as do most of the Code team members."

"Most?"

"As you know, we're supposed to wear our ID badges at all times, but, being human, sometimes the badges get left behind."

"And if you get caught without one, they dock your paycheck."

Ginny nodded. "Right, the idea being that knowing where the staff is helps keep the patients safer. It may even be true. The problem is that Dr. Jones left his in the ER. That's what he told Detective Tran anyway, and she tells me they found his badge exactly where he said he'd left it."

"Okay. So he was a naughty boy, but what has that to do with the video evidence? He's on patient-cam during the Code. Bound to be. He had to intubate."

"According to the team of investigators whose job it is to watch hours of security video and write down all the movements, he was in and out. He may have left the room, or he may have just stepped out of camera range. Detective Tran has a forensics specialist analyzing the amount of time it would take to leave that ICU patient room, walk to the break room, duck into the bathroom, strangle someone, drag her body into a corner, and get back again—oh, and put on and take off Personal Protective Equipment."

"PPE. Let's think about that for a minute. What evidence do we have that the murderer was wearing PPE?"

Ginny picked up the forensics report and flipped through it.

"Here. Traces of the nitrile gloves caught in the wire and bits of the paper they use to make the gowns under her fingernails."

"Okay. The murderer was wearing PPE. That's not uncommon in an ICU."

"No, it's not, but it's not common in an ICU *bathroom*. It would look odd if you took a set into the restroom with you, then put it on in there."

"Could the murderer have worn it in? I know we're not as careful as we should be sometimes. I've been known to strip my gown off while walking to my office, for instance."

"The rule is that you peel before you leave the patient's room and put a fresh set on before coming back in, to prevent spreading patient germs around. What's more, it would be unusual for Dr. Jones to leave the room during a Code."

"Unless he had to answer a call, nature's or otherwise." Jim's brow furrowed. "Can we eliminate all the men since they wouldn't go into the ladies' room?"

"Only if they're innocent."

"Well, isn't that the point?"

Ginny nodded. "What I mean is, a man could go into the ladies' room, wearing PPE, kill Phyllis, then nip into the men's room and come out drying his hands and no one would be the wiser, as long as no one saw him. Unfortunately, the bathrooms are not covered by the cameras."

Jim pulled over a yellow pad. "Can we safely say that anyone located by either badge or camera outside the bathroom during the Window of Opportunity can be dismissed?"

"Badge *and* camera, since, in addition to leaving them lying around, badges can be attached to other people."

"Hell. Of course they can." Jim modified his note. "Okay. That brings us to the WOO."

Ginny blinked. "The what?"

"Window of Opportunity. I just told you."

Ginny found herself laughing. "You said, 'woo.' You sound like a freight train."

Jim lifted a quelling eyebrow at her and Ginny subsided, still giggling at the acronym.

"As I started to say," he gave her a stern look, "the WOO begins when Phyllis enters the ladies' room. According to Detective Tran's notes, Phyllis—or her ID badge—entered the facilities at three-twenty a.m."

Ginny made a note of the time. "Okay. When does the WOO close?"

"Upper limit—when you found the body."

Ginny had known immediately there was no chance of saving Phyllis. Her body was already cool to touch, and blue, and starting to stiffen (they'd had trouble getting the breathing tube in because she'd been sitting up and her head had slumped onto her chest and her neck had wanted to stay in that position), but they'd had to try. She had dragged Phyllis out onto the bathroom floor and called for help. The day shift had responded with a fresh Code team, but that hadn't changed the outcome.

"I found her at ten minutes past seven that morning, but when the Medical Examiner saw her at eight, he said she'd been dead for at least two hours and more likely four. The autopsy says the same."

Jim nodded. "Okay. Pencil in the ME's estimate of when she died."

Ginny checked the notes she'd gotten from Detective Tran, then added *Time of Death between 0330 and 0600*. Her brow furrowed. "If she was dead before the four o'clock vital signs, who did them for her? The murderer?"

"It's possible."

"There was someone designated to watch her patients

while she ran to the facilities. There always is. I can ask around and find out who that was." Ginny made herself a note.

Jim nodded. "Okay, do we know the last time she was seen on camera?"

"I don't, but she was wearing her badge when I found her, and the data says the badge didn't leave the restroom, so I think we can safely say she went in and didn't come out again."

"See if you can find Phyllis on any image after three-twenty a.m."

They found Phyllis leaving one of her assigned patient rooms at three-fifteen, but no evidence she was seen on camera, alive or dead, after that.

"Which means," Jim said, "we're looking for someone who is unaccounted for between three-twenty and six a.m., just a bit over two and one-half hours. That's progress."

Ginny sat up straighter. "Yes, it is." She loaded the digital versions of the files and started searching. "I'm going to make some assumptions here. The first is that no one we eliminate was able to throw on a cloak of invisibility and sneak back into the bathroom without being seen. If they don't appear in the data, they weren't there."

"Agreed."

"The House Supervisor didn't linger during either Code, I find a mention of her at two fifty-seven, on the hall camera, leaving the Unit, then a badge ID marker for her at five a.m., coming back in."

"Scratch one House Supervisor." Jim's brown furrowed. "When did that second Code start?"

"Four forty-five."

"Can we safely say no one from the ER came up to the ICU except as a member of one or the other of the Code teams?"

"Let's see." Ginny searched the *Who Was Where When* file. "I don't see any ER people on this list."

"Which means no one on the *second* Code team was in the ICU soon enough to kill Phyllis."

"One of them might have left his badge behind, slipped in with no one noticing, done the deed, then gone back to the ER. Can you check to make sure all the ER people on Code Team 2 were actually in the ER until the Code was called?"

Jim bent to the task. "The police must have thought of that. It's all right here. No one missing from where they should have been from two a.m. until the Code was called." Jim let his satisfaction show. "All right! Scratch Code Team 2."

"Good!" Ginny peered at the next record. "Here. Tell me what this says."

Jim took the document from her and squinted at it, then took it across the room to the window. "Looks like Max Peabody."

"Oh! I know him. He's our night security guard, one of them. He would have been doing crowd control." She plugged his name into the search utility and was quickly able to tell that the security guard had arrived soon after the start of the first Code, then stayed, mostly stationed at the ICU door, until after six a.m. "I remember now. There was some sort of trouble with the visitors. I heard Max and the Supervisor talking about how the families who weren't involved in the Code wanted to wait at their loved one's bedside and the ones who *were* wanted to watch. He didn't actually threaten anybody, but he may have been tempted."

"Does his badge go into the break room?"

"Not even once. Does he appear in the images between three-twenty and six?"

It took Jim a minute to track the movements of the security guard. "Here he is, and he's wearing his badge. He doesn't enter the patient rooms, just hangs around, then leaves the Unit and goes to the Visitors Area, then back to stand just inside the main door."

"Can we eliminate him?"

It took the two of them another fifteen minutes to make sure the security guard's movements did not include using the ICU men's room, after which, they decided they could indeed scratch Officer Peabody off the suspects list.

"This is really slow going," Jim said.

Ginny nodded. "Who else can we eliminate? How about the HR guy, Isaac Zimmerman? When did he leave the Unit?"

"According to the date/time stamps on his images, the last picture he took was at two-twelve."

"Wait a minute." Ginny dug into the witness statements. "Here it is. Alice told the police she asked Officer Peabody to escort Mr. Zimmerman out of the Unit and lock the door behind him because he (Zimmerman) was interfering with the Code."

"Okay. Confirmed. His ID badge leaves the Unit at two thirty-five and is not seen again. Nor does he appear in any of the images that were taken after that time."

Ginny drew a line through Isaac Zimmerman. "Moving on."

Jim lifted his arms above his head and stretched. "I have an idea. Let's attack this from the other side. Who can we NOT eliminate?"

"Anyone who entered the break room between three-twenty and six-ish."

Jim's eyes narrowed. "We'd better change that to three-ish. The murderer could have gone in ahead of Phyllis and been lying in wait."

Ginny pulled up the badge locator data and fed it to Jim. In ten minutes, they had created a new list.

"Here's you," Jim said, pointing to an entry.

Ginny nodded. "I, too, had to answer the call of nature that night, though I don't remember lingering, and I didn't see anything."

"Ginny, look closer. Look at the time."

She peered at the entry. Three thirty. Ten minutes after Phyllis disappeared into the bathroom, never to return. She felt goosebumps rise along her arms.

"Jim! You don't think—" She stopped.

"That both Phyllis and the murderer were still in there when you arrived? I think it's possible."

"But I didn't hear anything! No gasping noises. No thumps. Nothing."

"Which probably means she was already dead."

Ginny swallowed hard. "According to these records, no one else entered or left the restroom at that time."

"Which explains why they spent so much time with you at first."

Ginny felt her chest constrict. "But I didn't do it!"

"And Tran knows that. Calm down."

"But Jim! That means the murderer was right there! Not ten feet away."

He rose and came over, pulling her to her feet. "I know. But whoever it was probably didn't know it was you. He or she would be hiding in the handicap stall with the door closed. They couldn't see anything and I don't know anyone who can identify a person from the noises they make in the bathroom. Not unless you have a distinctive walk or perfume or you sang to yourself, something of that sort." He drew her into his arms.

She closed her eyes and leaned against him until the shaking eased. He was right. All the murderer had heard was someone using the bathroom and washing her hands and leaving. Nothing there to tell him who might have seen or heard something. Besides which, she hadn't.

Jim bent down and planted a kiss on the top of her head. "I'm sure Detective Tran will understand if you want to back out of this investigation."

Ginny pushed herself out of his arms, threw her shoulders back, and took a deep breath.

"That won't be necessary," she said. "Mother is betting we'll catch this murderer before he can hurt anyone else, and she has the De'il's own luck. She never loses."

* * *

CHAPTER 30

Day 12 – Tuesday afternoon
Forbes residence

After lunch, Jim settled into the chair Ginny had provided for his use and tried to focus. His eyes were on the information supplied by Detective Tran, but his mind was elsewhere. While she was here, at home, and he could keep an eye on her, he was all right. The minute she had to go somewhere, somewhere he couldn't follow, he found himself unable to think.

They were both in danger. No one denied that. It was rational to be worried. It was irrational to think she was safe as long as she was with him. What could he possibly do to protect her the police couldn't do better? The DEA actually, but it amounted to the same thing, an armed escort everywhere they went. Until the cartel decided to show itself. Which might not happen. In which case, he would be completely mad before the year was out.

"Jim? Jim!"

He looked up and found her eyes on him.

"I can finish this alone, if you need to be somewhere else."

He shook his head. "Not until tonight." They were both scheduled to work tonight. He would drive and make sure their discreet tail would be able to see them safely into the building. After that, he would have to let her go up to the ICU. The same ICU where Phyllis had been murdered, and there was nothing he could do to prevent it.

He hadn't anticipated being jealous of his grandfather, but he could see there might be advantages to being Laird. If he got that job, Ginny would *have* to do what he told her.

He took a deep breath. "Let's see how far we can get before I go blind from looking at these images."

The corner of her mouth twitched. "Do you want a magnifying glass?"

"I'll let you know."

"Okay. We have a list of people we know went into the break room between three and six a.m."

"And we've been able to eliminate Code Team 2, the House Supervisor, the guy taking publicity pictures, the security guard, the patients, and the families."

She nodded. "Let's see who's left." She ran her finger down the list.

"There was a lab tech who came and went as part of the Codes, but he never went into the break room and he seems to have been in and out in ten minutes or less with each visit. Eliminate him. That still leaves Code Team One."

"Who was on that team?" Jim made notes as she read out the names.

"Dr. Jones, the ICU nurses, the ER nurses, and the two RTs. According to their badges, none of the ER nurses needed to pee while in the ICU. Let's see if we can eliminate any of them based on image records."

There were five nurses to be considered. Two male nurses, both assigned to chest compressions. Three female nurses; one on IV access and medications (assisted by Alice); one scribe (the person responsible for the Code record); and one who managed the crash cart, locating and handing over supplies. The last just happened to be Lisa Braden.

Jim blinked, reminding himself that the night Phyllis died was *before* Lisa had made her advances on him.

"I've just thought of something," he said. "If Lisa killed Phyllis, so she could marry John, she didn't need to chase me."

Ginny's brow furrowed. "Unless John told her to get lost, I agree with you. It weakens her motive. So did he?"

Jim shook his head. "I don't know." He added a note to the yellow pad.

"And," Ginny added, "the whole thing falls apart if Mary Jo is right and Lisa and Isaac are a couple."

The two male nurses were easy to eliminate. The patient hadn't needed cardiac compressions for more than a few minutes. They both left the ICU long before Phyllis disappeared, without visiting the break room, and were tracked from three to six a.m. in the ER in their proper places doing (one assumed) their proper jobs. Not murdering ICU nurses in any case.

The other three nurses, along with Alice, had continued to work on the patient right up until the transfer to the surgical suite, at which point two of the three (the scribe and the med nurse) had helped push the bed out of the Unit and down the hall, then gone back to the ER without returning to the ICU. Since that happened forty-five minutes before Phyllis entered the break room, all of the regular ER nurses could be eliminated. The police records again confirmed (badge and image data) that the ER people were located in the ER and not elsewhere for the remainder of the night.

Lisa was in charge of the Code cart, and the cart belonged to the Medical ICU, and it had to be restocked immediately after using it, so as to be ready for the next Code. She was, perforce, left behind to deal with that task.

Comparing image date/time stamps, they were able to track her movements (with the crash cart) from the patient's room to the supply room (first) and the med room (second) and confirm that she finished the task and re-locked the crash cart at two fifty-five a.m.

Ginny peered at the image on the screen. "I can't find Lisa's badge in this picture."

"According to the tracking data, it's in ICU Five."

"When does it move again?"

"Not until four forty-five a.m."

"Which means she left it in the patient's room and went back downstairs without it, missed it at some point, came back up to retrieve it, and we can't eliminate her."

Jim shook his head. "All these abandoned ID badges must mean something. Are they too heavy? Are the photos so bad people are hoping to lose them? Are they being used as a way to pass national secrets?"

Ginny looked over at him. "All good questions, but not on topic. Shall we continue?"

He bent to the task. "The police records for the ER say Lisa was definitely there by three forty-five, but that leaves plenty of time for her to nip into the bathroom, kill Phyllis, then get downstairs."

"Isaac Zimmerman told me he knew Lisa could *not* have done the murder, but he wouldn't tell me *how* he knew. Said it would be a breach of confidence."

"If he's the latest boyfriend, he might be making it up, to cover for her."

"True. I'm hoping I can get Lisa to tell me what he meant, or at least something that will make telling Detective Tran necessary."

Jim sighed. "Normally, there would be hallway images of everyone who came and went from the Medical ICU that night, but the lens on that camera was so dirty all they could see was blobs of color."

"Well, that's no help."

"It's also no help in identifying any stranger who might have snuck in." Jim leaned back in his chair for a moment. "If I were an assassin, coming to kill Phyllis, I'd disable as much of the surveillance as I could and dirtying the lens wouldn't set off any alarms."

Ginny met his eyes. "You're suggesting someone cased the joint?"

"It's possible. Disabling the hall camera in that way wouldn't require special access. No badge, no escort. Just ride up in the elevator, use a pole to reach up to the camera and dab some oily dirt on the lens. It could even be done in disguise, as a janitor or something like that."

Ginny nodded. "That's a lot of planning ahead."

"But if I'm a professional, I want to control as many of the variables as possible." Jim suddenly sat up and reached for his pad. "Let's ask Tran to follow up on visitors who had access to the ICU in the weeks before the murder. She'll love that. It widens the field to a few thousand or so."

"You're still thinking it was someone who came in from outside."

Jim nodded. "You don't like my idea?"

"What if the paid assassin was someone already on the staff? Someone with easy access to everywhere he needed to go."

Jim's brow wrinkled. "Did you have someone in mind?"

"Not really. I'm just thinking it would be easy to sneak someone into the ICU in all that bedlam, but getting out again would be harder. Someone might wonder why the stranger was leaving, rather than staying to help out. And they might remember. They'd remember maintenance, too. Anyone who got underfoot."

Jim nodded slowly. "It's a good point." He thought for a moment, then sighed. "Who's next?"

"Devlin Jones."

They weren't able to do as well with him. Try as they might, there were still large enough gaps in the visual record to allow him to slip into the break room, kill, and return before appearing in the next image.

Ginny made a face. "No location data, because he left his badge in the ER. Inconclusive video evidence because he wanders, until the moment we see him on the elevator camera, going back down to the ER. Which brings us to the written record. If we believe the Code record is accurate—and I have no reason not to—he was barking orders to the nurses right up until the neurosurgeon arrived."

"What time did they record as the end of that Code?"

"Two thirty-five."

"So DJ could have waved goodbye as they pushed the patient out the door, popped into the break room, then made his way back to the ER with no one the wiser."

"Except he didn't. The images suggest—and the documentation backs it up—that he sat down at the nurses' station, logged onto the computer, completed his charting, then strode out into the hall and down to the elevator. The computer entries all have date/time stamps that place him at the nurses' station until three-ten and the elevator image shows him heading down at three-fifteen. What's more, the computers are all tagged so we know which computer he was using."

She shook her head. "It's not really proof, but it's probably good enough to eliminate him. For Dr. Jones to be in two places at the same time, he'd need a helper on staff—one able to chart like an ER doc, and who knew how to read the Code record. No good murderer brings an accomplice with him."

Jim felt a weight lift within his breast. He hadn't wanted to believe Devlin Jones was a killer. "All right. Scratch Dr. Jones. Who does that leave us?"

Ginny looked at her list. "Both of the respiratory therapists, and four nurses. Alice took her craniotomy patient to surgery and didn't get back until almost four a.m. Susan and Grace never left the Unit. Neither did Dee. Peter helped to push the craniotomy patient's bed so he's in the same boat as Alice. And, according to the badge data, all of our remaining suspects (except, perhaps, Lisa) used the facilities between three-thirty and six a.m. at least once."

Jim pricked up his ears. "At least once? Someone went in more than once? That would be suspicious, wouldn't it?"

"It's possible someone had a stomach problem we know nothing about, or they just wanted to wash their hands and those sinks were closest."

"Who went in more than once?"

"Peter goes in twice, once at three-ten, just after the end of the first Code, to which he was assigned, then again around five-thirty."

"There might be something in the witness statements about it."

"Okay. I'll look. What's next?"

Jim sighed. "We're going to have to match images with location data for the remaining suspects. I'll do the two RTs and Lisa. You take Alice, Susan, Grace, and your boss."

They worked for the next two hours, comparing notes, cross-referencing, and brainstorming. None of the remaining suspects was completely accounted for, but none looked as if they were behaving suspiciously, either.

Jim tossed his pencil on the desk and stretched. "I need to go get ready for work."

"I had hoped to finish today," Ginny sighed. "But it's just too big a job." She gathered up the scattered papers. "We got something accomplished, though. We've narrowed the list down to seven people."

"Unless the murderer really did come in from outside." Jim's brow descended. "Either way, we're not close enough to point a finger at anyone in particular. He or she is still out there."

* * *

CHAPTER 31

Day 13 – Wednesday, two a.m.
Hillcrest Medical ICU

At two a.m. the next morning Ginny was still going through the witness statements, making notes and trying to compare them to the location data.

The police had spotted Peter's two trips to the rest room between three and six a.m. and asked him about it. He explained he'd just been diagnosed with high blood pressure and started on a diuretic. Since the point of a diuretic was to pull extra fluid out of the system, he was still getting used to the effects. He'd actually visited the men's room five times during that twelve-hour shift. In each case, he was located (badge data) in the *men's* rest room. On no occasion did his badge linger or enter the ladies' room. There was, of course, no video record to confirm that he was the one wearing his badge when he went in, while he was using the facilities, and as he came out again. The images didn't cover that part of the Unit. They just didn't. So he had to stay on the list.

Dee (the other Respiratory Therapist) bounced around in the records like a ping pong ball. This made sense, considering what she was trying to do that night, but made it impossible either to include or exclude her from suspicion based on the images and badge tracking. Ginny would have to ask Jim if he had looked at Dee's charting with an eye to tracking her movements. Her testimony should match—did match, as far as it went, but, like Peter, the job had proved seriously challenging that night and neither had stood still long enough to be caught on camera during the critical two hours.

Alice's images lined up exactly with her testimony. She had (within a minute or two) graphic evidence that she had been where her tracking data and official statement said she was. She had stayed in the Surgical Suite to finish her charting and was vouched for by the staff. She had visited the ladies' room, once, around four a.m., on her return to the ICU, then not again until the shift was over. So Alice could be eliminated.

"Ginny, have you seen Grace?"

Ginny looked up at the charge nurse. "Not since the beginning of shift. Is there a problem?"

Margot frowned. "I've got some family members that would like to talk to her and so would I. This disappearing during a shift is getting old. If you see her, tell her I'm looking for her."

"Will do."

Grace, like Alice, was accounted for, if you accepted the documentation as evidence she was where she said she was. Most of the nurses' charting was done on the computer and some of the room cameras caught the nurses making entries, but Hillcrest had both wall-mounted computers and computers on wheels, so the data wasn't consistent. She could have been doing something else for part of the time. Furthermore, her badge showed Grace entering the ladies' room at three-ten and not leaving again until four-eighteen.

When questioned by the police, Grace reported having left her ID badge in the bathroom (attached to her scrub jacket, which she had left hanging on the back of the door in the stall—NOT, she had emphasized, the handicap stall). She realized it was missing at four a.m. when she tried to swipe access to the medication system, and found it fifteen minutes later when she back-tracked her movements. The only image taken of her between those two times showed her not wearing her badge, which supported her testimony, and the next image after that showed her wearing both her scrub jacket and her badge.

Susan was easy to exclude. From the moment her cocaine-abusing admission hit the door at three a.m. until he was pronounced dead of his own lifestyle choices at six-ten a.m., Susan hadn't left the room. The gaps in her record could be explained by her moving out of camera range in the room, but she never darkened the door.

The last candidate on Ginny's list, the ICU Head Nurse, Marjorie Hawkins, was much harder to pin down. For one thing, she'd been doing quadruple duty. She spent some time in her office (presumably doing head nurse stuff), came out to help with the two Codes and the three admissions (charge nurse stuff), got a patient of her own, for whom she had to care (ICU nurse stuff), and dealt with Isaac Zimmerman, facilitating the publicity shots until he was thrown out at two-thirty (public relations stuff).

Ginny spent more than two hours studying the records on the Head Nurse and found just one discrepancy. Ms. Hawkins had reported to the police that she was in her office between three-fifteen and four-fifty a.m., working on charge and head nurse tasks, and her ID badge confirmed this. Which would have been fine, except that she appeared in the background on one of the photos taken in Susan's room during that time.

Ginny considered this. Ms. Hawkins could easily have sat down to write something and pulled her jacket off, which she might then have draped over the back of her chair. Then had come (perhaps) a plea for help from Susan, still dealing with the cocaine abuser, but not yet in full Code status, and the head nurse had gone to help for a moment, then gone back to her office. That could explain the discrepancy. But there was something else.

Phyllis' patients had their four a.m. vital signs and medications done by Marge Hawkins. The implication was that Ms. Hawkins had agreed to cover for Phyllis while she ran to the bathroom. There was nothing special in that. It happened all the time. What was odd was that Marjorie Hawkins didn't complain when Phyllis didn't come back.

* * *

Wednesday, two a.m.
Hillcrest Emergency Department

"We're blown." Agent DeSoto strode into the ER, fury radiating from every pore.

Jim looked up from the chart he was working on. "What do you mean?"

"Someone put the word out on the street that the police were waiting for druggies to show up at Hillcrest, to arrest them."

Jim's brow furrowed. "But that's not true."

DeSoto paced up and down in front of the desk. "It doesn't have to be true. They just have to believe it." He turned to face Jim. "We appreciate your cooperation, but there's no way we're going to find out anything here, not any more. We'll have to hope we have better luck at one of the other hospitals."

"We got two names. Those girls gave up their supplier and so did Corey Jones."

DeSoto nodded. "Both bottom of the drug business food chain. I was hoping for better."

He turned to the two undercover agents and started to speak, but was interrupted by what sounded like gunfire in the waiting room. "What the—?" He started toward the noise, then jerked backward and crumpled to the floor, blood spurting from his shoulder. The sound of the single shot was followed by a barrage as gunmen stormed into the treatment area.

Jim hit the floor, pulling his phone out in the same motion. He jabbed in the internal panic code, then followed it with a call to 9-1-1. There were screams, both men and women, coming from the waiting area, and curses, and the sound of flesh hitting hard objects.

Jim knew the thin wood substitute used in the ER desks would not stop a bullet of any sort. He needed a wall, preferably two, between him and the gunmen.

There was already a battle going on. Both DEA agents were fighting back. They had dropped two of the attackers and seemed to be making headway. Jim measured the distance between him and DeSoto, then to the treatment room on the other side of the desk. The bullets were flying, but not in his direction. The attackers were concentrating on the agents.

Jim slithered out from behind the desk, grasped DeSoto's shirt, dragged him into the treatment room, grabbed dressing supplies, and applied pressure.

"Hang in there," he told DeSoto. "If you have to get shot, this is the right place to do it."

He heard footsteps outside the treatment room and looked up in time to see one of the gunmen aiming at him. Jim threw himself sideways, hitting the wall just as the gun went off. He felt a searing pain in his arm and briefly wondered where the next bullet would land, but the gunman was already down, killed by one of the policemen, so there was no second shot.

It took the officers only fifteen minutes to capture or kill all twelve of the attackers who had smashed their way through the ambulance bay door, then through the security checkpoint, killing indiscriminately as they went. But the death toll was high: four patients, one nurse, and both DEA agents.

For the remainder of the night Jim worked on the survivors. Toward dawn he looked up to find Ginny's white face staring at him from the doorway.

She took a deep breath, then stepped into the room. "How can I help?"

"Hold this child."

When they had the sutures in place, she dressed the wounds while Jim examined the x-rays. The little girl had been thrown against the wall by her mother. It had probably saved her life, but had broken her arm. The mother had not been so lucky.

"Social Services is coordinating with the families."

Jim nodded, finishing off the edge of the cast. "I'm done here."

Ginny stepped into the hall and gestured for a staff member to collect the child. When they had gone, she closed the door and leaned against it, facing Jim.

"You're bleeding."

Jim tried to shrug it off. "Must be someone else's blood."

"It's on the inside." She came over, pulled his isolation gown off, lifted the sleeve of his scrub top, and removed the temporary dressing he had slapped in place over the bullet wound.

Jim looked down at the still oozing graze, then grinned at Ginny. "Shucks, ma'am. It's just a flesh wound."

She was not amused. "Sit down."

Jim started to protest, then realized it would be safer to comply.

She cleaned the wound and pushed at it, trying to bring the

edges closer together. "I'll be right back." She left the room, returning with Dr. Varma in tow. The older woman inspected the wound, then settled down to stitch it up.

"Tetanus booster. Oral antibiotic. Change the dressing as needed and daily for three days." She looked from Jim to Ginny. "You know what to look for." They both nodded.

She stripped off her gloves, washed her hands, then nodded at them. "Excuse me. Work to do."

Ginny closed the door on the other physician, then stared at Jim. "I saw some of the casualties," she said, her voice unsteady. "They were going for headshots."

"Come here, Ginny." He slipped his undamaged arm around her and lifted her onto the exam table. This brought them eye-to-eye. "Someone talked and I think I know who."

"You could be dead." She sounded strangled.

"But I'm not."

She sucked in a breath. "I didn't really believe, I didn't *want* to believe, that DeSoto was right."

"The man knows his job."

"But it's not *your* job. You have other obligations." He saw her swallow. "We need you, Jim, and you know it. *Why* did you risk your life like this?"

Jim found himself staring into her eyes. Her pupils were dilated, giving her a doe-like expression, vulnerable, frightened.

He took a breath. "Because it was the right thing to do."

The sound that escaped from between her lips was too soft to be considered a moan, but it had the same note of stifled grief.

"Listen to me, Ginny. All these things that have been happening; the murder, the bombing, this attack, they're all connected somehow. We need to find that link."

He saw her shiver and pulled her into a hug. "I'm all right, Ginny."

Her voice was muffled against his chest, but he heard her reply.

"No, Jim, you're not. We aren't either of us going to be all right until this is over."

* * *

Chapter 32

Day 13 – Wednesday morning
Hillcrest Cafeteria

Ginny looked up as Jim entered the cafeteria. He sat down next to her, his eyes on the woman across from them, his mouth pressed into a tight white line. The shift was over and Ginny had collared Lisa, bringing her down here and making sure she knew what had occurred in the Emergency Room.

"It's not *my* fault," Lisa shrugged.

Ginny scowled. "You're the one who shot off your mouth."

"You don't know that."

"We do." Ginny gave Lisa a hard look.

Lisa shifted uneasily. "Okay. Maybe I did tell someone, but I couldn't lie to *her*."

"Who was it?"

"Marge Hawkins. She called me in and asked me about it. She said she would speak to the agent in charge and told me to keep my mouth shut. Just like you." She looked over at Jim, her eyes lingering on the fresh dressing on his arm.

Ginny's eyes narrowed. "What exactly did you tell her?"

Lisa shrugged. "She wanted to know how long it had been going on, the sting operation I mean, and who was running it, and what they hoped to accomplish. I thought she knew. She used his name, DeSoto, and talked about the drugs and the dealers as if she already knew what we were looking for."

Ginny nodded. "So, you told her the plan, and about the vests."

Lisa nodded. "But she already knew all about it. Except for the fakes."

"*What fakes*?" Jim and Ginny had spoken at the same moment, and Lisa looked uncertainly from one to the other before settling on Jim.

"The fake fentanyl patches you brought in."

"How did you know about that?"

Lisa shrugged again. "The pharmacist came down and was asking questions. Had they come off the Internet? Had we seen anything like them before? You know."

"What did you tell him?" Jim asked.

"We told him no one knew anything about them. *He* told us *you* had brought them in." She stirred suddenly. "Look, this has been very upsetting. Can I go now?"

"After you tell us what you threatened Phyllis with."

Ginny watched Lisa's face, which had been rather pale, suffuse with a dull red, but her voice remained calm, almost disinterested.

"That's none of your business."

Ginny leaned toward her. "You can talk to the police, if you'd rather."

Lisa scowled. "It wasn't illegal."

"Then you won't risk going to jail if you confess."

Lisa fixed her eyes on the table. "I just wanted to hurt her, the way she'd hurt me. Him, too."

"What did you say?"

Lisa glanced up. "I didn't. I just threatened to."

"*What was it*?"

"Phyllis had a miscarriage, while she was in nursing school."

Ginny blinked. She hadn't known Phyllis well enough to be in on that secret. "And?"

Lisa screwed up her face, then looked directly at Ginny. "I threatened to tell John it was his and she'd killed it on purpose."

Ginny felt her stomach cramp. It was a nasty, petty, vicious little lie, but not, as Lisa had said, illegal. "How did you find out about the miscarriage?"

"I was at the gynecologist for a check-up and heard voices in the hall and recognized her voice. They got her out of there in a hurry, of course, and over to the hospital, but I'd heard enough to know she'd lost the baby. I got the rest in bits and pieces. She was arguing with Grace one night about going to the authorities."

Ginny's brow furrowed. "What authorities?"

Lisa lifted an eyebrow in her direction. "You didn't hear about the drugs they found in Phyllis' locker?"

"I did. What about them?"

"Grace got them on the black market. Grace was always getting drugs and other supplies that way."

"Why would she do that?"

"To give to her illegal friends. The ones that didn't want to go to the clinic because they were afraid of being deported."

Ginny felt a headache starting. "What has this to do with Phyllis?"

"One of the women, the illegals, was pregnant and having trouble. Phyllis was trying to persuade Grace to get her into the system, and Grace was refusing. Phyllis said she'd had a miscarriage and could have died if she hadn't been close to help, but Grace stuck to her guns, saying she wasn't going to abandon those people just because they're here illegally."

Lisa's eyes narrowed. "Phyllis raised her voice, well, hissed more loudly is a better description. She said if Grace didn't take that woman to get real medical care and the baby died, it would be her fault and that do-gooders like her should be locked up, since the road to Hell was paved with good intentions, or something like that. They were both livid."

Ginny took a moment to collect her scattered thoughts. "Grace was buying black market drugs."

Lisa nodded.

"And Phyllis knew about it."

"Yeah, and Grace put some in Phyllis' locker, for the police to find."

"Why would she do that?"

"To get Phyllis fired, of course." Lisa stood up suddenly. "I'm going home." She grabbed her bag and took off. Neither Ginny nor Jim made a move to stop her.

When she was gone, Jim turned to Ginny. "Grace on one side of the politics. Phyllis on the other."

"And Phyllis standing in for Clara. It's too much to be a coincidence, but I can't, for the life of me, figure out what it means."

* * *

Wednesday morning
Brochaber

Jim had dropped Ginny off at her house, then driven to his grandfather's. He now sat in the kitchen, a steaming mug of decaffeinated coffee in front of him, listening to the conversation between the other two men.

He'd been astonished to find Agent DeSoto already there, having talked his way out of a hospital bed and into the Laird's presence. The Laird, it seemed, was functioning in his capacity as chairman of the hospital board.

"It appears, sir, that the attack on the Emergency Department was arranged by someone on the Hillcrest staff."

The Laird's frown deepened. "What evidence ha'e ye?"

In answer, DeSoto slid a piece of paper across the table. The Laird picked it up and read it through in silence, then set it down. DeSoto picked it up again and put it away.

"After the attack, I remembered her visit and had the tech boys do a quick search. She sent that note and photos of Jim and Ginny to her home e-mail address, then to someone on the Dark Web. We've got our best hackers working on tracing it further. We've also been interrogating the surviving gunmen. They were told where the ER security was the weakest, and one of them volunteered they'd been called out in a hurry, a last-minute job. He blames the short notice for the number of cartel members who didn't make it out alive."

"Sae th' timing o' the event gi'es ye pause."

"And the specialized knowledge, yes, but we don't have any way to narrow that down further. There were too many people who knew we were there. All the ER staff, a few of the administrators, two ICU nurses, the patients. Any of them might have said something to the wrong person."

"Or called in a hit." Jim shared what Lisa had told them about her chat with Marjorie Hawkins.

DeSoto nodded then turned to face the Laird. "The plan is working; we've got their attention. We need to keep the pressure on so we can flush the rats."

"Th' blue envelope didnae help?"

DeSoto shook his head. "We found Luis' DNA on it, and what is probably his mother's, but no one else's."

The Laird sighed, his eyes settling on Jim. "I dinna like it. He's already been hurt." He looked back at DeSoto. "Sae ha'e ye."

DeSoto nodded. "And I have two dead agents to avenge."

Himself sighed heavily. "I canna speak fer my grandson, and he canna speak fer Ginny, but ye've my permission tae ask."

DeSoto turned to face Jim. Their eyes met. "Well?"

Jim's eyes narrowed. "If what you suspect is true, every minute Ginny spends in that building puts her at risk."

"Both of you."

Jim nodded. "I want it over with. I want that woman behind bars."

"We'll need more evidence before we can arrest her."

"She asked you for the ER schedule."

DeSoto nodded. "And gave me a valid reason for wanting it. Otherwise I wouldn't have handed it over."

"What about the tracker on Ginny's car?"

"Same problem. It's not legal to track a car you don't own, in Texas anyway, but we can't know whose name is on the account until *after* we look, and we can't look until *after* we prove we have probable cause."

Jim frowned. What DeSoto wanted, of course, was to continue using him and Ginny as bait.

"It will look odd if she disappears." DeSoto meant Ginny.

"I know that." Jim swallowed. "I hate to even suggest this, but it might be better if we don't ask Ginny first."

"Are ye suggesting she might no agree tae help?"

"No. I'm suggesting her face might give away the game, if she knows about it."

The Laird's brows drew together. "'Tis true she's no much o' an actress." He tapped his finger on the table as he thought. Jim waited.

"All right. I'll authorize th' extra help. Put in as many men as ye need."

"Thank you, sir. I'll make sure you know which of the strangers in your building are mine."

DeSoto and Jim both rose, took their leave, and headed for

their cars.

"Are you all right to drive?" Jim asked.

"I'll be fine."

"I think you'd be better off in the hospital."

DeSoto looked over at him and smiled. "I'll feel safer if I'm not drugged and wearing a flimsy gown that opens down the back."

Jim laughed. "At least post some guards."

"Already done. For you, too. Good night."

"Night."

Jim watched DeSoto drive off, then made his way home. He looked carefully around as he drove, and in the parking lot, and along the hallway at the apartment complex, but could see no one.

He stumbled over the threshold, locked himself in, stripped, and fell into bed. It had been a very long, very hard twenty-four hours. He was aware, intellectually, that gunmen might burst in and execute him in his sleep, or burn the building down around his ears. It was possible DeSoto's agents might be able to rescue him in time. It was also possible they would be the first to die. But he had reached the stage of exhaustion where he (almost) didn't care. He closed his eyes and was instantly asleep.

* * *

CHAPTER 33

Day 13 – Wednesday afternoon
Hillcrest Conference Room

Ginny dragged herself out of bed late on Wednesday afternoon, climbed into her scrubs, and headed for the hospital. She picked up a large cup of strong coffee on the way over, reflecting that she was in danger of overdosing on caffeine before she was allowed to sleep again, settled down in the third-floor conference room, and dialed the police substation.

"Detective Tran? I've sent some additional information to you." Ginny explained she had e-mailed her list of names that could be eliminated as suspects, with rationales, and a summary of what Lisa had told them that morning.

Detective Tran's voice responded. "I received it, and it is all most interesting, but I am afraid some of it is not accurate. The only fingerprints found on the drugs in Mrs. Kyle's locker were those of Lisa Braden."

Ginny blinked. "She lied to us."

"It would appear so."

Ginny's brow furrowed. "What possible use could it be to Lisa to lie about those drugs?"

"If she planted them, to deflect suspicion from herself."

"Well, yes," Ginny conceded. "What I mean is, she must have known Grace's fingerprints weren't on them, even if she thought hers weren't either. Why choose Grace? If she overheard Grace and Phyllis arguing about illicit drug purchases, why not say it was Phyllis, which is what it looked like in the first place, and leave it at that?"

"That is a very interesting question. May I suggest you ask her? And while you are at it, I would be most interested to hear how she opened the combination lock."

"I'll do that." Ginny heard a small hesitation.

"Miss Forbes, I am afraid I have unwelcome news for you. Maria Perez's car has been found, abandoned and stripped. The windows were shot out, and the doors ripped off."

Ginny caught her breath. "Was she—?"

"No, and there was no blood inside the vehicle. But I am afraid we have to be concerned about how she and the car became separated."

Ginny nodded into the phone, her heart sinking. "I'll tell Jim."

"I wish to repeat, Miss Forbes, that, although we appreciate your cooperation in this investigation, you are not obligated to put yourself in danger. It might be prudent to let us take over from here."

Ginny pulled herself together. "Detective Tran, I assure you, I have no intention of trying to play policeman."

"A wise decision. Good day, Miss Forbes."

"Yes, goodbye." At least she wouldn't have to worry about Jim being gunned down in the ER tonight. The police were all over the building and, if she read her laird correctly, there would be other guards in place as well. Angus, at least, was taking the threat seriously.

* * *

Wednesday evening
HQ of the North TX Distribution and Support Region

He sat behind his desk, his eyes on the Nurse Handler for the DFW area, carelessly tapping a pencil on the leather blotter, just fast enough to be irritating.

"You're sure you can do this?"

"I can make sure she's on that roof at that time. If he sets up with the helicopter pad on his right, he'll have a clear shot."

"You will escort her."

"I will."

He fell silent again. It was becoming necessary to act. "You have another problem, I think."

The woman in front of him shifted from one foot to the other. "It's personal."

He waited, letting her grow even more uncomfortable.

"You don't need to know about it," she said.

He set the pencil down, leaned back in his chair, and brought his fingertips together. "I know everything there is to know about you, señorita. I know where you go on your vacations. I know about the irregular bank account withdrawals. I know how you managed to get the jobs you have now—both of them." He watched as the color drained from her face. "There is someone blackmailing you."

The woman hesitated, then nodded, then stood up a bit straighter and faced him. "I can take care of it."

His eyes narrowed. "You killed a nurse, and drew the attention of the police, and the blackmail continues. This does not inspire confidence."

Her nostrils flared. "They can't pin that woman's death on *me*."

He studied her face. Arrogant and intractable, a bad

combination. "I must think on this. We'll speak again. For now, do nothing. Do you understand?"

She nodded, then turned and left the room.

He waited. Five minutes after her departure, the door opened again. The man who entered said nothing, just approached the desk and stood, waiting to be addressed.

"¿Escuchaste?"

"Sí, I heard."

"Will there be a problem?"

"No. I have already looked at the building. There is a parking structure across the street."

He nodded, then pulled a photograph out of his drawer and laid it, face up, on the desk. "This is your target."

"Sí, obispo. Sera hecho."

* * *

Wednesday late evening
Hillcrest Medical ICU

It had taken some doing, but Ginny had cornered Lisa in the medication room and barred the door, demanding that Lisa explain herself.

"I don't have to talk to you!"

Ginny's frown deepened. "I spoke to Detective Tran today. She said the only fingerprints on those drugs in Phyllis' locker were yours. She also wants to know how you got in. So, do you want to be taken down to the police station to explain that, or would you rather tell me?" She saw Lisa blanch, then flush, her eyes angry.

"You think you're so smart! Well, I've got news for you. You're not the only person around here with contacts. I have a few of my own."

Ginny crossed her arms on her chest, her back against the door. "Oh?"

"Yes! You might be surprised at what I know."

"What *do* you know?"

"I know your precious Dr. Mackenzie isn't as lily-white as he would have you believe!"

Ginny controlled her face. Jim was still a stranger in many ways, but she wasn't going to believe anything Lisa said about him, not without evidence and a full confession from Jim. "How would you know that?"

"Wouldn't *you* like to know!" Lisa was sneering now.

Ginny's voice grew quieter. "Yes, I would. Who've you been talking to?"

Lisa stuck her nose in the air. "Let's just say I have it on *very* good authority that *Dr*. Mackenzie could have easily ended up as *Mr*. Mackenzie, if not for a certain person's interference."

Ginny took a slow breath and counted to ten. Lisa was accusing Jim of having crossed a line that put his medical license in jeopardy. What's more, she was suggesting undue influence had been needed to get him out of trouble. It was possible, of course, but not relevant. Not at the moment. She decided to try a bluff. "You haven't told me anything I didn't already know."

Lisa's face fell, then stiffened. "You don't know what I'm talking about."

"I think you're making it up on the spot."

"That's not true! It came out when they did his hire-on paperwork. I've *seen* it."

"You're not on the committee. How did you see his paperwork?"

Lisa's eyes slid away. "I told you. I have contacts."

Ginny's eyes narrowed. "Someone in Human Resources."

"Yes! And that's all I'm going to say." Lisa tried to shoulder her way past Ginny, but Ginny didn't budge.

"How did you get into Phyllis' locker?"

Lisa smirked. "Do you have any idea how often kids forget their locker combinations? I used to charge them five dollars a time to reset those things. It's easy, when you know how."

"What about the drugs? How did you get your hands on them?"

"That's easy, too, if you know where to go and have the cash."

Ginny frowned. "Are you using?"

Lisa flared up immediately. "No!" Her denial was vehement enough to make Ginny wonder if she'd hit a sore spot.

"Lisa, if you have a problem, the Board has a safety net. They'll help you. All you have to do is ask."

Lisa's eyes grew cold. "Butt out."

Ginny took a breath. Lisa's transgressions, whatever they might be (short of murder), were not her responsibility. She steered the conversation back to Phyllis.

"Why did you say Grace planted those drugs in Phyllis' locker?"

"Because they hated each other."

Ginny's brow furrowed. "Why did you think that?"

"Because I saw them fighting."

"In addition to that scene about the miscarriage?"

"Yes."

"When?"

Lisa hesitated. "I don't remember the date."

"Where, then?"

"At the drug buy."

"How do you know they were buying illegal drugs?"

"Why else would they be there?"

Ginny could feel another headache starting. Lisa had that effect on her. "Did money change hands?"

"How would I know?"

"Lisa, you're accusing two ICU nurses of trafficking in illegal drugs. You can't do that without proof."

"I've got pictures."

Ginny was startled. "You do?"

"Well, not me, but someone I know does."

"What are we talking about here? A camera phone in the shadows under the bridge?"

"How did you know it was a bridge?"

From Corey Jones, Ginny thought, but didn't share. "Unless you have a seriously good camera, there won't be any way to tell who it was."

"Well, he does, and I've seen his pictures. He's got shots of the two of them arguing and there's one where Phyllis put her hand on Grace's arm and then Grace took a swing at her." Lisa's eyes danced at the memory. "You can see it clear as day."

Ginny was silent for a moment, thinking it through. Zimmerman, of course. Collecting images for the news media. "Was this friend of yours following Grace or Phyllis?"

"I have no idea why he was there. Let me go, I have to go back to work."

Ginny reached out and caught one of Lisa's hands, holding it up so they could both see there were no pictures on the now short and very clean fingernails.

"You broke a nail on the night Phyllis died. What happened to it?"

Lisa jerked her hand back. "Someone found it and turned it in to the Old Witch."

Ginny's eyebrows rose. "Did it have one of those X-rated scenes on it?"

Lisa's lips twitched. "Yes. She was not happy."

Ginny could well believe it. "Who found it?"

"She didn't tell me."

That could be discovered and whoever found the nail could tell them where. Ginny went back to the cocaine trap.

"Why did you put those drugs in Phyllis' locker? You must have had a reason."

Lisa sniffed. "Well, if you have to know, she was bugging me about getting counseling. I wanted her to get a taste of what it's like to be on the receiving end of someone's self-righteous attitude. She should have left me alone. Now can I go?"

Ginny nodded, stepping aside to let Lisa slip past her and out the door. Here it was again. Another example of a do-gooder who couldn't live and let live. But was it enough to get her killed?

Ginny shook her head at the problem, then went back to her own work. Sad, really, that the world didn't reward those willing to reach out to help others. But one had to accept that sticking one's neck out came with risks. There was always a chance someone would make sure you never did it again.

* * *

CHAPTER 34

Day 14 – Thursday morning
Forbes residence

Her shift was over and Ginny was already sliding between the sheets when her phone went off.

"May I speak to Ginny Forbes, please? It's Becky Peel from Austin."

Ginny sat up in bed. "Oh! Hello! What's up?"

"I thought you'd like to know we traced that Registered Nurse license number to one of the batch of Mexican graduates that came across the border last year."

"Maria Perez?"

"Yes, and son. Here on a work visa with a fast track option for citizenship."

"Anything fishy about her status?"

"No. She's clean and the whole thing looks like a win-win for the nurses and the long-term care facilities in Texas."

"Except that it's not."

"Well, that's what this legislation is about."

"When's the vote?"

"This afternoon. It's going to be interesting. You should see the crowds gathered on the lawn outside the capital!"

"Are they giving you trouble?"

"Not yet, but the police are taking no chances."

"Well, stay out of it. You still owe me a recording of the last day of the conference and a Continuing Education certificate!"

"I'll get right on that. Bye!"

* * *

Thursday afternoon
Forbes residence

Eight hours of sleep later, Ginny rose and pulled on sweats, then, coffee in hand, settled down at her desk. An idea had occurred to her while she was at work last night, but she'd been too busy to follow up on it. She brought up the images, summaries, transcripts, and badge data on the two respiratory therapists, then settled down to build a new timeline, starting with Peter.

Ginny went through every bit of data, locating, compiling, and transcribing the information. When she was done, she had a table showing where Peter was for each part of the window of opportunity. It had some gaps, of course, but it did what she had predicted it would do. She paged down and did the same thing for Dee.

When she was through with both lists, she printed the document and got out her colored pens. She highlighted each gap in the timelines, and noted how long they lasted, then marked how far from the restroom the two RTs were during the gaps.

She studied her handiwork, then did some rough calculations. When she was satisfied, she put her pencil down and leaned back in her chair. She was now prepared to swear that neither Dee nor Peter could have gone into the ladies' restroom, attacked Phyllis, dragged her into the handicap stall, locked it from the inside, crawled out underneath, removed the PPE, and gotten out into the Unit and back to duty in the time available. They were both just too busy.

That still left Marjorie Hawkins, Grace, and Lisa. More work to be done, but it was definitely progress! She put the investigation away, and turned her attention to her impending date with Jim. When the doorbell rang, she grabbed her evening bag, and headed downstairs.

Sinia caught them in the front hall. "I know you're on your way out," she said, "but come take a peek at the news before you go." She led them into the den where the announcer was reading a prepared statement.

"The rioting has been going on for more than four hours with no end in sight. The winners have retired from the scene, but the nurses on the losing side are not prepared to give up."

Far from giving up, they were locked in heavy combat with the Austin police department. Ginny shook her head.

"What good do they think this will do?"

"They think," Sinia said, "the end justifies the means. The problem is, history tells us they're wrong."

* * *

Thursday evening
Reunion / Jim's apartment

Ginny'd had trouble remembering to eat. Her eyes kept being drawn to the window and the view beyond.

"Like it?"

She turned to look at Jim, her face radiant. "I love it!"

He'd surprised her. All he'd said was, "Dinner." Then he'd brought her here, to Reunion Tower and the revolving restaurant at the top. The food had been excellent, the view spectacular. Christmas lights were up all over the county and the LEDs on the geodesic frame rippled with seasonal animations in bright red and green.

"I'd like to come back in daylight. I'll bet you can see all the way to Colorado."

He laughed and refilled her glass. "It's a date."

Ginny looked up as the waiter arrived with dessert, a watermelon-flavored sorbet with tiny dark chocolate 'seeds'.

"Delicious!"

They lingered over the wine, then Jim signaled the waiter for the check. He raised an eyebrow at the total. "This may have to be your Christmas present."

She smiled. "If so, I'm well satisfied."

"May I offer you coffee at my place?"

"If you don't think it will compromise my reputation."

Jim laughed. "We have a chaperone, you know. DeSoto's agents are still tailing me everywhere."

Ginny looked around. "How do you know? Can you see them?"

"Not usually. Every now and then one of them makes eye contact, just to let me know they're still there."

Once inside his apartment, Jim headed for the kitchen. "This will take a minute. Make yourself comfortable."

Ginny settled down on the sofa, slipping her shoes off and putting her feet up on the hassock. When the coffee was ready, Jim served her, then sat down facing her.

"I wanted a chance to talk to you in private."

She sipped at her cup. "What's on your mind?"

"I'm having trouble," he said, "reconciling my conscience. Risking my own life is one thing. Risking yours is another. I want you to tell Detective Tran she'll have to carry on without you. You can go to relatives or a friend or stay at one of the Homesteads, but I want you out of town until this is over."

Ginny set her cup down on the table. "Jim, you told me the only way I would get my confidence back was to take risks. Mother said the same."

"Reasonable risks, yes. I didn't mean taking on the drug cartel."

Ginny studied his face, then sighed. "I asked your grandfather to do the same—with you."

"But—"

She held up a hand and he fell silent. "He wouldn't do it." She put her feet on the floor and leaned toward him. "Neither you nor I is bulletproof, even with a vest on. The only way to make the problem go away is to eliminate it."

"That's not your job—or mine."

"I know, but would you rather be cannon fodder? Just waiting blindly for the bullet with your name on it? Or would you rather fight back?"

"You can still fight back, from a distance."

Her eyes narrowed. "Was I safer in Austin?"

"No, but that was because you were with me."

She took both of his hands in hers. "Jim, do you really think I can hide from the cartel?"

He blinked, then frowned, then dropped his eyes. "No."

"Then let's concentrate on removing the threat."

He studied her face, then took a deep breath. "The entire force of the federal government is working on that, specialists who've spent years training for the job. Why do you think you can do better than they can?"

"I don't, and it's not a competition." She paused, searching for the right words. "I can't get the sight of those rioting nurses out of my head. That level of civil unrest, among nurses, of all people, is scary." She swallowed. "I know those people. I'm one of them. We care, deeply, and we work every day to make our patients' lives better. But we don't usually resort to violence. It argues someone behind the scenes orchestrating the whole thing."

"The cartel."

"If Clara and Becky are right, yes. That makes it personal."

He was silent for a long moment, studying her face. "Okay. Let's assume you're right. How do you propose to deal with the cartel?"

"We need to take this fight to the enemy, to identify his weaknesses, vulnerabilities. What mistakes has he made? What challenges is he facing? If we can get inside his head, we can get to the next battlefield before he does, and stake out the high ground."

Jim frowned. "You sound like one of those crazy people who reenacts famous battles."

"You're not far wrong." She smiled at him. "My mother teaches history. Remember? And it's the lessons of history that military tacticians study. All we need to do is pay attention."

* * *

CHAPTER 35

Day 15 – Friday morning
Forbes Residence

The first step in a successful military campaign was gathering intelligence. Immediately after breakfast, Ginny tackled the cartel and its problems, starting with a list of the things she had discovered so far.

    1. The DEA was in Dallas because of suspected drug cartel activity.

    2. The cartel attacked the Hillcrest ER.

    3. Luis Perez stole fake drug patches from his mother, after which Maria Perez went missing.

    4. Maria said Phyllis was killed *because of* what she told her.

    5. Phyllis connected the Mexican drug cartel to the Mexican Nurse Pipeline in the BON article.

    6. Jim was asked to take evidence back to Dallas, but someone stole it out of his hotel room.

    7. Someone put a tracker on Ginny's car.

    8. Corey's drug supplier might be involved in a turf war.

    9. Lisa accused Phyllis and Grace of buying drugs illegally.

    10. Clara and Becky suspect cartel money is behind the Nurse Pipeline, but can't prove it.

    She sat back and looked at her list. She might have missed

some, but this gave her a good starting point.

The second step was to develop a plan of attack. How much of this constituted a problem for the cartel? She started another list.

a) If Maria was actually handling drugs for the cartel (and all they'd seen so far was fake fentanyl patches), then she could turn stool pigeon on them, and put at least some of the organization away for a very long time. Ginny frowned. Maria's car suggested the cartel had already handled that problem.

b) All of the criminals who attacked the Hillcrest ER were either dead or in prison. So the cartel was down a round dozen bad guys. How long did it take to recruit and train replacements? And re-arm them? Because all their weapons had been seized by the DEA. Possible personnel and equipment problems for the cartel.

c) Phyllis' Board of Nursing *Bulletin* article might be a problem for the cartel. The law might take the position that it was a dying declaration and admit it into court as evidence.

d) The cartel had recovered the evidence Jim was asked to deliver to Dallas. If they wanted to silence him, they should have done so before he talked to the DEA. Was that a problem for the cartel? Or Jim? Or both?

e) The tracker on her car. There was no way to classify that until the warrant came through so they could see who was keeping tabs on her movements.

f) The traffic in illegal drugs was an ongoing headache for everyone. But it was lucrative, so the cartel continued to offer the service. They were vulnerable because the users might talk, or the dealers might be picked up, or someone could get greedy. But none of those would lead to the main man. No obvious help there.

g) The money trail was a definite weak point. If the new legislation made it possible to find out where the money for the Nurse Pipeline came from and where it went, and assuming the cartel was behind it, the cartel was vulnerable indeed.

Ginny nodded in satisfaction. So far, so good.

The third step was to select a strategy to exploit the enemy's weaknesses. Ginny considered what tactics they might be able to use.

1) People talk. The cartel's usual way to handle that was to kill them before they could talk to the wrong person, and to scare everyone else into not talking at all. She needed to find someone willing to testify. Maybe one of Maria's coworkers, now that she knew where to find them. The textbooks called this tactic *subversion*.

2) The forensic evidence might still be useful. If they could trace those fake drugs, they might be able to cut the supply off at the source. *Divide and conquer.*

3) The legislation had passed and would take effect, but it might be years before it showed irregularities in the financial aspects of the cartel's business. Hmmmm. Technically another divide and conquer, but much too slow for her purposes.

4) Could the DEA put undercover agents in the place of the gunmen now dead or in custody? A tried and true method for defeating the enemy, *infiltrate* with saboteurs and spies and maybe traceable weapons as well.

5) *Set a trap.* DeSoto was already doing this, with Ginny and Jim as bait.

Ginny looked over her work, then e-mailed the lists, with a suitably respectful cover letter, to Agent DeSoto. She trusted him, but bringing down the cartel was a big job. He might welcome a fresh eye—and her role as staked goat was getting a wee bit uncomfortable.

* * *

Friday noon
DFW MegaMall

It was the next-to-last shopping day before Christmas. Faithful to DeSoto's instructions to do what she would normally do, Ginny had accompanied Jim to the mall and was mingling with the crowd, looking for the last few items on her list and admiring the decorations.

Santa's sleigh, suspended from the ceiling and drawn by eight full-sized reindeer rendered in pecans, was always a favorite. Actually, there were nine. Rudolph had been added years ago, and the artists had done a good job of matching him to the existing reindeer, but it was clear he was an outsider. His red nose was the only part of the display that used electricity.

There was another decoration she especially liked, a curtain of moving lights in red and green. Not the low-budget LED rotating rainbow, either. This was a *tour de force* of shimmering, vivid color that seemed to splash from ceiling to floor in a solid waterfall that parted as the shopper approached. No wires could be seen and, when one reached out to touch the lights, there was nothing there. Magical and (apparently) produced by magic. The only clue to its source lay in the dazzling white clouds that roiled across the ceiling just above the deluge. One had to approach from the south corridor because from the north side the whole display was invisible. There was always an audience in front of it, mesmerized, and Ginny joined them, fascinated by the spectacle, knowing it well, but gazing anyway.

When she'd had enough of that particular delight, she wandered on, looking in the windows, sometimes going in to handle an item that caught her eye, sometimes buying, sometimes putting it back. Ginny had no trouble spending money, but her Scottish blood demanded that it look like a fair price, preferably a bargain, and not much in this mall fit that description. In one of the shops she looked up to see a familiar face, apparently on the same errand.

"Hello!"

Grace started, looked up, then returned the greeting. "Hello. How's the Christmas shopping going?"

"Pretty well. I've got all the big presents done. Now I'm looking for stocking stuffers."

Grace raised an eyebrow. "Among the cashmere sweaters?"

Ginny laughed. "Busted! No, what I'm actually looking for is something I can throw in the washing machine. A petroleum product of some sort."

Grace gestured toward another rounder. "There are some over there, but I won't pay what they're asking for them. It's too easy to find the same thing in the thrift shops."

"You're so right! Maybe I can swing by one on the way home." Ginny turned and caught sight of another of their number, passing the plate glass windows. "Is that Marjorie Hawkins?"

Grace glanced over. "Looks like it." She turned back to her shopping.

Ginny hesitated, studying Grace's face. She looked as if she hadn't been sleeping well. Not surprising, really. Ginny took a breath then plunged in. "Grace, about the bombing, if you want to talk, I'm available."

Grace lifted her eyes to Ginny's for a moment. "No, thank you."

"It's normal to have a touch of PTSD after being caught like that. There's no shame in it."

Ginny watched as Grace's hands stilled on the rack, but all she said was, "I'm fine."

"If you change your mind, call me."

Grace nodded, but didn't look up.

Ginny gathered up her selections and headed for the checkout desk. Well, she'd made the offer. The next step would be up to Grace.

* * *

Friday afternoon
DFW MegaMall

Jim set his packages down on the table and lowered himself onto one of the dainty metal chairs provided by the café management for the use of its customers. He ordered coffee, then turned his eyes to the ice surface. He had no trouble spotting Ginny. She was wearing a bright red sweater that stood out from the everyday jackets of the other skaters.

She had Luis firmly by the hand and was showing him how to move his feet. As Jim watched, and to his very great surprise, both Mrs. Forbes and Himself skated up to join them. His grandfather knew how to ice skate? And still went out on the ice? At his age? Jim watched them move around the rink for several minutes, then decided he felt left out. He would have to learn to skate, too, enough to join family parties like this one.

At least he wasn't sitting alone at home waiting for a death squad to break down his door and shoot him. He glanced around uneasily. The DEA agent was still there, and there might be others. They had his back. The problem was that Jim would never see the attack coming. Or maybe he would, and would be a sitting duck here in the open. Maybe he should have stayed home. Or maybe it didn't matter. Maybe, when your time was up, your time was up and it made no difference where you were or what you were doing.

His eye was caught by a flash of red and he looked back in time to see Ginny fly past. Luis was now between Mrs. Forbes and Himself. His face was a mixture of fear and ecstasy. He shrieked as his feet got ahead of him. Then, as Jim watched, he shook off his escorts and struck out on his own. Jim smiled. A braw lad. Whatever his future held, he would be all right.

The sound was too small to be called a gasp, more like a hiss, the sharp intake of a breath. It caught his attention, though, and Jim turned to see Marjorie Hawkins staring at the ice, at Luis.

Jim's brow furrowed. Marjorie Hawkins had every right to be in the mall. She also had a right to enjoy a cup of coffee at rink side. So why did he feel a sudden disquiet at seeing her here, watching Luis so intently?

She stared for a moment longer, then paid her bill, rose and walked away. Away from, not toward, the ice surface. Jim watched her out of sight, then turned back to find Ginny waving at him from the barrier. He smiled and waved, then completely forgot about Marjorie Hawkins in the pleasure of watching Ginny skate. She was so sure, so deft in her movements. Back on the ice, in defiance of death, she glowed, and his heart glowed at the sight.

* * *

CHAPTER 36

The Cooperative Hall that night was bustling with the preparations for the coming holidays. Tomorrow was Christmas Eve and, in another week, it would be Hogmanay.

"How does this look?" Ginny asked.

"Up a little on the port side."

She grinned at Jim. "Port, huh? Feeling nautical are we?"

He smiled. "I was just thinking how much fun it would be to take a Windjammer cruise, with you."

"Those are the ones on the big sailboats, aren't they?"

"Ships. Tall ships, with real sails. The wind in your face, the sun on your back, the salt spray on your lips."

He helped her down from the step stool and Ginny found both of her hands captured and pressed to his chest, his eyes on hers.

"It would make a very romantic honeymoon."

Ginny lifted an eyebrow. "Judging by the look in your eye, a bride might wonder which you loved more, the ship or her."

He shook his head. "As lovely as a tall ship can be, no creation of wood and canvas can match flesh and blood. She would have no doubt who came first. But give me a bride who delights in the wonders of the world and I will make her a happy wife."

Ginny smiled up at him. "Here comes Caroline. You'd better give me back my hands or she might draw the wrong conclusion."

"Too late. I saw you two lovebirds." Caroline dropped into a chair set along the wall and looked from one to the other. "You'd better hurry up and get married and have children before you get yourselves killed."

Jim objected. "Wouldn't it be better *not* to have the children first, if all we're planning to do is die young?"

"Not for you. We need an heir. So you'd better get busy."

Ginny blushed. "Did anyone ever suggest you need a filter between your brain and your mouth?"

"Many times. I just ignore them." Caroline leaned forward, eyeing Ginny. "What *you* need to do is find out who killed Phyllis and get this whole thing settled."

"I'm trying!" Ginny protested.

"Okay, so where are you in the investigation?"

Ginny pulled a chair up and sat down. Jim straddled another. "We've narrowed the suspect pool to three."

"Unless you count the mysterious outsider who could have slipped in, done the dirty deed, and slipped out again unseen," Jim added.

Ginny shook her head. "I don't believe in him. Someone would have mentioned a stranger."

"So who's left?"

"Lisa, Marjorie Hawkins, and Grace."

Caroline chewed on her lip. "Well, if you ask me—"

"I didn't."

Caroline gave her a dirty look, then continued. "The stories all say the most likely suspect is the person who saw her alive last. So, who babysat while she went to the bathroom?"

"Marjorie Hawkins." Ginny frowned, remembering the discrepancy.

"What?" Caroline asked.

"It may not mean anything. She was in and out of almost all the rooms at some point that night."

"But?"

"She didn't sound the alarm."

Caroline gave her a shrewd look. "Explain, please."

"We cover for one another all the time, and sometimes things happen to pull us away, but if that happens to me, I go back later, just to make sure the patients are still alive."

"And she didn't do that?"

"I think she did. The four o'clock vital signs were done and she signed for the meds."

"So, where's the problem?"

"When the nurse I cover for comes back, she usually asks if anything happened. It's sort of a mini-report. Not formal and not documented."

"Okay. And?"

"I actually looked at one of those patients, after the day shift pointed out that Phyllis was missing. The patient was fine."

"That's good, isn't it?"

Ginny nodded. "The thing is, she shouldn't have been."

Jim was watching her intently. "Can you be more specific?"

"Well, she was on a ventilator and the respiratory therapists were managing those, so her airway was clear and the machine was working."

He nodded. "Okay."

Ginny screwed up her face. "She got her four a.m. medications and vital signs, which is also okay. But there *was* something odd, and I didn't realize what it meant until just now."

"Go on," Caroline said.

Ginny turned to her friend. "Do you know what TPN is?"

"No."

"It's a way of feeding a patient through a big intravenous line. The fluid is delivered via pump, because it's dangerous and needs to stay on schedule so it doesn't cause big shifts in glucose and electrolytes and fluid volumes."

"Sounds serious."

Ginny nodded. "When I got into the room, the pump had been set to a keep-open rate. There was still fluid in the bag, enough for several more hours, so I wasn't worried. I just told myself the oncoming nurse would deal with it. But it shouldn't have been set to run so slowly. You only do that when the bag is almost empty and you're waiting for the new one to come up from the pharmacy."

"Okay. So whoever changed the pump setting didn't want to have to deal with plugging in the new bag."

"It's more than just the bag. The tubing and dressing also have to be changed, to prevent infection. It's a routine night shift duty."

"What's your point?"

Ginny looked from Caroline to Jim, then back to Caroline. "Someone turned it down so she wouldn't have to do all that work."

"Again, what's your point?"

"In the usual course of things, anyone who had to respond to a low volume alarm would have raised the roof. Where in the hell was Phyllis? Why wasn't she doing her job? But no one said a thing. Whoever it was just turned down the pump and walked away."

"Would your Head Nurse have done that?"

Ginny gave a small shrug. "I wouldn't have thought so, but she was one very busy woman that night. She might have meant to follow up on it and been prevented."

Caroline leaned forward. "Is there some way to find out who it was?"

"I can look at the patient-cam images to see if the IV pump showed."

"Okay, so what will that tell us? There's a lazy nurse among you?"

Ginny was frowning now. "It should tell us who killed Phyllis."

Jim leaned forward. "How?"

She turned to face him, still trying to sort out the reasoning in her mind. "It's not just laziness. It's negligence."

Jim nodded. "Not following the doctor's orders, the patient could have been injured."

"Right. Which implies that whoever turned down the rate didn't want to draw attention to the fact Phyllis was missing."

"Sounds reasonable, but—?"

Ginny shrugged. "If it was the murderer, why didn't she just let the pump go dry? All she'd have to say is, 'Phyllis came back from the bathroom, and I went back to work.' That would have muddied the timeline considerably."

Jim nodded. "I follow."

"So do I," said Caroline.

"So where's the benefit in resetting the pump?"

"Other than delaying the alarm, you mean."

Ginny nodded, her frown deepening. "Why would someone kill Phyllis, then sneak in to take care of her patients? It would jeopardize the alibi if she showed up on camera in Phyllis' rooms, but failed to mention she was MIA. Would someone capable of strangling a fellow nurse care enough about the patients to take that risk?"

Caroline shook her head. "I don't think it can be the same person. There must be some other explanation."

Ginny nodded. "And I could still be wrong. It was a crazy night. Any one of us might have run in, made a temporary adjustment, meaning to come back and make a more permanent one later, and run out again, and gotten caught in the next disaster."

"So, does this exonerate all the nurses, on the grounds of conscience?" Jim asked. "Because, if it does, we have to look elsewhere."

Ginny sighed. "And I'm fresh out of suspects."

* * *

Friday night
Zimmerman residence

Marge Hawkins sat in her car on the dark side of the block and watched the front door of the house. Random cars turned into the street and cruised slowly past, looking at the Christmas decorations. She perched her phone on the steering wheel and made sure it was lit, so the curious could see what she was doing, be bored, and move on.

It had already been a long day. She'd completed her preparations for tomorrow, done some Christmas shopping, and paused for a late lunch, only to find Maria Perez's child right under her nose. She had followed the older Forbes woman to a children's shelter, and seen the boy turned over to the caretaker there. A bit of research told her the shelter was genuine, but private, under the control of the Scottish community. It seemed unlikely she would get a chance to speak to the boy, much less abduct him.

This target would be different. There would be no protector between her and him, but neither did she want to confront him. What she wanted was to leave a little early Christmas present for him, then slip away.

She'd seen him moving around inside and was beginning to wonder if he was in for the night when the door opened and he emerged, striding down the front walk, camera bag over his shoulder. He climbed into the car parked at the curb and drove off without paying the slightest bit of attention to her.

She waited for five minutes, then approached the door, tools in hand. The lock was a standard double-keyed deadbolt, no additional lock on the handle. The pick gun got her inside in less than twenty seconds. The keypad to the alarm was mounted beside the door, whining at her as the one minute delay counted down. She consulted her notes, then punched in the access code she'd gotten through the simple expedient of recording (using a bionic ear) the sounds made by Zimmerman as he enabled the device, then translating the tones to numbers and letters.

Once safely in, she headed for the kitchen. She'd read somewhere that the thing to do was to dip a spoon in the poison and let it dry. The substance would be totally invisible and all the victim would have to do was stir once. She opened the drawers in turn until she found the cutlery and a neat little stack of spoons.

She pulled the top one out and stepped over to the sink. She carefully poured one milliliter of the neurotoxin into the bowl of the spoon, then rocked it back and forth until it covered the surface completely. She had enough to anoint the back as well. She blew on it, to hasten the drying.

When she could see no more glisten of wetness on either surface, she put the spoon back on the top of the stack, set the alarm, and let herself out of the house. She could not lock the door with the tools she had, but he probably wouldn't even notice. He would put the key in the lock, turn it, and expect the door to open, and it would.

So now all she had to do was wait. It was lucky she'd made friends with that toxicologist on the last dive. He'd been most helpful in the matter of fugu poison. Quite knowledgeable and quite clueless. She should send him a small token of thanks and ask him where he was headed next. Perhaps they could go diving together again. With the blackmailer finally off her back—the right one this time—she'd be able to afford another trip.

* * *

CHAPTER 37

Day 16 – Saturday noon, Christmas Eve
Forbes residence

Ginny stared at the image. The TPN bag was clearly visible, as was the profile of the woman making adjustments to the pump. It *was* one of the Hillcrest Medical ICU nurses. It was *not* Marjorie Hawkins.

Grace was still in the running, of course. If she was the murderer, she might have set the various drips in the room to an ICU version of autopilot, to make sure no one went looking for Phyllis too soon. That would mean the TPN, plain fluid (for hydration), sedatives, and analgesics. But none of the IV pumps could be trusted completely. Grace would have to check on them at some point.

Ginny searched for evidence that Grace had returned to that patient's room, and found nothing. She had seen Marge Hawkins doing the four o'clock meds and Dee come in to suction the patient and check the ventilator, but that was all. No one else came or went.

She then followed Grace from Phyllis' patient's room to her own and watched for any sign that Grace was concerned about that TPN. Nothing. She seemed to have forgotten it.

It was possible, of course, that Grace had said something to someone else (out of range of the cameras), and that the someone else had ignored the question of Phyllis' absence.

That meant Marge Hawkins, the acting Charge Nurse for the shift. It would be her job to handle any problems and make sure the proper procedure was followed. Which, apparently, hadn't happened. Because no one had gone looking for Phyllis, and someone should have.

Ginny sat back in her chair and stared out the window. The winter sky was overcast, the clouds shifting shades of gray and white, billowing in the breeze. She watched the light grow as the clouds parted and a single shaft of sun poured through the gap, slid across the treetops, then faded as the clouds closed ranks again.

Illumination. That's what she needed. Her eyes drifted back to her computer. Information. Everyone was online these days.

It wasn't Ginny's habit to pry into the private lives of those she worked with, but maybe it was time she looked at a few of them. Marjorie Hawkins first.

The Head Nurse had a social media presence filled with images of her hobby, SCUBA diving in exotic locations. There were underwater images and topside images and after party images and in all of them she looked as if she was having a very good time. She also appeared on the Hillcrest Medical Center pages and at a variety of conferences. There were no images that looked like church affiliations, no candid shots taken at home, no picnics, no zoo, no concerts. Nor did she have pet pictures, unless you counted the tropical fish. There may have been pages hiding behind passwords, but nothing stuck out, and Ginny did not have hacking skills. She moved on.

Lisa next. Half an hour's searching added nothing to what Ginny already knew about Lisa.

The third search was more interesting. Grace, as it turned out, had something to say.

Ginny scrolled through the index of video clips, more like a video diary, really, since there were so many of them. They covered the last two years and all said very much the same thing. Grace thought the U.S. government was criminally liable for its treatment of illegal aliens fleeing war-torn countries, and that included Mexicans fleeing the drug cartels.

The U.S., in its arrogance and sloth, had forced the poor illegals to break U.S. laws just to survive. It was necessary that kind-hearted Americans also ignore the law and do the *right thing* instead. There was a lot more on the subject of following your conscience and not letting a piece of paper get between you and doing good deeds.

Ginny had heard it all before and knew that, far from ignoring the problem, there were more than a hundred agencies in the DFW area set up to deal with it.

Lisa had said Grace fought with Phyllis over this issue, Phyllis urging Grace to take her illegal charges to the free clinics and Grace arguing the illegals couldn't trust the charities.

Grace was a citizen and could not be deported, but she *could* be jailed. She had taken an oath when she got her nursing license. She was bound by law and, if she chose to break it, she could not complain about consequences. So was she being wise or foolish? Noble or wicked?

Ginny put the computer away and went off to find her mother. This was not the first time she'd had questions about the relative merits of good and evil. Sinia Forbes, with her vast knowledge of the history of man, understood human motivation, and could be counted on to provide examples of the consequences that followed following one's conscience. It was usually a sobering lesson.

* * *

Saturday afternoon, Christmas Eve
Hillcrest ER

Dr. Devlin Jones made his way to Exam Room Three, paused long enough to take a deep breath, then knocked.

"Come in."

He closed the door behind him and stood just inside the room eyeing the federal agent. The man rose and stood facing him, silent, waiting for him to begin the conversation. DJ looked around the room. There were boxes, and evidence of electrical work in progress.

"You're leaving us?"

Agent DeSoto nodded. "We appreciate your hospitality, but we no longer need a base of operations in this building." There was a brief silence, then, "Is there something I can do for you?"

DJ frowned, his eyes roving the room. It was hard to know where to begin. "Thank you, for what you did for Corey."

"You're welcome."

Another silence.

DJ licked his lips, then swallowed, then stuck his hands in the pockets of his lab coat. "You heard my son and Phyllis are— were cousins?"

DeSoto nodded.

"Phyllis was a good child. Always. Her whole life she was always being good, doing good. She was annoying."

DeSoto's mouth twitched, but he said nothing.

"Normal children get into trouble. They fight and whine and tattle on one another." He shook his head. "It was as if she skipped childhood and went straight to being an adult. She was the oldest, and there never was a more reliable babysitter. Her mother used to worry that she didn't seem to have friends her own age. I knew better. She had a gang."

DeSoto's brow rose. "A street gang?"

DJ nodded. "You know what those damned children did? They picked up trash. They passed out water to construction workers. They cut the grass for the handful of geriatrics that lived in the neighborhood. And she played nurse. Patched up elbows and preached healthy living. I don't know where she got it. The media, maybe, or the library." He fell silent.

"And?"

"When she got older, she went underground. None of us ever saw her doing anything she shouldn't, going any place dangerous. But she did. The other children were less discreet." DJ shifted his weight from one foot to the other. "She made contacts among the drug culture. Maybe through her volunteer work, homeless shelters, that sort of thing."

He took a deep breath. "Corey had gotten in with a bad crowd. She went in, more than once, and hauled his sorry ass home. Saved his life at least once. He'd bought some tainted crack and came very close to dying." DJ shook his head. "I loved my niece, but I didn't like her. None of us could live up to her example and that pissed me off." He looked up and met DeSoto's eyes. "But I didn't kill her."

The DEA agent nodded. "We know."

DJ nodded in return, then took another deep breath, pulled his hands out of his pockets, and crossed his arms on his chest. "I went to visit Corey's supplier, to settle the debt. He's out of the business, so I was dealing with a stranger. He said he appreciated my position and that Corey was welcome anytime, as long I remembered to pay the bill."

DeSoto's eyebrows rose, but he didn't interrupt.

"I asked him how they knew where to find Corey the night of the Christmas party and he laughed. 'Technology is a wonderful thing,' he said. 'You can track anyone anywhere anytime, as long as they're stupid enough to use their own phone.'" DJ found his eyes wandering the room, avoiding the agent's. "Corey told me what he told you. It's probably true. I don't really know what I said. I was so mad." He blinked hard, then looked back at the agent. "I didn't kill my niece, even if I threatened to. I'm sorry she's dead. The world needs more people like her. And I want a promise from you. I want that slimy bastard dealing drugs under the bridge to disappear. I would prefer dead, but life in prison will do."

Agent DeSoto nodded. "That's my intention." He came over. "I'm sorry for your loss. Can I count on your help?"

DJ swallowed hard, then nodded. "You've got it. Anything I can do."

Agent DeSoto smiled. "Thanks. I'll be in touch."

* * *

CHAPTER 38

Day 16 – Saturday midnight, Christmas Eve
Rooftop Helipad, Hillcrest Regional Medical Center

Ginny glanced at the clock. She had some things she had to finish before she could turn responsibility for her patient over to Susan, but she would make it to the helipad on time.

Every year, on Christmas Eve, Santa Claus arrived on the hospital roof with a helicopter full of donated toys, gifts, and food. It took a small army to get them all unloaded and distributed to the various floors, but it was one of the perks of having to work on Christmas Eve.

Every effort was made to send patients home for the holidays, but there were always some too sick to move, and more that came in through the ER doors because of loneliness or to escape the cold. Some years everyone was too busy to help. Not this year, though. The Unit was quiet and the patients mostly stable. What was uncertain this year was the weather.

"It's starting to snow!" Lisa came back from her foray to the window at the end of the hall.

"Will that interfere with the toy delivery?" June asked.

Lisa pushed one hand into the arm of her coat. "Too soon to tell. We're only supposed to get a dusting. Come on, Ginny. Get your coat."

"Coming." She turned to Susan. "We'll be back in an hour or

so."

"Take your time. I've got this."

Ginny hurried into the breakroom and pulled her winter coat from her locker, stuffing her arms into the sleeves as she ran for the elevator. There were already volunteers in the car, one of them holding the door open for her. They rode up to the top floor, then streamed out onto the brightly lit roof. The flood lamps were on to help the helicopter land safely, but they also caught the falling snow, making the air shimmer.

"Look, look!" Lisa was holding her hands out, her face tipped up to the sky. "We're going to have a white Christmas!"

"Come on, ladies. Say 'cheese'."

Ginny turned and smiled into the camera. "Hello, Isaac. Working late again?"

He shrugged. "Part of the job. We're supposed to be humanizing health care. Besides, it's not every day you get to see Santa climb out of a helicopter."

"True."

"Over here, everyone."

Ginny turned to find Marjorie Hawkins herding the volunteers into the shelter of the elevator canopy. She was passing out gay apparel: Santa hats, reindeer headbands, strings of flashing colored lights. Ginny had come prepared and was wearing an especially long candy cane pattern stocking cap that wrapped twice around her neck for added warmth.

"We need to stay out of the way until the rotor blades stop turning. As soon as that happens we can start unloading. Management wants pictures, so pretend you're having fun. Here, Ginny, you get to be Rudolph."

Ginny took the glowing red nose and placed it over her own, grinning at what she saw reflected in the Plexiglas wall. She felt a hand descend on her shoulder and turned to see Lisa, reindeer headband in place over her fur hat, her cheeks ruddy from the cold.

"No fair!" Lisa said. "I want to be Rudolph!"

Ginny sighed to herself then pulled the red nose off and handed it to Lisa. Anything for a little peace on Earth.

"Of course. It goes with your antlers." She smiled, trying to put some Christmas spirit into the words, then turned her back on Lisa and moved away.

The helicopter was landing. They all watched as it settled onto the helipad, the rotors kicking up the snow and making a very convincing blizzard around the familiar figure that was climbing out of the belly of the chopper.

"What's this? I thought you were going to play Rudolph?"

Ginny hadn't noticed Marjorie Hawkins standing just to her right. She turned and smiled at her boss. "Lisa wanted the nose to go with her antlers. I hope you don't mind."

"Lisa? Lisa Braden?"

"Yes. That's okay, isn't it?"

"Isaac! Take my picture!" Lisa pushed past Ginny, posing in front of the helicopter, waving at the camera.

"She looks cute, don't you think?" Ginny turned to her boss, then instinctively took a step back as the Head Nurse's cordial public face dissolved in fury.

Marjorie Hawkins grabbed Ginny by the arm, pulled her away from the shelter, then swung her around so that Ginny's back was to the edge of the roof. Ginny could feel Hawkins' fingers digging into her flesh, even through the sleeve of her coat.

"What do you think you're doing?"

"Let go of me!" Ginny tried to break the iron grip that held her.

"You were supposed to wear that red nose!" She pushed Ginny backwards, towards the edge of the roof.

"Stop it! Let me GO!" With a furious wrench, Ginny tore her

arm free and tried to run, but her foot came down on a slick spot. She fell, landing on the rooftop, just shy of one of the concrete wheel stops that kept cars from going over the edge.

There was a sound like a wet kiss, followed by a crack, then a small gasp. Ginny lifted her head and looked at the other woman. She was staring down at her chest.

A cheerful splash of red had materialized on her heavy white sweater, where the pendant of a necklace would have been, had the Head Nurse been wearing one. It might have been any Christmas themed ornament—a poinsettia blossom, a clump of holly berries, a red bulb off a string of lights—but it was none of the above.

Ginny saw the stain growing larger, but the meaning didn't sink in until she connected it to the sound. She watched in horror as the woman in front of her collapsed, landing just inches from her nose.

In the next moment, she realized there were other sounds: men shouting to get down, more gunfire, screams and cursing and someone calling for help and a stretcher. She turned her head toward the sounds and saw the volunteers running, cannonballing into one another as they tried to escape or reach the fallen, all of them in motion. All except one. She was lying on the roof, on her side, a man's arm around her waist. On her head was a pair of reindeer antlers and on her face glowed a bright red nose.

"Ginny, lass, talk to me!"

Himself knelt down beside her, his artificial beard pulled askew, his eyes shadowed by the arc lights behind him. In the same instant she saw him, the lights went out, to be replaced by flashlights wielded by men in uniforms.

Ginny felt arms slipped under her, turning her over, raising her head.

"I'm all right," she gasped. "I think."

"We'll get you looked at," someone said. "Come on."

"Ms. Hawkins—"

"We'll take care of her, too."

Ginny was hauled to her feet and supported into the elevator, then out again on the ground floor, into the ER, and straight into Jim's arms.

"Bring her in here."

In no time flat Ginny was bundled into the big scanner used to locate foreign objects in trauma victims. When Jim was sure she had not been hit by a bullet, he let her get dressed again, but would not let her go back to her floor. She sat in his office, wrapped in blankets, shivering.

"Drink this."

The coffee was warm between her hands, but he had to help her hold the mug still enough to drink from it. When she had managed to swallow half a cup, she pushed it away.

"Jim, can you get Himself down here?" she asked.

The Laird must have been nearby for he and DeSoto were there in five minutes. The Laird pulled up a chair and sat down, facing her. "Now, lass, tell us."

She took a deep breath, hiding her still shaking hands in the folds of the blankets. "It was an ambush."

Jim's face seemed to solidify into something harder than granite. DeSoto's registered a grim satisfaction. The Laird's did not change, though the shadows deepened. "Go on."

"It was supposed to be me, and it was Marjorie Hawkins who arranged it." Ginny explained about the Rudolph nose and how the Head Nurse had reacted when she found Ginny had given it to Lisa. "When she saw the red nose wasn't going to work, she hauled me over to the edge of the roof."

"What happened next?" DeSoto asked.

"I thought she was trying to push me off. I was fighting, trying to twist away. I slipped and fell."

"And in that moment, the shooter put a bullet in her heart. Interesting." DeSoto's phone went off and he stepped away to take the call.

Ginny turned to Jim. "What about Lisa? Is she dead?"

"She's in surgery. She had a stroke."

Ginny blinked. "A stroke? Not a gunshot?"

"No bullet wound."

Ginny fell silent, trying to make sense of it. Marjorie Hawkins clearly intended for the shooter to kill the woman wearing the red nose, but he hadn't aimed at Lisa, not for the first shot, anyway. If he had, she'd be dead.

DeSoto turned back to face them.

"Did you catch him, the shooter?" Jim asked.

"We found the sniper nest, in a van parked on the roof of the garage across the street." DeSoto slid his phone into his pocket. "He left the gun, the brass, everything. Which means we won't find a thing on any of it."

"A pro."

DeSoto nodded. "He rappelled off the back of the building, leaving the ropes, so the odds are we won't be able to trace them either, then slipped away into the night. Which means we can't ask him who his target was."

"Can you tell anything from the trajectory?" Jim asked.

"We've got the forensic team on the roof mapping the scene, but with so many people in such a small area, it's going to be hard to draw any conclusions."

He turned to face Ginny. "Except that she pulled you away from the others, toward the shooter, then turned your back to him, to make a large, well-lit target."

Ginny looked at DeSoto. "You think it was me." And he'd missed putting a hole in her back only because she slipped on the ice.

"We can't rule out that possibility."

Ginny's mouth felt dry as cotton. "So, I might be shot at again."

Jim jumped to his feet. "Not if I have anything to say about it!"

"Peace, lad." The Laird of Lonach rose from his chair and faced DeSoto. "Things ha'e changed. You and I need tae talk."

The DEA agent nodded. "Give me a couple of hours."

The Laird nodded. "'Twill gi'e me time tae distribute the gifts. I'll find ye when I'm done."

When the other two had gone, Jim pulled Ginny into his arms. "I don't think I can stand another fright like this. Please tell me you'll stay out of the line of fire from now on."

Ginny nodded. "I intend to. But Jim—" She looked up at him. "I can't live like this. It has to stop, and if I need to help make that happen, I will."

He drew in a shuddered breath, pulling her closer. "I know," he whispered. "God, help me! I know!"

* * *

CHAPTER 39

Day 17 – Sunday morning, Christmas Day
Neuro ICU, Hillcrest Regional Medical Center

A few minutes after five a.m. on Christmas morning, Ginny slipped into the Neuro ICU and approached the desk.

"Lisa Braden."

"Room four."

Ginny let herself into the glass-walled room and sat down beside Isaac. He looked over at her, then went back to staring at the figure in the bed.

"How is she?" Ginny asked.

Isaac sucked in a breath. "Too soon to tell. They've induced a coma and put her in therapeutic hypothermia." He looked over at Ginny. "I've never heard of that. Does it make sense to you?"

Ginny nodded. "They're trying to protect her organs—to minimize the damage done by the blood loss."

"Oh." He fell silent.

"Isaac, you told me there was a reason why Lisa couldn't have murdered Phyllis, but you couldn't break confidentiality to tell me what it was. Can you tell me now?"

He gestured at the woman in the bed. "That's why."

Ginny looked at Lisa's still form, then back at Isaac. "I don't understand."

"We were warned. Any exertion could kill her." His face twisted and Ginny found herself listening in growing distress to the tale of the aneurysm. Isaac shook his head. "She couldn't have strangled that woman without killing herself."

"Why didn't you tell Detective Tran?"

"Lisa wouldn't let me." He looked at Ginny, the tears welling up and spilling down his cheeks. "When the gunman opened fire, I grabbed her and pulled her down with me. Too hard. She hit her head. That's why it ruptured. It's my fault."

Ginny reached over and laid her hand on his arm. "No. You're not responsible. Not for the gunman and not for the rupture. Put the blame where it belongs and hang onto the hope she'll make a full recovery."

He wiped his face with the back of his hand. "You think there's a chance?"

"There's always a chance. The surgeon got to her almost immediately, and we have some of the best people in Dallas right here." Ginny put her arm around his shoulders and gave him a squeeze. "You must take care of yourself, too. She's going to need you when she comes out of this."

Isaac nodded, his eyes back on Lisa.

Ginny let herself out, her mind churning. Lisa's bizarre behavior had an organic cause and she, Ginny, had never once considered the possibility. She felt sick at heart. Here was a patient, in mortal danger, terrified, and angry, and lashing out, and all of those behaviors were understandable, in context.

She made her way back to the Medical ICU, completed the end-of-shift chores, then met Jim in the ER. She didn't want to talk about the events of the night and he didn't press, just took her home and said he'd see her at the kirk.

Her mother was almost as restrained, but her mother knew her better. She gave Ginny a hug.

"Let me know, darling, when you're ready to talk."

Ginny nodded, then slipped upstairs. She fell onto her bed and closed her eyes, wishing she had a magic wand she could use to make the whole thing go away. But she didn't. And it wasn't over. And now she had Lisa on her conscience, too.

* * *

Sunday noon, Christmas Day
Forbes residence

It was just after noon on Christmas Day and Ginny couldn't help wishing she felt better. Between the assassination attempt, the police, and Christmas Communion, she had gotten only three hours of sleep. The kirk had been awash with kilts and tartan sashes and it always did her heart good to see the Scots all dressed up, but she was glad it was behind her. At this point, she was wedged into the corner of the sofa, trying to keep her eyes open.

As per tradition, the stockings had been dumped, Christmas dinner eaten (and was doing nothing to help her stay awake), and toasts made to the assembled company. The final step in the festivities was the tree and the gifts beneath it.

Even the attendance of little Luis didn't bolster her spirits. He sat among the packages, poking listlessly at them, his eyes dry, but his heart clearly not in the celebration. Ginny's conscience smote her. She should try harder to be cheerful, for his sake, if not for her own.

Jim was handing out the packages. "Here's one for you. From Santa."

She looked up to find him bending over her, smiling mischievously. She pulled herself upright and took it from him, glancing around to find everyone except Luis watching her.

Ginny tore off the wrapping paper and examined the outside of the box. No clue there, just plain brown cardboard. She pulled it open, then slid a smaller box out and ran an appreciative finger across the purple velvet. It had "Edinburgh" stamped on it in gilt letters. She flipped up the lid and caught her breath. Inside was a silver brooch. It was a penannular, with a Celtic knot design stretching from finial to finial and a pin that glided sweetly from one end of the curved shape to the other.

"Oh! It's lovely!" She looked up to find her mother smiling at her. "Thank you!"

Sinia Forbes shook her head. "It wasn't me, though I may have given Santa a suggestion or two."

Ginny turned next to Jim, but he shook his head as well. "Nope. Santa."

That just left the Laird. Ginny let her pleasure show. "Tell me about it."

"'Tis a reproduction o' a family piece. Th' original was made in 1650 by a craftsman in Edinburgh, in gold. 'Twas too soft, ye ken, fer wearing. It broke and was mended many times and ended in th' museum, but I've always thought 'twould make up well in silver. I'm glad ye like it."

Ginny rose and went over to give him a hug and a kiss. "I love it! I'll treasure it always." She took her seat again thinking it was absurd to feel better because of a piece of jewelry. She shouldn't be so shallow. But, on consideration, she realized it was the care that had gone into the selection and production and presentation of the gift that warmed her heart. She loved it because of the love that had gone into it.

When Jim finished passing out gifts, he came over and sat down beside her, wrapping an arm around her shoulders.

"When you wear it," he whispered, "you'll be wearing a piece of Mackenzie history."

THE SWICK AND THE DEAD

Ginny snuggled closer. "I want to hear all about it, but right now I wish we could do something for Luis. He looks so sad."

Jim sighed. "Yes, he does."

It had been a hard Christmas for Luis. In early September, he and his friend, Joey Kyle, had been cast as shepherds in the Christmas Pageant at their church. Luis even had a speaking part ("Look! A star!"). After Phyllis' death, the Kyle boy had appealed to his grandmother, and his family had decided to let him participate as planned. He had insisted Luis be included.

So, on Christmas Eve, Sinia Forbes, in the company of the Kyle family, had taken Luis to the Roman Catholic Children's Christmas Mass. He would have preferred Ginny, and said so, but she was not available so he had condescended to let Ginny's mother stand in.

Ginny had asked her mother to keep an eye on the crowd, just in case Maria Perez dropped in to watch her son perform, but Maria hadn't appeared. After church, Sinia had brought Luis home so he wouldn't be in an institution over Christmas.

Both the Forbes and the Mackenzies had showered Luis with gifts, given him his choice of foods, and let him dictate the video specials he wanted to watch, but it was clear what he really wanted was his mother.

He was rolling a bright red fire engine across the rug, making small siren noises when his head shot up. "Mama!" he shouted. "Mama!" He jumped to his feet and ran toward the kitchen.

"Mama!" he said. "It's Mama!" He grabbed a chair and dragged it over to the counter, climbing up on it and reaching for the cellphone that lay there.

Ginny had found the phone in Luis' backpack on the first day. For two weeks they had been keeping the battery charged, activating the device at intervals, in the hope that Maria Perez would pick up the call or reach out to her son.

Each time the recorded voice had said there was no service and each time the hope that Maria was still alive had faded a bit more.

"It's *her* music, when she calls me it's *her* music!" Luis had the phone now and had it to his ear. "¿Hola? MAMA!" He launched into an ecstatic, then tearful stream of Spanish much too fast for Ginny to understand. She exchanged wide-eyed looks with Jim, then reached for the phone.

"Let me talk to her, Luis." She gently pulled the phone away from the child's ear and brought her own down close to it.

"Maria? Don't hang up! We want to help you. Maria? Maria!" The line went dead.

Luis went into hysterics. Ginny pulled the boy into her arms and tried to console him, kissing him, and telling him how much his mother must love him, and how wonderful it was to hear from her. She did not tell the child that she was relieved beyond measure to know the woman was still alive.

"We're going to find her, Luis. I promise!" She handed the phone to Jim. "Can we trace the call?"

"We can try."

Ginny took Luis back into the living room and settled down with him, letting him cry himself out while Angus contacted the authorities. Unable to raise either DeSoto or Detective Tran, he left messages, and grudgingly allowed the call to be routed to the officer on duty at the police substation.

"Can't we just hand it to the patrol car out front?" Ginny asked.

Himself shook his head. "They've orders tae stay here and stay alert. We dinna want tae distract them."

Sinia smiled. "You should have told me that before I took turkey and dressing to the pair of them."

Himself looked at her and lifted an eyebrow. "Ah, weel. I suppose e'en th' constabulary must eat."

The officer on duty at the station was very polite and asked them to bring the phone in, at their earliest convenience, and not to use it in the meantime.

Jim snorted. "Like we would! What does he take us for?"

"He works with the public," Sinia said, "and he's probably seen his share of contaminated evidence."

"I suppose so." Jim picked up his coat. "I can drop the phone off on the way home." He turned to Sinia and took her hand, engulfing it between his own. "Thank you for your hospitality and for including me. I wasn't looking forward to a frozen dinner alone."

"That was never going to happen," she said. "You're family, Jim, and always welcome."

Jim gave her a hug, then pulled on his coat. He made eye contact with Ginny. "I'll see you tomorrow."

"And sae will I," said Angus, planting a kiss on Sinia's cheek, then Ginny's, "but first I've tae see a man aboot a dog. Happy Christmas!"

When the men had gone, Sinia turned to Ginny. "I'll take care of Luis. You go get some sleep."

Ginny kissed her mother, then gratefully retired to her bed. The discovery that Maria Perez was alive meant she had some thinking to do, when her brain started working again. As she drifted off, she sent a silent prayer heavenward, mingling thanks and entreaty. It was a modified version of one of the O Antiphons. "O Heavenly Father, source of all grace and wisdom, show me the path to knowledge and give me strength."

* * *

CHAPTER 40

Day 17 – Sunday afternoon, Christmas Day
Brochaber

Jim yawned widely, forcing himself to pay attention. They were back in his grandfather's kitchen, miscellaneous drinks on the table in front of them. DeSoto was on his right, Detective Tran on his left, his grandfather across the table from him. A stranger lounged in the corner, sipping coffee.

"You will understand," Detective Tran was saying. "Even Bob Cratchit got Christmas Day off." She was referring to the crime lab staff, not herself. "The lab will be open again at six a.m. tomorrow. We can start then."

"Will this trace be the priority?" DeSoto asked.

She made a sketchy shrug. "Among the priorities, I should think."

He nodded. "Okay. I'll see what I can do with the FBI lab. We need to find this woman, alive, if possible."

"What o' Hawkins?" the Laird asked.

Detective Tran answered. "A forensics team has been at her house all day, taking it apart. Her computers are missing, but we have her purse and cellphones. The most interesting item so far is a tracking device like the one found on Miss Forbes' car. With warrants, we should be able to reach the account, which may give us additional clues to her identity. All of this is delayed by the holiday, of course."

"Identity?" Jim asked.

Detective Tran nodded. "When we ran her fingerprints, we found a discrepancy. They match a woman wanted in connection with the disappearance of another nurse sixteen years ago."

Jim blinked, trying to focus. "Disappearance?"

"The missing woman failed to go to work one day, sending a letter of resignation to her employer. She is supposed to have packed up her belongings and moved, leaving no forwarding address."

"How does Hawkins figure into the story?"

"The missing woman was named Marjorie Hawkins. The fingerprints on our corpse belong to a woman named Eloise Quinn. Ms. Quinn was a nurse who lived in the same neighborhood as Hawkins. She had her license revoked permanently due to a series of narcotics-related deaths."

"Wow!" Jim said. "Why didn't this come to light sooner?"

"All of the police departments in Texas are in the process of digitizing their paper files and that includes the paper-and-ink fingerprint cards, but it is a slow process. There are millions of archived files to go through. No one had run a search on Hawkins' fingerprints since the latest update, until now."

Jim frowned. "I wish I'd known. If we hadn't decided to keep our suspicions about Hawkins from Ginny, she wouldn't have been on the roof with that woman."

"Weel, if naught can be done 'til th' morrow," the Laird rose to his feet, "I thank ye all fer comin' and wish ye' a happy Christmas." He escorted them to the front door, all but Jim and the stranger. When the Laird returned to the kitchen, he gestured the stranger into one of the empty seats, then turned to Jim.

"I've a mind tae offer ye a bed, lad. Ye've had nae sleep and yer yawning yer heid off."

"I want to know what else you've got up your sleeve."

"Aye, but 'twill wait. Go. Sleep. I'll fetch ye fer dinner."

Jim rose reluctantly and headed for the stair. He had a pretty good idea why the stranger was here. He'd seen a holster when the man reached for the sugar and cream. He considered trying to eavesdrop through the kitchen door, but the house was too well built for that. He gave in, made his way to the bedroom he always used when camping out in his grandfather's house, fell into bed, and closed his eyes. Whatever they were cooking up in that kitchen would still be there when he woke.

* * *

Sunday midafternoon, Christmas Day
Refugee camp

Grace made her way through the waning afternoon, out to the snow-covered campground. She had filled the car with Christmas gifts, mostly for the children, but also useful things for the adults, clothes and tools and canned food.

She pulled in across a patch of muddy slush and parked, climbing out of the car with a big Christmas smile on her face. This was what she loved, what made it all worthwhile. The children thronged around, demanding gifts and sweets. She passed them out, enlisting the help of a pair of adults, to make sure the treats were evenly distributed.

There were new faces among the refugees. She looked over the crowd of children, counting noses, and her heart sank. She didn't have enough. She swallowed hard, forcing her smile back into place. She'd spent every penny of her Christmas bonus and half her paycheck on this project. She reached into the car and pulled out the last of her purchases, handing them to the adults.

"No más. Lo siento, eso es todo."

The children crowded around her, vociferous in their disappointment.

"Lo siento. Lo siento mucho." She looked around at the crowd of people, all looking at her, all waiting for her to produce more: more food, more toys, more money.

"I'm sorry." She retreated to her car, pulling free of the many small hands that tried to prevent her going. She backed out, and drove away, the entreaties following her long after the camp was out of sight.

* * *

Sunday evening, Christmas Day
Forbes residence

Christmas supper was always a picnic at the Forbes house. It was frequently consumed in front of the media screen in the den, giving the family a chance to relax after a hard day of celebrating.

Ginny settled down in one of the wing chairs with her plate on her lap, and pulled up the evening news. She was hoping to hear something of the shooting on the rooftop and she was not disappointed. The station had acquired a video of Santa's arrival. There was dramatic footage of the helicopter approaching, and a man in a red suit with the snow swirling around him, then a violent disruption of the image.

"Mother! Come look," Ginny called. Sinia had made sure Luis had turkey and a glass of milk (actually at the table, to facilitate getting the food into him and not on the carpet) then prepared her own supper plate. She brought it into the den and sat down in the other wing chair.

Ginny backed up the image and played it from the beginning.

"He makes a lovely Santa Claus, doesn't he?" Sinia commented.

Ginny nodded. The reporter was explaining what they were seeing.

". . . one women shot dead in what appears to be an assassination . . . another in critical condition . . . both employed at the hospital . . ."

"There's Lisa," Ginny said, her voice somber. After a long enough pause for the reporter to tell all that was known about Lisa Braden, the image changed to Marjorie Hawkins.

"Señora Jefa," Luis said.

Ginny jumped. She hadn't heard Luis come in and had no idea he was watching. "What?"

"Señora Jefa." Luis had Seymour in one hand and a slice of turkey in the other. He held it out to the turtle, who retreated into his shell.

Ginny scrambled for the remote control, found it, then backed up the transmission to the Hawkins image.

"You know that woman, Luis?" she asked, pointing at the picture.

He glanced up at it, and nodded, then went back to trying to feed turkey to the turtle.

"Can you tell me about her?"

"She's a bad woman."

"What makes you say that?"

"She made my Mama cry."

"I'm sorry to hear that. Why was she crying?"

"I don't know." Luis put the turtle and the turkey down on the carpet and came over, crawling into Ginny's lap. "I want my

Mama!"

Ginny cuddled him, kissing his hair. "I do, too, Luis. We're going to find her. I promise."

When the boy went back to playing with the turtle, Ginny went to the phone. She left voice mail messages on Detective Tran's and Agent DeSoto's machines, describing Luis' revelation, then dialed Jim.

"When would Luis have seen Marge Hawkins?" he asked.

"His mother had to get those fake drugs from someone, and the blue envelope didn't go through the mail. That implies a face to face handoff, a dead drop, or both."

"Too bad he didn't see a picture of her before last night."

Ginny nodded into the phone. "If Luis is right and Marge Hawkins was connected to the Mexican Nurse Pipeline, that's another connection between the Pipeline and the cartel."

"Something to do with those fentanyl patches, you think?"

"It's possible, but I still can't figure out what they're doing with fakes. The real thing is so much more lucrative."

"We need to talk to Maria Perez," Jim said.

"Yes." Ginny sighed. "We do."

* * *

CHAPTER 41

Day 18 – Monday morning, Feast of Stephen
Forbes residence

Ginny drummed her fingers on the breakfast table, thinking hard. "What will lure a frightened woman out of hiding?"

"Her child, of course." Jim helped himself to another mound of scrambled eggs. "Where is Luis, anyway?"

"Back in the shelter." Ginny's brow furrowed, returning to her puzzle. "Normally, I'd agree with you, but Maria dumped him at the hospital and disappeared, which implies she thought he'd be safer away from her."

"But she called yesterday."

Ginny sighed at the memory of Luis sobbing himself to sleep. Maria alive and in hiding was better than Maria dead, but not much, for the child involved. "What did she say to him?"

Jim shook his head. "I don't know. All I heard was Luis' side of the conversation and my Spanish is only good enough to catch one word out of three. I think he was saying he wanted her to come home, or he wanted to go home."

Ginny nodded. "Well, at least she knows he's alive."

Jim settled back in his chair, nursing his coffee. "I wonder if we can use that to our advantage."

"How?"

"You told her we wanted to help. She might have heard you or she might not have."

"And she might not have believed me."

"Right. Here's my point. What she *did* hear was a frantic Luis. If she thinks we're not being nice to him, maybe she'll come to the rescue."

Ginny nodded slowly. "I would, if it were my child." She chewed on her lip. "So how do we contact her?"

"If the feds can trace that call, they can try following her."

"If she has any sense, she'll have ditched that phone. We need another way." Ginny's brow furrowed. "I think I have an idea, but I'm not sure it's a good one."

"Let's hear it."

"An Amber Alert."

Jim frowned. "Those public service announcements that tell the entire world a child is missing?"

"Yes, those. If Maria is within reach of a highway or a computer or a cellphone, she'll get the message."

"They're designed to enlist the public as extra eyes and ears. We don't want everyone looking for Maria, just us."

"I know. That's not what I had in mind. Maybe we can send a message to her. 'Call this number. Luis needs you.' Something of that sort."

"Get a secured line and have her call in, to arrange a rendezvous?"

"Yes."

Jim nodded slowly. "It might work, but she's going to think it's a trap."

"It *is* a trap. We want to catch her so we can put her in protective custody. It will have to be clear she must risk the trap to save Luis."

"We can't threaten that child. He's been through enough

already."

"I know that, but Maria doesn't, and she seems to have a pretty poor opinion of authority figures."

"It's worth a try." Jim rose and headed for the front door. He turned on the threshold. "Grandfather asked me to remind you to stay home today. He'll catch up with you this afternoon. And, if I may be allowed to make a suggestion, you look like you could use some more sleep."

She nodded. She hadn't been really injured in the assassination attempt, just spooked, but he was right that she needed sleep. *That* had been hard to come by. She watched Jim climb into his car and drive off, nodded to the policemen in the patrol car parked out front, then closed the door and headed upstairs.

* * *

Monday morning, Feast of Stephen
Forbes residence

Ginny set the phone down and leaned back in her chair. Detective Tran had been very cooperative. She could issue the Amber Alert, but she would need to know when and what to say. Whatever they arranged, it would need a point person, someone Maria would be willing to listen to. What people in her life might she trust?

Phyllis, obviously, since Maria dropped Luis at Hillcrest based on Phyllis' recommendation. Not the police, since she didn't go to them, which implied she had something to hide— or something to fear.

Did she run because of someone or something at her job? Luis had identified Marge Hawkins as a bad woman who made his mother cry. That meant Maria and Marge had been face to face at least once. But did Maria know Marge worked at Hillcrest? Would she have dropped her son off there if she had known?

Luis had also said the fentanyl patches were for his mother. Which made it sound like someone was giving Maria counterfeit drugs. The only place a nurse would use narcotic patches was on the job. (Unless she was a drug addict and wanted them to feed her own habit, in which case the fakes were worthless.) Maybe Maria was supposed to swap the fakes for the genuine narcotics. There was a thought!

If true and Luis had interrupted her supply, maybe Maria was in trouble. Would whoever was behind a scheme like that forgive Maria for misplacing an envelope full of fake drugs? Or would they make an example of her?

Ginny sighed. If Maria's job was tied to the fake drugs, and Maria believed losing an envelope full of them would get her or Luis killed, it was unlikely she would look to a coworker for help.

Nor family and friends. That would be the first place an enemy would look. The inhabitants of that apartment complex would close ranks against an outsider, but they would talk to one another, and among the other children would be an obvious place to look for Luis.

Who else would Maria have contact with? The school? Did Luis have play dates? What other mothers had Maria spoken to? Or Phyllis, for that matter. Ginny suddenly wondered if Detective Tran had asked any questions at Luis' school. She picked up the phone again, but this time she dialed John Kyle.

Ten minutes later she hung up the phone, having found out what school Joey Kyle attended, that the police had not asked John for that information, and that the school was still closed for the Christmas holiday, so it was unlikely that anyone had been interviewed by the authorities. Ginny moved to the computer.

The school, Mater Dolorosa Montessori, was attached both physically and metaphorically to the Roman Catholic Church of Mater Dolorosa. It appeared to be a large, prosperous parish. There were lots of children in the posted images.

Ginny's eyes narrowed. If Maria attended services at this church, which made geographic sense (based on the location of her apartment) and would explain why her child was enrolled there, and if she and the clergy followed traditional Roman Catholic practices, then she would obey instructions from her padre. He would be someone she would trust.

They would need the padre's cooperation, of course. Ginny looked up his name, tried calling, found all the phones on voice mail (it was the day after Christmas after all), then decided to drive over and see if she could find anyone to talk to.

She paused for a moment to consider her instructions to stay home. There was no one at the church who knew her, and it wouldn't take long. All she wanted was someone who would tell her how to reach Father Ignacio Allende on his day off.

It was probably a wild goose chase anyway. She would probably find the doors locked and the lights out. She might be wrong about where Maria attended divine service (if at all), and Father Ignacio might refuse to help.

She wrestled with her conscience for a moment longer, then scribbled a note to her mother, grabbed her purse, slipped out the back, and headed for Mater Dolorosa.

* * *

Monday midmorning, Feast of Stephen
Mater Dolorosa Roman Catholic Church

Ginny worked her way around the edifice, trying every door. She found the kitchen unguarded. There was evidence of clean-up in progress, but no one in sight. She set off into the main body of the church, poking her nose into a series of empty chapels and meeting rooms.

She turned a corner and found a charming little fountain, the water stilled because it was a holiday and no public should have been in that place, but the greenery was flourishing, and the sight that met her eyes delighted her soul. In the middle of the fountain, on a marble plinth, stood a carved statue of Saint Michael slaying the dragon. His face was beatific in repose, his consecrated strength undisputed. One hand held the sword, plunged into the throat of the beast. The other gestured toward heaven.

In the space between the white marble fingers and thumb of the hand indicating the seat of divine power was wedged a coin. Someone, probably a daring child, had braved the waters and climbed the plinth and left an offering to God.

Ginny dug a coin out of her purse and tossed it into the fountain, with a silent prayer for Maria and Luis. As if in answer, she heard the sound of a door opening. She turned and followed it.

She tapped on the open doorframe. "Excuse me. I'm looking for Father Ignacio, and I'm hoping you can help me."

The eyes that met hers were astonished and unfriendly.

"How did you get in?"

"Through the kitchen." Ginny watched the two men exchange an uneasy glance.

"We're closed. Come back tomorrow." Their English was intelligible, though obviously not their native tongue.

Ginny nodded. "I understand, but there is some urgency. I want to speak to Father Ignacio about a woman in trouble, and I was hoping you could tell me how to reach him at home."

"Confessions on Tuesday and Thursday. Make an appointment. Tomorrow."

Ginny shook her head. "I don't mean that kind of trouble. This woman is in danger for her life. We're hoping the padre can persuade her to trust us."

They both shook their heads. "We cannot help you."

Ginny looked at the implacable expressions on their faces and decided she would get no further with them. She sighed, apologized for the disturbance, and turned to go. As she did so, her eye fell on a pair of men coming down the corridor toward the office, one bearing a striking resemblance to the picture of Father Ignacio she had seen online.

She stepped into their path and waited to be acknowledged, her eye drawn automatically to the second man, seeing one shoulder higher than the other, and tentatively diagnosing it as scoliosis. She let the thought slip from her mind as he moved back the way he had come. She turned her attention to the priest.

The two men from the office hurried to get between her and her quarry. They spoke rapidly in Spanish and Ginny saw the padre frown, his eyes on her. She saw also that the two minions were frightened. They were apologizing, pleading, excusing themselves. She did not need to understand the language to read the message. With an impatient wave of his hand, he stopped them and sent them away, then approached her.

"Father Ignacio Allende?" She introduced herself, apologized for the intrusion, and described her errand. At first he was as unhelpful as his staff, but when she explained there was a child involved, one who needed to be reunited with his mother, Father Ignacio seemed to become interested. He invited her into his office.

"This child was abandoned at the hospital?"

"With a note from his mother saying she would be back, but we were beginning to be afraid she was dead."

"Why have you changed your mind?"

"She telephoned yesterday."

"She is alive, then."

"Or was, twenty-four hours ago." Ginny explained again how urgent it was to coax Maria Perez out of hiding so she could be protected from whatever it was that was threatening her. "Will you help us?"

Father Ignacio smiled and nodded. "Willingly, my child. What do you need from me?"

A half hour later, Ginny took her leave, convinced she had never met a more charming clergyman in her life. Once he grasped the situation, Father Ignacio could not have been more understanding, more full of useful suggestions, more concerned for his parishioner. Yes, Maria was one of his flock and *of course* she must be rescued. That's what a shepherd did.

Ginny got into her car and headed home. DeSoto first, then Tran would need to be notified and both would probably want to meet Father Ignacio, but it could work. If Maria would just cooperate, they could get her back and Luis back into her arms. Suddenly, the promise of Saint Michael's upraised hand seemed to reach out to touch the endeavor. With the Lord's help, he seemed to be saying, anything was possible.

* * *

CHAPTER 42

Day 18 – Monday noon, Feast of Stephen
Forbes residence

Ginny parked the car, let herself in, and made her way to the kitchen, following the voices.

"Hello!" She smiled at Himself, then at her mother, who rose and gave her a hug.

"Thank goodness! We had begun to worry."

Ginny looked from her mother to the Laird, then to the stranger seated at the kitchen table.

"Sit down, lass." The Laird indicated a chair.

Sinia Forbes kissed her daughter's cheek. "I have some Christmas presents to deliver. Call me if you need me." She headed for the garage.

Ginny took off her coat, then sat down facing the two men. She waited for Himself to begin.

"Ye disobeyed me. Ye've been oot by yerself."

Oh, so that was the problem. She nodded.

He leaned toward her. "Ye decided, on yer own, tae approach a man ye didna know, in a place ye've never been afore."

Ginny had been looking forward to telling everyone about her success. Now it looked as if she was going to be punished for her initiative. Her brows drew together. "I didn't realize I was under house arrest."

"I didnae realize ye would tak' such a chance, sae soon after Saturday nicht." He indicated the stranger. "This is yer second cousin, Fergus Stewart."

She turned her eyes on the other man and saw that he did resemble her mother, a bit.

"He's a *gallóglaigh* and here at my askin', tae keep ye frae bein' killed."

Ginny started at his words. "Is that really necessary?"

The Laird gave her a hard look. "Aye and ye owe it tae him and tae me tae do as he asks."

So far, the stranger hadn't said a thing. Ginny looked at him and frowned. Was he a guest here? Should he be treated as family? He looked hard as stone and disinclined to conversation.

"Second cousins means we share an ancestor."

The stranger nodded.

Ginny tried again. "Presumably that means my Stewart great-grandfather."

Again, he nodded.

She studied him for a moment. He was darker than her mother, with chestnut hair cut very short and hazel eyes that seemed to bore right into her skull. Good bones, clean lines, maybe a year or two younger than herself. Not a soft spot on him. She turned back to Himself.

"He's a bodyguard."

"Aye."

Ginny knew the history of the *gallóglaigh*. They were mercenaries from the west of Scotland, arising in the mid-thirteenth century, and famous for their expertise and courage. The modern version was armed differently, but of the same mettle.

"I assume there are rules of some sort."

The Laird nodded. "Yer tae stay home, wi' the doors locked. Stay awa fra th' windows. Tell no one where ye are or tha' there's a concern."

"How am I supposed to get to work?"

"Yer off th' schedule 'til further notice."

Ginny blinked. She knew Angus had a great deal of power where the hospital was concerned, but they were short two ICU nurses and she had expected to be needed at her post.

"'Twill gie ye a chance tae catch up on yer sleep."

Ginny felt a stab of irritation. She didn't need any more Mackenzie males telling her she looked tired, and this one wasn't even a physician. "Is Jim going to be treated the same way?"

"Yer no tae concern yerself aboot Jim. We'll see tae him as weel."

Ginny found herself frowning. "I need to speak to DeSoto."

"He'll come tae ye."

"And Detective Tran."

"The same, or ye may use th' phone."

"I thought my phone wasn't secure?"

"We've taken steps." The *gallóglaigh's* voice resonated with quiet strength.

Ginny looked over at the bodyguard. His eyes were fixed on her, as if memorizing her appearance, or estimating how hard his job was going to be. She addressed her next question to him. "For how long?"

Himself answered. "Until th' crisis is past."

Ginny swung toward the Laird. "That could be months, years! I will *not* go into hiding for the rest of my life."

"'Tis wha' ye've suggested fer Maria Perez and wee Luis. Why them an' no yerself?"

"You know perfectly well why. Maria knows something. I

don't."

The Laird leaned back in his chair, the corner of his mouth twitching. "If I were th' cartel, I'd no believe it. Yer a nosy, interfering woman, and ye ha'e a history wi' th' police."

Ginny felt her cheeks flush, but Angus Mackenzie had been the Laird of Lonach all her life. He knew his charges better than they knew themselves. She conceded the point.

"I can't leave the house?"

Himself shook his head.

"At all?"

She saw the Laird exchange glances with the bodyguard.

"If th' need arises, we'll deal wi' it then." He rose from his chair. "I'll leave the twa o' ye tae get acquainted." He pulled on his Inverness cape, picked up his walking stick, and turned to face Ginny. "Ha'e ye any further questions?"

"Not at the moment."

His eyes lingered on her face, no doubt remembering every rebellious moment she'd ever had in her life. "I'll expect a good report o' ye, Ginny Forbes," he said.

She had risen when the Laird did and stood facing him, unhappy with the strictures, but knowing she would obey to the best of her ability. She took a breath, then curtsied as she'd been taught to do. "Aye, Mackenzie."

He nodded, then let himself out. Ginny stood where she was for a full minute, thinking about the scene on the hospital rooftop, then sighed, turned to the *gallóglaigh*, and addressed him. "Well, Cousin Fergus, where do we begin?"

* * *

Monday afternoon, Feast of Stephen
Brochaber

Jim put down his professional journal and picked up the phone, smiling as he recognized Ginny's number. "Hello!"

"Jim! Come rescue me!"

He sat up abruptly. "What's wrong?"

"I'm trapped in my own house."

Jim relaxed. "Oh, is that all?"

"All? Is that ALL? Do you have any idea how boring it is to sit and stare at the walls—and *don't* tell me to sleep. I can't."

"Where's your mother?"

"Out making Christmas calls and I wish I was with her."

"And your *gallóglaigh*?"

"You know about that, do you?"

Jim nodded into the phone. "Grandfather introduced me."

"Do you have one?"

"No."

"Then jump in your car and come get me."

"I'm not going to do that, Ginny. First, because I've promised not to, and second, because I like the idea of you safe at home until this is resolved."

"Then at least come over and entertain me."

Jim shook his head. "Can't do that, either."

"Why *not*?"

Jim couldn't help laughing at her tone of voice. "Because I'm not at home, either. I'm in residence at Grandfather's until this is over."

"Oh! So, house arrest for you, too."

"Sort of, only I have to go to work. Tell me about your cousin."

"I can't! I can't get him to talk to me. He's spoken eight words—I counted them—since he got here. Might as well be a brick wall."

Jim smiled. A bodyguard who couldn't be drawn into idle conversation sounded like a good thing. "Let him do his job, Ginny. Speaking of which, have you talked to DeSoto?"

"Yes. Did Himself tell you about my visit to Father Ignacio this morning?"

"You figured that out all by yourself?"

"Don't be snide. It was an obvious thing to try, once I eliminated all the other possibilities."

"The thing that sets you apart, Virginia Forbes, is how logical your mind is. It's most unwomanly."

"There you go, sneering at me again. I have half a mind to hang up on you."

"Don't do that! I promise I'll be nice. Tell me what DeSoto said."

Jim listened for the next twenty minutes to a description of Ginny's report to Agent DeSoto, his suggestions on how to set up the trap, Detective Tran's contributions, and a long string of things that could go wrong with the scheme.

"And the worst of it is, I can't go."

"It would be foolish to risk you. A female agent will do the job much better. I'm sure they've got one fluent in Spanish."

"Maybe so, but I wanted to see Luis' face when his mother appears. I promised we'd find her. I want to make good on that promise."

Jim felt his heart melt. "I know."

"Besides, all we expect is that Maria will try to sneak into the church, grab Luis, then sneak out again."

Jim shook his head. "No, what we expect is that the cartel will see our message to Maria, realize what it means and come prepared to kill her on sight. There's quite likely to be gunfire." Jim heard Ginny sigh.

"It's just so frustrating to be stuck here while all the action is going on somewhere else."

"How are you coming with the murder investigation? Have you figured out who killed Phyllis, yet?"

"The front runner is Marjorie Hawkins, but now that she's dead, I don't know how we're going to prove it."

"Can I help?"

"Not if you can't do errands for me. I can make my own telephone calls."

"If you need something, let me know and I'll run it past Grandfather."

"Okay." There was a pause. "Jim?"

"Yes?"

"You'll be careful? At work?"

"Of course, and DeSoto still has agents on my tail, so I'm not without help if I need it."

"Okay. Wish me luck with Cousin Fergus."

"You let him do his job!"

"Oh, I will, but I'm going to get more than eight words out of that man if it's the last thing I do!"

"Ginny—"

"Bye!"

Jim hung up the phone, a half smile on his face. That she sounded more like her old self again was a good thing. That she had decided to force the bodyguard to talk probably wasn't. Jim wished he could be a fly on the wall watching her try. Stubborn as Ginny was, Cousin Fergus had struck him as more so. It would be interesting to see who won that battle.

* * *

CHAPTER 43

Day 18 – Monday afternoon, Feast of Stephen
Ginny's residence

Ginny set down the phone feeling frustrated. She wandered over to the window and peeked out, being careful not to disturb the blinds. The *gallóglaigh* had spent the afternoon inspecting the house, making adjustments both inside and out, behaving almost as if she wasn't there.

"Step back from the window."

Ginny started, turning guiltily to find the man also moved like a cat, silent even on the staircase, which should have creaked to warn her of his approach. She stared at him, breathing hard, then moved to her computer and sat down, pulling up the genealogy files.

"Fergus Stewart." She dug into her database, but ten minutes of searching failed to find the man who stood absolutely still, absolutely silent in the doorway. She turned to face him.

"What am I overlooking?"

He lifted an eyebrow, but did not answer. She turned back to her machine.

"Starting with the shared ancestor, James Edward Stewart, my mother's grandfather, I find three boys and two girls. Of the three boys, the eldest died without male heirs. The second is my mother's father, my grandfather, Alasdair Stewart. The third is his youngest brother, Donald Mor Stewart." Ginny looked over at the *gallóglaigh*. "Your grandfather."

A nod.

Her eyes narrowed. "Mor, in Scots, means 'great.' I never met him. Was he a great man?"

"He was."

"What made him great? He wasn't christened 'Great,' was he?" She saw the man's mouth twitch.

"He weighed nine pounds at birth."

"Oh!" Well, that made sense. A baby that big might impress his mother as being worthy of the epithet. Ginny turned back to her files. "Donald Mor Stewart had three sons, John Edward, Alasdair Mor, and Donald Brian. Which of them was your father?"

"John Edward."

Ginny focused on John Edward Stewart. "No Fergus here." She spent another fifteen minutes sifting through the online databases, looking for a link, finding nothing. She swung around and faced the *gallóglaigh*. "If you're an imposter, Himself will have to be told."

The man smiled at her, then turned his back and went downstairs. Ginny frowned. Neither Himself nor her mother could make a mistake on a family connection so close to Sinia Stewart Forbes. There was a secret there, and he wasn't telling, and the others might not know.

Ginny crossed to the window again, in defiance of orders, but lingered for only a moment, then retreated into the center of the room. Her eyes ranged over the four walls and came to rest on a photograph of herself at one of the Scottish Country Dance Balls. It was full dress. She was in a floor-length ball gown of dark green velvet with her Forbes tartan flying behind her as she turned. Her partner was in dress kilt, complete with lace jabot, and looked good enough to eat. The next Tartan Ball was this Friday, followed promptly by the Hogmanay celebrations on Saturday night.

Ginny's eyes narrowed. She was *not* going to miss those parties! Even if she had to bring down the drug cartel by herself, she was NOT going to be locked up this weekend!

She metaphorically rolled up her sleeves, and went back to work. If the only way to be free was to do the professionals' job for them, then she'd better get busy. There was a lot to be done and not a lot of time left to do it in.

* * *

Monday evening, Feast of Stephen
Grace Edward's Residence and beyond

"NO! I'm sorry. I didn't mean to shout at you, but I can't come in tonight. You'll have to find someone else to cover for Ginny." Grace Edwards shook her head at the phone. "Personal business. No, I can't move it. Look, I'm sorry, but I CAN'T. Goodbye."

She hung up the phone wondering if they dared fire her. It wasn't as if she was just hanging around, doing nothing. She had to meet her supplier, then take the drugs to the *curandera*.

It would be full dark in another twenty minutes. She had just enough time to wolf down a sandwich, then get in the car and get over to the rendezvous point.

An hour later she was headed back, the precious drugs in the special bag she used for such things. It already had the rest of the items they would need: chemo gloves, IV supplies, antihistamine, antiemetic, more fluids. The latest supplies had been 'liberated' from the Hillcrest Medical ICU stock. She would have to find a way to replace them, but the need was great and urgent and the hospital could afford to lose one or two things. They could consider it a charitable donation.

She drove slowly along the narrow street, giving the neighborhood ample opportunity to look her over and identify the car. Just as she was about to run out of paved surface, a shadowy figure detached himself from a tree and sauntered over. She slowed to a stop, then reached up, and turned on the inside light, so he could see her clearly. He looked, then gestured for her to park the car and get out.

"Por aquí."

She followed him across the yard, along a dry creek bed, and into the shelter of a dense stand of old oaks. A few minutes walking brought her into the presence of a very old farm house. She hadn't been here before, and it was a mark of respect that she was being allowed to see this place. Her guide held the ancient door open for her.

She stepped inside and looked around. There was no electricity. Propane lanterns hung from hooks in the ceiling, and a log fire burned in the massive stone fireplace. A line of camp stoves were in use, making stew or soup, and boiling water for drinking. She'd taught them that. Texas wasn't a hot bed of dysentery, but the water still needed to be treated if it wasn't coming from the approved water supply.

"He is over here."

The *curandera* took her hand and led her to a pallet in the corner of the room.

The boy's eyes, dark in their sunken sockets, studied her without interest. The skin across his cheeks looked paper thin and taut and pale. Dehydration, she thought, and malnutrition. Probably, he couldn't keep anything down. A woman lay beside him, her arms around the child.

They had hung discarded curtains around the makeshift

bed, in an effort to make the corner warm for the child. The *curandera* placed her palms together and dipped them in Grace's direction. "Gracias. Thank you for coming."

Grace handed over her bag. "This has everything you will need. I've included written instructions, in Spanish, so you will know how to administer the medication." The old woman had started an IV before, with Grace watching, so she knew how. "Just follow the directions." She smiled at the boy's mother. "Rezaré por ti."

The woman kissed the child's head, murmured something to him, then climbed to her feet and came over. She grasped Grace's hand and kissed it. The *curandera* translated.

"She says, you are a good woman and she thanks you."

"Please tell her I'm happy to do what I can."

The healer nodded. "I am happy, too, that you are here." She held the bag out toward Grace. "I cannot do this. You must."

Grace tried to back away. "No. I got you the drugs. I can't do more."

The old woman caught her eye and held it. The fire glowed in the black depths of her gaze and Grace found herself unable to turn away.

"You are the *enfermera*. It is you who must save this child."

Grace tried again to make an excuse, to break away and escape this painful scene. "Take him to the hospital. That's your best hope."

The old woman shook her head. "They will take him and send us back." She held out the bag again. "You are the *enfermera entrenada*. It is you who must give the drug that will save his life."

Grace looked at the child on the bed. He was barely breathing. "It may kill him."

The mother gathered her son into her arms once more,

then looked up at Grace and spoke, the *curandera* translating.

"She says, she understands, and if it is God's will that he die, then that is God's will. But at least you will have tried." She held the bag out again.

Grace stood motionless, trying not to see the child, or the tears in his mother's eyes, or feel the weight of her vow to serve the sick wherever she might find them. Very slowly she reached out her hand and took the bag, then moved over next to the pallet and went down on her knees. She held out her arms to the mother. "Give him to me."

* * *

CHAPTER 44

Day 19 – Tuesday midmorning, Third Day of Christmas
Eternal Care Cemetery, Dallas

In the dead of winter, the dead, if they knew what was good for them, headed to Texas. Here the trees still rustled in the wind and lawns were green and winter roses bloomed. On this particular winter day, the weather was mild, with a soft breeze, azure sky, and blindingly white clouds billowing towards Heaven.

The population of the largest cemetery in north Texas had just grown by two. Lisa had succumbed on Christmas Day, quietly, in no pain and with no struggle.

It was Texas, so there were still many square miles of undeveloped land where one could plant a dead relative, but it was no longer legal. One had to go through channels and there weren't so many businesses devoted to dying as there once had been.

Therefore, Lisa Braden and Marjorie Hawkins (*née* Eloise Quinn) were both here, enjoying the weather and the impressive number of mourners assembled to say goodbye. By a quirk of fate, they would lie close to one another and, though the number of friends and family for Marjorie could be counted on the fingers of a man with no hands, the number of the curious was much greater.

Lisa, of course, had the usual turnout, supplemented by her own fame as the victim of a tragic accident, or mistake, or whatever it was, on Christmas Eve, no less, on the roof of the hospital, right here in Dallas.

Ginny had put on her little black dress and the sober jewelry she reserved for such occasions, and allowed the Mackenzies (and Cousin Fergus) to escort her to the graveside service. Lisa was unchurched and her memorial service had taken place on the grounds of the cemetery. Marjorie Hawkins was unclaimed and had been taken in, as an act of charity, by an ecumenical service held in the hospital chapel. Nice enough, but the real show was here.

Ginny looked around, estimating the crowd. The media was out in force, and so were the crowds of onlookers. Ginny didn't really object to strangers at funerals. It was something all mortals had in common. All would die and all were curious about it. She objected to the snickering, though. They should at least pretend to behave.

Lisa's family was genuinely bereaved. Funny how one didn't even think about the people who shaped the people one knew. A co-worker or a classmate was just that, no more. The extended families were invisible. But it was the extended family, especially the parents and grandparents, that resulted in the person you knew, with their manners and attitudes and opinions. Adolescent rebellion aside, every human being was the result of his heritage.

Ginny stood among the Hillcrest staff, flanked by Jim and Himself, Fergus prowling the edges of the crowd. Most of the night shift was here. They tended to bond over the midnight coffee and crises. Grace was missing. So, come to think of it, was Isaac. Odd.

She pulled her mind back to the draped coffins. The service

was starting. Ginny shivered and Jim slipped his arm around her. How close she had come! It could so easily have been her they were burying.

Instead, poor Lisa, ill and frightened and alienated from those who could have helped her, lay in the nearer coffin. It would be a long time before Ginny forgave herself for the ill will she had felt toward Lisa Braden.

In the farther coffin lay the liar, the one who had killed sixteen years before and stolen her victim's identity. She had fooled them all for years and might have gone on much longer had not Phyllis decided to study nurse imposters.

If Ginny was right, Hawkins had killed Phyllis to make sure her secret remained a secret. But with her death died any chance of a confession. Neither Ginny nor Detective Tran had the solid evidence necessary to put the guilt to rest with the body.

Ginny frowned. She hated unfinished business and this case looked to be already cold, the solution to the puzzle buried six feet deep and no way to dig it up again.

* * *

Tuesday noon
Forbes residence

Ginny heard the doorbell from her seat in the kitchen. She listened as Fergus opened to Himself and Agent DeSoto. "We'd like tae speak tae Miss Ginny, if ye'll allow."

She rose at the Laird's entrance.

"Ginny Forbes, I require yer assistance."

She nodded.

"It seems wee Luis willnae set foot outside th' shelter withoot ye. No even tae go tae his mither."

Ginny blinked. "I thought you were using an agent to escort him."

DeSoto answered. "That was the plan, but the boy won't cooperate." He scowled. "I can't have a hysterical child at the rendezvous, but if his mother doesn't see him, she won't come close enough for us to catch her. He needs to be there, and he needs to be kept quiet. Can you do it?"

Ginny looked from the Laird, to the DEA agent, then turned to Fergus. "Is it permitted?"

Before he could reply, there was a violent disturbance on her doorstep. The bell was rung repeatedly and she could hear a fist hammering, then a voice. "Let me in!"

The Laird's eyes drifted toward the ceiling, then he nodded. Fergus went to go unlock the door and admit a furious Jim Mackenzie.

He strode over to Ginny, then stood, fists clenched, looking down into her face. She could see fear in his eyes. He spoke without preamble.

"We talked about this. It's too dangerous."

"Wha told ye, lad, tae come here?"

Jim turned to face his grandfather. "Rose MacGregor called me when she couldn't get you on the phone. She explained what was going on."

Himself pulled out his phone and frowned down at it. "Th' battery's deid." He shook his head and slipped the device back in his pocket. "Weel, ye would hae found oot eventually. Speak yer piece."

Jim turned back to Ginny. "I don't want you anywhere near that church."

"I know."

"You'll be a sitting duck. All they have to do is bring in another sharpshooter."

"I know."

He reached out and put his hands on her arms, lowering his voice. "I have already been subjected to the lecture on how a laird must put the good of his people over the wishes of his own heart, but you won't do the clan any good if you're dead. And this cause is none of ours. Not Homestead. Not our people."

"Are you suggesting I break my promise to Luis?"

"All you promised was to find his mother. You didn't promise to die for him."

"He won't go without me and we need him to draw Maria out."

"She'll come no matter who's with him. They don't need you."

"Luis does."

"Why are you being so stubborn about this?"

Ginny sighed, then reached up and laid a hand on Jim's cheek. "You already know the answer to that. Because it's the right thing to do."

* * *

Tuesday midafternoon
Mater Dolorosa Roman Catholic Church

It was midafternoon on the Third Day of Christmas and, true to its nature, the Texas sun streamed through the clerestory windows, caught the dust motes, and turned them to powdered gold. Ginny watched as they drifted over the gallery rail, glittering as they sank toward the stone floor. Some completed the journey and were at peace. Some drifted out of the sun and were lost. Some caught a rising column of air and rode it back to the rafters, returning to darkness and dust.

Closer to earth, the sun pierced the jeweled panels and

brought forth the promise of resurrection. The stained-glass saints glowed on the flagstones, their colors as rich as their stories. Ginny's eye lingered on the familiar images, her mind on the never-ending struggle between good and evil.

She and Luis were in the back pew of the main sanctuary at Mater Dolorosa, tucked into a corner of the nave with a stone wall behind and another flanking them. She could hear the wind forcing its way past the edges of the massive west portal. The doors had been shut for this meeting, but the building was old and drafty, and it was the last week of December. She pulled the little boy closer.

Luis looked up. "Is she coming?"

"I hope so." Ginny gave the child a squeeze.

She looked around the cavernous space. There were DEA and FBI agents hidden in a dozen places, and police outside, under cover, waiting to close the trap once Maria was inside. They were prepared to wait all day, but Father Ignacio had specified a time and left the lights on so Maria could see her son when she arrived. The padre was waiting too, on his knees in front of the high altar, no doubt praying for a peaceful resolution to this dangerous plan.

Ginny could feel the cold creeping into her bones. If this went on much longer, she would be too stiff to move when the need arose. She stretched a bit, rolling her shoulders and head, then abruptly forgot her discomfort. She could hear the sound of the narthex doors being pushed open. Someone was coming in.

She put her hand over Luis' mouth, gesturing to him to be absolutely silent, then held him still, watching the strangers enter the nave and make their way up the main aisle toward the sanctuary, their footsteps echoing on the stone floor. Father Ignacio made the sign of the cross, rose from his prayers, then turned and came forward to greet them.

It wasn't Maria. It was a trio of men, the one in front wearing a heavy leather jacket and a crimson scarf. He walked toward the priest, seeming relaxed and sure of himself. He was accompanied by one of the policemen and another man, this one a professional of some sort. Ginny looked at all three figures as they advanced up the aisle and wondered what was niggling in the back of her brain. To her knowledge she'd never seen any of the three before.

The policeman spoke to Father Ignacio, appearing to introduce both men, then returned the way he had come. The second man, the professional, took a portfolio from under his arm, opened it, removed a sheaf of papers, and handed them to the priest. Ginny watched as Father Ignacio produced a pair of reading glasses from his pocket, put them on his nose, then held the documents under one of the altar lamps.

He took his time, turning the pages over slowly, asking questions. Ginny could see he was stalling and could see the first man growing impatient. The second laid a soothing hand on his sleeve. At length Father Ignacio sighed, nodded, and returned the papers. The second man, the one with one shoulder slightly higher than the other, put the papers away, then all three men turned to face the back of the nave, their eyes searching, finding, fixing on her and the child in her lap.

* * *

CHAPTER 45

Day 19 – Tuesday afternoon
Mater Dolorosa Roman Catholic Church

Jim's heart was beating as fast as if he had run up three flights of stairs. He cursed himself for a fool and peered out from behind the reredos, watching the scene unfold.

The sacred space in which he hid was fronted by a magnificent example of the sculptor's art. The massive gold cross drew the eye upward and served as a focal point for the rapture of the marble angels that surrounded it.

Jim did not share the angels' sentiments.

It had been the hostage negotiator's idea to put Ginny and Luis in that corner. It had solid walls on two sides and was tucked up under the loft staircase, which shielded them from casual view, and anyone approaching them would be seen, so they would have plenty of warning. But it also meant they had no easy escape route. To be free to run, they would have to slide to the end of the row and out into the main aisle, or crawl under the pews and wiggle out that way.

When the three humans on the other side of the altar turned to face the rear of the church, Jim felt goose-flesh rise on the back of his neck.

"I'm going with them," he whispered, but found his

grandfather's hand on his arm.

"Ye'll stay put 'til told ye may move."

Jim turned to look at his grandfather. Even in the dim light he could see the determination in the Laird's eye. He tried to explain. "We have no idea what's going on. She may need help."

"There's a score o' special forces round th' kirk. Let them do their job."

"But—"

"Haud yer wheesht, lad! I'll no hazard th' both o' ye."

Jim subsided, turning his eyes back to the trio headed toward the far corner. Ginny had apparently come to the same conclusion he had. She'd scooted all the way over to the aisle and was climbing to her feet, blocking access to Luis.

Jim watched Father Ignacio speak to Ginny, and her wary attention. She looked from one man to the other, then was handed the same papers Father Ignacio had examined. Even from here Jim could see her frown, then a half shake of her head, then puzzlement and a question. She was answered, but not to her satisfaction.

Jim felt a growing unease as he watched. He knew that look. He could tell from her expression and the way she held her head she wasn't going to cooperate. Father Ignacio waved the strangers off and spoke to Ginny in private for a moment, then drew her aside, allowing the man in the jacket to start down the pew toward Luis.

"What's this?" Himself asked.

The man had settled down in the pew facing Luis, speaking to him. The boy had backed up against the wall, almost disappearing from Jim's view as he tried to hide from the stranger.

"What's going on?" DeSoto had come up quietly behind them and was peering around their shoulders.

"No idea," Jim answered him. "Any news on Maria?"

"Nothing so far."

"Who's the man?"

"According to the police, *that* is Luis' father."

"Auch! Is't true?"

DeSoto shrugged. "He told the policeman he came to take his son home and showed him a birth certificate. I assume those papers he's been waving around give him the legal right to claim his abandoned child."

Jim frowned. By dropping her son off at Hillcrest and disappearing, Maria had given the State of Texas both the right and the responsibility to take the child and care for him as it saw fit. Unfortunately, this happened often enough that there were well-established guidelines for custody disputes across the Texas-Mexico border.

"Ginny is not going to like that."

"Apparently, neither does th' bairn." Angus nodded at the corner where the small drama was playing out.

The man who claimed to be Luis' father had taken the child's arm and started to pull him toward the aisle. Up to this point, the voices had been too low to be more than a murmur. Now Jim could hear the boy whining. He watched as Luis tried to pull free. Ginny, too, could be heard, arguing with Father Ignacio, the pitch rising as well as the volume. The third man had retired to the back of the church and pulled out his cell phone.

Señor Perez had made it to the aisle, pulling Luis behind him. The boy was screaming now, crying, in Spanish, but the meaning was clear to everyone watching. They were headed for the door when Luis started shrieking, "Mama! *Mama!*"

Jim caught the motion out of the corner of his eye and turned to see Maria Perez running along the aisle, dodging pews and stone columns. She was calling to Luis, "Ven, Luis.

Ven a mamá." She gestured for Luis to come to her.

Luis was struggling in the man's grip. As Jim watched, Ginny turned from Father Ignacio and lunged at the interloper. There was a collision. Maria flung herself toward her son and, in the same moment, Jim saw Perez straighten up and raise his right hand. The bullet hit Maria in the abdomen and she jerked backwards. Jim was out of hiding and running toward her before she hit the ground.

* * *

Ginny saw Maria pelting down the aisle toward Luis and responded without thinking. Law or no law, the desperate mother of that terrified child should have the right to hold her son. Ginny lunged, slamming into Señor Perez and knocking him into the pew. It threw him enough off balance that he loosened his grip on Luis.

"Let go of that boy." Her voice came out calmer than she had expected.

"I'll do as I please with my son."

"If he's yours, let him go to his mother."

"She, too, is mine, to do with as I please." He was on his feet again, the struggling Luis in one hand, the other drawing a weapon out of his pocket. He aimed the gun at Maria, and pulled the trigger.

"No!" Father Ignacio started toward Perez.

Perez turned the gun on the priest. "I don't wish to kill you, Padre, but I will if I have to."

"Put the weapon down, my son. This is a house of God. It is sacrilege to threaten a priest."

The corner of Perez' mouth turned up in a sneer. "A man of God? Is that what you call yourself?" He pulled the trigger.

The exchange gave Ginny the chance she needed. She

dropped her shoulder and rammed Perez, who staggered, losing his grip on the boy.

"Luis! Run!"

There was more gunfire erupting, the sounds echoing eerily in the vault above her head. Out of the corner of her eye, Ginny saw Jim kneeling over Maria and Angus scooping up Luis and heading for cover. Men were appearing from the woodwork, but she didn't have time to sort them out. Perez was turning his weapon on her.

She was too close. There was no way he could miss at this range. She stepped in, grabbed the front of Perez's jacket and brought her knee up as hard as she could between his legs, then grabbed his gun hand and twisted the weapon against his thumb, forcing him to let go. She heard the pistol clatter to the floor. He howled, then swore, wrenching his hand loose and reaching for something she couldn't see.

She let go and turned, intending to run, but he grabbed her hair, forcing her head back, a knife coming around from behind her and settling under her left ear. She knew enough to fall backward, against him, so that he landed on his tailbone on the edge of the pew, the knife sliding across the front of her neck as he did so. She felt blood running warm down her front, but ducked under his arm, and attacked again, intent on forcing him to drop the knife. The agents were closing in. All she had to do was keep the man occupied until they got here.

Perez regained his feet and came at her, swearing in Spanish. She caught his knife arm in both hands, deflecting the blow, but knowing he was stronger and she wouldn't be able to control him for long.

They were in the main aisle, with Ginny's back to the pews. Perez hauled his arm free and raised it, aiming the knife at her chest. She braced her hands on the wood behind her and kicked out at his leg, then lunged sideways, seeing his right knee buckle. He fell forward, hands scrambling to break his fall and landed, neck first, on the heavy wooden edge of the pew. Narrow, solid, impassive. There was an odd, choking sound, then he slid to the floor.

"Down! Get down!"

Ginny couldn't tell who was shouting, but the sound of a bullet smacking into the pew behind her made her turn. There was a man with a gun standing in the transept, pointing his weapon at her. As she watched, he fell to the floor, but there was another behind him. She dropped and rolled under the pew.

She lay on the floor, eye to eye with Señor Perez. He appeared to be having trouble breathing. He had his hands up, trying to pull his collar open, his eyes bulging.

Ginny swore to herself. She'd seen that look before. She rolled out from under the pew and knelt beside her attacker. A quick assessment told her he'd hit his Adam's apple when he fell. His airway was swelling and, without an emergency tracheotomy, he wouldn't last ten minutes.

Ten minutes. It didn't take her nearly that long to consider rolling back under the pew and slipping out the other side, leaving him to his fate. But there were those stained-glass saints watching. If she didn't even *try* to save this wretched man's life, which side of the battle would that put her on?

Perez had dropped the knife in his fight to breathe. Ginny slithered over and picked it up. She knew the theory of an emergency tracheotomy—make a hole so air can get in—but she'd never done one. This was Jim's department. She looked around, but couldn't see him. She handled artificial airways at work though, and knew where to look for an undamaged portion of the trachea.

She brought the knife up and saw her patient's eyes grow huge. He caught her wrist and tried to fight, but hypoxia was robbing him of his strength. She pushed the knife down, then through the flesh, then between the cartilage rings. There was an unpleasant spurt of blood accompanied by gurgling sounds and red froth, which meant she'd accomplished her goal, however inexpertly, but what *was* she going to use to hold that artificial airway open? In a fit of (probably) divine inspiration, she pulled the clip out of her hair and stuck it in the hole she had made. It was an ornamental twist of plastic with decorative pierce work. Perfect for letting oxygen molecules slip through.

"What the *hell* are you doing?"

Ginny looked up to find Jim dropping down beside her. "He fractured his larynx when he fell. He needed a trach." She sat back and watched as Jim assessed the situation. He looked up and their eyes met.

"Not bad, but I think you should let me take responsibility for this."

"No one is going to believe you could make such a mess of an emergency tracheotomy."

He shrugged. "No tools, just a killer's knife and a quick-thinking nurse with a handy hair clip." His eyes narrowed. "Is that his blood or yours?"

"A little of both, I should think." Her hands were covered in gore and there was blood on her clothing.

Jim moved over and took a look at where the blade had left its mark on her neck. "He did this?" He was frowning.

Ginny nodded. "How's Maria?"

"She took a bullet in her gut. We'll know more when they get her into surgery."

"And Luis?"

"He's fine, just upset."

"Poor thing."

"Father Ignacio is being looked after by the DEA. I don't think he appreciated being shot in the chest, even with a bulletproof vest on. The lawyer fellow is being detained by the FBI." Jim's mouth twitched. "DeSoto is going to have fun sorting this out."

Ginny was suddenly aware that Perez was making unhealthy noises. She frowned, not wanting to have anything further to do with the man, but her training got the better of her.

"Help me roll him on his side and watch his hands."

She was still making sure her patient was breathing when she became aware of an army boot that stopped beside her. She looked up into the face of the *galloglaigh*. He went down on one knee, leaning on his weapon, his eyes on hers.

"I could see you from the gallery, but there was no clear shot. You were moving too fast." He gestured toward the man on the floor. "Where did you learn to fight like that?"

The corner of Ginny's mouth curved up. "I have a brother."

"And he's still alive?"

Ginny laughed. "Yes."

"I don't see many people with that kind of courage," he said. "If you ever need a wing man, I'm at your service." He touched his cap. "Ma'am."

Ginny reached out a hand to stop him. "Wait! You haven't told me who you are, yet."

He smiled. "I was named for my maternal grandfather, Gavan Uisdean."

"Why 'Fergus' then?"

"My initials were G-U-S. The lads tried to call me Gus, but after I knocked them down a few times, we settled on Fergus, because of Fergus mac Ross."

Ginny smiled up at him. She knew the legend. "Thank you."

"You're welcome. Stay here until I get back."

By this time, the EMTs had arrived. Jim raided the trauma box, then put a hand behind her neck and applied gauze to the knife wound on her throat.

"I think you may need a stitch or two," he said.

She nodded, then watched his mouth curve into a smile.

"You and Alex? Really?"

"They were mock battles, just pretend."

"But this was the real thing." He shook his head. "I didn't know you had it in you."

Ginny looked from Jim to the man who had tried to slit her throat, now being loaded onto a stretcher for transport to the hospital, and shook her head. "Neither did I."

* * *

CHAPTER 46

Day 20 – Wednesday morning, Fourth Day of Christmas
Brochaber

Ginny ran a finger along the gauze dressing around her throat. It felt stiff-ish and alien.

"Leave that alone." Jim, seated next to her at the table, took her hand, inspected the torn knuckles she had acquired during yesterday's skirmish, then nestled her hand in his, smiling. He had reason to smile. The knife hadn't gotten to any of the large vessels in her neck, just little ones. Little ones that kind of hurt. A small reminder that she was still alive.

DeSoto was reporting, informally, to Himself.

"Maria and Luis are both in protective custody. She's expected to recover, but we've got someone with her, recording everything she says. Javier Perez is in the prison hospital and can't talk, but that hasn't kept him from singing like a canary. He's hoping for protection from his former employer, in exchange for cooperation."

Himself sputtered. "He tried tae murder Maria and Ginny and Father Ignacio!"

"And has killed others. He'll end up in prison, one way or another. In the meantime, he's being very helpful. We have an entire alphabet soup of agencies working on the information he's giving us."

"Can ye bring doon th' cartel?"

DeSoto hesitated. "We've already begun shutting down the money laundering side of the business—the IRS, Homeland Security, and Immigration agents are swarming the long-term care facilities."

"Where will th' auld folk go, then?"

"All of the patients are being re-evaluated and transferred. They'll be taken care of."

"And the nurses?" Ginny asked.

DeSoto looked at her. "We're handling them on a case-by-case basis."

"What about the drugs?" Jim asked.

"The Dallas police get the job—and the credit—for cleaning up the streets. They're out there now. But we believe the cartel was handling the importation and distribution, so that falls to the DEA. We've arrested seven of the mid-level managers."

DeSoto sighed. "We'd rather have caught the big fish, of course, but we may still get a break."

"Did you ever find out about the fentanyl?"

DeSoto nodded. "There was a new drug lord in town, willing to kill to drive the regular suppliers out of business."

"Where was he getting the pure drug?"

"Maria tells us she was switching the counterfeits for the real thing. All the nurses were."

"That explains why they needed fakes."

"Yes, but it's more complicated than that. The amount of pure drug the Pipeline nurses collected doesn't begin to cover the expenses involved in getting them up here. By forcing them to steal narcotics, the cartel had a way to keep them in line. They told Maria if she talked she would go to prison and Luis back to Mexico. She believed them, so she cooperated."

Ginny shook her head. "What a dirty trick to pull on

someone who just wanted a better life for her son."

DeSoto nodded. "The stolen narcotics were deposited in the BINGO box, and collected by the guy who ran the BINGO games. It's my theory he got tempted and decided to go into business for himself."

"So, what happens now?" Ginny asked.

"We've got weeks, maybe months of rounding up bad guys, then the lawyers will move in and that will take years. In the meantime, we keep on fighting."

"I meant, are Jim and I still in danger?"

DeSoto met her eye. "We don't think so. The small fry will be looking for new jobs. Any remaining mid-level managers will need to go underground or take a chance on being caught and prosecuted. Whoever is top dog in north Texas has just lost a major source of income, and his credibility. We think they'll all be too busy to care what happens to you."

He rose. "I'll need signatures on your statements so you'll be seeing me again."

Himself escorted the DEA agent to the front door, then came back and sat looking at Ginny.

"What?" she asked.

"'Tis progress, lass. Why do ye no look happy?"

"I'm happy," she protested.

Jim snorted.

"I am! We're alive, aren't we? Luis is back with his mom, and the bad guys are going to jail."

"But, 'tis no enough?"

Ginny sighed heavily. "Can *everyone* read my mind?"

The corner of his mouth twitched. "No yer mind, lass. Just yer face. Sae wha's th' problem?"

Ginny squirmed. "It's ridiculous, I know, but there are still so many unanswered questions."

"Like what?" Jim asked.

She turned to face him. "Like how do we prove Marjorie Hawkins killed Phyllis? How does Clara Carpenter fit into this story? Who was the brain-dead nurse in Austin? What about Isaac? He's supposed to have blackmail files on all of us. Where are they, and what do they say? Why did Javier Perez decide to come claim his son after all this time? Who's the head of the drug cartel in Dallas? Was I the target of that assassin's bullet, or was it Marjorie? How long do I have to wear this infernal collar? And I'm pretty sure I can come up with more questions, if I think hard enough."

"Whew!" Jim laughed. "Well, let's see if we can answer some of them. Javier Perez told DeSoto the cartel's plan was to use Luis as leverage, to draw his mother out."

"Which is what we did."

"Yes, and when they saw the Amber Alert, they tossed Perez on a plane to see if they could beat us to the punch. Detective Tran told us she's planning to interview Isaac. We'll see where that leads. The brain-dead nurse in Austin held the same position down there that Marjorie Hawkins did up here. She was in charge of the Pipeline Nurses and handled the fakes they had to switch for the real drugs. The dressing can come off as soon as the wounds are closed, about forty-eight hours. As for the rest of your questions, we may find out, in time." Jim stretched, yawning widely.

"You have to work tonight, don't you?" she asked.

He nodded. "Unlike some privileged characters who get taken off the schedule just because someone tried to shoot them, I have to work."

The Laird's mouth twitched. "Ye ken perfectly well, th' idea is tae keep her oot o' trouble until we're sure this is th' end o' it. Fergus can keep an e'e on her better if she's no at work."

"Where *is* Fergus?" Ginny asked.

"Up th' stairs, asleep." The Laird turned to Jim. "And tha's no a bad idea fer ye, as weel. Ye look beat."

"This week is catching up with me."

Ginny made a shooing motion with her hand. "Go take a nap. Don't forget we've got a big weekend coming up."

"I haven't forgotten." He climbed to his feet, then bowed to her. "May I escort you to the ball my lady, and claim the first dance?"

She nodded, smiling. "I would be honored, kind sir."

"I thank you! See you later."

When he'd gone, she turned to Angus. "We're down two ICU staff nurses and an ICU administrator. I really should be at work."

"And will be, lass. Just gi'e it a few more days. I've got th' shifts covered an' advertisements oot fer replacements. In th' meantime, rest, or see if ye can figure what the professionals canno'. And ye go nowhere wi' oot Fergus, ye ken?"

As if on cue, Fergus himself appeared, looking refreshed and calm and ready for anything. Ginny looked at him.

"He's likely to be very bored."

"I can stand it," he said.

She raised an eyebrow in his direction, then addressed Himself. "All right, if you insist."

"Aye, I do."

Ginny rose and started toward the door. "Come, Cousin," she said. "You can watch me sleep."

Fergus stepped in front of her, blocking her exit, and Ginny found herself looking up into a pair of hazel eyes that seemed to ignite at her jibe.

"I'd like that." He smiled.

Ginny caught her breath. "Just kidding!" She ducked under his arm and fled.

* * *

Wednesday morning
Forbes residence

Once safely in her own room, Ginny stood for a moment, examining her reflection in the mirror. It was true, she didn't look happy. Well, of course not. She hated loose ends. She frowned, then moved into the office.

Had she given everything she had to Detective Tran? Or had something fallen through the cracks when the cartel started to make a serious effort to kill her? And what was it Jim had said that set off an alarm bell in her head just now? Something about work. Something about her being taken off the schedule.

The schedule! She dove at her computer, pulling up her work e-mail and digging through the files. Yes, there it was, the Hillcrest Medical ICU shift schedule for January. No Phyllis.

Ginny whistled silently, then turned to the box of papers John Kyle had given to her, looking for Phyllis' day planner.

Her eye fell on the small collection of personal letters she had intended to return to John. It turned out Phyllis had kept a few of the letters from Lisa. Ginny looked them over, then decided John didn't need to see them.

She flipped through the remaining letters noticing that one had a single word in the area where the return address usually went. The word was "Perez."

John Kyle, in his role as executor of Phyllis' estate, had given her the envelope. That made Ginny a person who was legitimately dealing with a deceased person's affairs. But the sender wasn't dead. She had a right to privacy in her correspondence.

Ginny struggled with her conscience, then pulled the enclosed letter out and read it swiftly. It was a complete confession: names, dates, details, all having to do with the

Mexican Nurse Pipeline and its part in the cartel's drug trafficking in north Texas. It also explained Maria's plan to leave Luis with Phyllis for as long as it took to figure a way out.

Ginny reached for the phone. "Detective Tran? I have something for you." She explained about the letter and the schedule.

"I will be most interested to see them, but I do not understand the significance of the schedule."

"It means Marjorie Hawkins knew Phyllis wouldn't be available in January when she created this schedule."

"And?"

"And the date on the schedule is December first."

"Eight days before Mrs. Kyle was killed."

"Yes."

"That is suggestive, certainly. I have something for you as well. Something I think you will appreciate. When they did the autopsy on Eloise Quinn they combed her hair, looking for trace evidence, and found a thumb drive, disguised as a hair clip. It appears she kept meticulous files on all of the Pipeline nurses she was supervising. There is extensive demographic information on each of them, as well as distribution, collection, and payment records. Agent DeSoto was quite pleased to see the data."

Ginny smiled. She could imagine his expression. "It seems risky to keep evidence on a thumb drive."

"Less so than in a computer or paper file."

"May I look at it, when the lab is finished with it?"

"I expect that can be arranged."

"Thank you." Ginny hung up the phone, her mind on those meticulously kept records. She had seen the same coming out of the ICU Head Nurse's office at Hillcrest. Agendas and conference minutes, work assignments and instructions for continuing education classes, reorganization initiatives and staff pot-luck contributions. The woman was obsessive about her lists.

Ginny's eyes narrowed. Any woman who kept such perfect records in both of her jobs would have done the same elsewhere. You don't cast off a life-long habit of list-making just because you decide to commit murder. Where were the notes the ersatz Marjorie Hawkins had made in planning that attack on Phyllis?

Ginny pulled out her phone and called Detective Tran back. She could hear the doubt in the detective's voice.

"The police have already searched the house and it had been ransacked before we got there. It looked as if the cartel took everything that might conceivably be classified as evidence."

"Well, if there's no evidence for me to mess up, then may I go look?"

"What do you hope to accomplish?"

"I don't know. I just want to look around."

There was a short silence on the other end of the line, then Detective Tran's reply. "I see no harm in what you are suggesting, though I think you are wasting your time."

"I expect you're right."

"I will have an officer meet you over there in thirty minutes."

"Thank you!"

Ginny hung up the phone, gathered up the letters for John Kyle, grabbed her coat and purse, called goodbye to her mother, and headed for the garage. Fergus was waiting for her.

"My car."

Ginny didn't bother to argue, just followed him to the curb, climbed into the passenger side seat, and watched as he settled in to drive.

"What was wrong with my car?"

He glanced over at her and smiled. "This one's safer."

Ginny looked around inside the vehicle. Safer. More horsepower? Better tires? Bulletproof glass, perhaps? "What are we waiting for, then?"

"I'm not moving until you put your seatbelt on."

* * *

CHAPTER 47

Day 20 – Wednesday midmorning
Marjorie Hawkins' house

The police officer lifted the crime scene tape and allowed them to duck under, then unlocked the door and let them in. Ginny waited on the threshold while Fergus cleared the scene, then followed him inside.

The place was a mess. She walked through the rooms, seeing voids in the dust where a computer had been, desk and cabinet drawers open and empty, and the dead woman's jewel box on its side, the drawers gone.

Rugs and furniture had been moved, air conditioning vents pulled down, and holes punched through the wallboard. There were even some dangling electrical wires where the lamps and plumbing had been investigated. Very thorough.

There was fingerprint powder, too. What the cartel hadn't taken, the police had investigated.

Ginny pulled on a pair of nitrile gloves she had brought with her and began going through the mess, looking for clues. Her own notes-to-self tended to be jotted down on scraps of paper, then transcribed into the computer. She searched for anything that looked like a to-do list. Both men watched, but neither made a move to interfere.

Half an hour later, Ginny sighed to herself. This was getting her nowhere. She was standing in the room that had served as a home office, looking around. The thieves (and police) hadn't taken everything. The books sat on the floor in piles or lay scattered across the floor, the bookcases clearly the object of someone's interest. What could the books tell her about the dead woman? She began picking them up and putting them back on the shelves.

There were six books relating to Roman Catholic church ritual, the first catechism inscribed in a childish hand with a name Ginny hadn't seen before. It took her a minute to figure out it was in Irish Gaelic and translated to 'Eloise Quinn.' That implied Quinn's father was an Irishman.

There were a number of classic novels in the editions usually seen in high school classrooms, some of them in Spanish. One had a bookmark. She pulled it out and looked at the Christmas card featuring a family group; the Irish father, a woman who could easily have been Hispanic, and the very young Eloise. Ginny felt a queer sensation in the pit of her stomach. Such a pretty child. How had she ended up as Marjorie Hawkins, murderer? Ginny put the card back in the book and pushed the book into place on the shelf.

She worked her way across the carpet, in no particular order, finding a smattering of philosophies, one or two art books, and a large collection of paperback spy novels.

Many dealt with SCUBA diving and where to go for the best views. Ginny flipped through the travel guides, seeing Marjorie had added notes, highlighted items of interest, and flagged timetables—and was reminded why she was here.

She began to move faster, grabbing books at random, letting her mind wander, putting her subconscious to work on the problem. She hoisted a pile of reference books back into place, then reached for a massive tome, *The Complete Works* of *William Shakespeare*, with two hands, but when she lifted it off the floor it came up easily.

Ginny paused. She had expected that one to be heavy. She took it across the room and laid it on the desk, then opened it to find someone had cut out the middle, making a hiding space. It was not empty. Both men had followed her and were looking over her shoulders, one on either side. She looked from one to the other and smiled.

"Bingo!"

* * *

Ginny selected one of the slim volumes and opened it to the first page. It was a journal, lined, without pre-printed dates.

There were dates, however. Each entry started with one. They were chronological, too, in that each entry was later than the one before it, but they were not complete. The author had skipped some days and written very little on others. Ginny flipped through the pages, noting this volume covered five years, all of them long ago. She set it down and picked up the second. More of the same.

In the fourth, she found what she was looking for. The latter pages covered the time starting in the fall of the current year. Ginny read avidly.

> *I'm sick of having to pay hush money. I need to find a way to end this.*

A few pages later, Ginny found a list.

> *Things to consider:*
> 1. *Phyllis Kyle wrote that article for the BON and I have to wonder which of the Pipeline nurses she*

was talking to and whether her source mentioned me.

2. The tracker I put on her car, after the above, goes to Austin, to the capital complex, and to the Board of Nursing, where they keep records.
3. The blackmail started after the article was published.
4. Trips to Austin cost money and she never works extra shifts.
5. The blackmailer's voice on the phone is female and sounds like Kyle. Same word choices. Same accent.
6. She knows how a Swiss bank account works. I overheard her telling someone last month, at the staff meeting.

That entry was dated early in November. By Thanksgiving, they had taken on a sinister tone.

She stood right in front of me this morning, looked me in the eye, and told me she was planning to put an end to imposters in nursing. I'm not sure how to interpret this. If she's the blackmailer, then why tell me? Is she planning to screw more money out of me? If she's not, then how do I keep her out of the archives? Either way, she's a threat.

This was followed by several pages of lists, diagrams, and musings. Ginny frowned over the drawing of a garrote, with instructions on how to use it to best advantage. She turned another page and saw an entry for the day before Phyllis' death.

Okay. I'm ready. If she'd been satisfied with merely

blackmailing me, I could have overlooked it, but she's getting too close to the truth and that I cannot have. I've got people counting on me. I'm their contact to the money, to the good life, to not going to prison. They need me. The planning is complete. I have all my ducks in a row. With just a little bit of luck, by morning this particular problem will be behind me. So, off to work! Write at you later.

Ginny was beginning to feel queasy. She had worked with this woman for years, trusted her as one does a boss who doesn't make your work life a living hell, chatted amiably with her about her hobby. Ginny looked around, found a chair, dropped into it, then read the next entry.

I do NOT believe it! After all my careful planning, someone beat me to it! Phyllis Kyle disappeared into the bathroom and was not seen—alive—again. They found her body at change of shift. I don't know who saved me the trouble of putting her out of my misery, but someone did! I didn't know what had happened, of course. I was checking on everyone during the night. Around four I found that neither of her patients had gotten anything done for half an hour, so I know (now) roughly when she disappeared and I know (now) where she was. But I didn't at the time. I kept expecting her to show up so I could put my plan into action. I didn't want to draw attention to her, of course, so I did her four o'clocks and kept looking. By the time they found her, I had given up and was thinking how to try again later. Then, there she was, dead as doornail. Divine intervention, do you think?

Ginny took a breath, then another. She'd been right. Marjorie Hawkins had planned to kill Phyllis, but she hadn't actually done so. Which meant Ginny was also wrong.

"What does it say?"

Ginny lifted her eyes from the page to find Fergus crouching in front of her, alert, as always, the policeman hovering behind him. She turned the book around and handed it to him, watching as he read the entry.

When he was through, he looked up. "So, not guilty. Not this time, anyway."

Ginny nodded, then found herself blinking back tears. As long as she thought Marjorie Hawkins was the murderess, she could take comfort in the fact she was dead. No trial, no testifying, no chance she could kill again. Instead, the criminal was still at large, still a threat, and Ginny would have to go back to that mountain of evidence and go through it all over again.

"I'll take you home."

Ginny shook her head. "The police station. We need to hand these over to Detective Tran."

Fergus nodded. "All right. Then home."

Ginny nodded. Home, minus one suspect and the riddle still unanswered.

* * *

CHAPTER 48

Day 20 – Wednesday afternoon
En route to the police station

"STOP!" Ginny almost dropped the diary as Fergus slammed on the brakes. He pulled the car over to the curb, then turned to stare at her.

"Why?"

She pushed the book at him. Marjorie Hawkins had gone through Phyllis' papers, looking for evidence of blackmail, then come to the conclusion she'd been suspecting the wrong person.

He read the entry, his mouth settling into a tight line. "Which way?"

Ginny fed him the GPS coordinates. She didn't need to tell him to hurry.

He pulled up in front of the house, then slid out, motioning for her to stay put. She watched him circle the place, gun at the ready, peering into the windows, disappearing around the back, then reappearing. He paused at the front door, then opened it and slipped inside. A minute later he came out onto the stoop and gestured for her to join him.

"He's in here." Fergus led the way to the kitchen. "Don't touch anything."

Ginny could see they were too late. He lay on the floor beside an overturned chair, coffee and body fluids mingling beneath him, his face contorted in a rictus of agony.

Fergus had pulled out his phone and was talking to Himself. "Aye, dead and cold." There was a pause. "We let ourselves in. Will she overlook that?" He nodded into the phone. "All right. I'll call." He broke the connection then dialed again. "Detective Tran, please."

In spite of her medical training, Ginny was having trouble with the stench. She'd been trying to hold her breath and felt a bit dizzy. She turned toward the kitchen table, reaching for one of the chairs, but found Fergus' arm around her waist, holding her upright. He finished the call, then stuck the device in his pocket and turned her toward the front door. "Outside."

Ginny let him lead her back to the car and sit her down, with the door open to let the cold air clear the fog in her brain. When Detective Tran arrived, Fergus took point, handing the diary to her, and explaining what had brought them to the house.

She eyed Fergus. "Was the front door locked when you arrived?"

He nodded. "But the alarm was off."

"Will I find evidence of your entry on that lock?"

"Yes, ma'am. There were exigent circumstances." He gestured toward the diary.

She nodded. "Very well. What else do I need to know?"

"You will find my footprints and Ginny's in the front hall and the kitchen, but neither of us touched anything."

"You are sure of that?"

"I am."

"All right. Please wait here."

"Detective Tran," Ginny stopped her. "I want to look at that crime scene again."

The detective's eyes narrowed. "I will consider your request." She made her way into the house.

When the detective had gone, Fergus turned to Ginny. "Why do you want to go back inside?"

Ginny took a deep breath. "There were two photographs on the kitchen table."

Fergus' eyes narrowed. "Of what?"

"Of the inside of the Medical ICU break room."

Fergus caught his breath. "You're sure?"

"I'm sure."

* * *

Wednesday afternoon
Forbes residence

In the end, Detective Tran decided she could not allow an outsider onto her active crime scene. She did, however, promise to send copies of any photographs they found, and with that Ginny had to be content.

Lunch at home was the usual casserole, fresh fruit, salad, and hot bread. Usual in that on Wednesdays, Mrs. Forbes cooked after getting home from her teaching job. Ginny watched Fergus consume the double portions her mother still made because she had raised a son, even if he no longer lived in Dallas.

"Not hungry?" Mrs. Forbes eyed Ginny's plate.

Ginny still had the smell of Isaac's kitchen in her nostrils. "Maybe later."

She excused herself and went upstairs. She stood for a moment in the door of her home office and looked around. The normally neat, organized space was flooded with paper.

The stacks of white teetered, threatening to fall, festooned with sudden color in every shade of the rainbow from the sticky notes and flags and bookmarks in use. There were colored printouts, too, of her mind map, and timetables, and to do lists. The bookcases hid behind the work. The oriental rug struggled under its weight. The whole thing seemed to mock her, as if it knew she had failed.

With both Lisa and Marjorie Hawkins absolved of murdering Phyllis, the only candidate left was Grace. Ginny heaved a sigh, sat down at the computer, pulled up her files, and got to work.

There was nothing new in any of them. No clue to follow. Every item on her Action Plan completed. The mind map filled in and all the cross-links in place. Nothing that definitively pointed to Grace. Three futile hours later, Ginny picked up the phone and dialed Austin.

"Clara? It's Ginny Forbes. I have a question for you. Well, more like a plea. I'm desperate! Can you think of anything, anything at all, that might give us another clue in the death of Phyllis Kyle?"

"Like what?"

"I don't know, that's the problem. You said at first you thought it might be a case of mistaken identity. Did anyone threaten you?"

Clara's nod came down the line. "Oh, yes. There've been some very angry people down here. Nothing ever came of it. But—"

"But what?"

"I've just remembered. There *was* a woman making threats, but they weren't directed at me. She was threatening Phyllis."

"Was Phyllis pretending to be you?"

"Yes, but the other woman knew who it was. She called her by name."

"Can you describe the other woman?"

"Sure. A tall, elegant black woman. And I got the impression

THE SWICK AND THE DEAD

this wasn't the first time they'd argued."

Ginny pulled up the Hillcrest website and accessed the ICU staff directory. "Clara, if I send you a picture of a woman, can you tell me if it's the same one?"

"Maybe. Let me see it."

Ginny sent it over the wire, then waited for the image to arrive in Clara's e-mail box.

"Yes. That's her."

Grace.

"Can you remember what she said?"

"No. I'm sorry. I wasn't paying that much attention. I remember the other woman pointing her finger at Phyllis and poking the air with it. You know."

"Yes," Ginny had no trouble imagining that scene. "How are things going on your end?"

"We've had the most exciting day! According to the news, they've made twenty drug busts. It's as if the police suddenly had inside information on where to find the criminals."

"Are you out of hiding?"

"Sort of. The police have cleared me to go home, but I'm officially on vacation for a while."

"Give it a week. If I know Agent DeSoto, he'll have the streets of Austin safe to walk again before you can turn around."

"Just in case I want to turn streetwalker."

"Or saunter down Sixth Street, enjoying the evening air."

"That sounds nice. You should come down and join me."

Ginny promised to come visit, then hung up the phone and turned back to the investigation.

On the face of it, Grace was elsewhere when the murder took place. The evidence that supported her claim included the computer-generated date/time stamps, the images of her with her patients, the non-movement of her ID badge during the relevant times, the image showing her with neither her scrub jacket nor her badge, and the subsequent images showing her with both.

The evidence contradicting her story (if you were willing to give it such a strong name) consisted of the image of Grace making changes to the TPN pump in Phyllis' room at five minutes after three a.m., while Phyllis was alive and well and helping Susan with her admission.

Evidence of nothing in particular included images showing Grace in the scrum in front of the nurses' station each time there was a Code or an admission.

Evidence of a motive included Grace and Phyllis' animosity toward one another. They had been seen arguing more than once (Lisa's testimony about the fight under the bridge and Clara's report of Grace's threats toward Phyllis). But heated words do not prove murder. What in Grace's life could have made it necessary that Phyllis should die?

Ginny glanced at the clock. Three hours, minimum, before she could hope to catch Grace at work. If Grace was guilty, she would just deny killing Phyllis. But if she wasn't, she might say something different, or say the same thing a different way, and maybe it would help solve this case.

Ginny jotted a few notes down on a piece of paper and stuck it in her pocket, then rose from her chair and turned to find Fergus leaning against the door jamb.

"Going somewhere?"

"How long have you been standing there?"

"A while." He pushed off the wall and stood square in the doorway, his arms crossed on his chest. "Your mother asked me to remind you. John Kyle and his sons are expected for dinner."

"Oh!" Ginny had forgotten about the visit. Well, it didn't matter. She couldn't expect to find any of the night crew in place until well after seven p.m. "I'll be right down."

Fergus didn't move. "I'd like to ask you a question, if I may."

Ginny found her attention suddenly focused on the man standing in her doorway. She nodded.

"What's your relationship with Jim Mackenzie?"

"He's my laird's grandson."

"Nothing more?"

"He's a friend."

"He's in love with you."

Ginny took a grip on herself. A man like Fergus, trained to pay attention, could hardly have missed that.

"I know."

"So what's the problem?" Fergus uncrossed his arms and moved toward her. "Has he hurt you?"

Ginny found herself rooted to the spot, her eyes locked on his. She managed to shake her head.

He crossed the carpet and stood looking down at her. "Ginny, if you need help, tell me."

She swallowed, then forced herself to speak. "No. He's done nothing wrong. It's not him, it's me."

"Tell me."

She shook her head.

"You can trust me, Ginny."

She swallowed hard. "I know."

His brow furrowed. "You told me Lisa made accusations against Jim, but she didn't tell you what he's supposed to have done. Would you like me to find out for you?"

Ginny wasn't aware she had stopped breathing until the room started to spin.

Fergus put her back in her chair, then pulled up the other, and sat down facing her. "I have resources. Discreet ones. He would never know. Neither would Angus."

Ginny sucked in a breath. "I'm supposed to be learning to

trust him."

"That will be easier if you know the truth."

Her forehead was a collection of tight little knots. "Trust means not insisting on knowing."

He sighed. "Ginny, there's no man on earth, no man worth knowing anyway, who hasn't done something he'd rather not have everyone find out about. The best men confess to the women they love. Has he done so?"

Ginny swallowed and shook her head. "But he might."

"And you want to give him the chance."

She nodded.

Fergus studied her for a long moment, then nodded. "Okay. We'll wait and see what kind of a man he is."

"He will be Laird of Lonach."

Fergus raised an eyebrow, his eyes still on hers. "All the more reason to know if he's the right man—for the job—and for you."

* * *

CHAPTER 49

Day 20 – Wednesday evening
Forbes residence

Detective Tran kept her promise, sending a pair of digital images with a polite request that Ginny explain herself. The camera had caught the subject both coming and going. Ginny tucked the images into her bag intending to ask Grace about them when she caught up with her tonight. In the meantime, there were guests to be entertained.

Ginny, her mother, Fergus, John Kyle, and the two small Kyle boys were gathered in the den watching a recording of the Christmas Pageant. There was a lot of noise and movement in the room as the boys squealed in delight, or jumped up and ran from the room, then ran back in again, or climbed on their father's lap, then off again. Joey kept drawing the grown-ups attention to his part in the play.

"Look! Look at me! There I am!"

Ginny collared him at one point and pulled him up onto her lap. "Tell me who else was in the play."

"Luis was. See?"

"I see him. Who else?"

"Our whole class."

"Anyone else?"

The child screwed his face up, finding the question a bit of a challenge. "Lots of people." He squirmed loose and ran off again, his father in hot pursuit this time.

Whoever had put the video together had gathered clips from the parents. Each child was featured. The cameos were framed by shots of the set, the backstage action, the supporting adults, and the crowd.

Ginny almost missed it. The camera flashed to the audience, most of the faces hidden behind digital recording devices, but one in the clear. Grace Edwards, smiling at the woman sitting beside her. A sister, maybe, and a niece or nephew in the pageant. Grace was connected with Mater Dolorosa, the same church as Maria Perez and Phyllis Kyle.

Ginny shook herself mentally. She was fully aware of the Baader-Meinhof phenomenon, that quirk of the mind that makes it seem as if something you never noticed before suddenly crops up everywhere. Still, there she was.

The Kyle boys were young and their father took them home almost as soon as the video was over, apologizing, and expressing thanks for the company and the meal, and receiving hugs all around.

The minute they were out the door, Ginny grabbed her coat and her cousin.

Mrs. Forbes looked at her in surprise. "I thought you were off tonight."

"I am. Fergus and I are going to see if we can ask Grace a few questions. Don't wait up."

* * *

Wednesday evening
Hillcrest Medical ICU

Ginny led the way. "My car this time. I've got a parking pass for the hospital lot."

"May I drive?"

Ginny hesitated, then nodded. Hal had insisted he drive whenever the two of them were in the car together. Jim, too. She settled into the passenger side seat, rubbing damp palms on her pants and telling herself she was being silly. Probably he wanted to make sure he could get her out of danger if someone started to follow them.

"Talk to me."

Ginny looked over at her body guard. He was backing the car out of the garage and onto the street, expertly. He met her eyes as he turned forward again, then focused on the street.

"Why did you go pale when I asked to drive? I'm quite good."

"I can see that. Turn left at the next corner."

He said nothing more until they pulled into the Hillcrest lot and parked the car, then he turned off the engine, twisted in his seat so he could face her and said, "Thank you."

Ginny nodded. She knew, in her conscious mind, that she could trust Fergus with her life. It was her subconscious that hadn't caught up, yet.

They rode up in the elevator, Fergus keeping an eye on the surroundings while Ginny got her thoughts in order. She led him into the Unit and called out greetings to the staff.

"I've brought a visitor to see what mysteries occur behind closed doors." Several of the women looked up, then suddenly found they had time to come over and be polite. Ginny introduced them.

"This is Ann, and June, and Susan, and Margot." There were

three newcomers among the group of women now eyeing Fergus. Margot introduced them to Ginny.

"Janet, Maureen, and Thessaly are helping out while we're so short staffed, and might be persuaded to come onboard if we're nice to them." She turned to Ginny. "And on the same subject, when are *you* coming back?"

Ginny shrugged. "I haven't been released. Soon, I hope. Is it okay if I show Fergus around?"

"Sure, as long as he doesn't get in the way."

"I won't ma'am. I promise."

"Ma'am, is it?" Margot shook her head. "I must be getting old. Gray hair and a rocking chair for me."

Fergus turned to her, moving a half-step closer and smiling in a way Ginny hadn't seen before. He caught Margot's gaze and it seemed the temperature in the immediate area rose by several degrees. He held out his hand and Margot placed hers in it.

"I sincerely hope not," he said. "To deprive the world of those gorgeous eyes of yours would be a real shame." He lifted her fingers to his lips and saluted them. "I meant only deference to your skill in saving lives and mending broken bodies, for which I have a tremendous respect, having needed those services more than once in the past."

Ginny stifled a giggle as she saw Margot melt into his hands. It seemed even *she* was susceptible to charm on this scale. The others were openly drooling and Ginny had trouble extricating him.

"Nice women."

"And smart." Ginny grinned. "Usually. Would you like to see the scene of the crime?"

Ginny lead him to the staff break room, then into the women's restroom.

"This is where I found her."

He inspected the handicap stall, then nodded, looked around the rest of the room, then held the door for her to exit.

"This is the break room." Ginny turned slowly, studying the ceiling. "There!"

"I see it."

Fergus climbed up on one of the chairs, pulling a tool out of his pocket. He examined the device with a flashlight, then carefully removed it from its mounting, climbed down, and handed it to Ginny.

She ran her finger along the edge. "It's got a memory card."

"Hang onto it until we get home. Is there anything else?"

"Yes." Ginny pocketed the camera, led the way to the nurses' station, and located Margot.

"Is Grace available?"

"She was supposed to be on tonight, but she's a no-show and no one can reach her at any of her numbers."

"Is that usual?" Fergus asked.

Margot shook her head. "No. I can't think what's happened to her. She's been behaving weird recently."

"What do you mean?"

"Coming in late, disappearing during the shift, saying things that don't make sense."

"When did this start?"

"About the same time Phyllis was killed. I didn't think anything of it. We were all upset. But she's gotten worse."

Ginny's brow furrowed. A no-show and no one able to reach her. She felt a frisson go down her spine. There were too many bodies in this case already. "Where does she live?" she asked.

Margot dug into the files and came up with the emergency contact information on Grace. "Here's her address."

"Have you called the police?"

Margot's eyebrows rose. "Well, no. Why would we do that?"

Ginny thought there might be a good many reasons why her employer should report a missing nurse, but didn't say so. She gestured toward the patient rooms. "I just want to check one thing."

"Help yourself."

Ginny motioned for Fergus to follow her.

"What are you looking for?" he asked.

"EKG cables." She explained about the wire used to kill Phyllis, then slipped into one of the empty ICU rooms, pulled open a drawer, and rummaged around until she found what she wanted.

It had taken a while, but she'd finally figured out what those sheep had been trying to tell her. The murder weapon was something from the unit. Something only an insider would know was there.

"My subconscious has been giving me fits over this. I knew I'd seen it before, that I should recognize it, but I've been distracted. Then, when I told Detective Tran, she said they knew all about it, so I went away again, feeling foolish." She handed him the example.

"These cables are hard-wires for the old-fashioned EKG monitors. We use wireless now, but these are kept in each of the rooms as a back-up. Each cable has five wires, one each in red, black, white, green, and brown."

He tugged on the wires, finding that each one came easily out of the connection. "These are heavy."

"And long. Quite sufficient to choke someone with."

"And the one they found around her neck was a red wire."

"Yes."

"So all we need to do is find a set with a missing red wire."

"It's not that simple. They migrate from room to room. Right now, I'm just doing a census."

They spent the next half hour going through the drawers in

each of the twelve ICU rooms, at the end of which Ginny had discovered there were three rooms with a modified set; one had two greens and no red, one had two whites and no green, one had all but the red, the rest had the usual one of each color.

"Which room had only four wires and none was red?" Fergus was keeping track.

"Room eleven."

"Does that help?"

"Grace had rooms eleven and twelve on the night of Phyllis' murder."

"Would the murderer be able to count on a red wire being handy at need?"

"A wire, certainly. The color wouldn't matter."

"So it *might* have been premeditated, but it's more likely to have been a spur-of-the-moment murder."

"Yes." Ginny turned her head toward the nurses' station where a confrontation of some sort was in progress. "What's going on over there?"

"Let's go find out." Fergus led the way.

What they found was a visitor with minimal English trying to communicate with Margot, who had almost no Spanish.

"Senorita Grace, por favor.

"I'm sorry. She's not here."

"What does mean, not here?"

"I'm sorry." Margo spread her hands. "She's not here tonight."

"No here? Where is?"

"We don't know."

"I must speak."

"I'm sorry. I wish I could help."

"Debo hablar con la señorita Grace. Dime dónde encontrarla, por favor. Es importante."

"Excuse me," Fergus address the stranger. "¿Puedo ayudar?"

"Ah! ¡Sí!" The stranger launched into an impassioned string of Spanish, to which Fergus replied with courtesy, in the same language. After a minute or two of listening, he turned to Margot and translated.

"She says she must speak with Grace. That it's necessary she understand they do not blame her."

"Blame her for what?" Margot asked. Fergus translated the question, then the answer.

"She says, they don't blame Grace for the child's death. He was dying anyway and they knew she was trying to help."

"What child?" Ginny asked.

The conversation went on for the next fifteen minutes, during which Ginny learned that Grace had been providing chemotherapy drugs to a child who was in the country illegally; that the family had refused to take the child to the free clinic, for fear of deportation; that Grace had taken the child to the clinic anyway, when he got much worse; that he had died in the night in spite of everything the medical professionals could do; and that the illegal community Grace had been supplying with drugs and medical expertise did not blame her for the death, needed her help, and were begging her to come back to them.

Fergus assured the visitor that they, too, were looking for Grace, and would give her the message when they found her. The woman appeared mollified and went away, leaving the ICU staff to stare at one another.

"Did I understand her correctly? Grace has been supplying a community of illegal aliens with illegally obtained drugs?" Margot looked scandalized.

Ginny frowned. "More than that. I think she's been advising them, which would mean practicing medicine without a license."

"Surely not!"

Ginny's frown deepened. "When did Grace go missing?"

"She called in sick last night, then didn't show up tonight."

"I think we need to find her." Ginny looked at Fergus. "Let's try her home."

He followed her out of the unit, dropping his voice. "You think she may have fled?"

Ginny pushed the elevator button then turned to face him. "Let's just hope it's nothing worse."

* * *

CHAPTER 50

Day 20 – Wednesday late evening
Grace Edward's residence / Forbes residence

It was a small house, almost a cottage, with no signs of life. They parked on the street, got out, and approached the building, Fergus in front, his weapon out. Ginny watched as he looked around, then turned and gestured for her to join him on the front porch. He put his gun back in the holster, but Ginny noticed he didn't secure it.

"Try the doorbell," he said.

Ginny did. When that didn't work, she knocked, loudly. No response.

"Let's try the back."

Ginny again waited while Fergus checked out the area, then knocked. Still no answer. By now she was getting nervous.

"Guess we missed her," Fergus said.

Ginny looked around. There was no evidence of a disturbance, and it was possible Grace had suddenly decided she wanted to visit relatives. But without telling anyone?

She put her eye to one of the windows that flanked the door. The room beyond was in darkness.

"If she felt responsible for the death of that child," she said, "she might have done something drastic. I wish I knew whether she's lying on the floor in there or just out shopping."

She turned to find Fergus easing the door open. "Give me a minute." He pulled a set of night-vision goggles out of his jacket and put them on, then slipped inside.

Ginny leaned against the wall, listening to the sound of the wind in the dry trees and small animals scurrying for shelter, and waited. He was beside her before she knew it.

"There's no one home." He turned back to the door and closed it, making sure the lock engaged. "Her car's gone, too. The presumption is that she's left town."

"I thought only the guilty ran?"

"If she's responsible for that boy dying, she's guilty. If she's not, then she might still be guilty of something else."

"True."

They drove back to the Forbes' house, then climbed the stairs to Ginny's office. She pulled out the camera, extracted the memory card, and plugged it into the reader attached to her computer.

"Let's see what's on this." She scrolled through the images, Fergus hanging over her shoulder. "It appears to be motion-activated. Here's Lisa, planting cocaine in Phyllis' locker at three o'clock on the morning Phyllis died." Ginny looked up at Fergus. "You hadn't heard about that bit, had you?"

He shook his head.

"Here's someone in PPE entering the women's rest room at three-eighteen—which corresponds to the time Grace's badge says she entered—followed by Phyllis at three-twenty."

"You sound surprised."

Ginny's brow furrowed. "I should have thought of that earlier."

"Thought of what?"

"The Personal Protective Equipment is generally used to keep germs from spreading outside a patient's room, but there's an exception. If the patient is immunocompromised, the PPE is used to prevent the germs normal, healthy people have on them from reaching the *patient*. Reverse Isolation. Grace had an immunocompromised patient that night. It's the one time a nurse can wear PPE out of the room without getting fined for an infection control violation."

"Interesting." Fergus pointed at the next image. "There you are going in at three-thirty."

"And back out again at three thirty-five."

"You saw nothing?"

"And heard nothing. I thought I was alone."

They flicked through the images, all stills, since the camera wasn't set up for video. When they reached the point where Ginny found the body, Fergus dropped into the extra chair, and looked at her.

"Well!"

"It's not proof."

"It's proof she lied."

"But not proof she murdered."

"The images you saw on Zimmerman's kitchen table show Grace going in and Grace coming out, date/time stamped. That's evidence."

Ginny nodded. "Was he going to turn them over to the police?"

"I think not." Fergus stretched his legs out and crossed them at the ankle, his elbows on the arms of the chair. "Marjorie's diary said the blackmail demands didn't stop after Phyllis died."

Ginny nodded. "And I was present when she realized the perp might have been using a voice changer."

"So she looked elsewhere, and found Isaac."

"And eliminated him."

Fergus nodded. "Yes, but not before he saw these photos. I think he realized what they meant and was planning to use them to blackmail Grace. He'd gotten away with it once, or thought he had. Here was another ready-made victim."

Ginny frowned. "He got greedy."

"We don't know when he planted the camera trap. He might have just gotten lucky." Fergus stretched, then climbed to his feet. "It's after midnight. Why don't you get some sleep?"

"You go ahead. I have some thinking to do."

Ginny pulled up her files and settled down to add the new evidence. Along about one a.m., she descended to the kitchen, got herself a cup of coffee, then went back to work, smiling at Fergus as she climbed the stairs. He nodded, then went back to his magazine.

* * *

Thursday wee small hours of the morning
Forbes residence

In the deepest part of the night Fergus dropped into the empty chair in Ginny's office and faced her across the desk.

"How's it going?"

She sighed. "I'm in the same boat I was in before. When you line up all the facts, it looks like a solid case, but the evidence is all circumstantial. I know that can be enough in a court of law, but suppose we ask her and she denies it?"

"If she doesn't come back, it's as good as an admission of guilt."

"You don't know that. She might be ill or injured or dead."

He lifted an eyebrow. "The timing is suspicious."

Ginny leaned back in her chair and crossed her arms. "You sound very sure of yourself. Is this what you do, track down missing persons?"

"You mean for money? Occasionally."

Ginny's brow furrowed. "How do you find someone who wants to stay lost?"

He shrugged. "People go where they usually go and do what they usually do, thinking no one will notice. Also, there's a lot of psychology involved. It's human nature to believe what you want to believe."

The corner of Ginny's mouth twitched. "Like when you were teasing Margot this evening?"

He put his hand over his heart. "I meant every word. Most women are beautiful and don't know it. We men should tell them more often."

Ginny stared at her cousin. "Who are you? I mean, I look at you and see a soldier, not a poet."

He laughed. "My mother used to say I would have made a good bard, but the pay's lousy. I have a degree in philosophy and another in psychology. They come in very handy, most of the time." He lifted his ankle and set it on his knee. "Jim is easy to read. An open book. You, on the other hand, I'm having trouble figuring out."

Ginny's eyebrows rose. "I'm told my face gives away what I'm thinking."

"Oh, it does, but not why. For instance, I've seen you raise your voice to Angus Mackenzie, but not to Jim. Why is that?"

Ginny thought about it for a moment. "He has earned my patience."

Fergus nodded. "Okay. You have a history. I got that. But at some point you're going to have to confront him. What are you waiting for?"

Ginny's brow wrinkled, wondering just how much she wanted to share with this man. "I don't want to burn any bridges."

Fergus shook his head. "That man will go to his grave still

head over heels in love with you." He brought his foot down and leaned forward. "But, he doesn't understand you. You're going to have to teach him."

Ginny sketched a helpless little gesture. "I've tried."

"Can you give me an example?"

Ginny nodded, remembering and not wanting to. "He condescends, sometimes, because he's a doctor and I'm just a nurse. as if it was a second-class career choice."

Fergus lifted an eyebrow. "You're smart enough. Why did you choose to be a nurse, rather than a physician?"

Ginny took her time answering. "I was offered a place in medical school, but turned it down. Doctors don't spend much time with the patients. It's the nurses who are there 24/7; guarding, encouraging, grieving. Drugs and treatments can help, but it's the human contact that really matters." She took a breath. "Your turn. Tell me something about yourself. What's your relationship with Angus?"

Fergus' gaze turned inward. "He saved my life."

"Oh?"

"It's not a very original story. Adolescent rebellion gone too far. My father took the issue to our laird, who called Angus Mackenzie. He took me into the wilderness for a week of heart to heart man talk. I wasn't sure I was going to live through it. It really hurt to have to admit I didn't already know everything worth knowing."

"I know how that feels."

"He did it to you, too?"

"He did." She smiled across the desktop. "A wise soldier would make a good laird."

"In time of war, yes. Not in times of peace."

"We won't always be at peace."

"I'm not the heir. He's a good friend, though, and smart. I expect he'll let me help. I like to help, just like you." He leaned forward again. "So, are you going to let me?"

"Do what?"

"Help you make up your mind about Jim."

Ginny caught her breath. "What can *you* do?"

He smiled. "I can think of a half dozen things right off the bat, but let's start with talking. What are your reservations?"

Ginny stared at the relative who was a stranger and thought about family. "He's still new here."

"How long have you known him?"

Ginny felt the hairs rise on her arms. "That isn't the issue. You can know someone for years and not know them at all."

"True."

She was struggling to explain. "It's a huge risk, loving someone."

"Also true, but is it better to take that risk or stay safe?"

Ginny frowned. "The last time I took a chance on a man, I ended up regretting it and, no, it wasn't Jim. I'd be dead if it wasn't for him."

Fergus studied her for a moment. "He saved your life, but it wasn't enough."

"It *should* have been enough. I mean, if I were a normal woman."

Fergus' eyebrows rose. "A normal woman would have fallen at his feet in gratitude?"

Ginny squirmed. "Isn't that what the damsel in distress is supposed to do?"

He laughed. "I've rescued a few damsels and it hasn't happened to me, yet."

Ginny took a deep breath. "One of Jim's—our—problems is that he wants to protect me, to shove me into the nearest stockade and bar the door."

Fergus smiled. "And you're afraid you'll miss out on the fun."

"It's more than that. It means he considers me part of the problem."

Fergus sighed. "Well, I can understand his wanting to keep you safe. It's a male instinct."

"I'm perfectly willing to turn tail and run, if I think it's the best choice, but I want it to be *my* choice, not his."

Fergus' brow furrowed. "You're afraid marrying him will mean handing your independence over to him."

"Won't it?"

He settled back in the chair and crossed his arms. "It depends on the type of man he is. If all he wants is a dutiful wife who cooks and cleans and keeps the home fires burning, you may have a problem. A man who leaves his wife to do all the grunt work while he goes off adventuring is likely to end up with an unsanctioned playmate and an unhappy wife."

Ginny's brow furrowed. The idea of Jim cheating on her with another woman wasn't one she had considered.

Fergus continued. "If he's the kind of man who wants intellectual companionship, he won't find it by insisting he knows best. Sometimes smart women are smarter than their men."

"That's not the case. At least, I don't think so. But I do want his respect."

Fergus smiled. "Then tell him so, and I wouldn't wait too long."

Ginny sighed, then nodded. "It's not fair to keep him dangling if I'm going to decide against him in the end."

There was a pause. "Is that a possibility?" Fergus rose from his chair and started toward her.

Ginny watched him approach, a male animal, approaching the female, cautiously, aware she might run—or turn and rend him.

Some men, maybe most, would have stood over her and

looked down. Some might have perched on the edge of the desk, one leg dangling, still looking down on her. He did neither. He sank to his haunches and looked up.

Ginny found her heart pounding, the air between them electric. It seemed her psyche split into two personalities, one ancient and instinctual, the other modern and cerebral, at war with one another, and the older brain was winning. He held out his hand, palm up and she found herself placing hers in it.

"Whatever happens, Cousin," he said, "I want you to know you can call on me. Anytime, anywhere." He lifted her hand to his lips and Ginny felt her bones turn to water. He held her gaze for a moment longer, then released her, rose, and left the room.

Ginny felt dizzy, her head pounding. She gulped air and tried to talk herself down.

Men! She shivered, wrapping her arms around herself. Dear God! Why did He make men? Or women either, for that matter. And why this devastating hunger? Passion wasn't enough. You needed wisdom as well. Wisdom and courage and kindness.

She closed her eyes and let her head sink forward onto her arms. She wasn't at all sure this little talk with Fergus had helped. It had shown her how vulnerable she was. Trust Jim? What she needed was to be able to trust herself!

* * *

CHAPTER 51

Day 21 – Thursday morning, Fifth Day of Christmas
Forbes residence

At nine a.m. on the Fifth Day of Christmas, Fergus pushed open the door of Ginny's office and stepped inside. She turned bleary eyes in his direction, then went back to work.

He studied her for a moment. Angus had asked him only to keep her safe, but he was beginning to think he could do more. Starting with those dark shadows under her eyes. He walked over and ran a hand down her back.

"Come on. Bedtime. You've done all you can here."

She shook her head. "I'm missing something."

"Well, your brain will work better if you get some sleep. Why don't you try?"

She sighed heavily. "You're right." She stood up, pushing her chair back, and stumbled into his arms. He turned her toward the door, steered her down the hall, and made sure she entered her bedroom, wishing her a good sleep, then settling down in the chair he had positioned in the hallway, to think.

Ginny had chosen to trust Jim, but that didn't make him trustworthy. Fergus knew his job too well to take anything at face value. His eyes narrowed. There had been a moment when he'd seen Ginny flinch. Jim's response had been pain, then stoicism. Not satisfaction, not triumph. None of the usual marks of an abuser. But there was something there.

Fergus frowned to himself. He needed to know more. He pulled out his phone and sent a message to Angus. Within minutes he had an appointment to see the Laird. He rose, made his way downstairs and located Mrs. Forbes.

"I'm going over to Brochaber to talk to Angus. Ginny's in bed and should sleep. Can you stay here and make sure she doesn't leave?"

Sinia Forbes nodded. "School's out for the Christmas holiday and I've got plenty of things to do around the house. Let me know when you get back."

"Yes ma'am. Thank you."

Fergus let himself out and headed toward the Laird's residence. What he wanted was insight. What had Ginny meant when she said Jim had saved her life? Why was she afraid to confront him? And, if push came to shove, could Jim Mackenzie be counted on to have a man's back?

* * *

Ginny lay on her bed and tried to shut her brain off, but it didn't work. She'd been over those files a dozen times by now and could see them with her eyes closed. With Marjorie Hawkins exonerated of Phyllis' murder, the most likely suspect was Grace Edmunds. And Grace was missing.

Detective Tran knew all of this, of course. Ginny had held nothing back, except about Fergus breaking into Grace's house to make sure she wasn't a corpse. When did suspicion become probable cause and license to violate a citizen's privacy?

Because that's all she had. Suspicion. And she'd been wrong before. Terribly wrong. Stupidly, devastatingly, get-Jim-killed wrong. She shivered at the memory.

With the dawn had come additional images from Detective Tran. The police had found Isaac's stash of incriminating photographs. Tran had sent three showing Phyllis and Grace fighting under the bridge, two men in the background, watching. According to Tran, one was a known cartel drug dealer, currently enjoying the hospitality of the Dallas jail. They were working on identifying the man in the suit.

Ginny frowned to herself. It kept coming back to the cartel.

For most of her life, Ginny had heard the horror stories. No amount of law enforcement had stopped the river of drugs. The violence had ebbed and flowed like the sea, sometimes spilling over the border, leaving broken bodies strewn on the beachhead.

They—the cartel—had no conscience. They would protect themselves. They had just suffered a massive blow to the checkbook and would be like angry bees, looking for a target to vent their fury on. And Grace was missing.

If Grace had gone to the cartel to obtain black market drugs, then Grace knew too much. And she wasn't the kind of customer they could frighten into silence, not a druggie herself. So, either she was a member of the cartel—which Ginny had trouble believing—or she was in very great danger of being killed for her guilty knowledge.

Ginny turned over restlessly. She hated lying here, not sleeping, worrying. Was there anything she could do to help in the search for Grace? Was there anything she knew that she hadn't already shared with the police?

She hadn't yet told Detective Tran about seeing Grace in the Christmas Pageant video. It probably didn't mean anything. Someone's child had insisted everyone come and watch her perform. The place had been seething with families and those working the event. Ginny paused. There was a thought. Maybe Grace wasn't there as extended family. Maybe Mater Dolorosa was her home parish.

Churches had cultures, just like other organizations. If Dolorosa was Grace's home church, she might be well-known to them. She might be staying with one of the parishioners. Hiding out with one of them. Was there anyone Ginny could ask?

She sat up abruptly and looked at the clock. Ten a.m. He should be in his office by now, or at least reachable by phone. She climbed out of bed, looked up the number and reached a secretary. Yes, but not over the phone. He could spare her fifteen minutes if she could be there by ten forty-five. She could.

Ginny put her shoes back on and grabbed her purse. The hallway was empty.

"Fergus?" She wasted five minutes hunting for him.

"Mother?" No answer. Where was everyone? Well, she didn't have time to wait. Himself would just have to understand. She scribbled a quick note, posted it on the refrigerator, and headed for Mater Dolorosa.

* * *

Thursday midmorning
Mater Dolorosa

Ginny knocked on the office door and was invited in. Father Ignacio looked up from his work and smiled at her, then gestured at the chair.

"Just give me a minute to finish this."

"Of course." Ginny settled into the chair and waited until he set the paper aside and turned to her.

"Now. How may I help you?"

Ginny explained about her suspicions, that Grace had

somehow made contact with the drug cartel and might be in trouble because of it.

"And why did you come to me?"

"Because I think she is a parishioner here."

Father Ignacio raised one eyebrow. "Did she tell you that?"

Ginny shook her head. "No. I saw her on the video." She explained about the Christmas pageant and the two boys.

"I see." Father Ignacio studied her for a moment, then pushed a button on his desk, asking his secretary to send someone in to them. He turned back to Ginny. "Yes, she is one of my flock." His brow furrowed. "She came to me, on Wednesday, for guidance."

Ginny held her breath. Anything Grace had said was likely confidential and she could not expect a priest to break the seal of the confessional.

"She told me a child had died because of her actions." He spread his hands. "Unfortunate, of course. But I gave her absolution and penance." He leaned forward, his expression earnest. "Because she is a good woman and was trying to do the right thing." He smiled at Ginny. "Just like you."

The door opened and Ginny saw a well-dressed man in a business suit enter. He looked vaguely familiar.

"This is Raul Santiago. You may have seen him here before, on the day Maria Perez was taken by the federales. He is a lawyer."

Ginny nodded. "Yes." One shoulder higher than the other. Scoliosis. She had seen him three times before this one. The first time was here, in the corridor, the day she met Father Ignacio. The second time was in the sanctuary, where she had seen Father Ignacio introduced to this man as if they were strangers. But she'd been too far away to hear, so perhaps they had merely exchanged pleasantries.

The third time—

She froze. The third time she'd seen this man was this morning, in the photograph of Phyllis and Grace fighting. He'd been under the bridge, a smile on his face, standing in easy comradeship with the drug dealer as they both watched the two women indulge in a cat fight. He was with the cartel. And she'd missed it.

Ginny rose, stumbling over an excuse. "I don't want to keep you. Thank you for your time. Anything you can think of. Goodbye."

Father Ignacio's smile widened. "I don't know what an organization such as ours would do without the Good Samaritans of the world. So willing to fight for a cause."

The door opened again and Ginny could smell something sweet.

Father Ignacio hadn't bothered to rise. He was still smiling at her. A very self-satisfied smile. "And so trusting."

Ginny sucked in a breath, understanding flooding her with sudden horror. "It was you! You arranged the attack on me, Christmas Eve."

"I arranged the shooting, but you weren't the target. You just weren't that much of a nuisance, until now."

She turned to run, but the two men between her and the door grabbed her, one of them pressing a cloth over her nose and mouth. Chloroform. Sometimes the old methods worked best and they wouldn't care if they got the dose wrong.

She struggled, but it was no use. The room was swimming and she was cursing herself for making another mistake.

This time, she was the one who would die. Only fair, but what a stupid thing to do. She was still kicking her captors, and herself, when the room went black.

* * *

Thursday noon
Brochaber

"Jim? Jim! Where's yer heid, lad?"

Jim pulled his attention back to the kitchen. "I'm not sure. What were you saying?" He had given up on sleep and come downstairs to find his grandfather and Fergus discussing him.

"I was tellin' Fergus here aboot young Williams."

Jim looked at the other man, wondering just how much he needed to know about that. It felt private. Something he and Ginny shared.

"I was asking," Fergus said, "whether there could be a connection."

Jim shook his head. "I don't see how." He found Fergus watching him. "What are you doing here, anyway? I thought you were supposed to stay with Ginny?" Jim didn't mean to sound so peevish, but there was definitely something wrong with him today. Other than fatigue.

"Sinia's on guard, lad. She'll no let Ginny come tae harm."

Jim looked at his grandfather, wishing he believed that Ginny's mother could handle whatever the cartel decided to throw her way. "I think I'll check on her."

"Let her sleep."

Jim met Fergus' eyes, then dialed Mrs. Forbes.

"She's here. She's in her bedroom."

"Are you sure? Would you go look, please?" Jim was feeling more and more uncomfortable. There was a pause during which Jim endured the increasingly skeptical gazes of both his grandfather and Cousin Fergus.

Sinia came back on the line. "You were right, Jim. She left a note. She's gone to see Father Ignacio."

Jim felt his gut clench. "Do you know what it was about?"

"That co-worker of hers who's missing, Grace Edmunds."

"Why did Ginny think he'd know anything?"

"The missing woman showed up in the recording of the Christmas Pageant. I think she was hoping someone at the church could provide a lead. I don't know how she got past me. Please tell Fergus I'm sorry."

"I will." Jim hung up the phone. "She's gone to the Roman Catholic church, to see Father Ignacio."

Fergus rose from his chair. "I'll follow her."

Jim was struggling, hard, his mind and his emotions locked in mortal combat. "Wait." Both of the other men looked at him. "Wait a minute. There's something I'm trying to remember, something important."

"You can tell me later," Fergus said.

"WAIT!"

Fergus turned, startled, then looked at Angus. The Laird was frowning at Jim, his sharp eyes riveted on his grandson. "Wait a bit, Fergus, 'til we ken wha's goin' on here."

A tiny proportion, maybe two percent, of Jim's brain was paying attention to Fergus. The rest was working on his problem. He didn't know anything, not really, it was just that he had a really bad feeling.

The minute the words formed in his brain, Jim realized what was happening. It felt just as it had the night he flew to Austin. She'd been fine that time. Safe, just out of reach. She was safe now, he told himself. It wasn't real, he told himself. That wasn't even how the Sight worked, he told himself. But—

He grabbed his phone and dialed DeSoto. "What was the code name you got out of Luis' father, the one that was supposed to be the head of the organization up here?"

"The Bishop."

Jim let loose a very bad word. "Get your people together. I know who the head man is."

"Who? How?"

Jim ignored him. "No sirens. I'll meet you at the little park across the street from Mater Dolorosa. Fast as you can."

"Mackenzie! Report!"

"Ginny went in alone, to talk to Father Ignacio." Jim saw his grandfather's eyes register comprehension.

"Fifteen minutes."

Jim hung up the phone and looked at the other two. "Maria Perez and Grace Edmunds," he explained, "both go missing and the thing—the person—they have in common is Father Ignacio."

The Laird turned to Fergus. "Go, lad. Hurry."

"I'm coming with you," Jim said.

Fergus didn't even pause, just threw the words back over his shoulder. "Come on, then. But if you slow me down, I'll leave you behind."

* * *

CHAPTER 52

Day 21 – Thursday noon
Mater Dolorosa

The first thing Ginny noticed was the cold. The second was the nausea. She clawed her way to consciousness, trying to get her eyes open, to get to a bathroom, so she could vomit. She didn't make it.

There was a bucket sitting on the floor beside her. She grabbed it and vomited again, then heard a whimper from across the room and looked up. She was not alone.

"Grace?"

Ginny had heard that chloroform could make a patient so sick he could tear out newly inserted stitches with the force of the vomiting. She believed it. She vomited again, then pushed the bucket aside and gulped in air, grateful to find it (mostly) odorless.

"What are you doing here?"

The other woman crawled toward her across the floor, almost unrecognizable as the suave, sophisticated ICU nurse Ginny knew. Her hair was a mess, her clothes stained, her eyes haunted.

"I came to see Father Ignacio."

Ginny had her head in both hands, trying to avoid moving it.

"He told me." She peered at Grace with one eye. "Why?"

"Why did I come?"

"Yes."

"To make my confession."

Ginny had both eyes closed again, but her ears were working. "A dead child."

"Yes." Grace started crying.

"Is he a real priest or is he just faking?"

"I don't know."

Ginny had settled into a stillness that seemed to be working to keep the nausea at bay. She took a careful breath, then opened one eye. "Tell me what happened."

The old Grace would have refused. This one begged.

"At first, it was nothing. I heard some people talking about how hard it was for illegals to get good medical care in Texas. If they came for treatment, they got deported.

"Some of the stories were heart-breaking, but they were just stories. Then, one day, at church, I saw something I wasn't supposed to. They were in bad shape. I could see how dehydrated they were. One of the women was holding a baby. Just holding it. It was dead." Grace pulled in a ragged breath.

"I couldn't do anything, but I couldn't escape the feeling I should. I asked the woman I was with if there was any way I could help. At first, she said no. But I kept asking and eventually she told me they needed everything: food, water, clothes, medical care.

"I got hold of some of those brochures they're always pushing at nurses, and gave them to her, explaining there were charities in Dallas designed to meet those needs. She took the flyers, but shook her head at me. 'They won't go,' she said. 'They're afraid.' So, I started bringing things in and giving them to my friend, to pass along. Little things, at first, then bigger loads, then one day she told me to follow her in my car." Her face twisted at the memory.

"She took me to a part of Dallas I didn't know existed. Not south Dallas. Here. In this upscale suburb. You wouldn't believe the slum conditions. It wasn't just malnutrition. They were infected and infested. I looked at a few of the children and asked what kind of care they were getting. I was told there were old women who were considered healers, and there were benefactors who gave them money so they could buy over-the-counter medicines. Better than nothing, but not good enough.

"I started spending time with the healers. Some of what they did was harmless and some of it effective. Tar works, you know, on skin conditions, but they had no insulin for the diabetics and no antibiotics. They understood the problem. They just couldn't get their hands on the medications.

"I went home that day and started thinking. I didn't have the right credential to prescribe either drug. I'm not a Nurse Practitioner, but I know people who are." She brushed at the tears.

"I stole a script pad and forged a signature and used those to buy prescription drugs, out of my own pocket. And I kept urging the refugees to go to the free clinic. But they wouldn't. When the script pad ran out, I couldn't get another so I had to come up with something else. They were relying on me.

"About that time I overheard Lisa talking to the guy in Human Resources. They were in the cafeteria and I don't think either one of them knew I could hear them. She was saying he needed to follow Phyllis to the drug drop, to get pictures of her breaking the law, so she could be fired. He was arguing, saying he couldn't sell photos like that, not without losing his job.

"Anyway, I gathered that Phyllis knew where to buy black market drugs, so I followed her and got lucky. She led me to the dealer. I didn't let on, just waited until she was gone, then made my first buy. It was almost too easy. You can get anything you want." Grace shook her head.

"One night I was there, making a purchase, and Phyllis caught me at it. She thought I was buying recreational drugs and I didn't tell her the truth. She lectured me on the evils of a drug habit. I told her to mind her own business. But she was really angry and grabbed my arm. She broke one of the vials. That set me off and the two of us indulged in a very un-ladylike brawl.

"Isaac, the HR guy, had taken Lisa's advice and followed Phyllis, so he was able to get nice, clear shots of the whole thing." Grace frowned. "He offered to sell them to me. Probably did the same to Phyllis.

"Last week, one of the healers asked me to get her some chemo for a child with kidney cancer. I should have said no. That stuff is poison. But I did it and handed it over, with the instructions out of the drug handbook and a package insert I got off the Internet. I tried to walk away, but they kept begging me to set up the IV, to tell them how much, how often. Their English wasn't up to the task. I should have said no." Grace put her head down on her arms.

"He didn't do well, even with me staying with him, watching the IV, giving him the antiemetic. He got weaker and weaker and I got scared. So I drove him to one of the clinics, dropped him off, with his mother, and told her to pretend she had no English. Then I ran home."

Ginny watched the tears well up and spill down Grace's cheeks.

"He died in the night. I couldn't face going in to work, so I called in sick. That was Tuesday. By Wednesday, I couldn't live with myself, so I called Father Ignacio and asked for an appointment. He heard my confession, and gave me penance and sent me out to the Lady Chapel. I was on my knees, going through the prayers, begging for forgiveness when they grabbed me." She looked at Ginny. "Do you have any idea what they plan to do with us?"

Ginny took a careful breath. "If they're feeding you, they want you alive."

Grace frowned. "It looks like they think I'll go to the police, but the whole point of confession was so I wouldn't have to tell anyone else. A priest should know that."

Ginny felt a stab of annoyance. "They may not want to take a chance on you following the rules, since you didn't before."

"But this is different," Grace protested. "This is a promise to God."

If the situation hadn't been so grim, Ginny would have laughed. It was exactly the sort of naiveté that Father Ignacio had twisted to suit himself.

"I'm not sure they believe in God, but I'll tell you what they do believe in. Money. And you, my dear, with your *café au lait* skin and your almond shaped eyes and your long, lean, lithesome body, will fetch a pretty penny on the sex slave market." She saw Grace blanch, then swallow.

"I don't think I'd like that."

Ginny shook her head and found that she could do so without vomiting. Good. The drug was wearing off. It was time to think about getting out of here.

"Then we'd better do something about it."

* * *

Thursday, twelve-thirty p.m.
Streets of Dallas

Fergus wasted no time moving through traffic. Jim was leaning forward, watching the road. "Turn here."

"I know."

Jim bit his tongue. Both of them had visited Mater Dolorosa exactly once. They both knew the way.

They were less than a block away when Jim saw a white hatchback coming toward them. He saw the personalized license plate mounted on the front and the Cross of St. Andrew sticker on the windshield and stiffened.

"That's Ginny's car!" He turned in his seat to follow the vehicle with his eyes. "There's a man driving!"

Fergus reached for his dashboard and hit a button.

"9-1-1. What is your emergency?"

"Possible abduction/carjacking. White Volkswagen four-door hatchback. License plate CLANTX. Heading south on Sagebrush. The car is registered to a missing woman. Virginia Forbes, aged 28. Caucasian, blue eyes, long red hair. Check the trunk."

Fergus was still talking as they pulled into the parking lot to find DeSoto waiting for them. Jim almost fell out of the car.

"They've got her!"

"They've got her car," Fergus corrected. He explained about the 9-1-1 call. "They're already on their way."

Jim shook his head. "That's not what I meant. She's not in the car. She's here."

DeSoto looked at him curiously. "How do you know?"

"I'll tell you later. Let's find her first."

"Okay. On the assumption she kept that appointment, we need to find out where they took her." DeSoto reached into his vehicle and pulled out an electronic device. "This is a wireless bug." He plugged an earpiece into his ear and handed one each to Jim and Fergus. "We need to send someone in to plant this thing."

"I'll go," Fergus said.

DeSoto shook his head. "Sending a stranger after Ginny will just spook him." He turned and looked at Jim. "He knows Mackenzie. That could play either for or against us. He might just shoot him on sight, but I think it's unlikely. Gunshots inside the church are bound to be heard."

Both Jim and Fergus nodded.

"My people are moving into position now. Ask Ignacio if he's seen Ginny, but don't challenge him. Accept whatever he says."

Jim nodded.

"If we're lucky, Ginny's car will give us probable cause for a warrant. In the meantime, the law allows us access to any place open to the public. That's important because we don't want our perp to walk on a technicality. Can you two work together?"

Jim looked at Fergus and nodded. His grandfather trusted this man absolutely. Fergus hesitated a moment longer, then also nodded.

"Okay. Stewart, you've got Mackenzie's back. Stay out of sight, but it's your job to see he makes it out alive and in one piece."

Fergus nodded.

"Mackenzie, your job is to plant that bug and get out of there. Understood?"

Jim nodded.

"After that, I want both of you to come back here and wait for me."

* * *

CHAPTER 53

Day 21 – Thursday, one p.m.
Mater Dolorosa

"Are we still in Mater Dolorosa?" Ginny asked.

Grace screwed up her forehead. "I think so. I've been able to hear the bells for mass."

"Okay. Let me think." Ginny cleared her mind of all the trouble they were in and let her eyes do their job. Old paint on the walls, crumbling and peeling. An old ceiling, too, the plaster falling to make mounds of white dust on the floor. Storage shelves and a large, bare sink with large, bare faucets. A utility room. Rags and a jug or two of cleaning solution.

Ginny wasn't a chemist. Even if she could locate the right chemicals, the most she could do would be to combine ammonia with chlorine bleach and kill Grace and herself with poison gas. Not the best outcome.

She gazed up at the naked light bulb that hung over their heads. If she could reach it, she could short out the system and alert someone to come check on them. Also not the best outcome.

There were a few tools: a rubber mallet, a screwdriver, a paint brush. A quick check confirmed they had taken her coat, purse, phone, keys, watch, and the small gun she wore on her ankle when she went out. On a really good day she might be able to strangle someone with her bra, but this was not a good day. Nor would they come alone. They would come in pairs, and armed. Jumping them would probably only get her killed faster.

The church was old enough to have a historic marker. Solidly built, but more than a century and a half ago. Ginny's brow furrowed. What was it her mother had told her about this building? That the land on which it sat had subsided, because of the weight.

All the buildings in the north Texas area had similar problems. The clay on which they stood sucked up the water, then dried out, unevenly, and the foundations cracked. With a big, heavy cathedral-type structure, the weight had compressed the earth beneath it as far as it could go. It didn't rock back and forth, as the smaller buildings did, but it had settled five feet since it was built.

Meanwhile, Dallas had grown up around it. Over time, the streets had been repaved and drainage added and utilities buried and landscaping done. At the point where the entrance to the church lay fully below ground level, they gave up and made a new entrance on what had been the second floor. A magnificent staircase now invited worshippers to divine service, climbing toward heaven, rather than descending into the bowels of the earth.

Ginny blinked slowly, her eyes on the dust piles on the floor. They seemed out of place. The rest of the room was neat and reasonably clean. There was a broom in the corner, and a dustpan. Someone swept this room regularly. So why the dust? She crawled over to the nearest pile and examined it. A tiny mountain of white powder, a stream from the ceiling above.

Construction. There was always construction going on in Dallas. One could not escape it. In this part of town, Ginny knew, it was a subway extension. The Rapid Transit people had proposed a new set of rails, with a stop at the church. The tunnel had been dug. Once the rest of the infrastructure was in place, they would knock down a portion of the church wall and make a new entrance. That explained the dust. The heavy equipment needed to make a subway would shake this old building hard.

There was no work going on this week, of course. It was Christmas and everyone had the week off. So, no one to hear if they screamed. Thick walls, too.

Ginny's eyes moved from the floor to the walls. When the church was first built, this was the ground floor. Every room with exterior walls would have had windows. She climbed shakily to her feet, crossed to the shelves and tried to lift one end.

"What are you doing?"

"We need to barricade that door."

"What good will that do? They'll just break it down."

"It might give us enough time to find a way out of here."

Grace nodded and gave her a hand moving the shelving and supplies. The door opened inward, so it would take some time to push past the obstruction.

"Okay. Next." Ginny picked up the mallet. She rejected the wall with the interior door, turning her back on it, and facing the opposite side of the room. She walked over and began tapping, listening to the sound the small blows made. Small blows, because she didn't want anyone who might be outside that door to hear.

She moved methodically across the expanse, listening carefully. Windows were usually installed at waist level or higher. She estimated the distance to that naked light bulb. Not twenty feet. Might be twelve.

About one third of the way along, she heard a change in the resonance. She turned to Grace.

"Would you bring me that screwdriver and see if you can

find something to pry with? A crowbar of some sort?"

Working carefully, quietly, aware their captors could come check on them at any moment, Ginny and Grace broke holes through the wallboard, then peeled it away, revealing the original interior wall.

"There it is." Ginny pointed.

It was higher than she expected, about five feet off the floor, but clearly an old-fashioned window that was intended to be raised to let light and air into the room. Ginny climbed one of the racks and inspected it.

"Nailed and painted shut. We'll have to break it. Hand me that drop cloth, please, and stand clear. There may be flying glass."

Ginny laid the drop cloth over the ancient glass and gave it a sharp rap with the mallet. The pane broke sweetly and fell outside. Cold air rushed into the room.

"Okay. Turn out the light and come over here."

"If I turn out the light, I won't be able to see what I'm doing."

"It will give our eyes a chance to adjust to the darkness outside and will help to blind the bad guys if they manage to break through that door."

"Oh, okay."

Ginny knocked out the other five panes as quickly as she could, then broke the wooden frame, making a hole large enough for them to crawl through. That part of the process was noisy.

"Come on." She spread the drop cloth over the shattered edge of the window, then hoisted herself through, dropping to the ground outside. Grace followed.

"I think I've cut my hand."

"Me too. Let's go."

"Which way?"

It was a good question. They were in deep gloom, with no obvious way out.

"If this is the train tunnel, it has to lead somewhere."

"Are we in danger from the train?"

"No. The tracks haven't been laid yet."

"I wish we had some light."

Ginny looked both ways, shivering in the cold and anxious to get started. She touched her talisman, silently asking for help, then made a decision. "This way." If she was right, they would be heading further downtown and into a more populated part of the city.

"I think I see a light."

Ginny stopped. "Where?"

"That way."

"I don't see anything."

"Well, I'm going that way."

"Grace, wait." But she was gone.

Ginny hesitated for only a moment, then turned her back on the other woman and headed for downtown. She focused all her attention on the uneven ground, trying to make as good time as possible. Ten minutes later she was rewarded with a steady increase in the ambient lighting. Another ten minutes brought her to the exit.

The winter sun poured through the grille that separated her from freedom, showing her massive steel bars, and a chain with a padlock the size of Jim's fist. She examined the lock, wishing she'd learned how to pick one, but unconvinced that her hairpins would have been enough against this industrial-strength obstacle. The Transit Authority wanted to make sure no one came onto the construction site and got hurt. It made sense. It also made her heart sink. She examined her options.

The grille did not go all the way to the earthen floor or all the way to the curved roof. What's more, the ceiling looked like normal dirt. With the right tool, she might be able to move some of it out of her way. She looked around and found a discarded chisel. She climbed the grille, wedged herself into the space to see how much dirt she needed to remove, then set to work.

She was making progress. Her shoulder fit through the gap and her head almost did when she heard the pursuers coming down the tunnel. She could see flashlights waving around and hear voices, one of them Grace's.

Ginny abandoned her work and looked for some place to hide. The walls and floor were solid earth. There were no construction containers or huge spools of wire or anything else big enough to hide a full-grown woman. She looked up and found pipes and conduits running along the ceiling. If she could reach them, she could use them as a shield.

She swung off the grille and onto a pipe, climbed as high as she could, then squirmed into a spot between the big water main and the ceiling and settled down, prepared to stay very, very still. Maybe, just maybe, they wouldn't look up. And if they did, maybe, just maybe, she wouldn't show from that angle. She thanked heaven she had decided to wear dark sweats today. The pants and top covered most of her pale skin. She stuffed her hair inside her shirt, tucked her hands up against her chest, put her head down on the pipe, and tried to still her racing heart.

* * *

Thursday, one p.m.
Mater Dolorosa

Jim stood in Father Ignacio's office, trying not to give anything away.

"She never made it this far?" Jim studied the other man's face, looking for a tell. There! The break in eye contact, just for a second and back almost immediately. He was lying. He'd seen her. So where was she, and why did he have to lie about it? Jim leaned over the surface of the desk, toward the other man, sliding the tiny microphone under the edge and pressing it in place.

"Are you sure?" He tried for just the right balance of confusion, worry, and suspicion.

"We had an appointment, but she never came." Father Ignacio registered concern. "I do hope nothing has happened to her."

Jim straightened up, running his hand through his hair, and letting his anxiety show on his face. "Me, too. Will you let me know if you hear from her?" He took out a business card and handed it over.

"Of course." Father Ignacio rose and escorted Jim to the corridor. "I'm sure she'll be fine, but I'll put the word out immediately."

"Thank you." Jim shook his hand, then headed back to the car. He needed to be seen leaving.

Fergus beat him to it. "Get in." He handed Jim the second ear piece, let him close the door, then moved off.

Jim plugged the device in and was immediately rewarded. "Have you found them?" Father Ignacio's voice sounded in his ear. Then something in Spanish.

Fergus translated. "They pulled the wallboard off and broke a window. They're in the train tunnel."

Satisfaction in the priest's voice this time. "Excellent. They can't get out. Take as many men as you need. I want them both alive."

The reply came in Spanish, but Jim had no trouble translating this one for himself. "Yes, Bishop."

Jim grabbed the GPS and tapped until he got what he wanted.

"Which way?" Fergus asked.

"Turn right at the next corner. You're looking for the rail line. Unless you're planning to go sit in the park and wait."

Fergus' nostrils flared. "I don't work for that man."

They drove until they saw the *Coming Soon* signs indicating the subway extension.

"There are two places where you can get down into the tunnel. We have to choose."

Fergus pulled the car over and studied the map, then pointed at a spot on the enlargement. "This is where it joins up with the existing line."

He parked in the area reserved for construction vehicles, then jumped out, reaching into the trunk. He handed Jim a heavy set of bolt cutters, then slipped a pistol into the space in the small of his back, strapped a loaded thigh holster in place, filled his pockets with ammunition, and pulled a third gun (fourth, if you counted the shoulder holster he was already wearing) out of its case. He looked at the weapon in his hand, then at Jim.

"Can you hit what you aim at?" he asked.

Jim met Fergus' eyes. He was tempted to lie, to save face, but decided Ginny's safety was more important. "Not consistently."

The other man nodded. "All right, then. Let's go."

* * *

CHAPTER 54

Day 21 – Thursday, two p.m.
The tunnel construction entrance

Ginny held her breath as the voices came nearer. They spoke to one another, mostly in Spanish, but using standard English when addressing Grace.

"So where is she?"

"I don't know."

"She can't get out. What were you planning?"

"We didn't have a plan. Let me go!"

"Hey, Hector. Boss said he wanted them alive, but he didn't say in what condition. How about we have a little fun with this one. She's pretty, no?"

"She's pretty, yes, and you'd better leave the merchandise alone."

"Aw, come on. Just one little kiss. Ow!"

Ginny smothered a smile. That had to be Grace, expressing her opinion of the one little kiss.

"Why, you bitch! I'll teach you—"

"Not now, Diego. Later, maybe, after we find the other one."

They were almost parallel with her. Ginny held her breath. She could see them and, if they looked up, they would be able to see her. One of them peered out the grille. "I don't see no one."

"She wouldn't be over there, dumb ass. Didn't I tell you she can't get out?"

"Oh." He turned and scanned the tunnel. Ginny froze.

"So, pretty girl. Where did she go? With you, down the other direction?"

"I don't know!"

"I think you do." The ringleader brought his gun up and placed the barrel against Grace's cheek. "One more time. Which way did she go?"

"You won't shoot me. You'll get into trouble."

"Might be worth it. Or maybe the boss will understand. Or maybe I'll just shatter your jaw. All those pretty white teeth— gone. You won't be so pretty then, but you'll still be alive."

Ginny heard a cautious sound from the direction of the grille. From her vantage point she could see two figures, one on either side of the opening.

The one on the right held a set of bolt cutters. The one on the left was sliding the barrel of a largish pistol between the bars of the grille. She watched the barrel steady, then jump when the weapon was fired.

Bedlam erupted. There were howls of outrage and curses and the sound of bad guys hitting the ground. They were returning fire now. Lots of it. Ginny pulled her hands up and stuffed her fingers in her ears. When one of the bullets hit the pipe she was on, she gasped. She couldn't help it.

"Ginny?" Jim's voice. "Ginny!" Had he seen her?

"Ginny! Catch!" That was Fergus. She saw a pistol tossed through the bars of the grille and land almost underneath her.

Without thinking, she rolled off the pipe and fell to the earthen floor, then lunged for the weapon. She snapped it up, rolled over, aimed at the nearest bad guy, and fired.

There were two down already, hers made three, but the remaining gunmen were armed with rapid-fire weapons. She had two things going for her: first, submachine guns set on full automatic and in the hands of angry criminals were not known for exceptional accuracy, and second, Fergus was.

She saw one of them trying to find cover behind a low wall that stretched along the edge of the church property. She took careful aim and ended his personal reign of terror with a round that made him unrecognizable to anyone other than his maker. Fergus had loaded his weapon with hollow points. Ginny approved the choice.

At least one of them was still firing at her, spraying the area with bullets. They zipped past her ears, hitting the dirt, and the gate, and the cast iron pipe above her. She tried to aim at the bad guy's head, squeezed off a round, and missed.

Grace had been screaming. Ginny heard the sound stop, abruptly. There was a final round of shots, then silence.

Jim must have made a good job of the bolt cutters, for she heard metal cracking, then the sound of a chain being pulled through the grille. Then the gate creaked open and she heard footsteps coming toward her.

She lay in the dirt, her eyes, and the borrowed weapon, still trained in the direction of the bad guys.

Jim dropped to the earth beside her.

"Are you hurt?"

She shook her head. "I think Grace is."

Jim nodded, then hurried over to kneel beside Grace and assess the situation.

Fergus was examining the corpses, removing their weapons, making sure they would pose no further threat. Once that was done, he approached Ginny, carefully, from the side, his hand closing around the pistol grip. She left go. "Thanks."

"You're welcome." He unloaded the weapon and tucked it

away, then held out a hand.

"How did you find me?" she asked.

"It was Jim."

Ginny climbed to her feet, then found her knees buckling. Residual from the chloroform, perhaps, combined with adrenaline. With Fergus' help, she stumbled over and collapsed beside Grace.

She could see the point of entry and the spreading blood. Jim had pulled off his gloves and made a compression pad of them. She put her hands down on the pad and pushed while he called 9-1-1.

"What happened?" she asked.

"I think," Fergus answered her, "a ricochet off that pipe."

Ginny nodded, then turned back to the woman under her hands. "Grace can you hear me? Open your eyes."

Grace's eyes slowly focused. "Ginny?"

"I'm here."

Grace reached up and took a grip on Ginny's shirt, pulling her closer. "There's something I need to tell you, before I die."

"You're not going to die," Ginny said, then caught Jim's expression and knew it was a lie.

"Just listen." Grace swallowed, then closed her eyes. "Forgive me, Father, for I have sinned. It's been one day since my last confession."

"Shouldn't there be a priest?" Fergus asked.

"It's all right," Ginny told him. "God will listen." She addressed the dying woman. "Grace," she said, "you don't have to do this. He knows what's in your heart."

"But you don't. I murdered Phyllis Kyle."

Ginny let out a small breath. "Why?"

Grace swallowed. "I was eaten up with the sin of pride. I thought I knew better than the experts, that I could do what was needed and not hurt anyone. I broke the law and when

Phyllis caught me, I thought her life wasn't as important as the good work I was doing." Grace paused for a moment to catch her breath.

"Save your strength."

"No. Hear me out." She licked her lips, now stained with blood. "I was bragging to her, about all the good I was doing. She pointed out that I was practicing medicine without a license. I denied it, but she was right. She told me again—she'd said it before—that it was safer to use the free clinics. She was right about that, too. If I'd listened, maybe that boy would still be alive."

She coughed and blood ran down her cheek and onto the earthen floor. "She didn't threaten me. All she did was pull up the web site to look at the guidelines, but I panicked. I figured I had until the end of the shift. I was sure she'd turn me in the minute the office opened. Without my license and without my job, I wouldn't be able to do any more good for the refugees. They were relying on me. They needed me. They trusted me."

Grace's breath was now a harsh rasp in her throat. Her hand groped, seeking another, and Ginny took it, clasping it tightly.

Grace's voice was growing fainter. "God forgive me!" She gasped, then closed her eyes. "I see now how wrong I was." In a voice hardly more than a pale whisper, she began, "Lord, have mercy on me, a sinner." She struggled to pull in another breath. "Holy Mary—Mother of God—" Her voice faded out.

"—pray for us sinners now and at the hour of our death." Ginny finished the line.

There was a spasm, or maybe another cough. More blood ran from her mouth, then all was still. Ginny found tears running down her face. Holy Mary, Mother of God—Mary had watched her son be crucified, a horrendous death, slow and painful. At least this one had been quick.

"Who's in there?"

Ginny ignored the strange voice. Probably a policeman, come to investigate the noise.

The two men rose to deal with the newcomer. Ginny stayed where she was, letting the tears fall. After a while, she felt arms lifting her to her feet. An ambulance had come, silently, since there was no need for hurry. Someone sat her down on the ruins of the brick wall and washed her hands. They were covered in blood, Grace's blood.

The motto of the Forbes clan was, "Grace me guide." Ginny could not follow Grace into her sin, but she could try to follow her repentance. Pride was an easy sin to fall into and a hard one to recognize in one's self.

She was shivering with the cold and shock. But Jim was there, wrapping her in a heavy jacket, sitting down next to her, pulling her into his arms. Warm, strong, gentle arms.

She felt him enfold her and in that moment she understood. The problem between them wasn't trust. It was pride that had been keeping them apart, his pride and hers. They would have to work that out, or part company.

"Mackenzie! Forbes!"

She looked up and saw DeSoto approaching.

"We got him! We got the whole damned lot of them!" He strode up to them, then went down on his haunches. "If it were in my power, you would both get medals."

"Purple hearts?" Jim suggested.

"Medals of valor. You're both heroes." He stood. "I'll catch up with you later. Lots of work to do."

"Heroes." Ginny echoed the word. "I feel more like a fool."

"As in, 'Fools rush in?'"

"Something like that." She looked up at Jim. "Fergus said you figured it out."

He nodded. "It was a case of hiding in plain sight. DeSoto told me the boss' code name was, 'The Bishop,' but I dismissed

THE SWICK AND THE DEAD

a church connection as being too obvious."

"And I was unwilling to consider a man of the cloth as the evil genius behind all these deaths. He deceived us all." She sighed heavily. "I owe you an apology, Jim. I shouldn't have left the house today, not without backup."

"True, but you were following your gut. Trusting your instincts. Just like you used to."

She thought about that for a moment. He was right. The last three weeks had been terrifying, but each new challenge had helped rebuild her faith in herself.

"What's more," Jim continued, "if you hadn't gone after Grace and I hadn't gone after you, Father Ignacio would still be at large. Instead, the cartel is broken, and you caught Phyllis' killer. You should be proud of yourself."

Ginny watched the ambulance drive away. "I'm not proud of the mistakes I've made."

He pulled her closer. "Having the courage to try, even though you may screw up, is something to be proud of."

She looked into his face. Not conceit, not arrogance. That wasn't the kind of pride he meant. A reasonable self-respect, based on honorable actions. Too little of that sort of pride could be as bad as too much.

The police kept them answering questions for another hour, then agreed to let them finish up at the police station the next day. Fergus they eyed with suspicion, but the permits for his private arsenal must have been in order. They did not detain him. He turned his back on the officers and came over to where Jim and Ginny sat.

"Ready to go home?" he asked.

Jim nodded, then pulled Ginny to her feet, slipped an arm around her waist, and started toward the gate.

She put a hand out to stop him. "Give me a minute, Jim."

He paused, then nodded and moved off in the direction of

the car.

Ginny turned to Fergus. She took both of his hands in hers, then pulled him into a hug.

"Thank you, Cousin," she said, "for my life and my lesson."

"You're welcome. So, have you made up your mind?"

"Ask me again tomorrow."

The two of them turned and walked side by side, toward the tunnel opening and the last of the winter afternoon. Jim was waiting for them just beyond the entrance.

Ginny paused for a moment and looked around. The Christmas decorations were still in place downtown, awaiting the New Year celebrations, the rooftops heavy with faux icicles, every window display more elaborate than the last. Even the traffic lights cycled cheerfully between red and green. Peace on Earth.

She took both men's arms, pulling them closer. Peace sounded awfully good right now. "Maybe we'll get a vacation before the next body shows up," she said.

"No more murders for me!" Jim said. "I'm giving them up for Lent." He looked down at her. "And the next time Detective Tran calls you in as a consultant?"

"Oh, come on, Jim! How likely is that?"

"How likely was it you'd be involved in two murder investigations in less than three months?"

Ginny shifted uneasily. "It's still not my job."

"Oh, I don't know." Fergus looked along his shoulder at her. "Sometimes we find a job. Sometimes a job finds us."

* * *

CHAPTER 55

New Year's Eve, just before midnight
Forbes residence

"When is Alex supposed to get here?" Ginny threw her coat into the closet and hurried to help set up for the First Footing.

"He called from Denver to say the plane was delayed by bad weather." Her brother and his family had been spending Christmas with his wife's parents.

"I hope they don't have to spend the night in the airport."

Her mother poked her nose around the corner. "He'll let us know when there's news. How was the party?"

"Excellent! Some of the die-hards are still at it."

"It's too bad Fergus couldn't stay. He's dark enough to count as good luck." She was referring to the First Footing.

In the Scottish tradition, the first male visitor to cross the threshold on New Year's Day foretold the fortunes of the family for the coming year. A fair haired visitor meant ill luck, while a dark one, especially one bearing the traditional gifts of a lump of coal for the fire, shortbread, and whisky, assured good luck for the next twelve months. The fair-haired man was said to be a reminder of the Viking attacks on Scotland in the ninth century. The tradition persisted in spite of the number of blondes and redheads common among the Scots both before and after the Viking incursions.

Ginny smiled to herself. Fergus had certainly been good luck for her. He'd fulfilled his promise to Angus. No small feat, considering what trouble she had caused. And he had offered her his friendship. When they parted, he'd taken her face in both hands and kissed her, then given her a bear hug. "You call me," he had said, "day or night, if you need me." And she had promised she would.

"I'm sure they'll put him to good use in Georgetown," she said.

"Who's First Footing us?" Sinia asked.

"We've drawn Reggie MacDonald and he's going to be busy 'til dawn. I've seen his list."

Mrs. Forbes laughed. "He can handle it. What's our position?"

"Second."

Mrs. Forbes nodded. "Good. We'll be done before the bells have finished."

Ginny glanced at the clock. She'd broken away from the Hogmanay ceilidh with only fifteen minutes to spare. The clock now stood at five minutes to midnight. She grabbed the single malt and started to pour.

"His first stop is the Camerons, after which Caroline and Alan are coming here. Jim said something similar, though I think Himself drew Geordie this year and they may talk all night. I'm ready." She picked up the tray of wee drams and set it near the door. "There go the bells!"

They could hear the Auld Kirk bells begin to ring, first tolling out the old year, followed by a jubilant peal to celebrate the birth of the new one. Ginny watched the clock. When it reached midnight exactly, she lifted a glass to her mother, who returned the salute.

"Happy New Year!"

Ginny sipped the scotch, then turned as the doorbell rang.

"That was fast!" She pulled open the door then gasped. "No!"

Alex stood on the threshold, smiling. "We made it!" He started to enter, but Ginny threw her hand out to stop him.

"Wait! Don't cross yet!"

Alex glanced down at his watch, puzzled. "Why not? It's still last year."

"No, it's not! Have you forgotten the time change?"

He gritted his teeth. "Drat! Yes! We were so glad to be airborne I forgot to reset my watch!"

Ginny stepped out into the cold night air and gave her brother a hug. "Reggie will be here in a minute, after which we can all go inside."

"Aunt Ginny!" Three boys all embraced her at once, crowding around, then breaking away.

"Nana!" The youngest, George, made a beeline for his grandmother, who stood just inside the house looking out at the reunion taking place on her front walk.

"George, wait!" His father tried to catch him, but missed, and the rosy-skinned, blue-eyed, blonde was over the threshold and in his grandmother's embrace before they could do anything about it.

Ginny burst out laughing. "Does it count if the fair haired male is not a man?"

Sinia Forbes gave her a rueful smile. "Aye, it does." She kissed her grandson on the top of his head. "Well, you'd better all come in, then." She gestured them inside with hugs and kisses all around, followed by scotch for the grownups and ginger ale for the boys.

Reggie followed hot on their heels and was invited in for his own wee dram. Caroline and Alan were right behind him and Jim and Himself showed up fifteen minutes later.

The bells had been replaced by the boom of fireworks and with the front door open, they could see the rockets going up over the loch. Someone started singing Auld Lang Syne and they all chimed in.

Jim put his arm around Ginny's waist, then pulled her into a kiss. "Happy New Year!"

She looked up at him. "May it be quieter than the last!"

"You're not worried, are you? About George crossing the threshold first?"

She gave him a crooked little smile, then shrugged, her hand stealing up to the talisman around her neck.

"It's just an old wives' tale," she said. "No one believes in those things any more. Besides, with two murders in three months, we've used up our allowance of bad luck for a while. We should be fine."

"Just superstition, huh?" He took her hand and started to pull her toward the front hall. "Like the Sight? And your talisman?"

The door was still open and the brisk winter air stirred the mistletoe hanging above the threshold. Jim reached up and plucked a berry, then gathered Ginny into his arms. "They say that couples who kiss under the mistletoe will marry within the year and have a long happy life. Care to chance it?"

Ginny laughed, slid her arms around his neck, and gave him a mocking smile. "Why not? After all, it's just an Auld Wives' tale!"

THE END

GLOSSARY

Aboot – about

Ain – own

Ane – one (rhymes with "gain")

Aught – anything

Aye – yes

Bairn – baby

Bodhran – (pronounced "bow-rawn") a Celtic frame drum made of hard, circular wood with goat skin tacked to one side. It is supported on the body with hands and thigh and played with a wooden rod called a tipper.

Ceilidh – party

Curandera – a traditional native healer

Deid – dead

DFW – Dallas / Ft. Worth (Texas)

Didnae – did not, didn't

Dinna – do not, don't

DNA – Deoxyribonucleic acid

Dram – one sixteenth of an ounce (3.7 milliliters)

ER – emergency room

ETT – endotracheal tube, an artificial airway

Forbye – besides, in addition (to)

Gallóglaigh – Scottish mercenaries. The *gallóglaigh* arose in the mid-thirteenth century, originating on the western coast of Scotland, principally Argyll and the Western Isles (and believed to be the descendants of the Vikings). They were mighty warriors, famed for their strength and lack of compassion. There are references to them fighting in Ireland, Holland, Switzerland, France, and Sweden.

Gi'e – give

Gin – if (hard "g" sound)

GPS – global positioning system

Ha'e – have

Haes – has
Heid – head
Haud yer wheesht! – Be quiet!
HIPAA – Health Insurance Portability and Accountability Act – A law which defines protected health information and provides for penalties for improper disclosure.
IV – intravenous
Keek – peek, look
Ken – understand
Kilts – a non-bifurcated garment extending from waist to mid-knee, with pleats at the back and a flap across the front, secured with belt, buckles, and pins. The traditional dress of Gaelic men in the Scottish Highlands, it is usually made of wool in a tartan pattern.
MIA – missing in action
Na – no
Nae or no – not
NCLEX – the licensing examination for nurses
Nyaff – little nuisance (as in a person)
Penannular – having the shape or design of an incomplete circle
Pipes – bagpipes
PTSD – Post Traumatic Stress Disorder
Q&A – question and answer
Reel – a fast dance tempo in Scottish Country Dancing, also the name of a figure in which the dancers move in and out of the line of dance.
Richt – right
Rink – Scottish word for "course," used to describe the area where the game of curling is played
Slàinte – "good health"
Sporran – a traditional part of male Scottish Highland dress, a pouch that performs the same function as a pocket. The

sporran is worn on a leather strap or chain, conventionally positioned in front of the groin of the wearer.

Strathspey – a slower, more stately dance tempo in Scottish Country Dancing, with the emphasis on grace, body position, and elegant footwork.

Tot – seventy-one milliliters (in the U.S., a "shot" of whisky is 30 milliliters)

TPN – Total Parenteral Nutrition

Triage – A method of classifying patients to determine priority

Verra – very

Wean – child (rhymes with "gain") A combination of wee and ane.

Wee – small

Wee dram – an indeterminate quantity of alcohol

Wha – who

Worrit – worried

VIKING VENGEANCE

Ginny is forced to eat her words in her next adventure, *Viking Vengeance: Loch Lonach Mysteries, Book Three.*

The Up Helly Aa was not intended as a real Viking funeral. A least, there wasn't *supposed* to be a body tucked inside the ship the Lonach Homesteaders built and burned each January. But the discovery of a charred corpse hidden in the wreckage sends Jim and Ginny racing cross country in a perilous attempt to obtain justice for one of their own, with the law and divine retribution in hot pursuit.

Visit www.lochlonach.com for more information about Ginny, Jim, Himself, and the Loch Lonach Mystery Series.

About the Author

MAGGIE FOSTER is a seventh-generation Texan of Scottish descent. Her ancestors were in Texas before it was a Republic. In addition to being steeped in Scottish traditions and culture, she has spent a lifetime in healthcare as a nurse, lawyer, and teacher. Her interests include history, genealogy, music, dancing, travel, dark chocolate, good whisky, and men in kilts.

THE LOCH LONACH COLLECTION

The Loch Lonach Mysteries
- *The Arms of Death:* Loch Lonach Mysteries, Book One
- *The Swick and the Dead:* Loch Lonach Mysteries, Book Two
- *Viking Vengeance:* Loch Lonach Mysteries, Book Three

Loch Lonach Short Stories
- *Dead Easy*
- *Duncan Died Dunkin'*

CPSIA information can be obtained
at www.ICGtesting.com
Printed in the USA
BVHW041324200219
540740BV00013B/99/P